The Silver Castle

CLIVE JAMES

The Silver Castle

a novel

LONDON

First published 1996

1 3 5 7 9 10 8 6 4 2

© Clive James 1996

Clive James has asserted his right under
the Copyright, Designs and Patents Act 1988
to be identified as the author of this work

First published in the United Kingdom in 1996 by
Jonathan Cape,
Random House, 20 Vauxhall Bridge Road, London SW1V 2SA

Random House Australia (Pty) Limited
20 Alfred Street, Milsons Point, Sydney,
New South Wales 2061, Australia

Random House New Zealand Limited
18 Poland Road, Glenfield,
Auckland 10, New Zealand

Random House South Africa (Pty) Limited
East Wing, Endulini, 5a Jubilee Road, Parktown, South Africa

Random House UK Limited Reg. No. 954009

A CIP catalogue record for this book is available from the British Library

Papers used by Random House UK Limited are natural,
recyclable products made from wood grown in sustainable forests.
The manufacturing processes conform to the environmental regulations
of the country of origin.

ISBN 0–224–04384–6

Typeset by Deltatype Ltd. Ellesmere Port

Printed and bound in Great Britain
by Mackays of Chatham PLC

to Rita Guerricchio

con affetto

*

qui tocca anche a noi poveri la nostra parte di richezza

You can stand aloof from the sufferings of the world; you are free to do so and it expresses your nature; but perhaps that very aloofness is the one suffering you might have avoided.

– Kafka

1

THE PAVEMENT where Sanjay was born, and lived out his first difficult years, can only loosely be described as a pavement. Mainly it consists of packed earth, irrigated at intervals by rivulets of sewage. Americans would call it a sidewalk and be more accurate, because at least there would be nothing paved about the word itself. But in India the English language harks back to the Raj, so a stretch of hard dirt like Sanjay's birthplace will always be called a pavement, and give you the idea of something impermeable and slick instead of what it is – friable, porous, simply waiting to be washed away. About an hour and a half by bus out of downtown Bombay on a busy day, a right turn off the main road leading northish through the coastal suburbs takes you through yet more suburbs to an area where there are enough trees and scrub so that you can delude yourself for a few minutes that you have left the city. But leaving Bombay is never that easy. The ragged-edged asphalt two-lane road up through the low hills is heading for Film City, where much of India's enormous movie output for any given year is created in a concentrated version of that uniquely subcontinental business atmosphere combining somnolent chaos and last-minute urgency. For a long stretch, on the left side of the road as you drive up, a low-level shanty town scaled down for crouching people is laid out in a linear manner on the bare earth, a sort of ribbon development for the unfortunate. Nothing has been omitted from the picture of deprivation. There are garbage dumps with women pissing behind them and men pissing on top. Someone's mother-in-law is dying in full view on a spread sack in front of her front door while a couple of listlessly copulating dogs teeter past her mute scream. A little boy gets kicked in mid-shit by his elder brother. Meanwhile Film City, only a mile up the road, is providing an alternative and more easily contemplated reality. When Sanjay was tiny, the Film City back lot had just started to grow too, but like him it was unmistakably there. They both exuded the energy that makes growth seem inevitable. In India, where life is much chancier than we are used to in the West, the inevitability of growth is quite a thing to exude.

Sanjay, of course, didn't know that Film City even existed, even when he grew old enough to grasp what was going on around him. To start with he grasped nothing much except his mother's breast. There wasn't a lot in that, but luckily there was enough. Other children in Sanjay's row of hovels were given more water than milk. The water wouldn't have been sufficient even if it had been clean, which it never was, just as it was never cool. On the Bombay pavement, clean, cool water takes time and effort to come by. You can see a man selling it from a dented churn mounted on a cart. The sun heats the metal and the metal warms the water. Among the poor people of Bombay, systems gain heat, in a local reversal of the second law of thermodynamics. Sometimes only a wall away from them but many income levels above, air conditioning, with a soft roar and rattle, puts the law back into effect. The rich, the very rich, are cool. We can indulge ourselves, if we wish, in pronouncing it their fault that they breathe sweeter air, but to share that coolness out among all the mouths born to inhale the heat will take a better plan than any philanthropist has yet devised. It is said nowadays that general prosperity will work the trick, but the people who say so are already prosperous themselves, and few among them have ever lived on a Bombay pavement.

In the hovel next up the hill to the one inhabited by Sanjay's family, there was a little boy like Sanjay who didn't even have a mother. His father was a bottle-sorter in a reprocessing shed who had several older relatives living with him, so the baby was short of air as well as nourishment. One of the earliest sounds that Sanjay got used to was the sound of that little boy crying next door. On the

2

pavements, an expression like 'next door' must be used approximately. Really all the shanties join together. They aren't neat, separate constructions like the little cardboard houses that the Japanese builders' labourers from out of town put together for themselves every evening in the underground walkways of Shinjuku station in Tokyo. Bombay pavement shanties join together in long lines because they are all made of the same scarce materials: rags, bags, the ever-precious kindling and the very occasional, jealously guarded piece of tin or sheet plastic. Detached residences would waste a wall. By the same token, to make shared walls thick would be wasteful too, so they are composed of not much more than an old grain bag lined with a random collection of rags and paper stuck on any old how, usually just by accumulated dirt. It's caked dirt that holds whole houses together and joins them to the houses on either side, and so on until the pavement runs out at the next crossroads.

You can see these improvised sub-cities in almost every part of Bombay, even in the flash areas like Juhu Beach and the Malabar Hills. Except where the Parsees exert their influence, in the policed and barbered territories around the burial ground they call the Towers of Silence, the poverty of Bombay is always closing in on any new area of luxury and threatening to take over. In Rio, most of the shanty towns, the *favelas*, are up on the garbage tips above the city, and the majority of the little houses are made of colour-washed cement, so you will see a baby girl playing in pig-shit but at least she has a solid doorway to go back into when danger threatens, just like your daughter. But in Bombay the rag-and-bone suburbettes are all over the place, right in amongst the city like a parallel universe, and garbage is what they are made of. They have no colour except all the shades of dust and dirt. Dirty and dusty are often the same adjective in Hindi, reflecting the fact that the two substances are variations on a common theme. Just add heat or water to one of them and you'll soon get the other. Add too much of both and you get hot mud. When the monsoon comes the shanty towns in the lower-lying areas are the first to melt away, except for the few inspired constructions incorporating sheets of tin or hard plastic in the roof. In the monsoon it becomes easy to see why the pavement dwellers, though they are an

3

aristocracy compared to those who sleep on the open streets, are a hopelessly underprivileged sub-class compared to those who live in even the most noxious slum. Slums are not soluble. The shanties are, but in the long stretch of dry hot weather they look better than nothing, although only just.

Look inside one of them and you will usually see somebody sick: a grandmother getting ready to die, a teenage boy coughing like phlegmatic clockwork. When Sanjay made his first journey, about a yard up the slightly sloping pavement to the door of the next hovel, what he saw inside was a young version of himself lying naked and struggling. The baby's wailing and strangling noises were the audio accompaniment to Sanjay's first sentient year. Sanjay's mother told him not to look inside that resonant doorway but Sanjay, having been born with a contrary spirit, always did. He was fascinated by the waving legs. There were old women in there too, but they scarcely moved. When the baby's father cracked under the strain and lost his bottle-sorting job it must have been a clear choice whether to kill himself or the baby. He compromised by going begging, using the baby as bait. He worked the last set of traffic lights on the main road inland, before the turn-off. It was a cherished spot that he sometimes had to fight for. The baby acquired a conspicuous facial injury during one of these fights and its father noticed that his prospects for attracting donations correspondingly improved. It was a short step to improving the prospects further. Mysteriously, the baby lost its left hand. Bound up in a grey rag smelling of petrol, the stump was thrust by the father at the windows of cars waiting at the traffic lights. Cars containing western visitors to Film City were a sure bet. How the baby survived its early medical history is a puzzle best left to science. It didn't survive its later one, but by that time Sanjay was beyond regarding the short trip to the next doorway as an adventure. He had bigger plans.

During the day, Sanjay's father was seldom home to stop him wandering. Sanjay's father had a more or less steady job sorting plastic bags. Getting to the recycling shed, however, meant a long commute by bus that cost most of what he earned, and a newly acquired habit of drinking cost much of the rest. He was a man of disappointed hopes. He had brought his young wife and family in from the country with some confidence that he would find work washing clothes in one of Bombay's vast open-air laundries which the whole state of Maharashtra has heard about. But jobs at the laundries turned out to be booked up years ahead. He had found himself at the back end of a dispirited mob funnelled between walls, with a tantalising view over one wall of the laundry stretching away into the distance, the thousands of laundry workers swatting cloth against the smooth stone tables with the air of men who knew where their next meal was coming from, even if it came slowly. The whole place was running with water. The water was dirty yet somehow the clothes emerged clean. Again, here is something that makes India marvellous: dirty water can give you clean clothes. In mainland China, by contrast, a thousand million people previously world famous for their ability to do laundry are now, through the miracle wrought by Communism, unable to wash your white shirt without turning it grey, or to press it without crushing the buttons like aspirin in a spoon. In India they know how. Yet Bombay's gigantic open-air laundry system held no place for Sanjay's father. Having no work was a step worse than what he had left behind in his village, where the daily labour of scratching the earth was intolerable but at least tangible, and, if he managed to generate enough sons, might even one day offer rest. Here he was nothing. By the time his luck turned and he got the sorting job he had run through his capital. A room in a slum was out of the question. He could only just afford the shanty. He was at work the day Sanjay was born so he didn't see the dogs eat the afterbirth.

Sanjay's father and mother had left farming behind but not its mentality. There were up-to-date poor people in India who went on having children because they didn't know how not to, but might have stopped if they could have understood the technology. Sanjay's father didn't even have the desire to stop. He still thought of male children as a source of strength. That he did not arrange accidents for his female children he made a point of religious pride. He was a man of conviction. A reasonable number of very young pavement children are rounded up to be inoculated and sometimes even carted off to school, but such a fate had never befallen *his* children. He would not hear of it. If his wife had an opinion, she was given little respite in which to express it. As a consequence Sanjay was soon no longer the youngest child. When there were a couple younger than him, he was able to extend his voyages without fear of being missed, as long as he was back by nightfall. His father, when he finally got home, could often scarcely walk, but he could still count.

Sanjay's first big trip was across the road. He reached the other side on what would have been recognised as his third birthday, if anyone had known the date. The other side of the road was even more thronged than his own side. After running the gauntlet – toddling the gauntlet in his case – of the speeding buses, trucks, vans, cabs, cars and toot-toot micro-cabs, he emerged in another country. Instead of hovels there were places where people spread things out so that other people could look at them and sometimes buy them. There were all kinds of glittering things spread on mats and rugs. There were hundreds of different kinds of food. Some of it was being cooked right there where you could watch. Sanjay soon learned not to snatch at scraps. A slapped wrist stings. But sometimes he was given a scrap to eat because of his winning looks. Looks shape life and among the poor they help to stave off death. So on the pavement among the stalls Sanjay received the tiny amount of extra energy that made the difference between irreversible damage and the possibility of health. He was at knee height to the thousands of people passing along and he could look the stall-holders in the eye as they squatted. Some of them sat on low stools. One man sat on a painted stool with cards spread out in front of him that he could read, and so tell people what would happen to them in the future. The cards had lavish pictures on the back. The man said they were gods and goddesses. He had a parrot who would turn over the card that the client picked out. The man on the coloured stool was the one who told Sanjay that it would be better to take a shit on the rubbish dump near his home in the morning than to try and find a place to shit among all these stall-holders, because it made some of them angry and they would not feed him scraps. That was the first item in Sanjay's education, if you didn't count his mother's telling him not to piss inside the hovel. Not that she ever really told him: she just hit him when he did, whereas the man on the coloured stool had a kind voice and appealed to reason. As a consequence, Sanjay learned the lesson after a single telling, because his brain, against all the odds, was potentially as quick as his body was strong and healthy. Circumstances were contriving to undernourish them both, but the conclusion was not foregone. This was unusual, because on the Bombay pavements it almost always is.

2

THE FIRST TIME Sanjay ever saw the Silver Castle, he was about seven years old. By then he was used to travelling the whole length of the road on both sides, past all the shanties on one side and all the shops and stalls on the other, as far downhill as the crossroads and as far uphill as where the road was closed. It was closed by a guarded gate through which only those buses, cars, cabs and toot-toot micro-cabs could go that had permission. The people who had permission were all dressed as if they were rich. Some of them, the women who sat in the back seats of the cars, looked like the unimaginably rich goddesses who gleamed in gold and radiant colours on the cards the parrot turned over. All these rich people were going somewhere forbidden. One day Sanjay struck out along the wire fence that separated him from what he was not allowed to see. Eventually he left behind the last vestige of the area where the shops and stalls were, with all their own attendant shanties in an extended hinterland. It didn't extend forever, although it was a long way for his short legs. But eventually it turned into scrub land, just like the scrub land on the other side of the fence. So it was natural that when there was not much for the fence to shut out, it gave up. There was a whole section of it lying rusting in the scrub. Sanjay picked his way over it and headed up through the thick shrubbery. The occasional person was living there – there are few places in Bombay free of inhabitants – but on the whole it was the most unpopulated territory that Sanjay had ever seen. It was so unusual that he forgot to look around and take landmarks so that he could find his way out again. Perhaps he was just too small to think of it. Anyway, he kept going up and around the top of the hill, and then

8

suddenly he was looking at a stretch of road that he knew must carry the vehicles that were allowed through the barrier. There was a car going along it now, with a rich woman in the back seat. He could tell she was rich because of the gold and green and red shining from her sari, and because she was in a car. It was going somewhere. He looked to see where it was going.

There it was, at the end of the road, at the top of the next slope, rising far above the shrubbery, higher even than the trees. It was the biggest building he had ever seen. It had pointed towers at the corners and was all as brilliant and precious as a pile of crushed soft-drink cans, which up to then had been the most dazzling thing in his experience. Just by looking at this construction he could tell why he wasn't allowed to be there. It made him blink. Even as he blinked he went closer, keeping to the dusty edge of the road, off the hot asphalt. When a bus or a car or a cab or a toot-toot came along, he ran into the scrub, so it was in a zig-zag fashion that he approached the Silver Castle. His course was undeviating nevertheless, like destiny.

When he finally arrived at the wide stretch of bare earth before the castle, men were pouring out of its big front door and heading for the shade of nearby trees so that they could sit down and eat food from cardboard boxes. Sanjay had never seen men dressed like these. Most of them wore silver-studded black jackets, billowing red pants, and turbans with a black cone sticking out of the top. They all carried silver swords. Many of them had ordinary shoes or sandals on their bare feet but the tallest ones had shiny boots that went all the way up to the knee. There was a group of men who were not dressed like this but still looked rich. They were sitting around a table beside a white van and talking very loudly.

"We start again in an hour. An hour means one hour, not two. Ready or not."

"She won't be ready. She only just got here. It takes her two hours to put her face on."

"So we shoot around her."

Sanjay could hear all this but couldn't understand it. He was ready to scoot away if anyone tried to grab him but nobody seemed to care. Emboldened, he walked slowly close to the most magnificent of all the

9

men with swords. This man, instead of being dressed in black and red, wore a brown fringed soft-looking suit with very high brown boots that looked soft also and had, around their folded tops, fringes of their own. Even though he was sitting down, it was easy to see that he was tall. Elaborately flowing hair made him taller. He was looking at his hair in a mirror. He had more hair on his top lip, which he lifted so that he could look at his teeth. They shone. He shone all over. He was surrounded by other men wearing ordinary clothes, but richly clean and untattered, with proper shoes. One of these attendant men was talking urgently.

"They're saying she won't be ready for two hours, so we have to shoot around her."

"Then they can shoot around me too," said the shining man in brown, patting his hair. "I could be at the beach. I could be in Paris. Who needs it?"

This last phrase was said in a language Sanjay didn't understand, any more than he understood expressions like *shoot around* or *Paris*. He was to hear this language many times in the next hours. It was a special language they spoke here at the castle. The shining man put down his mirror, stretched back, pressed his fingertips gently to his eyes, lowered his hands, looked around and saw Sanjay.

"Who's the kid?"

Sanjay was all set to scuttle off but something in the shining man's tone encouraged a postponement. The shining man wasn't angry. He was like the parrot man. The grand total of people in Sanjay's life who weren't angry with him had increased to two.

"Some poor cockroach from outside the fence," said one of the shining man's rich companions.

"He doesn't look bad for where he's come from," said the shining man. "Bring him over and we'll get some food into him."

The shining man's rich companion walked towards Sanjay, who thought for a few seconds, decided he didn't like the look of the situation, and took off. When it became apparent that he wouldn't be able to outpace his pursuer by running in a straight line, he ran in circles. The shining man and his other companions were laughing and crying out.

10

"Go, kid, go!"

"Go right!"

"Left, left!"

"You're too fat, Deepak! Try lying down suddenly and maybe he'll run into you!"

Eventually the man dived, flung out a hand, caught Sanjay by the ankle and carried him upside down back to the shining man's throne.

"Take it easy, kid," said the shining man. "I just wanted to give you a bread roll. It's got a slice of cheese in it, see? American style. Ever see that? Take a bite."

Sanjay obeyed. The effect was strange but instantly satisfactory: a real mouthful, all the way down to the stomach.

"Thums Up?"

Sanjay had several times been offered a few mouthfuls of Thums Up by the parrot man but this was the first time he had ever been handed a whole bottle of it to keep. Also this time it was cold, not just cool. It was the coldest thing he had ever tasted. Thums Up is the Coca-Cola of India. Like all the world's countries which have ever been under the sway of the Soviet Union or even just loosely associated with it in an attempt to stave off the cultural influence of the United States, India had felt itself obliged to develop a Coca-Cola substitute. India's is called Thums Up and is one of the world's better local colas. Like all the others – try the Israeli version some day – it can be savoured on the teeth for an hour after it has been drunk, but at least it doesn't taste of petrol. To Sanjay it tasted like a new life. He was swallowing coldness.

"Wow, look at that stuff go down," said one of the rich companions.

"He needs six more bottles to wash himself with," said another.

"The dirt's holding him together," said the shining man. "He reminds me of what my life was like before I got into all this crap. Simple. The life of the senses."

"You're not telling us *you* were ever *poor*," said a special man who had just arrived. You could tell he was special because he had a special thing dangling round his neck.

11

"If you'd been my first director I would have ended up looking like this pitiful little bastard does now."

"Sure. You would have had only one BMW."

"Let's put him in the film."

"Not a bad idea. He certainly runs faster than you can. Probably acts better too. But he doesn't fit."

The special man walked back towards the castle entrance. The shining man rose from his chair, standing so tall he interfered with the sunlight.

"Dump some water over him and let him stick around. Useful reminder of the great public we're all working for."

The ordeal by water would remain in Sanjay's mind as one of the most intense of all the intense experiences that made up his initiation into the magic of the Silver Castle. Some of them were thrilling, some of them were shocking, but this one was devastating. Luckily they didn't try to get his clothes off. They just inundated him where he was. The sun soon dried him off, but the shameful memory remained of fingers being stuck in his ears and men showing the palms of their hands to each other after they had scraped at his arms and legs. He was on the point of heading home right there, but his trembling legs wouldn't carry him. That was lucky, because everything that happened next was wonderful.

He was taken inside the castle, which was even more dazzling inside than out. In actuality it was made of planks, roughly-dressed joists, plaster of Paris and frosty silver paint, and the film had to be finished before the monsoon came to strip the terraces and battlements bare of their glory and turn the patchy grass of the courtyard to uninterrupted mud. But to Sanjay it looked like the place where the creation of the Earth must have been planned, the fortress of the gods. There were armies manoeuvring inside it, marshalled by the special man, who would squint through his special thing and had a younger man to shout for him. The special man would say something softly and then the man who did the shouting for him would say it loudly. Then everybody made complicated movements on the grass and up in the terraces. Occasionally the shining man rose from his canvas chair and joined in. Sanjay was given a job. When the folding chair was moved to wherever the shining man was going next, Sanjay was allowed to help carry it. He could barely keep his end of it off the ground but apparently that was all that was deemed necessary, so that no speck of dust could be picked up from the chair and transferred to the shining man's impeccable person. It all went on for hours and Sanjay couldn't imagine how his excitement could grow any more acute. It did, though, because She appeared, the most beautiful woman in the world.

She appeared out of nowhere. All the soldiers were on the terraces with their swords drawn. By now Sanjay knew that the swords weighed almost nothing because one of the soldiers had let him hold one. It didn't cut you. It just gave you splinters. But the swords flashed in the sunlight when they were held up. The shining man was once again in position for the short walk and sudden pause he had been doing for half an hour. But now the beautiful woman was present and everything changed. Half the soldiers went away. They were replaced on the terraces by richly dressed women. None of these, however, was dressed half so richly as the beautiful woman was. Just the jewels on her slippers made her look as if she had stepped through a precious puddle. In her bare belly, above the billowing trousers and below her bejewelled halter, there was a plug reflecting different colours of light. When she smiled, her teeth looked as clean as the shining man's, although he was not smiling. But she was not smiling at him anyway. She was smiling at the special man, the director, who was squinting at her through his special thing.

"I think I dimly recognise you," said the director. "Didn't we once work together on a film?"

"I wanted to look my best."

"Well, you certainly look that, so we'd better get on with it. Re-set for the dance."

"Re-set for the dance!" shouted the man who did the shouting.

A large though not tall woman with bells on her fingers and toes joined the new focus of attention and began to make gestures, which the beautiful woman copied.

"What is happening?" asked the shining man, who with Sanjay's help had arranged his chair so as to be facing the other way.

"She's being taught the step that renders you helpless with lust," said one of his entourage.

"It will take forever," said the shining man.

The rest of the afternoon's work was consumed by the beautiful woman's seductive step. She had to repeat it ten times and it took ten minutes each time to get all the machinery ready. Some of it Sanjay was beginning to recognise. Everything seemed to revolve around the machine called a camera which was as big as a toot-toot and ran on rails that told it where to go. Sanjay had been taught not to get where it could see him. Otherwise he was free to move about. He watched in awe as the beautiful woman flung herself down the terrace, paused, looked at her own curved fingers, and undulated. When she had finally done that often enough, she did the same thing again, except that the shining man joined her with the same short run and pause he had been doing earlier. Sanjay was at a loss as to why everything had to be done over and over, but it suited him. His eyes could linger over it. When the beautiful woman and shining man were near each other, they smiled at each other until the director told them to stop, whereupon their smiles disappeared like drops of spit on a hot pavement. Until then, their radiant dental displays reflected each other. The air burned in the beam between. Then everyone started to go away. The shining man had been joined by the biggest car Sanjay had ever seen from so close up. It drove straight in through the gateway of the castle and stopped on the grass. Three families could have lived in the shade of it.

"Come back tomorrow, kid," said the shining man. "You're my lucky charm. Where do you live?"

Mainly by gesture, Sanjay explained that he lived outside the gate.

"Deepak! Get your gofer to drop the kid off."

The shining man was swept away in his enormous car, but Sanjay's exit from the castle was no less glorious in his own mind. He was sitting in the back of a toot-toot: something he had never done before although he had dreamed of it often. The toot-toot, or two-seater as it is known officially, is India's most salient example of that type of vehicular urban proliferation which is the infallible mark of all developing countries: the motorcycle trying to be something more.

14

The toot-toot has a motorcycle's single front wheel and suspension, but with two wheels at the back to stabilise its canopy, under which two passengers can sit behind the driver in relative comfort while the toot-toot pops along, producing a plosive profusion of polysyllabic vocables – Apocalypse, Papandreou, Popocatepetl – and occasionally, on a smooth stretch of macadam, threatening itself with apoplectic paralysis as its apocopated patter perks up to a peremptory peak, all the more pestilential for being practically powerless. Multiply the effect of this prose by ten and you'll be in a position to appreciate the quality of migraine that a single toot-toot can engender if it goes past you once. Toot-toots aren't allowed in downtown Bombay because their onomatopoeic prattle makes the air hideous and lowers the tone. But in the suburbs they swarm. In the suburbs is where a toot-toot belongs. A ride in a toot-toot is only one step up from running along the ground all by yourself. For Sanjay, however, it was a culmination: the shining man, the cheese roll, the whole bottle of Thums Up, Her, and now this. Perched cross-legged on the bouncing back seat, he was too proud even to grin. When they crackled through the area gate and started going down the street where he lived his first plan was to say nothing, so that the blissful ride could go on longer. Unfortunately his mother spotted him.

He climbed out, was interrogated for his story, and when his father came staggering home he was punished. Apparently his worst crime was having let a stranger bathe him. He had to promise that he would never go to the Silver Castle again. Next morning he could hardly walk.

3

HE COULD HARDLY WALK, but he went to the Silver Castle. It took him
most of the morning. His upper legs were bruised and if the parrot
man had not rubbed some ointment on them he might never have
made it. But after a long rest at the broken-down fence he
accomplished the second half of his journey just before the sun was at
its highest point overhead. The Silver Castle was still there. Sanjay
had been afraid that it might have disappeared in the night. It might
have gone back into the past. He had heard one of the shining man's
friends say that the area surrounding the Silver Castle was called
Long Ago. Obviously Long Ago was in a different country and
perhaps it was in another world. The castle was even more dazzling
today. Sanjay could barely look at it. There were soldiers on the
battlements blowing trumpets at the hot sky. The trumpets made no
sound. It seemed reasonable that magic trumpets would be silent.

This time Sanjay spent no time hiding. He limped up to the gate
and went through, confident that the shining man would look after
him. The shining man, however, was nowhere to be seen. Everything
was revolving around the beautiful woman. The small large woman
with the bells on her toes was undulating in front of her while she
undulated back, in a kind of silent conversation. A long line of
beautiful other women were undulating in the background. Loud
music was coming out of nowhere. Suddenly it stopped. Sanjay had
infiltrated while everybody else undulated, so he was just close
enough to hear the director when he spoke.

"OK, let's move the camera on that one to see how it looks. Tell
them we're going for a take."

16

"Going for a take!" shouted the man who did the shouting.

"Bring the kid over here."

"Bring the kid over here!"

Sanjay thought of running but he was picked up hugely from behind by a giant.

"Mister Rajiv Bharati is our fight arranger, kid," said the director. "Nobody runs away from him." But Sanjay knew it was going to be all right because the director was smiling through his beard, below which hung the fascinating special thing.

"You like the look of that? It's a viewfinder. Here, take a squint."

Sanjay looked through the special thing and saw a section of the terrace full of soldiers. He could see everything: the cracks in their teeth, the hair in their noses.

"Now take a look at Miranda. What do you see?"

He saw the beautiful woman. Her eyes were bigger than a sacred cow's. From the depths of their brown pupils came tiny bursts of light.

"You see trouble, that's what you see."

"I will be no trouble if this young man helps to carry my chair today." Sanjay would have felt her voice like an embrace, if he had ever been embraced.

"She sees him carrying Rahul's chair yesterday so she wants him to carry her chair today. What a surprise."

So Sanjay became the beautiful woman's second assistant chair carrier. Every time she sat down she was surrounded by people who did things to her hair and clothes. They did things to her skin, using thin paper – thinner than anything in Sanjay's experience. He picked up a crumpled piece of it after it had been discarded and it tore when he touched it. It smelled sweet, but not sweet like Thums Up: sweet like cool water. When he was close to her he could smell her sweetness. It was like ten different kinds of flowers mixed together.

"Fight scene and dance transition in one hour exactly!" shouted the man who did the shouting. "That means everybody! For the next fifty-nine minutes, lunch! Fifty-eight minutes if you hang around!"

The most amazing thing happened then. The beautiful woman took Sanjay's hand and led him away, the most privileged of her entire entourage. They all went to a house on wheels that stood near

17

the castle, a short walk from the gate, under the trees. There was a canopy spread out from the door of the house to give shade, with a table and chairs underneath it. Sanjay was allowed to sit on a box near the beautiful woman's chair.

"So you are the famous Sanjay. You held my chair very well. Therefore you may have an entire cheese roll all to yourself."

Sanjay attacked the cheese roll as if it were a deadly enemy.

"Slow down, slow down. You must learn to nibble at life. I am not so mean as that stingy pig Rahul. The cheese roll shall not be snatched from your lips. Here, wash it down with this."

This wasn't Thums Up but it wasn't ordinary water either. It contained countless small explosions. They tasted as brilliant as the bursts of light in the beautiful woman's eyes. Sanjay belched. Everyone cheered and clapped.

"His first word," said the beautiful woman. "He speaks to me of love." And indeed she spoke nothing but the truth. Deep inside the realm of her presence where the air smelled like flowers, he crossed his feet in contentment, having already learned that a smile from him earned a smile from her.

"For a blob of dust he has teeth like a tiger." The small large lady chinked and chimed as she laughed. "He will break hearts some day."

"Yes, every heart in the rubbish dump. What a world we inhabit." The beautiful woman lifted a plum to her lips. It was almost the same colour as they were. Her mouth and the fruit blended. Her fingernails must have been stained by the fruit. Her toe-nails too: did she eat with her feet? There was juice on her teeth. A woman reached forward with a piece of soft paper.

"Later, later. Fix it later. Let me live a real life for ten minutes. This afternoon I have to pretend that I love Rahul."

"It says here," said another woman who was reading from a variously coloured thin book full of pictures, "that the physical attraction between Miranda Dhaliwal and Rahul Kapoor is so intense that their latest film is behind schedule because they cannot be separated from their mutual embraces. It says that Rahul's girlfriend Navreet Tikmany has threatened to kill them both."

18

"Someone must have heard her threatening to kill another bottle of Chivas Regal. Does it say that I love him so much that when he touches me the contents of my stomach leap out and fall at my feet?"

"Speak of the Devil," said the small large woman, with a chink of bells. She had turned to watch the shining man's enormous car coming up the slope towards them.

"Speak of the Devil's latrine digger," said the beautiful woman. "Speak of the Devil's latrine digger's congenitally syphilitic illegitimate offspring."

Sanjay was shaky on the details of this conversation but he had grasped its drift. He had begun to wonder if the relationship between the shining man and the beautiful woman might not be marked by a certain lack of affection. He had not yet realised, however, that this could pose him a problem. He soon did. The shining man, in his full soft brown high-booted regalia with rustling tassels, came striding lithely near, with the sunlight rebounding from his midnight black bouffant and his teeth bared in a tightly clenched smile that shed no warmth.

"Miranda, darling, you've been looking after my chair-holder."

"For the first time in his life, I shouldn't be surprised."

"I think you'll find that Sanjay has his own opinions about that. An independent little man like him needs a big brother, not a mother."

"Well, he's certainly got something in common with you."

"And what might that be, pray?"

"Childishness."

"Miranda, you really are . . ."

"You really are required on the set as of now," said the director, suddenly appearing. "And so are you, Rahul. Bury the hatchet, please, my dears. This is the complicated bit where we actually need you both to be physically present at the same time, if you can possibly manage it. Let's go and block it out."

During the course of this long speech from the director the tension went out of the situation, at least for the time being. But Sanjay, who deduced meanings only from moods, found his loyalties cruelly divided. The shining man resolved the dilemma for him by leading him into the castle, where he joined his mentor's chair-holding team for what proved to be a long period of hard work, necessitating many shifts in the position of the chair. Rajiv the fight arranger was in charge of a sword fight, which took place between two groups of soldiers, one of them in pointed turbans and the other in tasselled coats. The shining man was the leading fighter of the group in tasselled coats. When the fight was at its bewildering peak of violence, suddenly the shining man held up his hand, silencing the fight with his authority. He had seen the beautiful woman running towards him from the terrace, followed by her attendant maidens. He threw his sword to the ground and stared at her. She stared at him. They smiled at each other. The music crashed into existence. Suddenly everyone was dancing except for the fighting men, who stayed where they were without moving, their swords still raised.

Everybody did all that twenty times while the director spoke instructions and the man who shouted for him shouted. Sanjay couldn't count to twenty but he knew that it took a long time. At one point the director picked up a trumpet which produced his voice, greatly amplified and crackling.

"Listen everyone, this is just a wide shot, all right? So nobody has to win an Oscar, all right? You just have to be in the right bloody *place*. Now let's do a real one."

They did a real one for another ten times. Finally there was a pause and everything was changed around. The shining man reclined into his chair with one long booted leg extended and the other crossed effortlessly over it. But his voice, as he spoke to his entourage, was nothing like so casual.

"You can't imagine what it's like to be so close to her for so long. You can smell the after-shave. It's like crushed toads."

Now the beautiful woman began to do something of her own. Once again it had to be done over and over. After the small large woman had shown her how, the beautiful woman took a few steps forward, stared, and smiled radiantly, as if the shining man were just in front of her. What she was staring and smiling at was the camera.

"She's better at this," said the shining man. "Now she's showing real animation. It's because she can see herself in the lens."

After a long time everything changed again. Now it was the shining

20

man's turn to stare and smile at the camera. For him to do this, it was necessary for some of the fighters to get into position behind him, raise their swords and stand immobile. There were many repetitions. Beside the shining man's empty chair, Sanjay let his attention drift to the beautiful woman, where she was sitting amid her entourage over against the opposite terrace. She sent him a smile that crossed the intervening space like a perfumed fireball.

"They'd better shoot this soon," said the fat man called Deepak, who never sat down in the shining man's chair even though he looked as if he needed to. "Rahul goes in half an hour."

"It's the light and the lens," said a smaller man who had just handed Sanjay a bottle of Thums Up with nearly two inches of cola in it for him to finish all by himself. "They're trying to get a split-focus effect in the background so that the fighters look frozen by magic."

"Fancy stuff. But they're going to lose their star."

Finally the man who did the shouting shouted that it was time to try a real one. At that moment, the beautiful woman crooked one of her curved, tapered, plum-tipped fingers towards Sanjay. He didn't know how to disobey. He didn't want to. So he headed towards her, crossing behind the fighters with their swords held up.

"Cut!"

Sanjay completed the remainder of his journey to the beautiful woman with his feet off the ground. The shining man was holding him by the back of his shirt, so that his feet were treading air.

"Here, keep him. Just keep him out of the damned shot, you jealous bitch."

"Good heavens, such passion."

"We wouldn't be pushed for time if you didn't need to be taught how to walk."

Sanjay stayed beside the beautiful woman's chair and watched with bewilderment while the shining man and the director and the fight arranger all talked, occasionally looking in his direction. Somehow he knew that they were talking about him. Then the shining man left, without saying goodbye. Sanjay's disappointment was doubled when he discovered that the beautiful woman had lost interest in him too. She had a new move to learn. She had to draw her clenched fists to her breasts, throw out her hands, turn and run. It took many repetitions and long pauses, but whenever she came back to her chair she never looked directly at him. Her deep, warm voice was aimed at everyone but him. After the real one she left without saying goodbye. Instead Rajiv the fight arranger came to see him. Rajiv filled the sky. There was no arguing with him and no running away.

"Time for you to go home, kid. Come on, I'll give you a ride."

Rajiv had a car. It was only half as big as the shining man's car but it was the first proper car Sanjay had ever been inside. While it was going he could hardly hear it. The softness of the seat was so deep that he couldn't see out. He would have been thrilled to be in the car if he had not been so concerned about the next day. He would have to make friends with the shining man again. It was clear that you could hold only one chair at a time. Yet how could he bear not to be in the beautiful woman's favour? He considered the possible rewards of being friends with both of them. Two cheese rolls. Thums Up *and* sparkling water. Perhaps he could belch for each of them separately. *Two* rounds of applause.

"Deepak's gofer says you live somewhere around here. Stand up and take a look."

The car had slowed down. They were indeed close to his home. He could see his mother. Sanjay instantly realised he had made a huge mistake. He would be punished again. He should have asked to be let off much earlier, walked home, and said he had been somewhere else. But stepping out of a car he could have come only from the Silver Castle. It was too late. His mother had spotted him.

Sanjay was wrong about this being the worst situation possible. Things got far worse than he could have imagined, because Rajiv the fight arranger got out of the car, not just to let Sanjay out, but to speak to his mother, telling her that they had enjoyed having her son at the Silver Castle, but that he was not to come there again because it was not meant for children. Sanjay's sense of betrayal was as great as his fear. Now he was for it, and it had all been for nothing. Sanjay's mother started slapping him before the car was even gone, so when his father came home after another long day of disappointment, the ideal outlet for his pent rage was already trembling in anticipation.

As always at the end of the day, Sanjay's father could hardly stand straight, but he could still hit. Sanjay's elder sister and his sick elder brother were both made to watch. No bones were broken, but it could hardly have felt worse if they had been. Next morning Sanjay left home, and was not to see the Silver Castle again for a long time, although in his mind it was always there, as the source of his grief and the object of his dreams.

4

Simply by leaving home, Sanjay became one of the children of the street. In Bombay the children of the pavement have somewhere to live. The children of the street live nowhere and everywhere, so if that is what they are going to be, it is best if they start early, because there is a lot to learn. At the age of seven and a bit, Sanjay was already a late starter. Luckily he was a quick learner. Above all he had an untapped natural capacity for theft. His quick mind could see an opportunity and his quick feet could carry him away from the consequences. The pavement stall-holders had managed to slap his wrists because he came at them from in front. Now he learned to creep up from behind, look innocent if he was challenged, and scuttle adroitly away with his booty when he was not. That way he managed to keep himself fed. But as one area of street learned to be on the lookout for him, he had to move on to another area where they had not. Thus he acquired a trajectory. He had no idea where he was heading, but a satellite overhead would have been able to predict his course if it had cared. He had made a left turn out of the teeming mile where he was born and was heading along the main road of the area towards the beach. It took him about three weeks to get there and by then he was already an expert at finding places to sleep at night. Paradoxically, the smaller children get the best positions, despite their lack of fighting strength. It is because they fit into smaller holes and can get under lower things. You might see a little girl living in an abandoned cardboard suitcase on a rubbish dump. When she grows too big, she has to move on, and then someone smaller will come along and take over. At one stage Sanjay lived for several days under a discarded slab of cement, until somebody dumped a lot of garbage that stopped up the gap between the slab and the earth. So he moved on. He had already forgotten his second name, which he had never heard used more than half a dozen times. At the beach he met some other street children and entered into the economy of Bombay.

The important thing to say about Bombay's economy is that it works. You are not dealing with some broken-down, post-political African country where the food has given out, the mad Marxist dictator has gone into exile with all the remaining aid money, and the people have no recourse except to lie down and die. Though malnutrition stunts the growth of millions, not many people actually die of starvation in Bombay, despite the fact that so many of its poorer people have come in from the country to escape precisely that possibility. Bombay can accommodate its continually burgeoning population because nothing is wasted. Everything is recycled. Bottles are re-used until they break. That happens in the West, too, but with us the bottle is usually re-used for the same sort of thing. In Bombay it is re-used for every sort of thing. When a Bombay bottle eventually breaks under the strain of having contained everything that quenches, inebriates, lubricates or scarifies, the broken glass goes into the furnaces and becomes part of another bottle, whose own event-strewn saga then begins, like a Maupassant story rewritten by Proust. Soft-drink cans are collected, crumpled and sold on from the single collector to the specialist used soft-drink can shop, and from there to the crushing plant, which in turn transforms all that silver flash and bright colour into useful metal. Nothing imperishable escapes collection, right down to the scrap of polythene, the nail and the pin. There are shops that specialise in dead batteries. Every form of rag is collected, and every form of paper. One of the results is that the rubbish tips on the pavements or between the houses are all organic – picked clean of anything inert, they are always rotting, but they never really grow. The little girl with the suitcase for a house had better not stray too far from it, or someone will take it away and sell it.

The solid junk of the city is forever being folded back in, and at every stage of an object's return journey to the source there is a trade-off, even if the value involved can scarcely be measured in the tiniest fraction of an anna. Sanjay became part of this process when he joined a gang of children scavenging the beach. He was never paid except in food, but not all of the food passed out by the gang's leaders was stolen from the bins at the back of restaurants. Some of it was new food purchased from street vendors. The purchase price came out of the profits after the gang leaders sold the day's haul of rags and paper and base but precious metals to the men in the shops who would sort it into categories and grades. Sanjay soon established himself as a key recruit. He could find significantly more negotiable detritus in a day of beachcombing than it cost the gang leaders to feed him. Sanjay was especially good at standing near picnicking families on the beach and looking longingly at the bottles they were drinking from. Often his winsomely charming vigil was rewarded by the outright gift of empty bottles whose owners could have returned them to the shop for cash on the nail, if they had not been rendered generous by the sunlight, the frivolity of the beach, and Sanjay's artfully yearning eyes. The gang leaders saw him in action and knew they had a star.

For the last weeks of the holiday season, when all of working Bombay wanted to sit on the sand on the weekends and the evenings, Sanjay's gang combed the beach all the way to Juhu, where the apartment blocks of the new rich rise side by side so thickly that the vertical slices of sky between them look drawn in with a blue pencil. At sunset, if you are on the beach and looking inland, the light comes in from behind you across the sea and sets the upper windows of the apartment blocks on fire as if they had been blinded by a death-ray in their ponderous advance to the water. One morning, on the beach below these apartment blocks, one of the gang leaders told Sanjay that the famous film star Miranda lived up in that apartment block there, the third balcony from the top. The whole day they were in the area, Sanjay's scavenging performance suffered as he checked the designated place with his glance. Towards the end of the afternoon he thought he saw her, and stood transfixed. He could tell it was a woman. Women curve, even at a distance. He strove to get her in focus, but the effort was doomed because she already was. She was

26

just too far away and too high up to be identified. Probably it was not her, because she just stood there instead of going back in and coming back out again ten times, the way she would have done if she was really from Long Ago. It never occurred to him that she might be some other film star called Miranda, and not the beautiful woman. He thought there was only one film star called Miranda. He thought there was only one film star. Finally the glass lit up around her and she disappeared into the silent fire of the reflected sunset. Sanjay turned around in defiance to face the horizon. Poised to vanish, the sun blinded him as if he, too, were a building – a little one, but similarly petrified.

That was the limit of the rich pickings. The logic of their trade took the gang of miniature scavengers south again, so as far as Sanjay's manifest destiny was concerned he was heading in the right direction when the monsoon came. The rain drove the gang members into holes under the esplanade as if they were crabs backing away from massed squadrons of hungry squid. Falling water washed them apart. Soon Sanjay was alone again, condemned to finding scraps that he could eat. Everything was wet, so he could drink at the same time. He scavenged and stole his way southwards towards the city. He didn't realise yet that he had only been on the edge of it. He had no idea how big it was, or how unfriendly. Perhaps it would have been better for him if he had never seen the Silver Castle, never felt a guiding hand, never blinked at an unstained smile. Then he would not have missed these things. It is just possible, however, that the memory of his first visit to Long Ago sustained him. Imagination and energy are part of each other, and few of us, even though we live in circumstances far more favourable, would ever get to where we are going unless a picture of it, however inaccurate, was already in our minds. If we had to, we too would have to dodge the rain between rubbish dumps, on the long journey back to the taste of a cheese roll, the tang of sparkling water, trumpets that crackle and toe-nails stained with plums. We don't have to, but Sanjay did.

27

5

By the end of the rains, Sanjay had still not reached the city, though it would soon be in sight. He had kept to the coastline, with the occasional foray into the suburbs in search of scraps, whose efficacy was proved by the increasing tightness of his clothes: he was growing as he moved. But before the northern suburbs of Bombay turn into the central immensity of Fort Bombay, the city proper, they first have to climb the hills of the Malabar peninsula, and Sanjay had to climb with them. That was how he found the Towers of Silence. They are really called that. It isn't a make-believe name like the Silver Castle. The Towers of Silence are a garden in the hills where the Parsees put out their dead for the vultures. Sanjay didn't know what a Parsee was. He barely knew that he was a Hindu, or that he spoke the Hindi language. But he could tell the Parsees were different because of their neatness. They lived in apartment blocks that were hard to infiltrate, and even the people who worked for them wore shoes, so a barefoot boy was very conspicuous. Sanjay was rarely able to get past the car-park under the buildings, and if he managed to penetrate into the stairwells and corridors he was soon picked up and thrown out. But what things he discovered! One day he reached a balcony where empty white tables surrounded by clustered white chairs were dotted along a narrow long green lawn whose deep green grass was made of prickly cloth that exuded a tiny sucking noise when he walked on it. There had been nothing like that even in Long Ago. From the balcony he could look a long way out into the sea and count the boats by ten. There were ten times ten at least. There were other countries out there. One of them had a city on it made of domes. They shone

28

white instead of silver but they reminded him of the Silver Castle in their splendid definition. From one end of the balcony, where it wrapped around the corner of the building, he could look back in the opposite direction and see another wonder. There was a huge garden, as big as a whole country, further up the hill. From the high balcony he could look down into it. It was full of flat spreading trees bigger than anything in Long Ago. Big birds were circling above it and would occasionally drop down into it, crying like sick children. Sanjay had only just begun to contemplate all these new phenomena when a man in white clothes suddenly appeared between him and his means of escape. He ran a series of small quick circles around the man, nipped back down the stairwell he had come up, and scooted out again through the car-park, noting freshly stacked sacks of garbage as he ran. That night he came back to pick a hole in one of the sacks and see what it held. The Parsees packed their garbage neatly. They had no rubbish tips: not, at any rate, of the sort you could live in. But if you chanced on a sack with food scraps in it they could be sumptuous. Sanjay found some melon rinds with a lot of melon still on them and some shards of nutshell still plump with meat. He stashed these treasures in his hidey-hole under a hedge and lived off them for two days before he transferred his residence higher up the hill, across the road from the wall that surrounded the Towers of Silence. There was no penetrating that wall if you were not a corpse, a funeral party or a vulture. It was a vulture that brought Sanjay his lucky charm.

This is not a superstitious book. Of all the countries in the world that need less superstition than they already have, India is up there near the top of the list. But nobody who believes in chance can rule out coincidence. It is one of the properties of randomness to produce patterns, and one of the patterns it produced in Sanjay's growing years can only be called his luck. The scrap that fell from the sky might have landed too far away for him to hear. Or it might have landed where it did, yet made no noise. The only reason it made a noise – an infinitesimal, single click – was that it contained metal. Sanjay bent to examine the rotten but still identifiable outline of a human ear. The metal was a tiny domed cylinder in its lobe. The tiny

29

domed cylinder gleamed with the same deep colour as the belt buckle of the shining man. The *look* of gold is plentiful in India. One of that country's many attractions is that a woman of no great wealth may wear a sari lavish with gold filigree even as she carries a basket of rotting fish on her head. The gods in the ashrams glow like El Dorado behind their smoke-screens of burning incense. But all that golden fretwork and folderol is no thicker than a molecule. The solidity of real gold is so rare that there is no mistaking it once you have seen the difference. You can weigh it with your eyes. Sanjay, an aesthetic instinct being one of his strengths, looked at the gold piece and knew that it was precious. He couldn't know its history, which was quite unusual. The ear came from the body of a Parsee girl who had broken her father's heart at least twice, the second time by dying young and the first by having her ears pierced in a completely unacceptable way during a trip to London. She had never been allowed to wear the earrings she brought home, but had argued successfully for the right to plug the holes, and after she had broken her father's heart again – ruinously this time, by succumbing painfully to a blood disease whose progress not even his fortune could halt – he expiated some of his anguish by allowing her to keep her twin miniature adornments when she was laid out to be picked apart. Where one of them had gone was known only to the vultures who were still busy at her corpse. But the other now lay at Sanjay's feet, where it started a new history, as his talisman instead of hers. He pulled it from the putrescent flesh and hid it in his secret compartment, a special pocket in his shorts just under where his belt would have been had he possessed one. The one thing he knew for sure about his gold piece was that he wouldn't keep it long if anyone bigger than he was saw it, and the world was full of people who answered that description. He didn't yet know that they were growing fewer. He didn't know he was growing. But he knew enough to be cautious. The concept of *coming in handy one day* was already present in his mind, another token of its precocity. Thus armed, Sanjay negotiated the last street of the peninsula which had until then been concealing from him a view of his next stamping ground. There it was, stretching away behind the gently curving beach into the far

30

distance, with buildings near the other end that were taller than the hills, and a hinterland going back to infinity that was packed with nothing except more buildings, which experience had already taught him must be packed with people, who would also proliferate in all the streets between. It was bigger than the sea. It was Bombay.

6

Sanjay went down into the main part of the city and his real education began. Some of it even included the kinds of things that we call education when they happen to our own children. Most of it, however, was, for want of a better word, informal. Sanjay learned to beg by watching other beggars. He soon learned that his charm did something to offset his principal disadvantage, which was that he had nothing obviously wrong with him. Foreign tourists are at their most generous to beggars with limbs twisted or missing. Sanjay didn't fit that description. But he had a soulful look that appealed to the more discriminating. Soulfulness works better than cheekiness. Foreign tourists soon learn that they can't give something to every cripple in Bombay without courting penury in their turn. Having learned to hold back from the halt and the lame, they won't fork out for the facetious and ebullient, in however small a package. But a little boy who looks spiritual is in with a chance. Tourists were attracted to Sanjay as he was attracted to them. At first he met them only at the windows of the cabs and buses. A demand in search of its supply, he panhandled his way instinctively southwards towards the big hotels, from which the tourists began their journey into the city and its hinterlands. Before he quite got there, however, he was detained for a season at Chowpatty Beach.

Chowpatty is much more down-market than Juhu. The people who go there to relax and be entertained are ordinary citizens of Bombay who have little money to spare for the poor, from whom they are only a step up, but there is money to be made in supplying them with drink, food and spectacle. In addition to the regular funfairs with their donkey rides, Ferris wheels and shooting galleries, the beach offers a copious supply of freelance side-shows. Anyone who can do anything to hold a crowd can just move in and start work, provided he can find a space. At any one time in daylight, and far into the evening under the light of lamps, the beach will feature the acrobatic family, the troupe of flagellant dancers, the man buried alive, the snakecharmer, the strong man who ties knots in an iron bar, and any other routine even mildly interesting. Around each act, a crowd forms three deep in a talkative circle. At the busiest times, on rest days, the crowds practically touch each other. If you aren't tall, it's like fighting your way through a crowd without even knowing why it's there, until suddenly you burst through into a clear space and find a man sitting in the middle of it with a fire flickering on his turban while he kisses a cobra. Sanjay, being the reverse of tall, could see between people's legs, but it was still hard to guess what he would find next. Lucky as usual, he found a family of magicians on the very afternoon when their youngest son was discovered to have grown too big for the disappearing trick. He could still get into the box all right but when he curled up in the secret compartment he couldn't uncurl afterwards. The boy was handed over to a nearby fakir in the hope that he could be straightened out. The father of the family was worrying about how to replace him at the exact moment Sanjay showed up.

Sanjay proved a natural for the act. The father of the troupe taught him to look apprehensive when he climbed into the box and to look pleased later on when he jumped out of the bag. But it was Sanjay who added the little skip of delight, the finger pose and the flashing smile. The usual murmur of wonder elicited by this apparent teleportation was boosted by Sanjay's antics into a round of applause and a detectable increase in revenue. None of the money trickled down to Sanjay, but at least he was fed, and for a while he took advantage of the corner of the family hovel that was assigned to him for sleeping quarters. They even had a blanket. Until then, Sanjay's method of getting warm on a cold night had been to shiver until he was exhausted. He might have settled in to stay if the older boys in the family hadn't made life miserable for him. They were envious and strong – an unbeatable combination. Sanjay lasted only one season. One of the older boys, however, had friends in a scavenger gang, to which Sanjay, making a quiet deal behind the older boy's back, transferred his allegiance. The gang worked the esplanade all the way south to the point, and then back again on the inside of the harbour to the small peninsula jutting out in front of the Taj Mahal hotel, usually called the Tajma for short. In front of the Tajma, the Gateway to India stands, marking the place where invaders have come ashore since the time of the Portuguese. Once the British army landed there. In recent times, European and American television crews have pretended to arrive there by boat even though they really drove in from the airport. It is Bombay's heart, into which Sanjay, at the age of about nine, was eventually drawn like a blood corpuscle. The analogy is useful, because a heart pumps blood corpuscles out as well as in, and Sanjay wasn't there long before he was driven out again by the force of the competition.

Rounded by the sea wall, fronted by the towering gate, and backed up by the cliff-like Tajma, the foyer of Bombay is the big time for the city's beggars, the Broadway of their essentially histrionic profession. It might look like a casual assembly point for strolling buskers, but in fact it is all staked out. Below the sea wall, the big motor launches take on their passengers for the trip out to the islands that guard the harbour, the islands which Sanjay had thought were other countries. In the tourist season, visitors of every nationality crowd the upper decks of the boats. While waiting for their trip to start they watch small boys jumping and diving off the sea wall into waves the colour of mud. The cleverest of the boys can catch coins on the way down. There is always at least one boy who can somersault – quite a thing to learn by yourself if you have never been in a swimming bath, or even in a bath. It all looks spontaneous and joyous but any boy who tried to join in unasked would face a pitiless interview panel after the first jump.

Inside the parapet of the sea wall, on the broad flag-stoned expanse around the gate, all the stall-holders have their assigned pitch. The snakecharmer wants no other animal act near him. Coiled hissing in his basket lies the means to discourage rivals if it ever comes to the point. The little boy who blacks your shoes doesn't own his kit. His protector does. There are only three men doing lightning sketches and there is no place for a fourth. Women selling trinkets from glittering mats are evenly spaced, with never two mats adjacent. The boys selling fake bottled mineral water to the foreign boat-trippers are working for the man who has the monopoly on buying the used cloudy blue plastic bottles, filling them with very ordinary tap-water, and capping them with the old machine his brother stole for him from the factory. (The fake bottled water trade rather depends on the unwitting purchasers not catching anything more serious than hepatitis, so amateur fake bottlers – bogus fake bottlers, as it were – are not encouraged, for fear they will lower the standard.) The beggars look less well organised than the merchants and entertainers but a new arrival still has trouble getting started. There are only so many spots for crippled women with babies. The star amputee can paddle his trolley fast enough to keep up with a taxi as it slows to turn beyond reach into the guarded driveway of the Tajma. He would paddle it just as effectively straight at any other trolley that tried to crowd his pitch.

Isolated and insulated in your hotel room, you can look down into this open-air theatre and gradually work out how its cast is able to stage such an all-feature-player, no-star spectacular without a single shout from a producer. Devoid of any ambition except to continue, inspired by nothing except its own customs and system of seniority, the show is an infinitely renewable yet entirely outdated automatic perennial, in the way that the Moscow Arts Theatre lived on without Stanislavsky, the NBC Symphony Orchestra without Toscanini, and the Glenn Miller big band without Glenn Miller. Such reflections are a luxury you can afford. Your mini-bar is full of real Pepsi, a touch of the remote control will bring you MTV, the BBC and all those wonderfully terrible Indian movies, you will sleep between sheets and soon you will be going home. But for them down there, this is home: a self-regulating economic system within pitiably diffident limits, desperation only a breath away. If a group of visitors tries to undertip the snakecharmer after he shows them how the mongoose bites the head off the new-born cobra, he will follow them with a writhing sack

35

held high until they get the point. The policeman on the beat will be slow to intervene.

Sanjay tried begging from a taxi full of visitors turning into the Tajma and had his ankle skinned from behind. The amputee on the trolley shook his head with firm regret. Since his head was one of the few moving parts he had left, the gesture was doubly emphatic. Sanjay tried a few other dodges but everything was taken. The heart was pumping him out. It was all for the best. He wasn't ready for the major leagues. An overriding consideration was that there was nowhere to hole up. Every niche was occupied. The elite of the younger beggars and thieves slept on the roof of the public toilet in the square to one side and just inland from the Tajma. It was the top spot. On hot nights, the sea breeze filtering across the roof did much to offset the piercing salience of the odour rising from below. Savvy and cocksure, the ruling clique smoked heroin off silver paper, swapped gossip and made plans for the next day. Listening from a distance, Sanjay was attacked by the envy that fuels ambition. Vowing to come back, he moved on for a few blocks inland, where he providentially arrived at the crucial open area in front of Victoria Terminus, the biggest railway station in Bombay.

As its name implies, Victoria Terminus is a leftover from the Raj. Like all the big imperial buildings in that area of Bombay it has the polychrome brick texture of Victorian architecture at the height of its confidence and the depth of its pocket. At a glance, and if you could filter out the people, the general effect of the area would be to remind you of the South Kensington museums, except on an even grander scale and less invaded by anachronistic disimprovements. In the principal Victorian buildings of London all the architectural styles of Europe were transferred through time to a harmonious meeting point. In Bombay the same transference occurred not just in time but in space. Historic Europe took off like Laputa and landed seventy-five degrees of longitude to the east, in the wrong context but the right atmosphere. The buildings look worn, but they have worn astonishingly well. A bit of dirt and a few cracks hurt them less than a too-meticulous restoration might have done. In Kensington you can see the danger of re-pointing: heritage is stripped of history, and what

36

was once created in the full flush of practicality starts looking as re-created as any too-clean Californian simulacrum of the Globe theatre, saved from belonging to Disneyland only by the absence of Donald Duck. No such danger threatens Bombay's imperial centre in general or Victoria Terminus in particular. The station, indeed, is an ideal example of how such a building should age – in its own time, like the human face, with no nips and tucks. It can't be denied, however, that when you get close up you can see how erstwhile grandeur has fallen on hard times. The great station no longer plays hostess to great trains. This is appropriate, because there are no longer any great people to travel great distances. When the grand go a long way, they fly. Into Victoria Terminus nowadays come the commuters from the suburbs and the visitors from outlying districts. Only the commuters can be relied on to go out again, and they will be coming back in next morning, more of them all the time. So Victoria Terminus, even more than the bus stations and much more than the airport, is a funnel to force-feed Bombay with people. The more prosperous the city gets, the more they come, to generate poverty in step with the wealth. Just how poor some of them are going to get is indicated to them as they arrive. They debouch into the yammering propinquity of the station concourse, stiff at all times with beggars, very small-time merchants and con-men so giftless they can't fool a foreigner. Gangs of scavenging children work the tracks to gather the detritus of the trains bulging with people. But the most edifying hint of what the city holds in store lies in the square outside and its attendant roads. It lies there to sleep through the hot nights. It is the population of the asphalt and the concrete. They curl up to sleep on the footpaths and traffic islands.

Sanjay slept on a traffic island for a few nights while he spent the daylight doing a reconnaissance in depth of the station concourse and all the surrounding area. His first sight of the imperial buildings had overwhelmed him. If they had been painted silver he would have thought he had arrived at the capital city of Long Ago. Victoria Terminus was not only ten times as big as the Silver Castle, it had a roof, so that when he got inside it he experienced its vastness like an absurdly expanded room. But he soon began to suspect that he had

37

come to the wrong place. Begging opportunities around the station were thin. He had long before realised that an Indian reduced to begging from his fellow Indians was fated not to prosper. On the other hand, opportunities for trade seemed to be all wrapped up. The scavenging gangs of children who worked the tracks made it painfully clear that they weren't taking on any new recruits for the present. Outside the station, business prospects were all the more bleak for being lit up by the unrelenting sun. Starting near the station concourse and stretching away past Azad Park on the Mahapalika Marg, there is a footpath bazaar whose personnel hold qualifications fit to stifle the hope of the most ambitious interloper. Here, the fortune teller has three parrots. The painter of miniature portraits has a different brush for each colour. The shoe-shine man has polish of every colour and can actually mend shoes with real tools, including a new-looking hammer free of rust. Sanjay was particularly impressed by the dentist. At the time we are talking about, India's economy had not yet been deregulated. That inevitable change was already imminent, however, and small businessmen were beginning to appear all over the city. But the really small businesses, run by solo entrepreneurs with a single carpet doubling as their open-air office and show-room, had always been there, long before they were supposed to be, and would probably go on being there tomorrow even if the country were ruled from Beijing. The pavement dentist has been tending teeth since before Independence, providing a service that no government-controlled economy had ever managed to extend to the less well-off, despite loudly dedicating itself to doing so. He is still there now, ready to remodel mouths that have unaccountably failed to catch their share of the wealth which in theory has already begun to trickle down, nay gush, from the new prosperity. Sitting cross-legged on his mat with his back against the railings, surrounded by an appreciative crowd, he pokes the gaps in a squatting patient's dentition with his experienced fingers. From a tin can full of teeth extracted from previous patients he finds one to fill the empty space. He glues it into position and the patient goes away happy. Patients needing an extraction are less happy because the dentist has no anaesthetic, but he doesn't charge much either, so it balances out. For

38

customers with a lot of teeth missing he can offer upper and lower plates with roughly the right number of teeth in the right place. For customers with no teeth at all he can offer a complete set. It used to belong to somebody else, but what he does not offer is an explanation of how he got hold of it. In Cairo, as Naguib Mahfouz tells us in his great novel *Midacq Alley*, the dentists in the bazaar notoriously rob graves. A Bombay street dentist is more likely to have his sets of false teeth willed to him by patients to whom he only hired them out in the first place, on the understanding that they will revert to him upon the patient's demise. Whatever way he gets them, he's got them. They are all there on the mat beside him, marshalled in ranks, a cheerful collection of Cheshire smiles. On the day Sanjay came by, the dentist was fitting a shoeless man with a new upper left incisor. It had once been somebody else's upper right incisor but with a bit of chiselling it filled the gap. Sanjay was impressed by how the dentist, without taking his eyes off the patient's open mouth, rinsed his instruments in an enamelled tin bowl full of water before drying them with a rag and laying them out. For almost the first time in his life, Sanjay made a verbal suggestion.

"Can I do that?" he asked, pointing to the rinsing bowl. "I can do it."

The dentist, still holding his squatting patient's jaws apart with the extended fingers of one hand while he wielded a probe with the other, glanced at Sanjay and made a lightning calculation. The dentist knew that rinsing the instruments made no real difference because the water was changed only once a day: it was just for show. And the boy was filthier than the water. But his smile was a potential drawcard. His teeth blazed. So the dentist nodded and Sanjay joined the act.

It should have worked out. The crowd responded to Sanjay's subtle histrionics. Sitting beside the dentist, he frowned suitably when a new patient opened his mouth to reveal the nagging damage. When it had been repaired, Sanjay held up an approving thumb and flashed his smile. Also he made a great show of precision when rinsing and drying the instruments. By the afternoon of his second day on the job he had learned their names and could hand them up when called for. Viewed as a spectacular, the dentist's routine had gained a new dimension of expressiveness. But to please the crowd was not the principal object. The number of customers did not increase, so at the end of the day Sanjay was paid off with a few annas and a small photograph of Rajiv Gandhi at his most radiant – one of a supply of celebrity snaps which the dentist drew upon to help convince customers, against all likelihood, that he had once plied his trade in high circles. Another photograph Sanjay might have asked for was of the shining man, his smile white beneath his moustache like the moon cut off by a black cloud. But when Sanjay saw that face he felt betrayal. It was a familiar feeling. All over the city there were big pictures with writing on them up on the walls of buildings. Sometimes the pictures were of the shining man or the beautiful woman. Sometimes they were together. Sanjay rarely looked up at them for long. They made his eyes wet.

That, for a while, was the end of Sanjay's career in the acting profession. A foundation had been laid, but for some time he was not to know that. It was his closely allied talent for deception that led him into his next phase – providentially, because what he now needed most in life was a new set of clothes, and helping out with street theatre would never have brought him that. Retiring, temporarily defeated, from the stage, he went back into the echoing, Acherontic ostinato of Victoria Terminus just in time to be adopted as a decoy by a shoe-stealing gang. The gang worked the trains on their way to the outer suburbs and beyond. Commuters flush enough to own shoes often took them off to rest their feet, especially if, by some miracle, they had found room to stretch out. Most of them were on guard against losing their shoes while they were awake. When they slept, they were open to having their shoes lifted by the dab hands of the shoe stealers. Good shoe stealers could steal a man's shoes even when they were still on his feet, provided he was sufficiently drowsy or distracted. Sanjay got the job of being distracting. It worked all right the first day, but on the second day the older boy to whom he had been apprenticed made the mistake of working a compartment that was merely full instead of bursting. There was room for the insufficiently unwitting victim to lunge. He forfeited his shoes, but he came up with Sanjay, who found himself travelling back to Victoria Terminus in the company of a policeman.

It was a turning point, because Sanjay might have gone to children's prison right then, without going to school first. Luckily the police were sufficiently sadistic to believe that school might be a worse punishment than the cane, though they caned him for a while anyway, just to show him what he was being spared. As a resident of the second biggest traffic island in front of Victoria Terminus, Sanjay was not strictly within the catchment area of the Bibhuti Road Youth Club, a Christian foundation which offers a day of schooling once a week to any street children within a mile radius. From Victoria Terminus to Bibhuti Road is more than a mile. But he was delivered there anyway. If schooling were all that the Youth Club offered then no child would go near it except at the point of a policeman's whippy stick. Nor is the initial compulsory rub-down with soap and water an enticement. Once the muddy suds are sluiced off, however, the bounty starts to flow. On first attendance, and once a year thereafter, the street children can choose a new set of old clothes to replace their old set of old clothes. Set up in the courtyard there is a small Ferris wheel – a child of the big one on Chowpatty beach – on which they are allowed to play so long as they don't fight. At the apex of the day there is the irresistible prospect of an actual meal, with several different kinds of food on the one paper plate: a cornucopia that adds up to more than most of them have eaten for the rest of the week. To sit and learn for an hour or so is a small price to pay for all that. There are other penalties too: the man with the booming voice who runs the place unaccountably feels compelled to make you sit in line, segregated by sex, and recite votes of thanks aimed at someone in the sky, the performance climaxing in a mass cheer which he induces by swinging his right arm many times backwards in a blurred circle while rising on his toes as if the action were pulling him off the ground. Sanjay moved his mouth at the right times. The policeman had made it clear that a bad report from the man with the booming voice would result in worse punishment than this.

Sanjay's level of rebellion had been unnaturally low ever since he had been pushed through the gate along with the hundred and fifty

41

other children streaming into the Club. He had been the only one accompanied by a policeman and obviously the only one who didn't know where he was. Along with a batch of boys, he was pushed into a walled-off washing area and given a preliminary dousing with his clothes still on. A big boy in a white suit attacked him with a bar of soap. The object seemed to be to get his clothes clean before he took them off. Everyone else was yelling so he felt less self-conscious than he might have done about yelling as well. Judging by the noise coming from the other side of the wall, a batch of girls were getting the same treatment. When he had to remove his sodden clothes he complied, whereupon the soap was applied directly to his person. The big boy seemed intent on removing his cane-weals along with the dirt. Creamed thickly, Sanjay had his eyes shut when the waterfall from an abruptly upended bucket descended on his head. Only the deeply etched memory of his first day at the Silver Castle made this comprehensible. Otherwise he might have tried to run off naked. But that would also have meant leaving his gold piece behind. When he was told to put his sodden clothes back on again, he checked to make sure the gold piece was still there. The next thing that happened was comparatively pleasant, although still bewildering. He and the rest of his batch were released into the playground to dry off. He was taught to take his turn on the small Ferris wheel by being punched when he tried to jump the queue. When he lost at a game of checkers, he had his ear twisted to dissuade him from calling his opponents cheats. Bruised but clean, he was in mixed spirits when he was led inside the hall. But the next thing was amazing.

There was a table of clothes and a woman in a sari to help him choose some to fit. She explained that they had to be a bit bigger than seemed right, because they had to last a year, and he didn't want them to get as tight as the ones he had on now, did he? Her voice was strict but her movements were kind. His only real concern was to transfer his gold piece safely from his old pair of shorts to the new pair. This he accomplished, although he was worried that he had nowhere to put it except into the empty depths of a side pocket. Later on, when he got the chance, he would find a secret compartment. "We might manage some form of footwear, later," said the strictly kind woman. "After school." What she said was too complicated to follow. His punishment, he now found, was only beginning, because he was marched over to sit with twenty or so other boys in front of a big blackboard held off the floor on a wooden stand. The strictly kind woman covered the board with a stiff piece of paper full of pictures and signs as if the parrot man's cards had been stuck together edge to edge – and what was to pass for Sanjay's formal education commenced.

7

Sitting down cross-legged and looking up, Sanjay was faced with the Hindi alphabet. Although he was weeks behind the rest of his class, he caught up half the distance in that first hour. Along with a good memory he had the priceless extra quality which is best described as a knack for language. Talent is too exalted a word for it: there are people who can learn a dozen languages without effort but are unable to say anything of interest in any of them. The knack for language is, however, a characteristic which, like musicality, can look like magic to those who don't possess it. Long before the obediently chanting Sanjay had memorised all the symbols of the alphabet, he had already figured out that this must be a system for writing down and reading out the same things that he could say. Each letter of the alphabet was represented on the chart by a thing whose name began with the letter. Sanjay soon grasped that the rest of the name must be composed of letters too. Rapidly he arrived at the point of being able to guess what the next letter to be learned must be, because he had already seen it as part of the word written out in full under a previous thing. This process was made easier for him by the nature of the Hindi alphabet, which is phonetic: the letters are really the invariable symbols of a syllabary. Phonetic alphabets may look different from each other but they have the advantage in common of providing an exact transcription, syllable by syllable, of what is said. Written down, Hindi looks like rows of little pots with lids and farm implements hanging from their handles, the lids and handles all joining up in a straight line along the top, like a shelf. Gujarati, the other main Indian language of the area, looks like Hindi but without the shelf.

The resemblance is not surprising because both Hindi and Gujarati are derivatives of Sanskrit. If Bombay, as might have happened, had joined the state of Gujarat instead of the state of Maharashtra, Sanjay might have been learning Gujarati. He would have found it just as easy. If he had come from a Muslim household, he might have been learning Urdu, which sounds the same as Hindi, but is written down in Arabic notation. Written Arabic looks like the rippled patterns of sand under clear water, and sometimes the ripples combine into intricate whorls of linked arabesques which take a certain amount of unscrambling, but basically a phonetic script is what it is: you say what you see.

All over the world there are phonetic alphabets and each has its individual beauty. Hebrew looks like flames, and the only reason it is hard for the foreigner to learn is that the sparks – the dots indicating the vowels – are usually not presented, because it is assumed that you know where they must come, having grown up watching the fire. Hiragana, one of the two phonetic alphabets which combine with the Kanji characters to form Japanese, is already graceful even before you can read the poetry that is partly written in it, whereas Katakana, the other Japanese phonetic alphabet, is already a memorably sharp collection of knives and hooks before you can read the foreign loan-words it so aggressively transcribes. If Japanese were written solely in one of its phonetic alphabets, or even in both, anyone could learn it. What makes Japanese impossible to learn quickly is the Kanji – a set of complicated ideographs which have to be memorised separately and in combination, like Chinese only more so: Japanese children spend ten years of school learning the first thousand, with thousands more still to go. It sounds hard to do and it is. Yet people brought up in the English language often fail to realise that they learned their own language in the same way. The alphabet in use throughout western Europe comes close to being a phonetic transcription only in those languages which, like Italian and Spanish, offer you the advantage of saying more or less what you see. But in English you can do that even less than you can do it in French, and far less than you can do it in German. English could be learned much more quickly if it were written down in the Russian Cyrillic alphabet, the only logical aspect of the Russian language. In English, learning the alphabet is only a small first step towards learning to read, because in actual words the letters are often used in combinations which have to be memorised like ideographs. A little word like 'phlegm', for example, contains two of them: a one-syllable word with five consonants in it, like a whole family of circus dwarves in their trick car. It is no wonder, then, that with the decline, in many ways welcome, of prescriptive schooling, the English-speaking countries now produce generation after generation of people who are at a loss to read as well as they can speak, and that foreigners studying English have to be trained scholars in the first place if they are ever to read anything complicated. One of the most unpalatable facts about the great synthetic nation of India is that its lingua franca, English, is written down in an alphabet so insanely unfaithful to what is said, whereas the principal sectarian languages can, in their written form, be mastered with comparative ease. So the alien language which was meant to unite India has turned out to be universal only in its frustrating elusiveness, whereas the languages which divide it have one dangerous element in common – they feel like home. Chanting along with his Hindi class for one hour of one day of each week for a month, stocking the shelves of his mind with all those pots and tools, Sanjay made a good start on building for himself a house to live in – the one house to which he would ever enjoy the undisputed title. The house was only in his mind, but at least he would be able to find his way about in it, as so few of our own children really can. If English had been the first language that the strictly kind woman had tried to teach him, he would have got nowhere, because time would have been against him, as it always was, even before he was born.

The strictly kind woman had seen many bright street children come and go. There was always at least one of them in each class. The bright boys might go on to become better equipped thieves than they would otherwise have been, the girls to become slightly more liberated child prostitutes. Even more than her husband, the strictly kind woman had learned to temper boundless hope with realistic expectations, and to regard the small improvements she could make as an absolute good, without brooding about the consequences.

46

Sanjay was one of those exceptionally bright boys who made her fear for them almost as much as she feared for the girls. His astuteness was pure, like virginity. She enjoyed his smile but found it untrustworthy, as well she might have done, because it had come in useful too often: it had the look of knowingness about it. He had learned his shy charm in a different and harder school. But a thirst for knowledge is not the same as knowingness. For as long as the first burns, the second evaporates; and there were moments, as he sat in class, when a flash of comprehension transfigured his face, replacing the self-conscious giving out of delight with the far more delightful forgetfulness of a revelation taken in. At those moments she enjoyed him without reserve. Though she loved her own children they were lifeless by comparison. Sanjay's hand would go up automatically when he knew the answer. He would come to the blackboard as if drawn by a magnet. Only on his way back to his place, after explicating the chart with a speed and certainty that left his classmates variously awed, envious and annoyed, did he once again adopt the smirk and swagger that marked his pleasure in his own energy. After his first few classes, when some of the older boys had often enough taken him aside in the playground to encourage greater humility, he took care to mask his satisfaction, converting the swagger into a casual walk and the smirk into a look of near contrition. The strictly kind woman easily guessed that these new attitudes were as posed as the old. But when he made a new connection there was no disguising his radiant surprise. He sat there like a little Buddha with the light flooding into him instead of out.

The strictly kind woman was thought by all the children, including Sanjay, to be without variable emotions. She just stood there conducting the lesson, deploying praise and blame with an even hand, in an even voice. She was always careful to play no favourites. In her mind, however, she cherished Sanjay and resolved to give him what extra treats she could, if only to ensure that he would come back, and not go to waste immediately as most of the brighter boys did eventually, just like the dull ones. At the end of the first hour she made sure that he got a pair of sandals. At the end of subsequent hours she coached him for ten or fifteen minutes of private

47

conversation, correcting his sentences without letting it feel too much like a lesson. She asked him where he was living.

"I sleep in front Victoria," he said.

"I am sleeping in front of Victoria," she said, strictly but kindly. In Hindi the continuous form of the verb is marked by a suffix, rather the way it is in English. Sanjay absorbed the construction and soon started using it with other verbs as well. The capacity for generative grammar is meant to be a human characteristic but some humans find it easier than others and Sanjay seemed to find it as easy as breathing. Moved to a rare concession, the strictly kind woman told him that outside of class he should call her by her first name, Sabbandra.

"Sure, Sabbandra."

"Don't be so cocky. It makes a bad impression. Just say yes, Sabbandra."

"Yes, Sabbandra. I sorry."

"I *am* sorry."

"I *am* sorry."

"No. Just I am sorry. Don't emphasise it."

"I am sorry."

"That's perfect."

Sabbandra pretended that Sanjay's new T-shirt didn't fit him. Actually it did – it was about two years' too big, which was even better than one year too big – but secretly she thought a plainer design would be more attractive. She found him a plainer, pale pink T-shirt in slightly better material and made him change into it. Giving him extra food would have been too blatant.

So Sanjay had a guardian angel. Unfortunately her sphere of influence stopped at the church gate. Outside he was back in the real world, which was getting harsher as he grew. When the monsoon came again he was washed off the traffic island in front of Victoria Terminus and had to trek a long way before he found shelter he could occupy without a fight. He ended up under a fishing wharf further around the harbour and back in an inlet. It was a long way to school through the rain but he only had to make the two-way trip

48

once a week and by now he was much less likely to get lost: a map of the city was forming in his mind.

Meanwhile the wharf gave him shelter. There were at least fifty other street children there to fill the places not occupied by fishermen's dependants who had gathered when the rains started and had found no room in the hovels. Yet Sanjay had been able to find a good spot against a piling and had formed alliances to protect it when he was away. Most of the street children belonged to gangs. One of the gangs worked the tourist boats out to Elephant Island. The gang's leader was an older boy called Dilip. He had a very dark, pitted skin and wore long pants. His gang must have been doing well because he smoked all the time and sported a heavy signet ring with his initials on it. Dilip took a fancy to Sanjay, who in this case, it must be confessed, found it diplomatic to make himself fanciable. Dilip's demands in that regard were not excessive. In the darkness he asked only to be stroked until some stuff came out. He held up a lighted match so that Sanjay could watch it happen. Dilip in turn made sure that Sanjay got a good share of the stolen fish. The fishing went on even in the rain. There were tubs of small fish everywhere. Big fish lay piled on planks. Sting-rays with their tails cut off were spread out on the sand like thick mats. The fishermen and their families couldn't watch it all. Dilip's gang usually had a fire burning somewhere or other so they could eat their fish cooked. Sanjay was interested to discover that the fish tasted better that way. Though the stench under the wharf was paralysing, it would last only for a season, and soon the tourists would be on their way again to Elephant Island. Dilip invited Sanjay to join his gang when the traffic resumed. One of the other senior gang members was annoyed that he had not been consulted. Dilip reconciled him to the situation by stubbing out a cigarette on the back of his hand.

The rain stopped and the boats leaving from the Gateway of India once again began to fill with tourists. First of all, however, the gang had to build up a bank, because it was hard to get on a boat without a ticket. Dilip had money. He had shown it to Sanjay. It was a sodden pad of blue fifty anna notes kept in a purse. But he wanted to hang on to it. So for a week the gang scavenged along the railway lines of the suburban stations a mile inland. The pickings would have been better in Victoria Terminus, but in Dilip's view it wouldn't have been worth a fight with the gangs that were there already, especially with so many police around. Sanjay was relieved: he didn't want to meet that policeman again. The suburban stations were slow work but steady. You just had to be careful about listening for a fast train. They lost one gang member that way. "Best thing, really," said Dilip. "Anja always was too slow on his feet."

Their best prize was a wallet with half a dozen brown notes in it – one of them for a whole ten rupees – that must have fallen out of somebody's pocket as he clung to the outside of one of the scrums around the train doors. Everything else was junk they had to trade in. Eventually they had enough to buy tickets for the whole gang, now reduced from seven boys to six. With Dilip in the lead they trekked on foot to the Gateway of India and waited amongst the hubbub for the right boat.

"The Japanese are useless," Dilip told Sanjay. "They never give you anything unless their group leader tells them to. If their group leader tell them to jump in front of a truck they all do it. Otherwise they do nothing. What we want is Europeans, especially Italians."

"How can you tell which is which?" Sanjay was fascinated.

"By the way they sound. You'll pick it up."

In the middle of the morning the top deck of one of the boats filled up with a lot of different groups of people speaking English and one big group speaking the language that Dilip said was Italian. So the gang got on board too and climbed to the top deck, where the Italian group had taken the seats and benches at the back. Another ten minutes went by before the boat cast off. Small, nearly naked boys were jumping off the sea wall into the muddy water beside the boat. One of them could do a somersault. The Italian men threw coins to the boys on their way down. The Italian women clapped and laughed. One of them cried into a handkerchief when a boy swimming back to the stone steps was thrown against them by a wave and skinned his leg from knee to ankle.

"Perfect," said Dilip. "Go and stand in front of the women and give them a smile. But don't ask for anything yet. Wait until we get to the island."

Sanjay did some smiling as the boat headed out into the bay. The women adored him. He could tell that, even though the words were strange.

"*Poverino! Che bello!*"

He adored them, although in a different way. It was their clothes and their skin. The materials were so soft and clinging, and there was so much skin left uncovered. Their sandals had fine straps that crossed and re-crossed over their ankles like basket work. His own sandals smelled of rotten fish and were already falling apart. One of the men tried to give him a fifty anna note but he shook his head. He could tell straight away that this made a good impression. Dilip was clever. Sanjay went back to join him near the front of the top deck.

"Just right," said Dilip. "Well done. On the island you can take what they give and it will be more."

The boat chugged past a headland behind which a huge grey ship rode at anchor.

"Aeroplanes land on that ship," said Dilip, who knew everything. Sanjay looked hard but could see no aeroplanes. He knew what aeroplanes were because he had seen them in the sky. They were silver, so he had always assumed that they came from Long Ago. Halfway to Elephant Island they passed the smaller island on which, at the water's edge, stood the domed white city he had once seen from the apartment block near the Towers of Silence. From close up it looked a bit less like Long Ago than it had from far away. Dilip could see that he looked puzzled.

"That's the atomic power station."

"Do people live there?"

"They have to wear white suits."

Perhaps it was Long Ago after all. Sanjay shelved the question when some of the English-speaking people loudly called him over to join in a photograph.

"They're Americans," said Dilip. "You can tell by how loud they are all the time. The Australians talk loudly when they're drunk. The

English talk softly except if the men have short haircuts. Be shy for a while and then go over and do some smiling. Don't take any money."

Some of the other gang members were doing their best to ingratiate themselves as well. They had had more practice, but Sanjay did better from the jump, especially with the women. It was the last year of his cuteness. Soon he would be good looking, which is a different thing, and more threatening.

The boat docked beside the long stone jetty that serves Elephant Island. From the lower deck the Indian passengers streamed ashore. The European passengers shuffled down the wide staircase beside the wheel-house to follow them across the gangplanks and up the stone stairs from the landing to the level of the causeway.

A whole family which just happened to be washing its dishes and clothes at the water's edge successfully demanded compensation for being photographed. They got a rupee for each *ooh* and *aah*. Already the chair-bearers and the merchants were yelling at the Europeans from the jetty. Leaning against the railing at the head of the staircase, Sanjay smiled at the Italian women as they descended. He could see down their blouses and marvelled at the firm roundness, the skin you could look into. Under the skin he could see little branches of sky.

"You're too old to suck on those," said Dilip. "Too old and too young."

On shore, some of the Americans had hired carrying chairs. Each American got into a chair and was lifted up by four chair-bearers, one at each end of two long poles that supported the chair. Under the weight of one of the American men, a giant, the poles curved and creaked. He looked pleased instead of angry when the American women laughed. There were only a few chairs but not all of them were hired. Most of the Europeans elected to walk, first along the jetty and then along the causeway leading to the island. Beggars and merchants accosted them as they walked. Some of the merchants would set out a stall, wait until everyone had gone by, fold up the stall, run ahead, and set it out again. The Italians joined the end of the procession. The woman who had cried at the injured diver waved at Sanjay as he was crossing the gangplank. She was waving him towards her, shouting a word he didn't understand.

"Vieni! Vieni!"

"She says come, come," said Dilip.

"She is saying come, come."

"Don't correct me again or I'll smash your head, you little turd. Now get after her and hold her hand."

Adopted by the Italian woman, Sanjay accompanied her group as it made its slow way up the hill on the stone path. Dilip and the rest of the gang went ahead to stay near the Americans and the English. From both sides of the path, peddlers and beggars vocally assaulted the tourists. Souvenir shops gave way to trinket sellers as the path zig-zagged upwards, often in the form of a staircase whose stone steps were worn concave. The tourists walked the gauntlet, the more gullible weighing themselves down with knick-knacks as they ascended. Sanjay stayed near the hip of his marvelling woman. It was all new to him, too, so he was glad of the company. At the top there was a stone-paved plaza among the trees. Monkeys came to be fed. The tourists bought bread to feed them. Sanjay was given bread too. He could tell that the woman feared him less than she feared the monkeys.

In the cave at the top of the hill a temple to the gods had been fashioned out of the living rock, long before the Portuguese came. When they came they hacked off the faces and breasts of the female gods together with all their attendant erotic minor statuary. The defaced deities sit there in semi-darkness, inscrutably resisting the last erosion, a steady murmur of foreign voices that swells and ebbs with the seasons of the year. There is not much left to be astonished by. Bombay is not the place to come to if Indian art is what you're after. Sanjay's woman did her best. She *ooh*ed and *aah*ed, in a soft register overwhelmed by the boom of the Americans. The Italians were last in and last to leave. As they were leaving, Sanjay felt a tug at his sleeve. Dilip drew him behind one of the thick columns joining the floor to the roof.

"Wait until they get outside," he said quietly, "and then go and give them this."

It was a wrist-watch. From his point of concealment Sanjay could see his woman looking around for him. Now that she was alone, the heels of her sandals could be heard clicking on the stone floor. Finally she seemed to assume that he had gone ahead, and she went out into the sunlight.

"Wait for a minute," said Dilip. "Wait until he realises he's lost it. He'll start yelling."

There were raised voices outside.

"Now. Just show it and tell them you found it. Don't hold out your hand afterwards. They'll give you something anyway."

It all worked out the way Dilip said. "*Tesoro! Tesoro!*" wept Sanjay's woman. He could tell it was a kind word. Once again Sanjay was impressed by how clever Dilip was. Sanjay didn't mind, later on, when Dilip took all the money off him and put it in his own pocket. That was a right conferred on him by his cleverness and long pants. On the way back down the hill the woman held Sanjay's hand except when she was buying souvenirs. The Italians bought so much merchandise they needed the rest of Sanjay's gang to help carry it. Sanjay ended up carrying an elephant covered all over with mirrors and coloured thread. By the end of the boat ride back to the Gateway of India, all the boys had been given money, even if it was only a few rupees.

For weeks Dilip's gang worked these tricks and many others, shuttling back and forth to the island with a constantly changing cast of tourists. Sanjay developed a few tricks of his own. He could cadge the boat fare to the island just by standing near the gangplank and wiping tears from his eye. He learned his come-on in English, parrot fashion.

"I am living on island. They are taking my money."

Even when the English-speaking tourists didn't believe him they couldn't resist his act. Sanjay put his heart into his new trade. He didn't miss a day with the gang except when it was time to go to school. But the gang didn't work the boats every day. When they had built up a sufficient bank they went to the movies. Dilip was so rich he could have paid for them all to get in. He made them pay anyway, in case they got lazy. The rule with all the street gangs in Bombay is that they feed themselves mainly from the rubbish bins behind restaurants and hotels and they spend their money on the movies, although some

54

of the older boys smoke heavily as well. Even the boys who smoke heroin, however, go to the movies regularly, because the cinema is where you can find what you can't beg, steal or inhale – luxurious surroundings, the faces and extensively bared bodies of giant women, their stunning loveliness.

Sanjay was astounded by his first movie. He started being astounded at the entrance to the Palace cinema. He had never been among so many people trying to get into one place. It beat Victoria Terminus during the rush hour. When all the soldiers and dancers at the Silver Castle had broken for lunch it had been like this, but there they were fighting to get out of an open door, whereas here they were pushing against a closed one. In the foyer there were smaller versions of the huge posters in the streets that carried the stars' faces and the names of the films – names which Sanjay could now sometimes read. The faces of the stars were painted on the posters. Rahul Kapoor, the shining man, and Miranda, the beautiful woman, were both often represented, but Sanjay was never shocked into particular recognition, because the truth is that the film poster portraits are so indifferently painted that everyone looks the same. He still found the posters a continuous source of fascination. In the streets, they lined his path with enchantment. When he looked up, it was as if he were an ant walking through a tunnel made from the cards of the fortune teller. So the foyer was in some sense familiar. But when the gang got inside and raced for seats along with everyone else, Sanjay found something he had never experienced before except as a passenger in the car from Long Ago – the luxury of a soft seat just for himself. It was soft under his bottom and soft behind his back. Around and above him, the pillars and vaults of the Palace soared and swooped. Darkened by dirt, flaky with neglect, nevertheless the old art deco extravaganza found in Sanjay its ideal admirer. The architect, if he could have come back from oblivion, would have been pleased. At Nuremberg rallies there had been young Nazis less impressed by the dome of searchlights than Sanjay was by these cliffs of curried plaster. Their creator would have thought that his masterpiece had been distempered with dysentery. Sanjay thought he was in heaven. Better

55

than that: he was back in Long Ago, and this time there were no uncertainties and humiliations, only reassurance and delight.

Working the boats almost every day as the tourist season picked up, Dilip's gang could afford to go to the movies twice a week: sometimes three times. And Sanjay was still making it to school once a week. It added up to a busy schedule. Sanjay, although keen to learn, was no saint in the making: he would probably have cut school if Sabbandra had not known how to blackmail him with a laden paper plate. But he would never have missed a film. For a long time, almost the whole of that first year, he found it hard to believe that what he saw on the screen was the result of the kind of work he had seen done at the Silver Castle. He found it hard to believe even when he recognised Rahul Kapoor and Miranda, which he did often, because they were in many films, although more often separately than together. Unlike in the film posters, on the screen they were disturbingly real, just as he had once seen them. But their surroundings were different. Even when he thought he recognised the Silver Castle, only bits of it appeared. All the essential components were missing: the camera, the director, the small large woman and the crackling trumpet – they never appeared. The magic trumpets on the battlements produced sound instead of silence. It was a puzzle. There was an older boy, another gang leader called Sunil, who claimed to have the solution. Sunil's gang often sat in the row behind Dilip's gang. Dilip said that Sunil's gang were rent boys and always getting thrown in gaol. Dilip despised Sunil for not being clever. And indeed no other gang leader was as clever as Dilip: Sanjay could tell that. Only Dilip could have figured out that if you stole things from tourists and tried to sell them you would get caught, whereas if you found them and handed them back you would get paid. But Sanjay could also tell that Dilip had another reason for hating Sunil. Sunil was handsome whereas Dilip was not. Sunil's skin was as smooth as smoke and his teeth were straight. Sunil had charm. He was interesting. He plainly had access to all kinds of information denied to Dilip. Sunil had been places. Sunil had not actually been to the Silver Castle, but he seemed to know all about it. He said that there was no difference between what happened there and what happened on the screen. At the Silver Castle everything might happen ten times just as Sanjay had said, but later on, according to Sunil, they joined it all together so that it happened only once. Sanjay, without quite believing him, was very interested in this theory. Dilip, seeing that Sanjay was interested, grew annoyed. Sanjay learned not to turn around in his seat when Sunil was expounding, otherwise Dilip would take reprisals. This behaviour confirmed Sanjay's impression that Dilip didn't really like the idea of Sanjay's having had any life at all before he first came in under the wharf and out of the rain. Dilip was possessive, like Sanjay's father. It was advisable to be circumspect.

One afternoon Sanjay forgot his caution. The gang had arrived late at the movies and missed the opening titles of the main feature. Sanjay knew from the publicity that Rahul Kapoor and Miranda were both in it and that it was not new. But he was not prepared for the moment when the swordfight stopped, Rahul and Miranda locked eyes, and everyone began to dance. For Sanjay it was as if years had collapsed. He recognised every movement. He was so transported that he even forgot how what he was watching had led to his humiliation. He remembered only the enchantment of it all. He experienced the acute satisfaction of someone for whom a mystery has explained itself simply because its component parts have been moved sufficiently close together. Many times during that year, in half a dozen different films, he had seen Miranda's plum-stained lips part in a smile. But for *this* smile he had been *there*. When the screen filled with nothing but Miranda's face, and then with nothing except Rahul's face, as if the two faces were looking at each other, Sanjay was in delighted possession of the secret information that they weren't really looking at each other at all. They were just looking at the camera. He *knew*.

Sunil's gang was not sitting behind Dilip's gang that afternoon, but after the film the two gangs met each other in the crowd outside. Sanjay made the mistake of telling Sunil about his moment of truth. Sanjay spoke as off-handedly as possible but could not keep the excitement out of his voice.

"That was the film they were making when I was there."

57

"What did I tell you?" said Sunil. "She still lives down at Juhu. I know someone who has been in her apartment, delivering groceries."

Dilip overheard this conversation and seemed tolerant at the time. Later on, when he got Sanjay alone, he still didn't look angry. He just looked cold. First he positioned Sanjay carefully, almost clinically, against a wall. He cracked Sanjay's nose with the first blow of his fist. Before Sanjay had even raised his hands to hold the injured area, a second blow from the same fist split the skin above his left eye. Dilip walked away wiping blood from his heavy signet ring. Sanjay was left alone to slump into a sitting position against the wall with blood and tears seeping through his hands, as if what he had seen on the screen, multiplied in its impact as it sped out of the past, had exploded in his face like a revelation.

8

SCHOOL WAS FOUR days away, so by the time Sabbandra saw Sanjay's injured face the cut above his eye was already infected. He had been sleeping in the open again, which didn't help. She dressed the wound to the best of her ability, but when it healed there was a scar: a clear channel running obliquely through the eyebrow. She sent him to a doctor to help mend his nose. Whatever the doctor did, it didn't help. When the swelling finally went down, Sanjay's dead straight nose had healed crooked: not by much, but by enough to spoil his looks. He still had his allure. It was just a less symmetrical poem. Previously he had grown more handsome as you looked closely. Now he grew less so. Yet he was still enough of a catch for Sunil to take him over. They met a few weeks later at the movies when Sanjay was sitting alone, as many rows away from Dilip's gang as he could get. Sunil's gang was sitting behind Dilip's. Sunil left his gang and came to sit with Sanjay. The movie was a favourite for both of them, *Andaz Apna Apna.* It was the usual story of a frustrated love between a prince and a princess, played by Chunky and Poojah. First they hated each other, singing and dancing separately, but after the princess had disguised herself as a boy and run away to join the bandits, they fell in love properly in the middle of a battle. Then they danced together while their royal fathers looked wisely on. No story could have been more predictable. The singing and the dancing, however, were exceptionally fine, and Poojah's celebrated breasts were given many opportunities to dominate the screen. As was mandatory, they were well covered, yet their shape was so salient that there could be no doubt, in Sanjay's opinion, that the rumours were all wrong about her bodice being padded. Sunil had never believed these rumours anyway. He seemed to know everything about Poojah, and all the other stars as well.

Sanjay joined Sunil's gang in the coveted position of favourite. During the hot months Sunil's inner cabinet lived on the roof of the Tajma square toilet, the very place which Sanjay had once enviously marked down as the object of his aspiration. Now he was back to stay if he wanted to, because Sunil reigned supreme up there. There were never fewer than twenty boys in residence and they all deferred to him. Sunil had the best sleeping position, near the end of the roof where the bough of the tree spread low overhead to provide a kind of canopy. He gave Sanjay the place of honour beside him. Sunil wanted a little more from him than Dilip had but not much more. Some nights he wasn't even there. When he was, he required Sanjay's mouth as well as a helping hand. It was no great price to pay for the hospitality and Sanjay even found it emotionally satisfactory, because Sunil did things to him too. There were no tangible results, yet the excitement was intense: a kind of fever that made his head throb in the dark, under the stars.

It was a good place to sleep. The smell from below was significant but not overwhelming – certainly less pervasive than the smell under the fishing wharf where he had lived with Dilip. The olfactory truth about Bombay is that for all its squalor it doesn't smell very much. It's too hot for that. Organic waste rots quickly and evaporates. Odours get eaten up. Some of the odours rising from the toilet took a lot of counteracting but it was worth it for the sea breeze. The toilet roof was at just the right height to catch it. Only a hundred yards away the tourists in the Tajma were living in air-conditioned luxury. Sunil knew all about how they lived. He had friends, he said, who had actually been in there: one of them had an important job tending the minibars. Sunil knew everything. If Sunil said that the toilet roof was as comfortable as the Tajma, it must be so.

"Of course in the Tajma," Sunil said when they were smoking one night on the toilet roof, "you can get room service."

"Of course," said Sanjay, not really knowing what room service was but reluctant to display his ignorance.

"You can't get that here," said Sunil, releasing a slow stream of smoke after the last word. They were smoking heroin, one sip at a time from the same paper tube, in the cautious manner which Sunil favoured.

"No," said Sanjay, "but here you've got the breeze." He, too, strove to release the smoke in the most miserly plume possible.

"Some people go crazy from smoking this stuff," said Sunil. "People with no control. You have to take things a bit at a time. Then you last. No use going places if you can't last."

"No use," said Sanjay. "You said it."

Though heroin has always been cheap in Bombay, Sunil wasn't making the kind of money to buy much of it, so Sanjay was scarcely in mortal danger. But Sunil did well enough. Compared to Dilip, Sunil was a big operator. His rackets were small-time and unsubtle, but there were a lot of them. They added up to an empire. He would split his gang up into sections so they could work different tricks in different places. That way they didn't present too conspicuous a target for the police. It was through Sunil that Sanjay first cracked the big-time begging and con-trick spot: Victoria Terminus. Sunil taught Sanjay that it wasn't enough to cry and pretend you had lost your ticket home. You had to be in the right spot at the right time so as to catch the right people who were catching the right train. Sanjay did well with the women. They all travelled in the two carriages at the end of the train, so as to be unmolested by the male commuters. Sanjay worked below the windows of these two carriages before the train pulled out. All he had to do was think of his nose being broken and the tears came in floods. Sometimes one woman would give him the whole fare. Another of Sunil's begging units concentrated on small tourist buses. When a small tourist bus left from one of the downtown hotels, Sunil would know its itinerary and send his troops to the last stop: Gandhi's house, for example. Outside Gandhi's house the begging was always good after the tourists came out – good because their consciences were bad. You could even get something off the Japanese without having to steal it. At other places you had to work harder. Unlike Dilip, Sunil was not above encouraging his troops to steal. Some of the troops would distract the bus minder by annoying a tourist, usually a female, who was too bus-sick to go into the museum or the temple or whatever the place was, but who couldn't stay in the bus because while it was stationary with its engine off there was no air-conditioning and it heated up like an oven. So she would be standing out on the footpath and they would gang up on her. The bus minder would go to her assistance and a couple of other troops could be into the bus long enough to lift something good. Once they got a whole camera bag with everything in it, including the camera. Theft from tourists was a hard assignment because the police were merciless. Sunil had seen his people go to gaol in batches. But that was the point: he had seen *them* go to gaol. It was a long time since he had been there himself. Sanjay was impressed by Sunil's capacity to divide and rule.

One time Sunil sent Sanjay to learn the bottled water business. There was a lot involved. The scavengers would turn up with pale blue plastic bottles rescued from garbage dumps. After a bottle had been filled with tap water, the man with the bottle-capping device – the key item of equipment – capped the bottle so that it looked professional. But he couldn't distribute the finished product himself. That was where the gangs came in. Sunil told Sanjay that everything depended on whom you approached, and when. Sophisticated tourists would never fall for it, and not even the stupid ones wanted to know at the start of their day. You had to catch them at the end of a long walk, but before the heat went out of the sun. Sunil had a list of the places and the times. He had thought it all out. It wasn't Sunil's fault that Sanjay got caught. The police just happened to be making a sweep of the Malabar Hills at the very time that Sanjay and three of Sunil's troops were working a big bus load of Germans. It was hot enough to make you sweat just from carrying the bottles, so they were making sales. Unfortunately they were making one when the police showed up in a van.

Sanjay was in gaol for three weeks, which meant that he missed three days of school. He got another kind of education instead, one that taught him to stay out of gaol if it was at all possible. There were five hundred boys in the cage and the police seemed determined to beat all of them every day. The gaol was a pit. For someone like

Sanjay, used to the luxury of sleeping on top of a toilet, being obliged to sleep inside one was a severe come-down.

During his final week of captivity, as a sort of grand finale, he was sent on a closely supervised pick-up detail along the railway tracks that skirt the miles of docks before they head out into the Greater Bombay suburbs that never seem to end. The task was to pick up the pieces of passengers who had fallen under the wheels of the trains. It happened with some frequency because in the rush hours there weren't just people clinging to the outside of the trains, there were people clinging to those people. Sanjay was glad that his detail had hit a quiet patch. Only one body was found. But it was very widely distributed and it took two days to find one of the feet. The foot finally turned up in a culvert. Sanjay was glad he was not the one who found it. He saw it though, held up by a laughing policeman: a severed, withered cow's udder in a plastic bag full of water. Reminded of the ear that fell from the sky, Sanjay checked the lucky charm in the belt-band of his shorts. He wasn't feeling very lucky.

9

SANJAY'S SPIRITS rose again after he was released, because Sunil showed sympathy. Sunil had not taken another favourite while Sanjay was away so it was good for both of them to be back together. Sanjay was restored to his place of honour on the toilet roof. His reception at the Youth Club school was less heartwarming. Sabbandra had found out that he had been in gaol. She let him rejoin his class but there was no extra conversation afterwards. It took several weeks before he got back into her good books, and by that time the monsoon had come again.

The monsoon washed Sunil and his inner cabinet off the toilet roof and away into the streets. Sunil, as always, had a course of action all worked out. His gang scattered all over the district to improvised shelter. He himself, however, had a proper place all set to receive him. It was a back room in one of the hundreds of slum houses packed together along the north bank of the outlet from the Love sewage plant, where the outlet apes a river before it meets the sea. Under the eye of eternity, the Love sewage plant slum village is no picture of loveliness. It is more likely to strike you as a kind of flameless burning ghat in which people are consumed alive by squalor, instead of dead by fire. The river trickling past it, in the middle of a deep, wide culvert, is less like water stiffened with sewage than sewage diluted with water. The houses share their cement walls like a sick beehive. The alleyways are never wider than two men and every one of them has its own channel of slime cut down the middle. Where the slum village and the foetid river both reach the sea, there is a breakwater built across which is used at night as a latrine by people too poor to have lodgings in the slum: people who dream of getting into it the way the people who live there dream of getting out. It is not a beautiful area. If you are attracted by the redemptive, ecstatic qualities of Indian poverty, it is the kind of place that might make you think again. Yet for Sanjay, who had never before slept in anything approaching a proper room, it looked like a big step up. Street children dream of pavement shanties, and the children of the shanties dream of a room, or would do if they knew about such a thing – a room with a door. Behind a door you can accumulate goods. Sunil's door had a lock on it. When he opened the door, all kinds of things were revealed. There was a mattress, a box for his clothes, a mirror, a dish for washing. More amazing still, there was a stack of movie magazines. Sanjay had seen movie magazines on news-stands. Sometimes he had managed to hold a magazine long enough to half work out a few sentences in a story, before he was chased away. The occasional magazine had circulated on the toilet roof. Now, suddenly, he faced a glut of what he had thought was a rarity. For access to this treasure, whatever Sunil asked of him was a trifling fee.

When it was raining too hard to work, they read the magazines. Sunil knew every story inside out. By nature Sanjay found it hard to admit it when he could not understand something. He struggled to overcome his reluctance. His curiosity demanded satisfaction even at the cost of handing Sunil such an inestimable advantage. Sunil became his second tutor. Sunil didn't know how to read as well as Sabbandra but he was there every day. Sunil was surprised by how quickly Sanjay caught up. Except when he was sent off to forage for food, Sanjay did nothing in the daylight hours except read the magazines. If Sunil was out, Sanjay would underline words he didn't know and ask Sunil what they meant when he came back. From being able to work out a sentence he progressed quickly to being able to work out a paragraph and finally a whole story. The feeling was almost as voluptuous as looking at the photographs of Madhuri and Poojah, Sridevi and Karisma, Manisha, Meenakshi, and the strangely named, sumptuously loveable Dimple.

When Sanjay went to school, Sabbandra was bowled over by how

65

quickly he was coming on. As always she tried hard not to let her excitement show. It wasn't just because of her natural reticence. Sanjay was going to be twelve soon, or perhaps he already was, and the Youth Club offers no help for children beyond that age. Soon she was going to lose him and she didn't want it to be too much of a wrench. She was sparing with her compliments and affection. When the time came for the year's set of new clothes, however, she made sure he got some good ones. Again he conducted his secret annual ritual, the transferral of his gold piece to a safe place.

After the rain stopped, Sanjay accompanied Sunil back to the toilet roof. Sunil had sworn him to secrecy about the room in the slum. According to Sunil, the rank and file of his gang would not work for him properly if they knew he had a solid refuge. So the two friends reoccupied their elevated positions and the year settled into a pattern. Though Sunil had lieutenants who did more of the organising than Sanjay, nobody was closer to the throne than he. Sanjay was the nearest gang member to Sunil, whether the gang was on duty or off. At the movies, Sanjay sat beside Sunil. When they played cricket in Azad Park at the weekend, Sanjay was vice-captain, even though, as a late starter from out of town, he was initially not much use as a cricketer. If jealousy was aroused, it did not show. Sunil severely discouraged jealousy. It was the only time he was ever severe: he had none of Dilip's cruelty. He did not even feel, as Dilip would certainly have felt, threatened by Sanjay's increasing capacity to absorb any information available to him. Sometimes when the gang members were scattered all over the central district pulling their different tricks, Sunil and Sanjay went home to the slum with a new batch of magazines and worked through them one by one. By now Sanjay could read a story as fluently as Sunil. It got to where Sunil would lie back and smoke while Sanjay read out loud to him about the sexy, wild behaviour of one of the new female stars. It was about this time that the first scandalously suggestive songs were cropping up in the new films, and the magazines would print lines from the lyrics as captions to the photographs of the latest rising starlets as they aimed smouldering glances out of the page above a readily detectable cleavage. Sunil, with his pants around his ankles, liked to be jerked off

66

while being read to. Sometimes, as the critical moment neared, he demanded that a specific passage be repeated. It was during one of these colloquia that Sanjay himself first produced fluid at the moment of maximum interest. Sunil looked proud, almost fatherly. Sanjay found it difficult to imagine his real father being so pleased.

Taking his cue from Sunil, Sanjay also was now smoking nicotine with some regularity. The extent of his habit depended on how much money Sunil allowed him to keep. He was unable to smoke as much as he would have liked. Possibly he would never have been able to do that. It is often thought that smokers miss the breast. Heavy smokers seem to miss more than that: they need not just their mouths full but their lungs also, as a way of getting back into the amniotic fluid, a dry re-run of that first drowning. For Sanjay, birth had been the beginning of a permanent displacement. Smoking took him back beyond it. Reading was part of the same relief. It took him out of himself. "Speculation about the Poojah Bhatt-Bobby Deol marriage continues to gather momentum," he would read. "While neither has come up with a definite yes or no, many insist that they are lawfully man and wife. In fact, one very reliable insider ..." Reading this, Sanjay would release smoke from his mouth, suck it back through his nostrils, and feel that he was a very reliable insider himself. Then he would turn the page, be confronted by a photographic portrait of Miranda, and the feeling of displacement would return with renewed intensity. Once, in reality, that dreamed-of face had smiled on him, and when he had reached out for it he had been rejected. It would have been better if all that had never happened. If he had never told Dilip about the Silver Castle, Dilip would never have broken his nose. Sanjay was glad that he had told Sunil so little. He should have said even less. What beauty, though, in Miranda's lips and eyes. She was more beautiful even than Sridevi, whose mouth, though as lush, was not so subtly plump in the lower lip. Miranda was far more beautiful than Zeenat, Mamta, Parveen, Nanda, Sadhana, Vajyanthimala, Waheeda ...

Repeatedly read, soon the magazines fell open by themselves to reveal female film stars in their full-page glory. Sanjay found the male film stars interesting too, but mainly for what they wore, how their hair was arranged, and what they possessed. Akbar Khan wore a black silk shirt open at the neck to show a gold medallion; Chunky's hair was very full at the sides and back; Faizal Khan owned a foreign car with its seats covered in white fur. The way they looked could make Sanjay envious, but never set him dreaming. The women carried him away. His eyes could taste them. It was the taste of Long Ago.

One of the magazines had the new teenage sensation Mumtas on the cover. She was wearing a short-sleeved white shirt and jeans cut down to frayed-hemmed shorts, western style. She was holding one knee up with her long-nailed hands as she sat on the other leg. He could see between her legs, where the swell of her light skin emerged from the fray. She was looking at him defiantly, as if he were one of her enemies who were listed in the article inside. Below her delectably open legs there was a line of English print he could not quite understand. "I Care A Damn For These Slimeballs!" He looked at the cover picture of Mumtas so often that the words were committed to his memory along with every detail of her succulent appearance. He would mouth her name. Mumtas. Moom-tas. Mmm. Umm. Mumtas!

From the films, from the magazines about the films, from the film posters in the streets, hundreds of names and faces had entered Sanjay's memory and accelerated the process of converting his frame of reference from the abstract to the concrete, the mythically sweeping to the empirically meticulous – which in itself is a dry, empirical way of talking about lost innocence. The Silver Castle was no longer the central building of Sanjay's mental city: it had been joined by the toilet roof, the concourse of Victoria Terminus, the gaol cell in which he had slept with life crawling over him, the room in the slum beside the putrescent river. The Silver Castle was losing its strangeness. Its significance had become specific. From those days, only his gold piece still held for Sanjay the unplumbed allure of the inexplicable: only his gold piece, and the look of lovely girls. About anything else, in all other respects, he was becoming a realist, an analyst. Surrounded by millions of people who were susceptible to every astrological cult and fad, he was immune. Even the hard-headed Sunil was a mystic beside Sanjay. Sunil thought Vishnu and Krishna mattered. He had been known to visit the ashram even on those nights when food was not being handed out. Sanjay, too, enjoyed the spectacle in the ashram: the floodlit cows, the fires and the bells. But Sanjay, just by thinking about it, knew that it was all nonsense. With no religion, with no memory even of belonging to a caste, he was a born rationalist. Yet it was not by rational analysis that he understood how only an increased access to information could increase his powers of thought. It was by instinct. Here was Sanjay's true uniqueness. Though his awareness of his own sharp wits made him cocky – and sometimes, on the inside where it didn't show, drove him to private ecstasies of superiority – he was never satisfied with what he already knew. A gift for unravelling mysteries didn't slake his thirst for more of them. He was always on the road to Long Ago. Sabbandra knew this about him. At the church school which he was no longer supposed to attend, she had made her dispositions so as to be able to break a rule on his behalf. She had persuaded her husband, who ran the mission and of course commanded her life, to let Sanjay in for an extra year. Her plan was that he should learn English.

He couldn't learn it all, of course. Not even the English can do that, unless they go to school every day. Sanjay rarely managed more than half an hour a week under Sabbandra's personal supervision. While she conducted the Hindi class from which he had nothing left to learn, he sat to one side looking at an elementary text book and not, at first, getting very far with it on his own. Not getting past the first page, really. After the class was dismissed she would spend some time with him, taking him first of all through the alphabet and then later, in the weeks to come, through the first reading passages, where it turned out that the different letters of the alphabet were not always pronounced in the way that he had learned them. He made some progress but it was very hard: much, much harder than Hindi, because he had heard so little of the spoken language to back it up.

Eventually Sabbandra found the burden of an additional, individual pupil too much. Her husband was looking at her askance, something that his burning black eyes equipped him very well to accomplish. The rest of her work was suffering. So she passed Sanjay on to one of the rich daughters who did volunteer work at the mission. Enlightened middle-class families of Bombay commonly sent their sons and daughters to help at the mission for one day a week. The sons and daughters wore special uniforms; white or tan shirts and trousers for the sons, grey shirts and skirts for the daughters. The sons and daughters weren't always rich – sometimes their families were only professionals of the middle rank – but to Sanjay and the other poor children anyone was rich whose shoes laced up. The rich daughter to whom Sabbandra consigned Sanjay was called Pratiba. Though only three years older than Sanjay, she might have been his mother where education was concerned – except, of course, that his mother had had no education. Pratiba was not good looking and very conscious of the fact. Among the other rich daughters there were always two or three beauties in attendance at the mission at any given time, and even the least pretty among the rest of them had a refinement of features and extremities that Pratiba conspicuously lacked. In one of the most subversive and shocking passages of his great novel, Flaubert tells us of Madame Bovary's astonishment when she discovers that the rich are more finely formed than the poor. In India the discrepancy is not so obvious. The sari is a great equaliser. There is many a penniless rag-picker's wife who carries a plastic bag full of bottle-tops on her head as if it were the turban of a Mogul's favourite concubine. Nevertheless the women of the well-to-do are often marked by their unmarked faces and finely tapering hands. Pratiba had pitted cheeks to go with a set of features which avoided distinction by all possible means short of deformity. Nor was her thick-set body endowed with any special agility to make up for its lack of grace. Her hands echoed the characteristics of her torso: the fingers were short, fat and awkward. She was a human demonstration of the self-similarity so noticeable in the natural world – a branch is like a tree, a twig is like a branch, a leaf is like a twig – except that in her case it was the negative quality of clumsiness which was repeated at each step of the scale from the totality down to the part. Her spirit, however, redeemed her appearance, if not in her own eyes then in the eyes of others – although never, naturally enough, in the eyes of her father, who thought only of her future marriage, and therefore correctly assessed her readiness of wit as a negative attraction. And indeed her own opinion of herself was that she would have been better off pretty like all her friends, and that her friends would have been better friends to her had that been so. But her mother had prepared her well for the harsh truths about appearance and reality. Pratiba could take a detached view of her condition and even laugh at it. She had a sense of humour. It was the first time in his life that Sanjay had encountered such a thing.

At first he was not sure that he liked it. Next to the kitchen of the church hall there was a small room half full of spare pews, piles of prayer books and stacks of chairs made out of brown painted pipe and once-cream canvas. Sabbandra had assigned this room to Pratiba and Sanjay. On a pipe and canvas chair each, they sat facing each other across a small table. There was always noise from the kitchen, where paper plates of food were prepared which would, as has been said, constitute, for all the children eligible to visit the mission, their only square meal of the week. But with the door closed – although never, naturally, locked – teacher and pupil could concentrate on their difficult task. Pratiba's teaching methods involved a good deal of laughing at Sanjay's ignorance and lack of manners.

"If you must pick your nose," said Pratiba off-handedly, "do you really have to look at your finger afterwards? Can't you tell just by feel whether you've succeeded?"

Sanjay didn't enjoy this initially. After the first lesson he was rather hoping that there would not be another. But after a while he got into the swing of it. It helped that she could be just as cutting about herself.

"Today we're going to start reading a story about a prince who falls in love with a princess in disguise. She is so beautiful that even when disguised as a boy she entrances him with her charms. Try to imagine me dressed as Yasser Arafat and you've got it."

Sanjay had no idea who Yasser Arafat was – possibly some American film star – but he still appreciated her capacity for self-mockery. Though it was not the way he really felt about himself, he incorporated it among his own armoury of devices for staving off wrath. Charm can't be taught to those born without it, but in those

71

who have it as a gift it can certainly be cultivated, and by no method more effectively than from example. Sanjay absorbed everything about the way Pratiba talked. Since the price of the extracurricular lesson was to make progress with the curriculum, he had an extra motivation to get ahead with his English. For a good part of each lesson Pratiba spoke to him in that language, doing her best not to break back into their shared speech in order to explain difficulties – the constant temptation for the untrained teacher of languages.

"You can run your finger under the line when you are reading it out," she would say, "but I would have preferred it if the finger had been cleaned first. This text book belongs to me. There is a useful English expression: a poor thing but mine own."

Pratiba was a great influence on Sanjay's standards of personal hygiene and mode of dress. Due to lack of resources he was in no danger of turning into a dandy, but to accompany his naturally good eye for simplicity and elegance she helped to bring out in him a care for detail. When the annual day came to choose a new set of old clothes, she was there beside Sabbandra to help make sure that Sanjay got the best. Later on he was in their tutorial room and just completing the change into his first ever pair of long trousers when Pratiba entered.

"Even as his legs are covered up, in compensation the superb muscles of his upper body are revealed to the world at last," she said, closing the door behind her. "And I was *extremely* glad to see that his hands had been washed without any prompting."

Sanjay was wrong-footed. In his new trousers he felt doubly conscious that his chest was uncovered. Worse, he had not yet quite finished transferring his gold piece into a small gap he had just found in the stitching of his waistband. So he was fumbling at his waist and shuffling in his new sandals.

"Why so nervous?" asked Pratiba, laughing because she didn't really mean it. But when he said nothing, she realised that he actually was nervous, and her face fell. She was standing quite close to him so he decided to kiss her. They had been reading about the prince and princess doing this. Unlike in Indian films, in English stories everybody seemed to kiss all the time. Sanjay and Pratiba had shared several jokes about how it must taste. "It probably tastes like whatever they ate last," Pratiba had ventured. But Sanjay had thought at the time that Pratiba looked unusually thoughtful even while she wove these fantasies, so now he dared, and discovered to his surprise that it didn't taste like anything.

It *felt* like something. It felt like softness in depth, warmth in density. All the gradations of sweet touch were there that he had felt when acting on the instructions of Dilip and Sunil, together with the airy tension that had sometimes invaded his own head on those occasions, as if his body was concentrating in his brain. In addition, there was the shock of experiencing so much sensation by making physical contact with someone he had not longed for, dreamed about, or even really noticed. Pratiba just stood there lumpishly with her eyes closed. After a few seconds she broke off the kiss, moved her head back a few inches, and looked at him. He did not find her face any prettier than it had been before. There was a difference though. She looked guilty. She glanced at the door. Suddenly looking resigned, she reached around him and ran her hands quickly all over his back, then just as quickly all over his shoulders and chest, as if blindly trying to memorise every thin contour. Finally she moved against him for one more kiss, and this time he could distinctly feel her breasts against him. He was still getting over the shock of that after she had broken away and sat down.

"Put on your new shirt," she said, pretending to be looking for something specific in the text book. He put on the shirt, tucked it in, and sat down too, managing to do so with a swaggering flourish that he didn't really feel.

"Don't you ever dare do such a thing again," she said.

Sanjay, under the impression that she was the one who had done it, showed his confusion.

"And don't look so sorry. It wasn't that bad, was it?"

He showed more confusion. Her expression softened. After glancing at the door again, she reached out with her left hand and stroked his right wrist.

"Don't worry. I just couldn't resist these pretty bones. Some of us are less lucky with our skeletons. Now let's find out what the prince

73

and princess are doing this week. *She asked him back to her castle.* Start from there."

"She asked him back to her castle," Sanjay pronounced haltingly. It was the precise thing that Pratiba could not do. Her castle was her parents' apartment in that swanky curve of the beach between Chowpatty and the promontory, and he would never be allowed into it. If her parents found out that he had so much as touched her it would mean serious trouble for them both. Besides, she was not his princess. He had no personal feelings for her beside his acute curiosity as to how she would react physically when he did things to her body, which for purposes of experiment he was prepared to regard as desirable. Intensely focused on himself, he tended, like most children and some adults, to believe that everyone else felt and thought as he did, so he assumed that she, too, had a purely exploratory interest. It seemed that way. In the ensuing weeks and months, each lesson would include a short period of physical communication to supplement their verbal interchange. She, much more than he, was likely to keep an eye on the door that they could shut yet not lock. Fearful of interruption, she would not permit any noticeable adjustment of her clothing. But progressively, from occasion to occasion, he was permitted greater intimacies with her well-developed breasts. Though their large size was part of her awkwardness, he forgot that fact while cupping their warmth under her blouse and squeezing their hard nipples to make her gasp. It was a month before he was allowed to advance his stroking of her spread thighs to the occasional light stroking at the inner edges of her panties. It was two months before he could begin to press between the edges with the side of his finger and feel a softness even warmer than a breast. The way she breathed altered radically in just the half a minute that she allowed him. It gave him the beginnings of an actual experience to illuminate some of the things he had been reading in Sunil's movie magazines, about ecstasy, about being carried away. ("The fact remained that she was not strong enough to resist what happened. It was an explosion of her inner being. She yielded to him as if gasping for air after holding her breath for too long. Oh, Mohitlal!") It gave him a version, drained of all beauty but injected with tangible actuality, of those open-mouthed expressions he had looked up at in the darkness of the cinema. He was fascinated. He always wanted more. No matter how demanding of concentration the rackets in which he was engaged, he looked forward all week to going further with his invasion of her person. But because, for him, the adventure was in no way connected with her personality, he assumed that she felt the same detachment. It never occurred to him that Pratiba would have permitted none of these familiarities had she felt indifferent. He assumed that she was seizing the only possible access to such pleasures that she would ever get.

If Sanjay had feelings of love, they were directed towards someone else. A street girl in her last year at the school, her name was Urmila. For the previous two years he had seen her around the place but suddenly she had flowered into his consciousness. Even in her rags she had uncommon grace. She was almost like one of the rich girls in the way she moved. Though Urmila rarely smiled, her mouth and eyes were an enchantment to him. Perhaps the lack of happiness in her face was the secret of her appeal. She had melancholy, yet without vulnerability. It was a self-possessed sadness. Her figure was still slight even though her breasts had become unmistakably divided and prominent under her faded lemon threadbare dress. At the mere thought of touching them, he felt a hungry tenderness which the actual touching of Pratiba's breasts did not produce. To go with *this* princess to her castle seemed something worth dreaming about. But to spend even a little time with her was difficult. He would arrive early and manage to be with her for a little while between the end of her class and the start of his. Sabbandra, however, did not favour the friendship, and Pratiba was positively put out by it. A few words with Urmila cost him ten minutes of cutting remarks from Pratiba at the start of the class, and sometimes it was the end of the class before he even got to touch her, and without her touching him in return. A tradition had arisen that she would stroke him for a little while through his trousers as part payment for what he did to her. Careful management was necessary because the results had to die down before the door was opened at the end of the class. But he had learned to depend on the excitement, and to have it withheld was a serious punishment. Though he had learned to say that he was in no way interested in Urmila except as a friend, Pratiba had a way of accepting the explanation without being satisfied with it.

"Sheep's eyes for your friend and a dog's breath for your teacher. Thanks for the favour, but are you sure she's stupid enough for you? There's still a chance she might learn to spell before she gets out of here. Still, I suppose you'd feel at home if you could get a look at the piddle-stained pants she's wearing under that rag. If she's wearing any." Sanjay would have been withered by such invective if Pratiba's anger had not been accompanied by the incipient tears he could see glinting in her eyes. They helped to tell him that she would not be bothering to speak at all if she had not been dependent on him. His only mistake was to believe that her dependence was like his, detachable and transferable, a mere indulgence.

Urmila, however, was an obsession in the making, and all the more so for being elusive. There came a time when he would break off his afternoon participation in Sunil's rackets to be at the gate of the school when Urmila came out and walk with her to where she lived. While they walked, he tried to charm her with his newly learned self-deprecation. It seemed to be working. "My shoes don't look magic, do they? But they always take me to you. Watch this." The magic shoes idea was a good one: he had got it from a story in the English text-book. Urmila still didn't smile, but at least she didn't send him away. Capering and joking around her while she walked in a straight line, he travelled twice as far as she did to end up in the same place. Her castle was a hut in one of the most populated shanty-town alleys of central Bombay. They are not alleys *in* a shanty town. Each alley *is* a shanty town all by itself, with strips of joined-up hovels on each side leaving only enough room down the middle for push-carts and a central gutter in which urine and washing-up water form that oddly milky effluvium everywhere recognisable as the world-girdling river system of poverty. You can see it flowing down the middle of the street in Palestinian refugee camps, in the favelas of Rio, in the alleys of Shanghai on the banks of Shouchu creek, in the grim clusters of fibro-and-corrugated-iron gunyahs on the outskirts of Australian country towns, in the backyard improvised villages of Nairobi where the piece-workers live who spend their day carving wooden animals

76

in the souvenir factory. But in flat central Bombay it doesn't flow. It just lies there. If the heat were not so intense you would catch a disease just from looking at it. Urmila's castle had this for a river view. Her family included several brothers, so Urmila at first found it prudent to say goodbye to him at the mouth of the alley. Gradually, as the weeks and their walks continued, he accompanied her further in. Only after months had gone by did he get her all the way to her door. Urmila introduced him to her mother as the young man who had been assigned by the school to see her home safely. The mother barely grunted. The father, luckily, was not at home. The eldest of the three brothers present looked darkly suspicious. Fortunately there was an old dying female relative lying on a pallet in front of the hovel. She took a turn for the worse, which occupied everyone's attention. Sanjay volunteered to fetch some medicine. At the far end of the alley, around the corner in the main street, there was an apothecary's shop that sold Love Care energy cream, whose efficacy was so unimpeachable that it was advertised on the bottle in the English language. "Yes, Love Care energy cream fulfils you with a new joy and great feeling of life in its prime. Made most scientifically with the latest technique on advanced machines." Sanjay understood only some of these words, but they were repeated in Hindi with a longer description besides. It was made exhaustively clear that Love Care cured everything. To buy a bottle of it used up most of the money in Sanjay's pocket. Luckily he managed to steal another bottle while the apothecary was wrapping up the first one, so things evened out. When Sanjay got back to Urmila's home and presented his bounty, he found himself, if not precisely celebrated, at least less disapproved of. The contents of one of the bottles was rubbed on the face and limbs of the patient without causing any noticeable worsening of her condition. The other bottle was held in reserve. Urmila was allowed to accompany Sanjay when he left. Though she went with him no further than eyeshot of the darkly suspicious brother, it felt almost like being alone with her.

"Thank you," she said. "You have been very kind."

"I would like to kiss you," said Sanjay. "I know how."

"I do not," said Urmila. "Pretend that you were doing so. What would you be doing?"

"I would be breathing your breath," said Sanjay, quoting a magazine story without acknowledgment. Afraid that two small boys staging a pissing competition in the gutter nearby were spoiling his effect, he brought out his best phrase. "There would be an explosion of your inner being."

He got the sense that Urmila had not fully understood what he had said but was impressed anyway. She allowed him to linger. Standing there in the crowded thoroughfare, they talked for a little while that for Sanjay lasted a sweet always, like one of those magazine love dialogues that stretched out into the time it took to read. These were not magazine-like surroundings. Nor were the circumstances of her family life, as she recounted them, particularly glamorous. Her brothers worked at sorting plastic bags and dead batteries, when they worked at all. Only one of her elder sisters had a job, in the Falkland Street prostitution trade. Her father came home intermittently and more often to get money than to bring it. All this would have bored Sanjay if he had not loved her voice and her appearance. But he did, and that transformed everything. His love for her was all the more intense for being so pure. The small curves of her breasts under her ragged dress, the way she swapped her light weight from one hip to the other as she stood, turning out the opposite foot on its heel so that the toes waved above the hot asphalt – it was an exalted display of light and line, an aesthetic aurora that consumed desire like cold flames. When he left her he took a hundred memories with him, pictures to leaf through in his mind. The thought of touching her was almost too beautiful to bear.

So he touched Pratiba instead. In this way his emotional life was neatly divided. If he had been a grown-up poet – to the extent that poets ever grow up – Urmila would have been his muse and Pratiba his wife: a classic dichotomy which has little to do with personal appearance, and all too much to do with a fear of finality. All Sanjay's interludes with Urmila were spent in a timeless, directionless haze of barely articulate afflatus, punctuated by his carefully rehearsed poetic borrowings from such clear springs of literary feeling as *Cine-Blitz*.

78

With Pratiba he made strictly diachronic progress in the finer uses of his native language, the elementary capacities of English, and the study of heterosexual physical sensation. This demanding curriculum was made easier to cope with by Pratiba's sense of humour, which he would have valued more highly if he had realised how rare it was. But his having met it only once was not yet enough to tell him that he would meet it seldom. A sense of value is not one that young men, be they ever so precocious, can be expected to possess. Even if deprived, they haven't lost enough. It takes time to build regrets.

The disjunction of Sanjay's emotional life between Pratiba and Urmila was strict but equal. Just as strict, but far from equal, was the discrepancy between his emotional life and his practical existence: the daily, continual effort to stay alive. Though less of a struggle than it had been, this still took almost all his time. To keep well in with Sunil, to keep him sweet, to keep a grip on all the privileges that accrued from the relationship – the best place on the toilet roof, the first choice of food, the precious hours off in the slum room with its treasure trove of darkly printed words and glowing photographs – Sanjay had to work the rackets. Sanjay was quite the young man by now, with an Adam's apple showing above the collar of his pale shirt and always, it seemed, another half inch of ankle appearing below the cuffs of his long trousers. His voice had cracked and deepened, giving the built-in thunder of his Hindi an extra boom which from now on he would always have to hold in, or else offend his own sense of propriety. He had already noticed how the best foreigners flinched from too much volume in the voice. Not even the Americans liked to be shouted at. They preferred to do the shouting.

Sanjay was watching himself, grooming himself. He spent time in front of Sunil's mirror. Sunil took him to a barber. In the course of time Sunil also took him to a fellow gang chief called Ajay, an older boy, a young man really, who ran a racket known as the Arab Season. Sunil rented Sanjay out to Ajay on a part-time basis. Ajay's slum room was even more splendid than Sunil's, with a bed held off the floor by short wooden legs. After Sunil discreetly withdrew, Ajay poured Sanjay another beer and gave him a packet of cigarettes that was almost full.

79

"Keep these," said Ajay.

"I appreciate it," said Sanjay, lighting one.

"There's plenty more where those came from," said Ajay. "All you have to do is please the Arabs."

While they smoked and drank, Sanjay was told what was involved. When they had finished their cigarettes, he was shown. Kneeling on the mat with his upper body on the bed, he could see what was happening in the mirror. He didn't much like the look of it but it felt less bad than he expected.

"It won't hurt so much next time," said Ajay. "Soon it won't hurt at all, as long as they use plenty of jelly. You carry the jelly with you just in case they haven't got any. Tell them they'll like it better that way."

When Sanjay had pulled his trousers back up they sat together on the edge of the bed and had another smoke while they finished their beers. "Quite often they don't even want that much," Ajay explained. "You just have to pull them off or suck them. It's money for nothing. Just remember the money goes to me and then I pay you. But after you give Sunil his share you're still going to have more left over than you've ever seen before, believe me."

"How much, exactly?"

"You're going to be able to get into any movie you want. Put it like that. And into any girl too. Some day soon you'll be able to wander down Falkland Street and take your pick."

Sanjay didn't attain to that latter luxury immediately, partly because he wasn't sure he knew how it was done and didn't want to make a fool of himself; partly because Pratiba and Urmila combined to regale his divided sensuality and reverence with enough stimulus to be going on with; and mostly because a sudden hike in discretionary income faced him with more pressing possibilities. Arabs who regard Bombay as a source of sexual opportunity are not necessarily of the highest rank. Like the Japanese who go to Bangkok in search of the satisfactions so misleadingly promised by their pornographic magazines at home, the Arabs who come to Bombay are not rulers, merely servants. They own no oil-wells. They shuffle paper. Though their wealth seems unimaginable to the Indian boys they come in search of and easily find, they do not always stay in the very best hotels. But the second-best hotels were still a revelation to Sanjay, who had never seen a clean sheet in his life, or even two pillows against the same headboard, let alone four – with a bed covering that did nothing more than cover the bed when it was not being slept on. When he took his turn in the bathroom he would stand in awe, bathed merely by its clean brilliance: he did not have to run the water to feel cleansed. In the beginning he was offered only a few appointments a week, and sometimes he was one of a group, which lowered his cut still further. He still had to spend most of his time working the rackets. It is galling to spend a long morning on the trail of a tourist bus or acting out tragedies at train windows when your head is full of the previous afternoon's air-conditioned luxury: cold bottles of Limca freely available, a television set showing interesting foreign videos, the puffy carpet underfoot running all the way to the wall. But soon the balance of his activities had tilted far enough towards this unprecedented abundance for him to contemplate satisfying his new, bold ambition for a slum room of his own, thus to emulate the privilege that really fascinated him about his hosts: not their promiscuous pleasures, which in truth left him cold, but the pampered solitude they could enjoy after he and his friends, and then their own friends, were all gone. They even had their own telephones in there. They could connect themselves to the world by wire if they wished, and, even more enviably, shut it out by speaking a command. They could be alone with everything they wanted, and close the door on anything they didn't want. They were in paradise.

So Sanjay made a veiled suggestion to Sunil that he, Sanjay, might rent a room of his own, not far away in the same slum. Dilip would have greeted such a suggestion with violence. But Dilip was a figure of the past, even though Sanjay still saw him occasionally at the movies and never looked in a mirror without remembering him vividly. Sunil, as always, was a better psychologist. Realising that the best way to keep his burgeoning puppy was on a long leash, Sunil made the arrangements for a room in the next alley but one. It was a smaller room than Sunil's, and of course far smaller than Ajay's, but it had a door. Sunil gave him a padlock as a housewarming present, and passed on a small stack of some of Sanjay's favourite magazines to be the seed corn of his own library. It was agreed that though Sanjay's income did not as yet match the rent, the difference would be an interest-free loan. Since Sunil was lying slightly about the rent, and Sanjay had been holding back some of his take from the rackets, both were satisfied. A certain degree of mutual chiselling can be a useful prophylactic against bad blood: by the time both parties find out that they are entangled, it feels like fellowship.

In his exiguous spare time Sanjay happily occupied himself with furnishing his room. He accumulated a pallet to lie on, a palliasse to cover it, a basin to wash in and some boxes for his belongings. He even found some broken bits of a mirror, which, by resting their edges on half driven nails, he managed to attach to the crumbling concrete wall in sufficent proximity to one another to give him an image of himself: fractionated, but then so was he. None the less he felt more of a piece, and at one with the world, than he ever had before. This was lucky, because it was around that time that a few things in his emotional life went wrong, and he might not have been able to sustain his losses so easily had he felt less secure in the material sense.

It was near the end of the scholastic year when Sabbandra caught him with his hand down Pratiba's blouse. Things might have been worse. He might have been on his knees beside her with her dress up around her waist as he pressed her panties into her to make them wet. They had done that only the previous week. That would have been very hard to laugh off. Even as things were, there was big trouble. Sanjay's explanation that he was looking for his pencil was not accepted. Sabbandra slapped him repeatedly without speaking. When she spoke, it was worse.

"I gave you my trust. I gave you my *trust* and this is how you repay me." The Hindi word for trust stung like a stroke from the cane. Pratiba came in for abuse too, but Sanjay was able to stave some of it off on her behalf, by saying it had all been his idea. Sanjay did not know it, but here he was at his best. He did not want her to suffer and was prepared to pay the price. Pratiba, in loud tears, with her head in her hands, did not participate. She was still sitting there when Sabbandra ushered him out of the room and rapidly through the crowded church hall, with everybody watching the commotion. She marched him all the way out into the yard, pushed him through the iron gate, and shut it behind him. The policeman on duty tapped his cane speculatively against his own hand and asked if she required assistance. Luckily she told him no in a loud, impatient voice. Then she whispered to Sanjay through the bars. The whisper was a hiss.

"You are on your own."

For a while Sanjay felt that he really was, but after a few weeks the sense of loss faded. After all, he had other means of continuing his education. He soon forgot most of his embarrassment, and nearly all of Pratiba's, although to do him credit he was relieved to find out that she had not been expelled. One day when he was lurking across the street waiting for Urmila, he saw Pratiba come out with a couple of her glamorous friends. As always she looked like the odd girl out – what she would call *the gooseberry* – but at least she was there, and not noticeably miserable. She and her friends went off northwards to their rich lives. He made a vague plan to trail her home one day and try to catch her alone so as to apologise and perhaps pick up where they had left off. Urmila, however, was a more pressing issue. He would have to be careful about making any actual physical contact with her in sight of her family. It did not occur to him that this more spiritual relationship might also go wrong, if in a different way.

What happened was painfully simple. Urmila's glowering oldest brother had somehow found out that Sanjay was not the school's official appointee to walk her home. He had found out that Sanjay had been lying through his teeth. Unaware that he had been detected, Sanjay was particularly eloquent as he walked Urmila home along the mile of crowded broad pavements that led to the narrow alley. It was a perfect day: not so hot that Urmila really needed the second-hand sandals she was wearing, although Sanjay was pleased to see them on her pretty feet. They made her look even more lissom and luxurious, as if she were a rich girl going to a party, the way they did in the magazines. As the pair of them entered her alley, Sanjay was quoting to her some lyrics from one of the latest hit movies that she herself had not yet seen, and probably never would see. He did not try to sing them, but he could recite them as if they were poetry, which to him they seemed to be. In English translation they might seem slightly ridiculous, but in his own language they had a mellifluous ardour which his new deep voice was well equipped to bring out.

"Your sexiness," he intoned, "triggers procreation in the world." Hearing this, Urmila hung her head as she walked, but she was smiling as much as she ever did, and in an appreciative way, too, as if struck by the rhythmic aptness of the phrasing.

"Life without you is like a cactus."

She was fascinated. Sanjay in his turn was fascinated with the effect he was having. He watched her downcast eyes as they tried not to shine, her tongue as it fought not to lick her lips. So neither the princess nor her troubador was looking ahead, or they might have seen her big brother working his way purposefully towards them through the late afternoon crowd. The first thing Sanjay noticed was his head ringing from a blow to his right ear. Urmila wailed softly but already from a distance. Sanjay was on his way out of the alley even faster than he had left the school.

"You are *poor!*" shouted her brother. "You are not really rich *at all!*" Her brother could kick like a sacred cow demolishing a cake stall. Sanjay had to dodge and run with his left leg almost entirely out of action from a kick under the buttock.

"She is not for *you!*"

Sanjay limped home with wounds in places he couldn't lick. They were superficial, but they hurt, and the humiliation hurt worse, lingering long after the physical pain had ebbed, as a line of jetsam marks the long reach of the tide under the wharf.

10

Sanjay found it hard to accept that he had seen Urmila for the last time. It was several days before he was able to go back to earning a living, so he had to hustle hard when he did. He could not really afford the time to hang around the vicinity of the school on the next day she would be there, and wait for her to come out. He did so anyway, until he noticed that one of her brothers had turned up. There was another brother the following week. She was a family asset. They had plans for her. They weren't going to let her be wasted on a nobody. So Sanjay shelved the project. He postponed his love, telling himself there would be another day. Besides, he had another area of interest. Throughout this period of disappointment he had continued to participate in weekend cricket matches. He had developed into a reasonable batsman who could hit the ball in some way or another every second time. As a bowler he could at least project the ball in the right general direction. For cricket as played by the Bombay rag-tag and bobtail, these were high enough standards, and he was content to field for hours on end while he occupied himself with his own thoughts. It was a time he could spend considering his life. One afternoon he realised someone else was considering it too.

Weekend cricket in Azad Park is not much of a spectacle unless you are actually participating. There are a dozen games going on at once, with far more than the regulation number of players in each team. It is quite possible, indeed frequent, for a fielder to be active in several matches at once. The ball is only a tennis ball. There is no effective umpiring except by gang leaders. Superficially the whole arrangement looks like a shambles, but closer inspection reveals it to be nothing as grand as that. It isn't a broken down system. It never was a system. The occasional talented boy might show up but in these circumstances he won't develop. The cricketers who become national heroes start off in less humble circumstances and get better at playing the game because the game they play has some degree of organisation to it. Apart from the very occasional natural, nobody who plays cricket in Azad Park is going anywhere. Their game is like their lives. Nothing happens that is worth looking at, so anyone who wanders by and stops to watch must be curious about something else. This spectator obviously was.

He was a foreigner. When Sanjay realised that the man was looking at him, he returned the scrutiny, and detected all the signs of someone rich from England. The man wore a suit but it was light in colour and weight, well adapted to the heat. Though tall, stooping and half bald in that typically English way, he was well groomed. As with all people of European origin it was easy to tell his age. He was no longer young, but not yet in decline. Sanjay found the man's shoes especially telling: a sort of soft, unpolished, cloth-like leather that the very rich Indians sometimes wore to establish their connection with the glories of past times. These shoes, together with a certain limpness of gesture and an unduly fond smile, convinced Sanjay that the man was interested in boys. After half an hour there could be no mistaking that Sanjay had been chosen. It was so noticeable that some of the other boys had started to laugh. So Sanjay abandoned his position and strolled over to where the man was standing at the notional edge of the field. One of the other boys whistled as Sanjay went by and he paid the whistle back with a subtle but obscene gesture formed by the fist and extended knuckle.

"Well," said the man, in English. "I must say I've been admiring your fluent style in the field."

"A poor thing but mine own," said Sanjay.

"And your English is beautiful too! You're beautiful all round. A beautiful all-rounder, if I can allow myself the pun."

Sanjay sensed that the man was unsettled and talking for the sake of talking, so he took the initiative.

"My name is Sanjay."

"Mine's Rochester. Edward Rochester. Rochester *sahib*, I suppose they would say here. But I want *you* to call me Ted."

Ted also wanted Sanjay to come back to the Tajma for a drink. Sanjay was in his second-best clothes and guessed that he would not get past the door even under his new friend's guardianship. He said that he would have to go home and change. Mr Rochester, as Sanjay preferred to call him, insisted on coming along. Sanjay was at first worried that the sight of how he lived might put his companion off. During the long walk to the slum, however, Sanjay, obliged to use up most of his English phrases in a heavily edited recounting of his life story, discovered that Mr Rochester, far from being repelled by details of street life, was attracted by them. When they reached the slum and plunged into its festering interstices, Mr Rochester's interest intensified to excitement.

"My *dear*!" he exclaimed. "This place does wonders for my *nostalgie de la boue*. In fact I'm not sure I've ever had this much *boue* to be nostalgic *about*, if you get me."

Sanjay didn't get him. Mr Rochester's use of the English language was unfathomable for threequarters of the time he was speaking, which was nine-tenths of the time available. But his emotions were easy to read. When Sanjay unlocked the door of his little room, Mr Rochester's excitement was at fever pitch.

"Oh my darling! You mean a lovely beast like you strides out of *this*? But no, it's perfect. It's your *gouffre obscur*. Don't change a thing."

Sanjay caught the word 'change' and said he had to change his clothes.

"You go ahead. I won't watch. I'll turn away. But there's not much of an away to turn *to*, is there? I'll keep my hands over my eyes."

Sanjay took off his sweat-shirt, dropped it on the bed, and lifted his best shirt reverently from one of the stacked cardboard boxes that formed his cupboard. When he changed his trousers he would have to be careful about transferring the gold piece. Then he realised that Mr Rochester had been looking into the fragmentary mirror through his fingers.

"You look like one of those cubist photo-montages that dear David

87

Hockney does. Only much, much prettier. *Such* skin. Subcontinental blend, ground fine."

Mr Rochester wanted only to be stroked and sucked and to do some stroking and sucking: nothing compared to some of the Arabs. Afterwards he lay replete on the bed while Sanjay knelt beside him on the mat. But Mr Rochester, except when his mouth was full, never stopped talking for long.

"And to think I'm only going to be here for another ten days. I could have found you a week ago. Think of the *time* we've wasted."

Sanjay politely stroked the strange, brindled hair showing in the space of Mr Rochester's still unfastened shirt, although the belt buckle below had been done up again with hasty modesty.

"*Ma femme est morte, je suis libre!* A poet you perhaps don't know. Baudelaire. You can't imagine how poignant that line seems at this moment. Do you realise I've got a wife and three children? Used to, anyway. My elder girl is your age by now. Probably looking for a young man like you. But *I* found you, didn't I?"

Sanjay was already getting used to Mr Rochester's habit of asking himself questions. A nod of assent was usually sufficient reply.

"Finish getting changed and we'll go back to the Tajma for that drink," said Mr Rochester. "But you promise me I'll be coming here again, won't you? With the emphasis on the coming, if you'll permit the pun."

With his new mentor as a sponsor, Sanjay at last penetrated the sacred gate of the Tajma, whose façade had dominated his existence for so much of his life. The giant bearded and turbanned guardians of the forecourt looked at him sideways but did not raise a gloved hand to bar his way. Reverently manhandled by flunkeys, the glass doors sighed open and he passed through into the conditioned air of the lobby. On the left, stretching away into the distance, was the front desk, with a number of beautiful women behind it and an even greater number of beautiful women standing in front of it, all modelling the same wealthy pattern of sari. The rest of the vast floor space was full of chairs and couches radiating their own plump softness. Rich people of all nationalities sat quietly drinking or moved unhurriedly about without once raising their voices. All that could be heard was a plush murmur, as if sound had been conditioned like the air. Sanjay blinked. Mr Rochester, who was not entirely without sensitivity, realised that his protégé was suffering from shock.

"I suppose this must be like an air-lock to a space station if you aren't used to it," he said. "Why don't we sit down for a little while here and have a drink or two before we go up and see my room?"

The waitress brought Mr Rochester something low and glowing in a heavy glass and Sanjay a Limca colder than its own ice-cubes: it numbed the hand with which he picked it up and the first mouthful left his lips tingling.

"Put it on the coaster so it won't leave a ring," said Mr Rochester strangely. "Pity to mark that teak. Comfy?"

The couch was so soft in texture that Sanjay felt he might have fallen through it if it had not somehow buoyed him up with its puffy inner being. His eyes were everywhere. It was an effort to stop his skull swivelling to follow them. Luckily he was facing in the right direction to see the young women at the desk without having to look over his shoulder. They all looked like film stars. There was one who looked like Sridevi. Perhaps it *was* Sridevi. Following Mr Rochester's lead, Sanjay reached into the bowl of nibbles and crammed a random selection into his mouth. One of them tasted like cheese. For the first time in a long while, he was back in the Silver Castle.

"Did you know it could be like this in your own country?"

"No," said Sanjay, and he was not just being polite. He had had glimpses. He had peered into forbidden places. In the hotel bathrooms of Arabs he had pocketed toothbrushes wrapped in thin plastic. He knew. Knowing, however, is not the same thing as experiencing. There were more experiences on the way along the main corridor linking the new wing of the hotel to the old. There were banks and travel bureaux and shops. He had seen something like them in the streets, but nothing like them for their opulence. There was a shop full of gold: not the filigree gold that you could see at street-side wedding ceremonies, but solid like his gold piece – solid and wrought into the shapes of elephants and tigers, devils and dragons, fighting fish like contending treasures, birds whose tails spread in a fan of glory like a paralysed sunrise. They came to another lobby that opened on to a huge courtyard in which a swimming-pool as big as a small ocean lay glittering with a deep coolness the thirsty sun could not suck up inside a year. A slim western woman climbed out of it. She was wearing almost nothing except two stripes of lime. She had come from another temperature. Mr Rochester tapped him on the shoulder.

"More of that some other day. Dream about them in your little room. *My* little room is four floors up."

Sanjay had been in a hotel elevator before but not like this one. Six Japanese men in suits followed them into it and there was still room to spare. The Japanese men stayed in it when it reached the fourth floor. Sanjay followed Mr Rochester along a railed walkway skirting an atrium. Sanjay had seen a hotel atrium before but not like this one.

"Splendid creation isn't it? This was the old part of the hotel, all built like a barracks. The *sahibs* used to be in here like a separate world. Those were the days. All it took was the occasional Amritsar massacre and the whole system went like clockwork. Tickety-boo."

Sanjay had no idea what Mr Rochester was talking about but didn't care. He had already guessed that Mr Rochester would say everything again eventually, or something very like it. 'Tickety-boo' was probably a way of indicating 'here we are', because Mr Rochester had taken from his pocket the key that he had picked up at the desk, and was fitting it into the lock of the door to room 419. Mr Rochester held the door open and politely ushered Sanjay ahead of him, into the most astonishing experience yet. "*My* little room," Mr Rochester said again.

It was a palace. The room was huge and there was another huge room beyond it, through an archway. Each room had windows from which Sanjay could look down on the world he had left behind, as if he needed reminding of the contrast. He was looking down on crowded hard stones where he had once not even been rich enough to beg. Now he had carpets underneath him like compressed clouds. In the first room there were chairs and couches and cushions, but none of it was of leather as in the lobby: it was all done in some costly material with flowers imprisoned in the weave. On the walls there were square and oblong pictures like magazine pages, except that

90

they were framed and you could see their texture, as if they were inviting fingers as well as eyes. There was a bowl of fruit that would have fed him for a week. There was a television set in each of the rooms. Not even the Arabs had had two television sets. In the second room, the bed was big enough for a game of cricket. There was a bathroom he could have lived in if he had sunglasses to shield his eyes. He fought to stay calm, but was sensible enough not to overdo it: indifference would not have been welcome. Mr Rochester obviously wanted him to be impressed.

"How very different from the home life of our own dear Queen. The little room of our own dear little queen. For as long as I'm here I want you to make yourself *zu Hause*. It's the least I can do for you."

"Thank you. You are very kind." Sanjay was guessing, but it sounded like the thing to say.

"Really, your English is astonishing. You really are the most astonishing young man, aren't you? On top of your beauty. Which is where a lot of people I know would like to be, believe me."

After they had both consumed what Mr Rochester called a real drink, they did things on the bed. Mr Rochester wanted something extra this time but Sanjay did not mind. The real drink had left him slightly abstracted. It completed the distancing effect induced by his new friend's almost incessant stream of chatter. Whether verbally or physically, the only participation required was essentially passive. Sanjay grew alert again, however, when Mr Rochester began to indicate that the afternoon sojourn was nearing its end.

"We must make arrangements to meet again tomorrow. But just in case you should think better of it, perish the thought, I want you to have some money. I can't transform your existence. I only wish I could. I'd like to give you wings so you could fly home beside me. My desolation angel. But at least I can do this much."

Mr Rochester was offering a fortune. Sanjay looked at the proffered notes and had to catch himself or he would have licked his lips. He was looking at six months of idleness. Just in time he remembered Sunil's teachings.

"It is too much. Just this much." He took the smallest note and handed back the rest.

"You really are the *sweetest* boy. I'll take you down to the lobby and see you away safely."

Keeping pace with the long, satisfied strides of his protector, Sanjay retraced his adventurous course along the corridor of jewels and precious metals to the pavilion of women. He knew he would be coming back. There had never been any danger that he would think better of it. Mr Rochester might have, but would not now. It was the boy, not the man, who had made a slave.

11

"So THERE SHE WAS, the biggest soprano still in existence," said Mr Rochester with an expansive gesture, "and they'd given her a shelf of rock that a *lizard* couldn't have slept on without *falling off*. It was like a *playground slide*. I thought she was going to come zooming down it and *plug the orchestra pit*. Believe me, darling, you're in the right place. Seven thousand miles east of Covent Garden is exactly the right place to be. Half the world away from those Marxist maniac producers. Bloody Krauts. What did that Australian critic say? Nowadays they produce operas because they aren't allowed to invade Poland? Thank God the Wall's down. Now the Poles can invade *them*. Give the mad bastards something else to think about. All that and a Wotan who sings the way I do. A truly *hideous* evening."

If this speech of Mr Rochester's had been aimed solely at Sanjay it would have been greeted with respect for its torrential fluency but with little comprehension. Sanjay, however, was only a spectator. Mr Rochester's real interlocutor was an American called Adrian Desmond. He was much younger than Mr Rochester, possibly still in his thirties, but clearly of a similar persuasion, although his voice swooped less and he looked, on the whole, more conventionally masculine. It was his eyes that gave him away. They strayed towards Sanjay at the slightest opportunity. Mr Rochester and Mr Desmond were seated opposite one another in Mr Rochester's hotel suite sitting-room. Every time Mr Rochester found a reason to get up – to fetch more drinks, or a book he was recommending, or to adjust the air-conditioning, or simply to rearrange cushions elsewhere in the room because they had been allowed to remain undisturbed by his electric energy for too long – Mr Desmond's gaze transferred itself to Sanjay, who, smoking with elaborate casualness an imported cigarette, was comfortably seated in his own chair, square on to the one-sided verbal contest. But when Mr Desmond was given a chance to speak, he too spoke well, and for Sanjay's purposes he spoke better, because his forms of expression could be appreciated even when the subject was a mystery. It was the afternoon before Mr Rochester's frequently advertised and loudly lamented date of departure. After more than a week of his company, Sanjay was exhausted. This visit from a third party was a nice rest.

"But that's enough from me," said Mr Rochester uncharacteristically. "And I suppose you get most of the Euro-news anyway. You must be well settled in by now."

"Oh sure," said Mr Desmond. "But the more I blend in with the landscape the more I hanker after gossip like this. I'll be here another year at least and I'm already on the phone for an hour every day just finding out what's going on back home. Finding out how Dan Quayle gets his rocks off, for example. Stuff like that. The *International Herald-Trib* has all the juice squeezed out of it."

"What are you working on now?" asked Mr Rochester, with the strain that always marked his voice on those rare occasions when he asked a question he did not intend to answer himself. "A terrible pity you were out of town. You could have shown me."

"Still the same book. It's getting longer. There's a collection of miniatures here that has some of the key pictures for studying one of my manuscripts, the *Gajendra Muksha*. That's 'The Deliverance of the Elephant by King Gajendra'. An episode of the *Baghavata Purana*, you know it?"

"Vaguely."

"One of the most informative pictures is in the Jagdish Goenka collection, right here in Bombay. I can walk there from my apartment. Nothing like as lush as the stuff they have in Jaipur or the Banares Hindu University in Varanasi. But important. The miniature of the Elephants and the Water Sprites is *really* important. And when I'm through with that I'll stay on here and finish the book even if I have to make the occasional trip to Delhi or somewhere. I just like it

94

here. There's something about the place." At the end of this last sentence he cast a glance at Sanjay.

"Isn't there though?" said Mr Rochester, with what seemed to Sanjay like a mixture of pride and regret. "But there aren't many quite like *him*. A sexual omnivore, this one. You should have seen him eyeing the lobby girls the first time I brought him here. Drinking in the female talent. Kind, generous, respectful and bent both ways, the little darling."

"Kim."

"Exactly. How very perceptive of you, as always. There was a time when I would have been teaching him the Great Game. Only now the game's different. And he seems to have learned it all by himself, haven't you, love?"

Sanjay caught enough of this to know he was being patronised. He also caught Mr Desmond's discomfort. Mr Desmond could be embarrassed, in sharp distinction to Mr Rochester, for whom there was nothing between overweening confidence and utter humiliation.

"I'm going to give you Adrian's address," said Mr Rochester after his friend had gone. "I want him to look after you. I'll die of jealousy but at least I won't die of shame. You'll never know what it means, saying toodle-oo to you."

Mr Rochester was right. Sanjay never did find out what saying 'toodle-oo' meant. But in that last evening together he got the general idea. There were a lot of tears, all of them from Mr Rochester. Some of them soaked the palliasse on Sanjay's pallet, because Mr Rochester insisted that their last encounter should take place in the slum.

"So *real* here," sobbed Mr Rochester. "For once in my life I have lived in reality. *Ange plein de gaité, connaissez-vous l'angoisse?* No, of course you don't. Dear, dear boy. Isn't it funny? I used to feel this way about Adrian. A thousand years ago. But he grew up. And you never will, because I'm going to leave you. So you'll always be like this, won't you?"

"Yes," said Sanjay, because when Mr Rochester was talking it was always a safer response than no.

Early the next afternoon Sanjay accompanied the departing Mr Rochester to the airport. It was by far the longest ride Sanjay had

95

ever had in a wheeled vehicle. The vehicle was the more luxurious, or at any rate the less austere, of the two types of taxi available in central Bombay. Not counting the toot-toot, which is confined to the city's outskirts, there are basically only two types of taxi in Bombay even today. At the time we are talking about, before deregulation, there were really only two types of car altogether, even among those owned by private individuals. A few film stars owned imported cars, but otherwise everything on wheels was of state manufacture. Both types of car were copied from obsolete western models. So there were a small type of taxi and a slightly larger one. The slightly larger one resembled, and indeed actually was, the English Morris Oxford dating from about fifteen years back. Robust, simple enough to be repaired by its owner, it was short of frills. But at the small price of doubling its fuel consumption and halving its acceleration, it had been given air-conditioning. Hence it was known by the shorthand name of an A/C car. For Sanjay, the splendour of being in an A/C car while travelling such an incredible distance was in itself worth all the trouble of having had to listen to Mr Rochester for more than a week. Up they went over flyovers to see the city spreading everywhere except into the ocean. They travelled slowly single file through miles of roadworks, with hundreds of men and women shifting stones while Sanjay, nominally their compatriot, sat back in luxury to watch them toil, every puff on his cigarette tasting all the sweeter for his comparative idleness. Or else they travelled quickly in multiple lanes of traffic, edging past other cars, zooming past trucks that threatened to spill loosely tied loads of junk. The vibrating drivers of the trucks looked down and sideways resignedly, disowning the accident that would soon fall off the back and happen to someone behind them. The A/C car's driver spoke good enough English to reassure Mr Rochester they were going in the right direction. Eventually there was confirmation: the whistle and silver gleam of huge aircraft strangely close to the ground. Some of them, more than strangely, were actually *on* the ground, moving around on wheels, like enormous cars. Sanjay was enthralled, but retained enough of his wits to stop Mr Rochester paying the driver far too much money. The driver's parting glare at Sanjay was not fond. Mr Rochester's was. Inside the airport building, after all the formalities at the desk, Mr Rochester gave him a small but heavy parcel and made a farewell speech.

"It had to be this way. You do realise that, don't you? I could never bring you home legally. And I couldn't bear the thought of you sitting there in quarantine at Heathrow while they killed themselves laughing at your fake papers. I just can't imagine you – dear, darling, fastidious you – squeezed into some airless container with fifty other people. Squashed between two fat women with condoms full of heroin in their stomachs. Just part of another juggernaut load of human misery that gets stopped at Dover. And suppose you made it? Freezing in Neasden with socks and sandals and seven sweaters. You're too fine for that. This is your country. Be beautiful here. Live beautifully for India."

There were tears to accompany all this. Sanjay could tell that most of them were inspired by Mr Rochester's profound appreciation of his own threnody. But there was real affection too. The money Mr Rochester offered him was proof of that. This time Sanjay took it, and not just with the satisfaction of a successfully completed manoeuvre. He knew that he could do nothing more generous for his departing friend at this moment than to accept his bounty.

"Adrian will look after you. I have to go. Fled is that music. If only we could kiss. Kiss me, so long as but a kiss may live. But this will have to do."

They shook hands. Mr Rochester turned and went, leaving Sanjay embarrassed, speechless and rich.

Mr Rochester had ordered the A/C car driver to wait and take Sanjay back to town. Along with his tip, the driver had been given enough to cover the return fare. Sanjay negotiated with the driver to get this money back. After a protracted shouting match he managed to secure almost all of it. Followed by the driver's curses, he caught a rattletrap bus all the way back through the gathering darkness to Victoria Terminus. From there he walked to the slum, where he at last opened his parcel. It was a thick book called *The Concise Oxford English Dictionary*. Not knowing what concise meant, he looked it up, the way Pratiba had taught him. What a useful book. He put it on top of his pile of magazines. Then he spread the money out on his bed,

97

one note beside the other, in rows. Gathering the notes up again, he neatened them into a wad, tucked the wad under his thin pillow, and slept on it. Next day he would have to work out how to keep it safe when he was not at home.

12

IN THAT DEPARTMENT Mr Desmond was a great help. He opened a
bank account in Sanjay's name. Sanjay was given a little book with
his name on it. Because he had forgotten, or never known, his second
name, Mr Desmond advised him to fulfil the requirements by giving
his first name twice. In this way Sanjay Sanjay was enabled to limit
his pay-off to Ajay and Sunil. Sensibly he did not try to avoid it
altogether. The price in resentment would have been too high. Sanjay
calculated their respective kickbacks nicely, so that even if they
suspected that he was holding out on them, they were pleased enough
with what they received to 'let sleeping dogs lie'. That had been one
of Pratiba's phrases. Sanjay resolved to see her again, a resolution at
odds with the quiet life he was now enjoying for the first time since he
had been too young to think. He had a nice thing going with Mr
Desmond. It was a smooth inheritance. Mr Desmond did not
demand very much, and his first-floor apartment near the West End
Hotel would have been a pleasure to visit even if agony had been the
price. It had three rooms as well as a bathroom and a separate
kitchen. To Sanjay, whose previous standards of expansive domes-
ticity ran to a two-room hotel suite at most, three rooms seemed
like eight. There were couches, cushions, pictures, books in several
languages, cigarettes in a silver box, and a small forest of bottled
drinks whose labels were like pictures too. If this was Mr Desmond's
idea of 'camping out', as he called it, how must he have lived where
he came from? The apartment had rich, sophisticated people drifting
in and out of it all the time. There were more men than women,
naturally enough, and more westerners than Indians, but those of

Sanjay's compatriots who were in attendance were of a splendour and cultivation that he had not previously encountered. His own role, when he was there, was to be a sort of moveable fixture: part of the furniture, but dancing attendance, helping to fetch things, being Mr Desmond's right-hand man. He attracted a certain amount of curiosity, and more than a little envy, but he offset it by his attentiveness. He drank in the conversations even when he did not understand them.

"You can see the sky-dwellers and the nymphs up here," said Mr Desmond, showing spread pages of a big picture book to one of his Indian friends, Suresh, a radiant young man in a black silk jacket. "That's Mara and the rest of the gang leading their heavenly existence. But the Crocodile Demon is lurking in the depths, you dig? So the Elephant Boy has to be saved by Vishnu. Vishnu gets off his butt, swoops down on his birdman steed like Flash Gordon, and slices off the beast's head with a well-flung quoit. Which are you, the croc or Garuda?"

"Who was Garuda? I thought that was an airline." Bent over the picture, Suresh reached up to take a drink brought to him by Sanjay. "You know more about our culture than we do. It's too shaming, actually."

"Well, *you* probably know more about *our* culture than *we* do. That Oxford education of yours wasn't available where I came from, believe me. I was in my sophomore year before I heard of Georgia O'Keeffe. And there weren't too many mullioned windows on the subway to Columbia."

"I wouldn't overrate the dreaming spires. All I ever learned at Balliol was how to piss in the sink."

Sanjay understood only enough of conversations like this to reinforce his feeling of being left out. By now he had learned that he belonged to a country, not just a city, but he had also learned that he knew little about his country beyond the growing realisation that it stretched back into time as well as an unfathomable distance into space. Yet to know that you did not know was better than not knowing. It was painful, but it was better. And on those occasions when he was alone with Mr Desmond he received many an invaluable lesson in language. It was not an exchange lesson. Mr Desmond's Hindi was fluent. But he was generously good at teaching little tricks to help with colloquial English.

"The gas gave out, the motor gave up, and I gave in. But maybe you should say the petrol gave out, not the gas. Gas is American English. And we're teaching you English English. Try it."

"The petrol gave out, the motor gave in, and I gave off."

"Nice try. But say the motor gave up. And gave off is something else. Like you might say the motor gave off fumes. But you won't need that one. Try again."

"It's hard."

"Yeah. I know. It's the little things that are the hardest. Give up and give in are practically the same anyway, but let's hasten slowly. Try it again. The gas gave out, the motor gave up, and I gave in."

This time Sanjay got it right. He enjoyed his visits to Mr Desmond, who called them visits with. With his inborn canniness, Sanjay was careful not to visit every day. There were evenings when he made himself unavailable. He did not let his new mentor take him for granted. One consequence was that Mr Desmond was generous with money. Another was that Sanjay had time on his hands.

Mr Desmond never came to the slum. Unlike Mr Rochester, he had no interest in exploring the realities of his protégé's everyday life. Quite the opposite: he expected standards of dress and fastidiousness that Sanjay, despite his gift for neatness, sometimes had trouble meeting. It was not enough to have clean fingernails. Mr Desmond expected them to be filed. There was nothing as formal as a personal inspection at the threshold: Sanjay was always welcomed with something as close as his undemonstrative host could manage to open arms, but there could be sharp words waiting among the soft furnishings. This particularity on Mr Desmond's part would lead to serious trouble later on, but for the moment Sanjay was relieved to be left alone: he could lead his life unobserved, and with a hitherto undreamed-of freedom to dispose of his own time. Since he did not count his relationship with Mr Desmond as part of his emotional life – it was purely practical – his thoughts naturally turned to unfinished business. Pratiba and Urmila both fell into that category, and Sanjay

101

was surprised to find that the matter of Pratiba was the more urgent. Perhaps it was not so surprising. When Sanjay dreamed, he usually dreamed of choking, of falling, or of being beaten with canes by yelling policemen. Sweet dreams were rare. He would dream of Urmila, but only of her outline: the sweep of her dusty black hair, the swing of her dress over thin limbs lithely rearranged, her bare foot pivoting on its heel with toes turned up. Dreams of Pratiba were more specific: her breath deepening, her nipples hardening, her hips moving vividly with his hand between them. Sometimes he would wake up to the feeling of his wet right hand and find it under his dribbling mouth. Desire does not outrank love, but often does precede it. Sanjay, better fed than ever before in his life and older by several pairs of trousers, had sex on his mind. Studying photographs of Mumtas was no longer enough. He wanted the living, breathing girl, and he wanted her breath to change because he had caused it. He wanted that feeling of tender power. There was also the consideration that he missed the way Pratiba talked. Like Mr Desmond she could talk sharply, but the way she did it did not sting.

Sanjay prepared carefully with a new haircut from the pavement barber. By now the proud owner of three pairs of trousers, two to switch and one kept for best, he wore the second pair, just back from the open-air laundry with a sharpish crease. As always he transferred the gold piece with ceremonial care. His peppermint green shirt, newly bought, featured a very fine wavy gold weave that he thought Pratiba would admire for its subtlety, or at least not mock. "Will it be the crisp look or the unsculpted look for you?" an advertisement in one of the English-language film magazines had asked. He had begun a tentative acquisition of second-hand English-language magazines even though he could barely puzzle out a paragraph. The words in the advertisements for men's clothes were especially incomprehensible, but always worth half an hour with the dictionary which he was slowly realising to have been the most precious among Mr Rochester's final shower of gifts, up there with the expensive pair of rubber thongs which Sanjay now regularly employed for the long trip to the latrine. For his new shirt he had chosen the unsculpted look. The spare cloth in the sleeves, he thought, gave an air of understated flamboyance, of 'devil-may-care' as the advertisements put it. His black shoes, though not lustrous, were at least clean, set off by thin grey socks that were almost new. Thus attired he took up his weekly position opposite the Youth Club and discreetly trailed Pratiba's group of privileged girls on their long, laughing walk home to the apartment blocks on the esplanade of Back Bay where the languorously extended sweep of beach begins its curve to the peninsula. Having arrived in that blessed area, the group began to split up. They all lived in different apartment blocks. Strangely, these buildings, though not identical, were united in a style unlike anything else in Bombay. Sanjay was not to know that they were unlike anything else in India, except perhaps the old cinemas and administrative buildings left over from the last glory of the Raj. One and all, they were perfect expressions of art deco. Today they strike the western eye like the row of small hotels along Miami's South Beach, but without the dubious charm of over-restoration. The pioneering blocks of home units on Port Philip Bay in Melbourne have been too meticulously maintained to acquire the appropriately distressed air of the past tense: it all looks as bright and fresh and unbelievable as the Recoleta district of Buenos Aires. A closer comparison, for their mood of a suspended dream, would be with the buildings along the Shanghai Bund and old hotels like the Jing-Jang, or, in old Saigon, the Majestic, now known as the Nine Dragons. The diplomatic district of Cairo provides an even closer comparison, because there, as in Bombay, it has been the very effort of underfunded upkeep which has provided the patina of time's damage: spare windows plugged with breeze-blocks, unfortunate additions, the wrong paint. In Cairo, however, the doors are guarded by soldiers with loaded rifles and there is nowhere for the common run of humanity to set up camp. In Bombay, as always, the common run of humanity is unstoppable. There they are, swarming at street level, penetrating into every crack, while above them the façades of the West's most exuberant modern architectural style deploy their geometric flourishes in patterned brick, cement rendering and discoloured plaster – cornices curved like the bumper ends of pre-war Detroit cars, free-floating entablatures like laminated ziggurats, blind portholes from Cunard liners made of tiles, vertical grilles of crushed glass brick that once filtered light instead of dust. Inside these superannuated fantasies, beyond the heavy doors of the apartments, dwell the comfortably off, looking down from various but equally unattainable heights on all who are not so: the millions who may not enter but will not stop trying. Pratiba's family lived somewhere up one of those sets of chipped stairs and Sanjay would have to step lively if he was to catch her alone. The moment she separated from the last of her friends and turned into the communal foyer of an apartment block still wanly flaunting the last vestiges of its original pink and sea-green plaster, Sanjay crossed the street and walked quickly in after her, the hands in his pockets meant to make it look as if he belonged. He caught her halfway up the first set of stairs. Between him and her was a man evidently meant to be on guard. He seemed to have his own family with him along with some of their furniture: the staircase was in the process of becoming inhabited. There was enough confusion for Sanjay to slip through and softly call Pratiba's name.

"Oh no! What are *you* doing here?"

Sanjay had not expected to be greeted with pure pleasure, but the look on her face was undiluted fright.

"Quick, come down this way," she continued, recovering her wits with an urgency plainly induced by apprehension. "And look casual."

Sanjay, having taken his hands out of his pockets, put them in again. Pratiba led him back down the stairs and through the foyer towards the rear of the building. She pushed open a door and suddenly they were among parked cars. They must belong to the people upstairs, thought Sanjay: people like her family. There was a man slapping at one of the cars with a dirty rag. He turned to look at the intruders on his labour. Another car was missing its wheels and appeared to have people living in it. Pratiba took him through another door, up a short flight of cracked steps, and through another door held open with a bucket. She brought the bucket inside with them, into a store room lit only by a small window at shoulder height, some of whose glass had been replaced with plywood.

"This is the only place to be alone," said Pratiba, "and not for long." She was already kissing him. She had her hands on his behind.

"I am sorry to have frightened you," said Sanjay, having withdrawn his tongue after going further with it into her mouth than ever before.

"Your shirt would have been enough to scare me witless."

"It is the unsculpted look."

"It is the pits. But your English is coming on. Quick. Touch me here."

Sanjay did. It was happening just the way it did in his dreams, only much faster. But even as her hips moved she kept talking.

"This is crazy. If that bitch Sabbandra had told my parents they would have married me off to a shit collector. There. Not so hard. If we get caught now I'll be killed. And so will you. Harder. This is so crazy. And I love it so much. I've been thinking about it so much. So much."

She had one arm around his neck and with her other hand she was squeezing the swelling in his trousers hard enough to hurt. Half the time she was looking down into his shoulder and he couldn't even kiss her. But his fingers were inside her panties and one of them was inside her. He thought it might break when she finally convulsed, letting out a long sob that made him worry about the man cleaning the cars. Her plainness was transformed into an abrupt beauty. Then, just as abruptly, prompted by the reassembling of her dispersed panic, it returned to what it was. With a haste that struck Sanjay as bordering on the ungrateful, she led him back down the cluttered steps, past the cars, through the foyer and out into the street.

"Stay a few feet away from me in case somebody can see us," she said on the way. "If my parents weren't away I wouldn't even have turned around to say hello. Now please go away quickly. Please. *Go.*"

Sanjay guessed that she would like to make another appointment, as long as it was not here. He suggested that after her tour of duty at the Youth Club the following week she should leave her friends on some pretext and walk in the other direction. He would be watching and he would take her to where he lived, a room with a lock. Or perhaps they could make a rendezvous earlier: tomorrow, for example.

"Good heavens no. The rest of the week they watch me like hawks.

Next week, then. I'll walk the other way. For a little while, you understand. And you can't have any more than this. Now go. *Please.*"

Sanjay was confident that she would give him more. She had made the connection between the swelling in his trousers and his finger pushing up into her soft wet. He would get it into her. It was a sure thing, as Mr Desmond would say. Meditatively Sanjay sniffed his fingers. Essence of wharf. Beneath the callous certainty of his thoughts there was the disorienting softness of feeling that he always had when he had been with Pratiba. Something about the way she had been moved had moved him.

Children imitate their parents' emotions, and when they have no parents they imitate the feelings of people they meet. Much depends on who those people are, and what they do. It's a matter of luck, which more than it ought to has to do with looks. During that week of waiting, a further threat, comparable to Dilip's fist, materialised to Sanjay's personal appearance. When visiting Mr Rochester at the Tajma, Sanjay had been impressed to discover that a couple of opulently wrapped foreign chocolates appeared by magic on the pillow of the enormous double bed at some time between the afternoon and the evening. Mr Rochester, moved by the innocence of Sanjay's awe, had offered him the chocolates, two for every day of their relationship. Sanjay had always taken them home and eaten them in solitude the last thing before he went to sleep. The immediate result had been an intense rush of well being, like heroin you could chew. The long term effect was a decayed incisor. Feeling the pain, Sanjay looked closely into a piece of his multiple mirror, and thought that he could see where the pain was coming from. Nothing stopped it, not even Love Care smeared on thickly. Mr Desmond said that he could recommend a dentist. Sanjay, with an ill-timed show of pride, said that he already had a dentist of his own. But the pavement dentist was better at replacing missing teeth than he was at repairing a tooth *in situ*. The way he chiselled off the affected part was hard on the nervous system, and the wedge of amalgam he cemented into the gap was even harder on the eye. When Sanjay squared up to his multiple mirror again he could tell straight away that the repair would not pass muster: he looked as if he had been trying to catch a bullet in his teeth. Shame-faced, he climbed the stair to Mr Desmond's apartment. Mr Desmond made his distaste obvious. Though he also kindly made quick arrangements to have the damage repaired properly, it was his look of annoyed disappointment that Sanjay remembered. Sitting there with his mouth open while the proper dentist chipped out the botched plug and replaced it with something more fitting, Sanjay had never felt more powerless.

"You're lucky," prattled the dentist, "to know someone who can pay for this. Quartz doesn't come cheap. Whoever stuck that thing into you should be repairing locomotives. Some relative of yours?"

Sanjay could give no answer beyond a gargle. As often happens, a feeling of impotence in one area led to delusions of grandeur in another. The injection wore off, the edge of his tooth gleamed like new, and he had become a person who had his teeth seen to while reclining in a special chair instead of squatting on the pavement at the centre of a small crowd. There was a swagger in his step when he intercepted Pratiba as she walked in the wrong direction from the Youth Club. For her this was already an unprecedented boldness. It needed tentativeness from him to match her mood.

"You're awful when you're cocky. At least that's a better shirt."

He adjusted his features to a suitable solemnity. Yet somehow, as they walked, things were already not quite right. They got less right when Pratiba saw the slum, and not right at all when she saw his room.

"Oh no. This is hopeless."

Sanjay made a mistake. He should have played for sympathy and waited. But he tried to repair the situation by kissing her immediately, and there was angry impatience in the kiss. She felt it and broke away.

"No. Don't. Let's sit down for a minute and talk." She made it clear that even to sit on his bed was a large concession on her part. The cover was relatively clean but she didn't want to rest her shoulders against the wall. He sat down beside her as her eyes went from the fractionated mirror to the neat heap of magazines. Unfortunately Mumtas was on the cover of the top one, showing her legs.

107

"And I suppose you play with yourself while you look at these. I suppose I'm just the 3-D version. Are you all swollen up now?"

This time he had the sense to do nothing except look charmingly lost. It was the expression he had perfected outside train windows and beside the boats to Elephant Island. Pratiba's hand strayed to his trousers as if it were only visiting. But as always she was interested in what she found. The situation was partly restored. Sanjay helped her to open his trousers.

"It's the first time I've actually seen one of these. Is it clean? How do you get *anything* clean in a place like this?"

"It's as clean as a whistle," said Sanjay. The use of one of her own phrases made Pratiba smile and lent generosity to her hand. It felt much better than anyone of his own gender doing it. There was a puffy tenderness to it. Luckily he had a sort of towel within reach.

"What a flood. Oceans of *stuff*. How very weird and wonderful. And rather revolting, really."

She said this last part with a rueful smile, to take the sting out of it. But things were still out of synchronisation. The scene, he now realised, had been played fatally in reverse. It should have started with her. Now it was as if his satisfaction had been hers. When he tried to touch her she was thoughtful, instead of seized by the thoughtlessness that sanctioned her usual abandonment. She was self-conscious. She wanted to go home. When they were standing up he made one last effort. There was something mechanical about it, and again she felt it.

"You just want to hear some heavy breathing. Save it for your magazines. Save it for Mumtas."

Had he commanded the words for his deeper feelings, he would have told her that while it indeed made him feel powerful to render her helpless, her satisfaction was more important to him than his; that it was the moment when the world revealed its full strangeness and a plain girl became beautiful. Perhaps it was lucky that he could not articulate this unflattering thought. Anyway, it was certainly the wrong moment for a cockroach to run down the wall. Another one chased it.

"I have to go. Now. I have to go home."

All the way to the main street through the noisy, noisome labyrinth of the slum, Sanjay tried to fix another appointment. But Pratiba was vague. In the narrow alley she only just managed to dodge a peeing little boy without getting her shiny shoes wet. Sanjay cuffed the little boy but scored no points for gallantry. When they got to the street she hailed the first taxi that came by.

"It's just best that we don't see each other for a while." Her eyes were wet. "It's a terrible risk for me. And it *is* all wrong, you know. You do know that, don't you?"

He shook his head but he had nothing to say. She got in and went.

So Sanjay had never even seen what he had so often touched. Reluctantly but firmly he wrote Pratiba off. After all, it was not as if he loved her. There were many girls he could have now. One hot afternoon he took a walk along Falkland Street to look them over. Some of them were very pretty. They stood at the doorways so that potential customers could choose. Some of them wore exciting western-style dresses. One of them daringly wore a pair of tight trousers. Sanjay found such plumage too strident for his taste. But there was a strong contingent of pretty, reasonably reticent-looking girls, most of them no older than he was, and some of them conspicuously younger. All of them, even the most modest-looking, smiled and beckoned. "You're more beautiful than we are," one of them shouted. "Put on a skirt and come to work." Giggles crossed the crowded narrow street. There were dozens and dozens of them: a whole harem just for him. It was a slack part of the day and he was the centre of attention. He could just about afford one if he wanted to. He decided to put it off. It would eat into his nest egg. And you couldn't be sure how clean they were. The VD clinic was the busiest looking building in the street. On the toilet roof, Sanjay had heard a lot about sexual diseases during long discussions in the haze of heroin. Apparently the worst diseases came from girls who had had abortions. Also some of the girls tried to make you wear rubber things that were diseased. Sanjay could think of a dozen reasons for postponement. He put on a look of someone who just happened to be going along Falkland Street on the way to somewhere else. The truth was that he was shy about making a fool of himself. It was an area where he needed guidance but he no longer had that subservient relationship with Sunil and Ajay. He had established himself as their equal. It was too late to become a pupil again. And although Mr Desmond knew almost everything about almost everything, this was scarcely one of his areas of expertise. Once again Sanjay was paying the penalty of being out on his own.

13

"DON'T BE QUIXOTIC," said Mr Desmond one evening. "There's no poverty in America that couldn't be fixed somehow, except maybe for the blacks. The poverty in LA is Mexican, not American. Real poverty is endemic. Real poverty is *here*. This is a country where a kid as smart as this doesn't even get to go to school. He doesn't even get to *fail*."

As so often during these soirées, Sanjay was being referred to rather than addressed. The addressee was another American, called Scott, which was apparently his first name even though it sounded like his last. The good-looking Suresh was there again, and another Indian young man fully as splendid. But all paled beside the splendour of Scott. He was a head taller than anyone else, and the head was as magnificent as his body, which filled his fine tan clothes with muscle. His hair and moustache were blond like the good straw used to pack plates. From the stretches of conversation that he could understand, Sanjay had deduced that this creature from the clouds was on television in America. Sanjay found it hard to imagine how. He had seen something of Indian television, whose on-screen personnel, though sometimes quite good looking, all behaved as if they had been drugged into submission. Scott was alive. It was just that he was so unlikely, as handsome as an advertisement for American cigarettes in a foreign magazine.

"I never said America had the poverty of *want*," said Scott, confusingly pronouncing it *warnt*. "What we have is the poverty of abundance. We're insulating our kids from the world as thoroughly as the poor nations are. *More* thoroughly. The average kid in the US

111

right now has far more electronic equipment in his bedroom than there used to be on an aircraft-carrier ten years ago. He can't do without all that stuff. You can switch him off at the wall. So what does he know about the real world compared to this little faggot?"

"The American kid has much more information," ventured Suresh. "He can press a button and see how big India is. Sanjay can't do that. How big is India, Sanjay?"

"Very big."

"Very big, India," giggled Suresh.

"He's the new Noel Coward," giggled Suresh's friend.

"Give him a break," said Mr Desmond, who liked to hold the monopoly on making Sanjay feel uncomfortable. "Scott has a point. Sanjay can look after himself on the street. And we're talking about a *Bombay* street. An American kid the same age wouldn't last five minutes on Fifth Avenue. He'd be lost without his electronics."

"He's lost *with* them," said Scott. "Alienated. I never thought a Marxist word like that would pass my lips."

"Has anything else interesting passed your lips since you got here?" asked Mr Desmond, to universal laughter in which Sanjay politely joined. It turned out that Scott would be in Bombay for two weeks to film a report on Bombay's poverty, an increasingly popular subject for foreign television crews, especially if they came from countries whose inner cities were no-go areas. A more liberal Indian government was now letting them in, and paying the usual penalty of seeing everything that used to be even worse held up as the worst thing in human history. Scott was just a particularly imposing soldier in a growing army of occupation. Sanjay was given the job of fixing him up. Sensibly Sanjay decided to consult Ajay, who was delighted to make an appointment. Ajay thought that a meeting in the slum would be a bad idea. He specified the steps of the Jahangir art gallery, a place which for some reason was a centre of attraction for educated foreigners. The next afternoon Sanjay walked Scott to the appointed place.

"Adrian's very jealous about you," said Scott as they walked. For Sanjay it was like walking beside a living statue. They had their own small crowd going with them, pushing through the larger crowd going the other way, some of whom turned around and joined their crowd. "I've never seen him like that before. You must really have something. What do you know about him?"

"He is a kind man."

"Oh sure. He's that all right. A little bitchy, but nice underneath. What he really is, though, is smart. The smartest. Smarter than a poem by James Merrill. When I first knew him he was a boy-wonder professor at Barnard. I was just in from the sticks and here was this guy barely older than I was who could talk about *anything*. Isaiah Berlin's philosophy, Richard Feynman's physics, John Rawls's political theory, Diane Arbus's photography, Diana Vreeland's lipstick. He talked about them all as if he knew them personally. And Jesus Christ, it turned out that he *did*. If they were still alive of course. Can you imagine the impact?"

Sanjay, for whom Jesus Christ had been the only even vaguely recognisable name in this catalogue, was reminded of Mr Rochester all over again. Luckily this time it would be Ajay who would have to deal with the flood. Where did all these talkative foreigners find the time to listen to one another? Then Scott said an interesting thing.

"A kid like you would make a good runner for us while we're here."

"I can run very quickly," said Sanjay with some truth, neglecting to add that he ran most quickly when holding someone else's property.

"I bet you can. But it's not really about running. A runner goes to find things, or minds the truck. That kind of stuff. I'll talk to my producer about taking you on."

Sanjay filed this away for the future. At the museum steps he handed Scott over to Ajay. It was instantly apparent that the two of them would get on well, and Sanjay was not surprised to hear later on that Ajay, instead of passing his new client along to one of his subsidiaries, offered himself personally for the task and was accepted. The immediate result was that Scott more or less disappeared. Several days went by before the message was passed through Mr Desmond that if Sanjay wanted some casual work as a runner he should report to the Tajma at the time specified.

"This could be the beginning of a whole new career in the mass

113

media," said Mr Desmond as they lay in bed with a window open to the soft roar of the warm evening. Sometimes, in the right weather, Mr Desmond liked that sound better than the rattle of air-conditioning. Lulled by the second orgasm and the third Martini, Mr Desmond was disposed to talk nonsense. "Don't stop talking to me when you're famous."

Sanjay laughed dutifully but wondered for the first time what fame would be like if applied to himself. He saw himself riding in the back seat of a foreign car with Urmila beside him, richly dressed. When he showed up in front of the Tajma the next morning, however, it turned out that none of the big cars in the forecourt belonged to the American television crew. Scott and his associates were all grouped around a minibus with its back door open. Already it looked like hard work. Big silver boxes were being loaded into the back of the bus by two fat young American men wearing loose trousers and sweat-soaked T-shirts marked with giant initials. Though their shining cargo evoked romance, their groaning and grunting indicated effort. Sanjay cannily made a gesture towards helping with one of the boxes that was still on the ground. All set to pretend that he couldn't budge it, he was relieved to find that no pretence was necessary. It was as if set in concrete.

"Leave that to these guys," said Scott with a laugh. "All you have to do is help the driver mind the truck when we're out of it. Mitch, Thad, this is Sanjay. He's our new Indian guide."

"Indian guide, huh? Hi there, Kemosabe," said the fat one known as Mitch.

"How," said the fatter one known as Thad.

"And this is the person in charge, Melanie," said Scott, introducing a slight young woman whose initialled T-shirt and tennis shoes were separated by a pair of trousers, as if she had turned into a man halfway down.

"Goodbye," said Melanie in Hindi. Sanjay, quickly realising that she had misplaced the word for hello, adroitly converted his puzzlement into a look of astonished appreciation. "How's my accent?" she added. There was that word 'how' again, but this time it was comprehensible.

114

"Your Hindi is coming on," said Sanjay.

"Wow," said Melanie, raising her dark glasses. "We have a *genius* here. You sure can pick 'em, Scott baby."

"Sanjay picked himself," said Scott. "He's one in a million."

"One in twelve and a half million, according to the latest official estimates." It was another young woman talking. As fat as Thad and Mitch put together, she too was wearing trousers, but her trousers were tight: a miscalculation on a monumental scale.

"And this is our researcher, Barbara Tibbets. But we all call her Boots."

"Hello," said Boots in Hindi, thereby placing Sanjay on the horns of a dilemma. How could he show his appreciation of her use of the right word without indicating that the person in charge had used the wrong one? He tried a subdued look of amazement incorporating a wry awareness that his native language was unduly rich in words of greeting. It was not a success. Luckily Melanie's impatient wince was not directed at him, but at Boots. There seemed to be some kind of rivalry going on.

Sanjay was allocated a small jump-seat near the front of the crowded bus, at a convenient angle so that its driver could ignore him. The driver obviously resented having his position as sole local eroded by a minor. Once they were under way, however, Scott's overwhelming bonhomie soon suppressed all tensions. With the fluttering and hammering hands of beggars filling the windows at every intersection, after only twenty minutes they were at their destination. Disconcertingly it was the very alley-way shanty town where Urmila lived. Sanjay was glad that their parking place was not too close to her house. It would have been a bad start to his new career if one of her brothers had seen him sitting there, helping the driver to mind the bus. Nor does minding the bus mean that the minder can always crouch inconspicuously inside. If the bus has to shift position, the minder has to get out and supervise the crowd while it reverses, otherwise there can easily be a time-consuming incident. But on the whole Sanjay was happy to stay with the bus. Immobility here was better than mobility further in. It was better than going down under a flailing heap of Urmila's brothers. Everyone else had got off and headed along the alley in a tight group clustered around the camera. Around this tight group was clustered half the alley's mobile population, so the centre of attraction was soon invisible. Sanjay concentrated on not letting anyone into the bus on any excuse. Since he knew all the excuses, he was an ideal doorkeeper. People took up their beds and walked towards the bus. He turned them around again and sent them back. When the inevitable underoccupied policeman demanded that the bus be repositioned, Sanjay could spot exactly which child was likely to run expensively beneath the wheels as it reversed. He slammed sliding windows expertly on the necks of aspiring thieves. A poacher turned game-keeper, he enjoyed the feeling of respectability.

The most interesting part of the day was the lunch break. Everyone came back to the bus and they all sat in it with the air-conditioning roaring while the windows filled with constantly shuffled hands and faces, a sky of flesh. Sanjay was given a bread roll with sliced egg in it and his choice from a big styrofoam box full of canned and bottled soft drinks packed in ice. For once he passed up his beloved Limca. There were cans of Coca-Cola in there. He had only ever seen Coca-Cola in the form of advertisements, decorating English-language magazines from abroad. He had never tasted it. The taste was stunning. It was like Pepsi Cola speeded up. It was taste times texture: a compressed fizz, half of which went into the hollow passages of the head while the other half went down like a barely controlled explosion, a gas grenade. Sanjay belched stealthily through his nose but Scott must have seen his nostrils flare.

"The taste of America," said Scott, barely fitting under the roof of the van even though he was sitting down. "You've got it coming, kid. Well minded. You're a good minder. Isn't that the English word?"

But that was as long as the attention was on Sanjay. A heated discussion started that he couldn't follow for a minute. Americans always shouted at each other. He should have been used to it. But he could never get used to the way they shouted at each other even when they were close together.

"NBC will shut down the bureaus even if News makes a profit," shouted Boots.

"Why should they do that?" shouted Melanie. "Who says so? They can't."

"They can. Because GE calls the shots and Welch is a cost-cutter. News *costs*. Goodbye baby and amen."

"What about CBS?" shouted Scott. He didn't usually shout, but he had to shout now because the women were shouting. The bus was rocking to their shouts.

"CBS will close the bureaus because Loew's calls the shots and Tisch is a cost-cutter," shouted Boots.

"I've met him," shouted Melanie. "He's a nice guy."

"Like Charles Manson is a nice guy!" shouted Boots.

"And what about us?" shouted Scott.

Sanjay was not to know that he would have failed to understand this conversation even if he had understood the words. All he knew was that he did not understand. It felt like failure.

"Dearly beloved ABC will keep the bureaus open because Cap Cities calls the shots and they know something about television," shouted Boots. "And also if anyone tries to shut *me* down I'll pour gasoline on myself and give CNN the exclusive rights to the footage. Kaboom!"

"Bwah!" shouted Thad.

"Pfwoosh!" shouted Mitch.

"Anyway," shouted Scott slightly less loudly, "when did *you* meet Tisch? When did you just happen to start playing footsie with the head honcho of a rival organisation? And what were you wearing at the time? Clothes?"

"Oh, a while ago. Just socially."

But by this time Thad and Mitch were shouting about something separate. Sanjay's incomprehension switched to them. They were using a small TV set in a steel box to look through all the pictures that they had taken that morning. Sanjay had his eye on the street just in case Urmila showed up, but he knew she wouldn't. She would hide. She was gone, he felt. Meanwhile his ears were fully occupied with what Thad and Mitch were saying. The team had been joined by a rich young Indian woman in western clothes. Scott, Melanie and Boots engaged her in a long discussion about the locations she had

117

been scouting, whatever that meant. Thad and Mitch were left alone with each other at the back of the truck, walled off from the others by the stack of equipment, shut in from the world by rear windows full of hands and faces. Through the soft roar of the air-conditioning, Sanjay eavesdropped on them with fascination. This was more like it. Full of names and initials, their conversation was impossible to follow in detail, but they talked with such concentration that Sanjay knew it must be important.

"Kim Basinger," said Mitch, "has the lips."

"Too *big*," said Thad. "The mouth is too *big*, man. That broad is just Mick Jagger with better skin. Demi *Moore* has the lips."

"A hunch-back."

"It's just the way she stands. She's guarding those perfect jugs."

At this point Sanjay began having problems with the vocabulary.

"How can you say she's not a hunch-back because it's just the way she *stands*? That's what a hunch-back *is*, for Christ's sake."

"Listen, this is an argument about delicious young female screen hopefuls who are going to make it, right? Well, Demi Moore has already *not made it*. She gets married to *Bruce Willis*. Of her own free will! That is *already* not making it."

"Wait for *Die Hard*. Willis could be huge."

"Wait forever. The woman who is really going to make it is Mary Elizabeth Mastrantonio."

"Oh *yeah*. Now we're in agreement. Very spiritual stuff. After she changes her name."

"After she changes her name why?"

"A name like Mastrantonio will never make it on the marquee. Sounds like Marcello Mastroianni having a period."

At this point Sanjay began losing the drift.

"Wrong. *Very* wrong. What that name says is, this broad is *exotic*. Like Isabella Rossellini. Like – get this, here it comes – Nastassia Kinski."

"Now *there* is a pair of lips."

"Polanski. He finds them by radar. He's down there at pussy-sniffing level. You see this new broad he's gonna marry?"

At this point Sanjay began to wonder whether they were still speaking English.

"How old? Thirteen? Twelve? Go on, hurt me. Tell me she's *eleven*."

"Take it easy, she's eighteen. But exotic. With lips."

"Bridget Fonda is going to make it. You seen *Shag*? Great teeth."

"Yeah. Great mouth. And – this is important – *delicately shaped pubic area*. Looks excellent in panties only."

"Like Geena Davis. Also Brooke Shields will be enormous."

"Only in the physical sense. Too many peanut butter sandwiches."

"Regular sex with me will solve that problem."

"OK you guys," said Scott. "Back to reality."

Sanjay was relieved. The rest of the day was like the start of the day and lasted even longer. They went to several locations, all poor. Sanjay had spent time in all of them and was sometimes able to make suggestions about where the most foetid cul-de-sac was, the most pitiable heap of dust. The rich young Indian woman did not seem pleased at first, but Scott declared Sanjay invaluable and Sanjay, though he modestly shook his head, found it hard to disagree. This was, after all, his area of peculiar expertise. The rich young Indian woman, who had an English name, Elizabeth, eventually seemed reconciled to his presence.

For as long as the Americans were in the city Sanjay was busy. Truck-minding was taxing work. The monetary reward was not all that high. It was not like being handed a wedge of notes by a weeping Mr Rochester. On the other hand Mr Desmond, who seemed to be more amused than angry at Sanjay's new ambition, did not cut back on remuneration for services rendered, so when the two sources of income were added together Sanjay was out ahead. After the Americans left there was a welcome lull. Ajay, reputedly, was distraught: Scott had supplied him with a new wardrobe from top to toe and apparently there had been a promise, alas unfulfilled, of a motorcycle to match. Ajay went incommunicado. Sanjay, for his part, was well content. There had been suggestions that his name would be passed on to other foreign television and film crews. As a truck-minder and all-purpose guide to Bombay poverty his career was launched. So he relaxed in the grand manner. He bought himself one or two new items of clothing. Having the great virtue of a sense of proportion, he was not carried away by the advertisements in the English-language glossy magazines. He merely permitted them to stoke his initial excitement.

"Image Incarnation," he read. "A line of suits and prime sophisticate signature style blazers for the connoisseur. And trousers that flow like Chablis. In provocative textures and colours. A timeless, urbane look that doesn't wear out. For the gentleman who goes against the grain. His just deserts. Image Incarnation. Punctuate Your Personality."

Then he would go and buy himself a timeless, urbane pair of socks. Sanjay, who by now was reading his English magazines almost as fluently as, or with no greater lack of fluency than, he could read their Hindi equivalent, knew when to call a halt. He couldn't have everything all at once. Ajay had lost his head: powerful evidence of the appeal of foreign glamour, because Ajay's head had previously been famous for being level. You had to stay calm. It helped that the glamour of the gossip columns, even abetted by a dictionary, was sometimes so hard to puzzle out that the ardour and envy had time to cool.

"With things going great guns for momma," one paragraph began, "daughter *Twinkle* couldn't be too far behind. In case you've forgotten, she's still going strong with *Gattu* and they're even doing a film together. Plus they make it a point to go out every other night. Call it love, bubble-gum style hons. It's a dream-team alright."

The dictionary advised him that 'hons' was an abbreviation of 'honours'. He didn't quite see how that fitted in. But on the whole he was at home with the Bombay film world and all its offshoots. From the semi-comprehensible conversation of Thad and Mitch he had deduced that there was another film world, a foreign one, full of strange names and unimaginable attributes, such as perfect jugs. At the time we are talking about, with deregulation on the horizon but not quite arrived, the quota system was still so strict that hardly any American films reached Bombay. It is questionable whether Sanjay would have been impressed even had they done so. They would have

120

lacked the support system of the local product. The newspapers and the magazines flooded the city to almost its lowest levels with information about the Bollywood stars. When Sanjay went to the movies, as he did every day in these days of leisure, he already knew the name, face and biography, official and unofficial, of everyone he was going to see on the screen. He had the same information about some of the people in the audience. One of them was Dilip. There was a late afternoon when Dilip accosted him after the movie finished.

"Bet you got hard looking at Nagma," said Dilip. "Bet Sunju wanted ten takes of that shot where she gets on the horse. What a pussy. Like a lychee wrapped in muslin. Kiss kiss."

Sanjay said nothing. Dilip had a couple of his toughest boys with him. Besides, Sanjay *had* got hard when he looked at Nagma: not when she had climbed on the horse, but when she and Sunju had almost kissed at the end of the last dance. Their open mouths had been on the point of touching. They must have been able to taste each other's breath.

"By the way," said Dilip with elaborately affected casualness. "That girl of yours that you used to fool around with at the Youth Club. What was her name, Urmila?"

Sanjay said less than nothing.

"I hear she's got a job in Falkland Street. About twenty chaps every day using her as a toilet. Easy come, easy go. Nice socks you got there. Business must be brisk, dick-licker."

Dilip had gone before Sanjay could react. He wasn't sure he knew how to. Dilip's parting shot had hurt him like being hit in the nose all over again. At least it was a clear indication of where she was. He went to Falkland Street next day. He spent a long time looking for her. If she had already been working there when he helped to guide Scott's television crew as they made a pass down the road in their truck, it was no wonder that he hadn't seen her. The girls standing at the doors amounted to only a fraction of the number of those concealed inside in little rooms one customer in length, off dark wooden staircases one customer in width. The rooms were just big enough in plan form to contain the bed, with a few inches to spare in

121

both dimensions and a bucket in the corner. Customers could get past each other in the stairwells and corridors if they cooperated. Most of the girls had less freedom of movement. At busy times they just stayed where they were. Pretending to be a choosy customer, Sanjay attracted much vilification as he searched.

"You think she is not good enough for *you*? She was good enough for Rajiv Gandhi! Get out! Don't come back!" It turned out that more than a hundred girls had each been the love of Rajiv Gandhi's life. It was a long and weary morning and half an afternoon before Sanjay found her: two floors up, the third crib on the right, in the pungent semi-darkness.

Sanjay was a man now: sixteen years old at least, and because so much had happened to him his eyes were older still. He was looking through those eyes when he saw her again, and what he saw was someone who had left him behind. She was still pretty; she was still graceful; but what had once been mystery, a holding back, was now an emptiness. Her potential was gone. She was finished. She looked at him, remembered him, yet did not seem able to connect him with anything that had ever been hopeful or joyful. The woman in charge named her price. Sanjay met it with everything he had in his pocket and was left alone with Urmila in her little box of a room. It was like a box open at the top. It was made of partitions that ended well short of the roof. There were rafters up there, and cracked tiles that let in daylight. As well as the bed, the room contained the usual bucket. A westerner would have deduced, correctly, that hepatitis hung in the air like a fine mist. Sanjay, whose accustomed body had antibodies to spare, breathed in nothing except the proximity of her sweet look. She still looked lovely, despite everything. Her eyes had gone dead but she still brought him alive.

"I work here every day except the weekend," said Urmila. Her voice, which had never been big, was now the merest gesture: something to do instead of not talking.

"I am glad you have employment," said Sanjay.

"It is for my family," said Urmila. "You had better do it with me or I will get into trouble."

Sanjay did it with her. It was not difficult to achieve a state of excitement: she was as pleasing to be near as she had ever been, and more so when her dress came off over her head. She was wearing nothing else. At last he saw what he had so often thought of. He piled his clothes at the end of the bed because the floor looked inhospitable. Entering her was very easy. Dilip had once explained that to rape young girls was impossible because they were too tight: hence any rape stories were fantasies on the part of the girl's family. Sunil, during an especially long night-time symposium on the toilet roof, had once delivered an extended speech on the necessity of foreplay. Illustrating this lecturette with a wiggling forefinger, he had caused such hilarity that one of his listeners had fallen off the roof, never to return. Ajay, on the other hand, had warned that virginal young women had an extra set of baby teeth down there, which did not drop out until after they attained womanhood. When Sanjay had objected that he had found nothing like this in the case of Pratiba, Ajay had countered with the information that the teeth were usually made of gristle rather than bone, and did not manifest their rigidity until the male member had been inserted beyond the chance of withdrawal. Sanjay was relieved to find all this advice was irrelevant. It was easy. It felt light, soft and sweet. He was pleased. My just deserts, he thought. It was only after he reached a quick climax that he found anything amiss. What he missed was any sign of pleasure from Urmila. He had not missed it at the time, but thinking back on it he missed it now. Perhaps Pratiba had spoiled him. Perhaps Pratiba was the only one like that. But Sanjay had read about it too often in the magazines to be in any real doubt. "You may think this is too sweeping a generalisation," said *Savvy* magazine, "but too many Indian women are robbed of ecstasy by male partners with a *tandoori*-and-scotch breath." Women were supposed to be driven mad with passion. They were supposed to thrash about in frenzy.

"You never moved," murmured Sanjay, just managing to lie beside her on the narrow bed. Even replete, he found the delicate shape of her pubic mound an aesthetic miracle to be contemplated endlessly, with his fingertips the antennae of his eyes.

"For everyone else I have to," said Urmila. "They check up on me and make sure I do."

"Then for me you must not," said Sanjay. "For me you will just think."

"You are coming back?"

"I will always come back." Sanjay had borrowed this line from a film, but he delivered it with sincerity.

"You must not try to take me away. For my family this is very important. My brother will hurt you worse than before. Much worse."

"I understand. I won't try."

The sad fact was that he didn't want to. It suited him for her to stay where she was. When Urmila's keeper saw him down the stairs, telling him that Urmila was one of Rajiv Gandhi's favourites, Sanjay had already realised that Urmila was one among thousands, a cliché. He still felt tender towards her: she had an accommodating, untroubled spirit, and nothing short of violence could ever injure her grace. Only a few yards down the street there was the special clinic where all the girls went once a week to have their diseases taken out. She would be looked after. She would not die the way these girls used to. But her mystique was gone. It had gone before he reached her. It had all drained out of her as casual familiarity was pumped in. Sanjay was a romantic. He would come back; he would be kind; but he would not risk his life to rescue a life that was already over. Urmila was a casualty of the streets, and Sanjay was not that: not yet.

In fact for a street child Sanjay was doing so amazingly well that it was possible to forget his origins. Another monsoon came and went. His roof kept him dry. His clothes by now could get him through almost any door. They punctuated his personality. They flowed like Chablis. He had found out from Mr Desmond what Chablis was: it was a French drink. The year began in which Mr Desmond would go back to America, leaving Sanjay without protection. But Sanjay had resources to see him through. There was a certain small amount of capital which could be reached through his bank book. On top of that there was his income, which was earned on the truck, the van, the bus or whatever the foreign TV crew happened to call the vehicle in which they travelled around. Sanjay had become an established truck minder, runner and assistant fixer. The rich young woman, Elizabeth,

124

who had done the fixing for Scott's crew, had been very snooty at the time, always looking at Sanjay as if she had just scraped him with difficulty off the sole of her sandal. Of mixed Indian and Portuguese background, wearing a little cross around her neck like the one on the spire of the Youth Club, she came from a place called Goa, and apparently she was 'acatholic'. Assuming this word was an adjective, Sanjay was not able to find it in his dictionary, but guessed that it might mean snooty. It had turned out, however, that such was only her manner. For the new season she made a point of asking for him to join each new documentary unit to which she had been appointed fixer. Since Elizabeth was the first choice for the best crews, this meant that Sanjay rode in all the best minibuses. Almost all of them did the poverty tour, so Sanjay became increasingly skilled at knowing just where those extra vignettes of squalor could be found which would give the sequence the seal of authenticity. While he was helping the television crews, the television crews were helping him, even if they didn't know it. He listened in on all their conversations. In this way he picked up something of their languages to go with his smattering of English. At the same time his smattering of English became better than a smattering. It did not, and never could, amount to mastery, but it got him by. It came in especially handy with some of the foreign crews when he had little of their language and they had none of his. For communicating with the Japanese and Germans it was a big help. After several trips around the poverty circuit with the different Japanese channels Sanjay picked up quite a lot of useful set phrases and made a start with generating simple sentences from the two main verbs. *Asoko ni ikenakucha* he would say. We must go over there. Unfortunately the Japanese, while keen to demonstrate how impressed they were when a westerner showed himself willing to grapple with their language, felt no such compulsion when someone from the East did the same. From the Japanese, amused tolerance was the warmest emotion Sanjay seemed able to arouse. Laughter filled the *basu*, their word for the bus. Luckily he, and they, had English to fall back on, although their English was often fiendishly difficult to understand, and became more so if his face displayed puzzlement. Similarly with the Germans: he had to be ready to ask

125

for clarification in English, and then, if the clarification was not clear, to take the chance of doing the wrong thing. But whereas the Japanese spoke English with the vital 'l' sound transposed to 'r', the Germans merely swapped around a few sounds that didn't much matter, and sometimes their English was startlingly good. There was a crew from ZDF who spoke better English than the English. After Sanjay said *Guten Morgen* in the morning, he didn't have to venture anything else in their own language until he said *Auf Wiedersehen* in the evening. Meanwhile he picked up all kinds of useful little bits just by listening, and then later on he would score points and a further tip by using them in the right place. *Einverstanden* was a good one. I understand. Quite often he didn't, but he had made the gesture.

The ZDF crew were in town for two weeks doing the entire poverty tour, with nothing left out: in the fishing village they waited for more than an hour until a seagull plucked a dead fish from the crippled little girl's hand. They would have given the little girl's mother enough money to start a riot if Sanjay had not stepped in. Their researcher was very apologetic. Her name was Trudeliese and she had long blonde hair held back with a velvet band. She wore an apricot T-shirt that showed off her breasts, khaki slacks that showed off her hips, and American deck shoes that showed off her access to dollars. Sanjay had never seen a western woman so beautiful, not even the Italian woman who had once held his hand on the boat to Elephant Island. While the crew was out shooting in the tumultuous heat, Trudeliese would often sit in the cool of the *kombi* and read, seemingly undisturbed by the press of faces and hands against the window. For a few days in the second week there was a young Englishman called Rupert who came along in the *kombi* with the Germans and wrote down what they did. He was writing an article for an English newspaper about foreign coverage of poverty in Bombay. It soon became clear that he was highly appreciative of Trudeliese. While the crew were out of the *kombi* shooting, Rupert usually found a reason for staying on board, so that apart from the driver and Sanjay there was nobody else there except him and her. Rupert would speak tenderly to her, as if they were alone. Sanjay could hear the solicitation in Rupert's voice even when they spoke

126

German. When they spoke English, Rupert's regard became even more evident.

"One of the most beautiful sights in the world," said Rupert, "is to watch a girl like you reading *The Magic Mountain* for the first time."

"It's my second time, actually," said Trudeliese in her clear English. "And stop sounding like my uncle."

"It must be wonderful to read it like a native. I had a hell of a time with the vocabulary."

"So do we. Some of the words you can't find in the dictionary. He made them up."

"I can remember what a relief it was when Hans and Claudia started talking French together. A nice holiday from all that tangled syntax. A bit like the French conversations in *War and Peace*. It gets you out of wrestling with Russian for a few blessed minutes."

"You were learning Russian too?"

"My people were dreaming of the Foreign Office."

"The whole British people were dreaming about you?"

"It's a way of saying my parents. There are certain aspects of English usage that not even you can master by intuition."

"A class thing, yes? Like your Foreign Office. Like this place."

"What place? Bombay?"

"Yes, Bombay. Isn't this yours, really? Fort Bombay? Your Empire in the East?"

"I suppose so. Once upon a time. Although, if you'll forgive me, and I don't mean your generation of course, but if you think of *your* Empire in the East, say about January 1943 . . ."

At that point a sympathetic conversation about a book turned into an acrimonious argument, but Sanjay was struck by the way the underlying emotion, on Rupert's part anyway, failed to change. It was all love play. Sanjay began to see that a conversation need not necessarily be concerned with its nominal topic, and that the language of affection can be spoken in tones as much as actual words. For the moment, however, this was an insight he had no occasion to apply. His affection for Urmila demanded practical expression. As the Italians succeeded the Germans, the French the Italians and the

Spanish the Japanese, Sanjay went on acquiring his useful smatterings, improving his English, and saving money, although less money than he would have saved if he had not been visiting Urmila in Falkland Street. This last activity was the only one in which he felt that he was not getting anywhere. There was no progress to be made. It was a kind of desperate standstill. Twice a week – which was as often as he could safely afford – she would greet him as a saviour. Saving her was exactly what he could not do. Even if he could have afforded to burden himself with her, her family would not have permitted him to take her away. Yet he found a sense of having failed hard to quell. In one way he did try to help. An American woman photographer, who loudly proclaimed herself to be famous in her own country and something she called The Whole Civilized World, wanted to take photographs in the house where Urmila worked. The proprietor and the two proprietresses formed a committee to choose which girl should be photographed while working. Urmila was their choice. Several of Urmila's regular customers were approached with regard to their possible participation. All of them, for various personal reasons, declined to be included. Sanjay heard about it and volunteered. It made Urmila feel slightly less miserable about the whole project, and Sanjay had a plan which he thought might make her eventually feel that she had done a good thing. Sanjay negotiated his personal fee separately with the photographer. The committee was initially not happy with this idea but as a regular customer, and one used to bargaining with foreign media people, he was able to put the deal through with a businesslike briskness. After much noisy preparation, the photographer, who luckily was not as large as many of her countrymen, climbed up into the rafters. She was wearing dark green clothes with random brown patches on them and a hat to match, so she was hard to see up there in the half light, especially since there was so much direct dazzle lower down. She had erected special hot lights on thin metal stands in the corners of Urmila's little room. Sanjay manfully did it with Urmila while clicks, grunts and instructions came from above, even after he had finished and was lying beside her.

"That's it, Mack. Now you're drowsy. *So* drowsy. You got what

128

you came for and now you're thinking of tomorrow. Can you tell her to move her hand off her snatch? Off her thing?"

The business took a couple of hours so there would have been real money involved even just counting Urmila's time. On top of that there must have been a lot more. The house got nearly all of it, of course. But since Sanjay's fee came direct to him, when he and Urmila were finally alone together he was able to give all the money to her. That had been his plan all along. Her misery, however, was not alleviated. She was not in tears or even close to them. She looked beyond that, as if staring at desolation. In a voice that went on vanishing in the direction of its source she said she had nowhere to keep the money; nowhere to go and buy anything with it; nowhere to go. Sanjay wondered if it was not time to give up on her. He left her lying there, holding her unexamined wedge of precious brown ten rupee notes up beside her shoulder as if it were a torch she might as well set alight, so as to see at least a little further into the darkness of her future. Her toes were curled tightly, as if in pain. Sanjay, as always, said he would be back, but he found it hard to believe himself. He could hear doubt in his voice.

Sometimes he even doubted himself. Not long after the bad afternoon with the photographer he had a whole bad fortnight with an English television crew. They had come to make a television programme for the BBC based on Mr Rupert's newspaper article about the foreign television coverage of poverty in Bombay. Their researcher was very nice. She was also very pretty, almost as pretty as Trudeliese, and like Trudeliese she read a book during her spare time alone in the van. It was called *Out of Africa*. Her colleagues kept saying that the book they wanted to read was called *Out of India*. They were not enjoying their visit. They didn't like the accommodation, the food, or even the water. Nor did they seem to much like the people. They were quite nice, but like all English television crews they posed an acute problem to Sanjay: it was the way they spoke English. Their lighting man, officially called Sparks, but confusingly addressed as Harry, often turned out to have meant something crucially different to what he had said. "Leave it out," he said testily when Sanjay tried to remind him of a heavy silver box that had not been loaded on the van. So Sanjay left it out, and they almost set off without it. It turned out that Sparks had merely not wanted to be reminded, because he was doing something difficult at the time. So everyone ended up laughing at Sparks, and Sparks ended up not liking Sanjay. To multiply the confusion, the English spoke at least two different versions of their own language. The people in charge put in all the consonants but used their own peculiar grammar. "Do you want to wait here?" meant "Wait here"; it wasn't a question, it was an order. The people who were not in charge left out half the consonants and used a different grammar altogether. "Do me a favour" was another version of "Leave it out". It meant to stop doing something; it wasn't an order, it was an admonition. Sometimes both kinds of people would use the same language but they both used it in reverse: "charming" meant "not charming", and so on.

"I just finished framing up on this little bugger when he squatted down and shat."

"Charming."

"I got the whole thing with a slow zoom out."

"Did we get it on sound?"

"Nobby was reloading. But you wouldn't have wanted to hear it, believe me. Sort of liquid rush."

"Sounds lovely."

Then they all laughed. Why did they do that? And Nobby was the sound man, so if there was no sound how could it sound lovely? None of it made sense. But sometimes Sanjay heard phrases that he could store away with some confidence for future use. "You're beautiful when you're angry," said the cameraman to Sparks, one of the least beautiful Englishmen that Sanjay had ever seen. That was a good one. It meant the opposite of what it said, but there was intimacy underneath. You couldn't say it to a stranger. Sanjay would save it until he met someone who was not a stranger.

What Sanjay could not know was that the English language of Britain, quite apart from all the English languages of the old Empire, had become a world of its own, with its own countries, all held at a distance by mutually incomprehensible accents. The accents and the idioms of the classes and regions within Britain have generated

130

internecine borders that only the classical language can cross, except that there is almost no one left to speak it. The reason why Sanjay could make himself understood to all the different kinds of Englishmen was that the Americans actually spoke English with all the sounds left in. Thus Mr Desmond, in this respect as in so many others, was a stroke of luck. By unintentionally assimilating the way Mr Desmond spoke, Sanjay, as he had from Pratiba, had learned a pedantically inclusive pronunciation which enabled him to speak a form of the language that made him comprehensible to all the different kinds of English speakers even when they could not comprehend each other. His vocabulary was limited and his grammar often patchy, but what he said was clear. He knew that he owed some of this to Mr Desmond even if he did not know quite why. What he now had to face was the loss of his surest guide. The time approached for Mr Desmond to go home to America. He had finished his book. There was a party to celebrate this accomplishment. The apartment was crowded. A large part of the crowd consisted of one man: an unbelievably tall Englishman called Mr Cuthbert. The middle part of him was folded into a soft chair in the corner of the sitting-room, and the rest of him went halfway up the wall and a good way towards the centre of the room. His head was framed in a mirror and his feet were crossed on the carpet in front of a couch full of Mr Desmond's rich Indian friends, the ones Sanjay had grown to like no better as time went on. But he liked Mr Cuthbert immediately. Mr Desmond seemed to hang on his every word, so Sanjay tried to do the same, even though he couldn't tell what any of it meant. Mr Rochester had been a miracle of clarity compared to this.

"You can't *imagine* how *sick* I got of Buenos Aires. I was dying of envy every time I thought of you surrounded by these delightful people. Especially *this* delightful person. I certainly guessed right about *him*."

"Give me a break," said Mr Desmond fondly. "You used to tell me how that place had everything."

"That was before I got there, sweetie. It's got everything if you like eating burnt steak on the back of a polo pony that can dance the tango. Otherwise *nada*."

Up until this point, Sanjay had more or less understood the conversation.

"What about Borges? Did you finish the book?"

"You were writing a book about Borges?" piped Suresh. "I admire his short stories so mu . . ."

"Hold it," said Mr Desmond, and indeed he held up his hand as if he was holding something back. Good phrase, thought Sanjay. Hold it. The same as leave it out, but the American version was better. "Let Ian complain," Mr Desmond continued. "He has a complaint."

"Don't talk to me about Borges," said Mr Cuthbert.

"No, *you* talk to *us* about Borges. The great passion of your life, as I remember."

Sanjay was ceasing to understand, but he tried not to show it.

"It's *too* sordid. I just got sick of him. I couldn't keep track of all those dialogues. They were coming out in Spanish twice as fast as in English. That stuff in the *New Yorker* was just the tip of the slag-heap. The older he got, the more there were. *Last Dialogues with Borges, Absolutely Last Dialogues with Borges, Dialogues with Borges On the Point of Death, Dialogues with Borges When Actually Dying.* And then he croaked and the production line really speeded up. *Dialogues with Borges Shortly After Death.* And then they started publishing the books he'd repudiated, followed closely by the books he'd never published at all, with good reason in most cases. And I started thinking, who the fuck needs a book about Borges from *me*?"

"Yours might be the sensible one."

Sanjay had ceased to understand altogether, but he adopted a look of comprehension.

"Fat chance. I just lost sympathy with the whole mad scramble. And you know, I ended up not even *liking* him any more? Is any of his stuff really *about* anything? Games with mirrors. That sodding labyrinth. Bifurcation. As if reality wasn't already bifurfuckingcated enough. Here's a man who never rode a horse in his life and he was still glorifying these long-gone gaucho knife-fighters when the soldiers were clipping electrodes to girls' nipples only a few blocks from his *house.* Deflowering virgins with electric cattle prods because they'd been caught reading Simone de Beauvoir. What did he ever say about *that*? He just wrote fairy stories instead. Or articles proclaiming the genius of Wilkie Collins. Spare us."

Flying blind, Sanjay essayed a small laugh of delight: very small, in case it was a bad guess. But it turned out to fit the mood.

"You got too close," said Mr Desmond, sounding more fond still, evidently enjoying the way Mr Cuthbert was whipping himself up. "What did you expect him to do? Right from the jump he said he loathed Peron. Peron could have killed him for that. Peron killed his own brother-in-law for less. And Borges was an old man when the generals took over, but he still came out for human rights."

"He sucked up to Pinochet."

"He didn't. He just didn't know what was going on in Chile. How can a blind man read newspapers?"

Sanjay nodded in agreement. How *could* a blind man read newspapers?

"He could hear."

"Anyway, he admitted his mistake about Pinochet."

"In some damned dialogue. But the sheer bloody *frightfulness* of that whole stretch of his country's history didn't touch his creative work one little bit. Brilliant language, of course. Bloody floods of that. The dazzle that conceals. Like those tremendously sexy lines in American movies but they screw each other with the sheet up around their waists. You can search the stories and poems from end to end and never find any horrors that didn't come out of Edgar Allan Poe."

"But that was the point, wasn't it?" asked Mr Desmond. "The regime *did* come out of Edgar Allan Poe."

Again Sanjay nodded in agreement, as if backing up Mr Desmond's opinion from his own experience.

"Quoth the raven, never more," said Suresh's friend.

"I think you'll find that 'quoth' rhymes with oath, not cloth," said another young rich Indian. He was not as handsome as Suresh or his friend but Sanjay knew that he was very clever. His name was Gupta and he had been in the apartment quite often recently. He had a disdainful face and never seemed to enjoy himself except when someone else felt at a loss. Mr Cuthbert went on as if nobody except Mr Desmond had spoken. Sanjay realised that this was because they were old friends. As Pratiba might have put it, they were on the same wavelength.

"I wish you were right, but the fact is that when I got deep enough into the dreadful reality I couldn't escape from the conclusion that the old man had dodged it. When I started using *On His Blindness* as a working title for my book I realised it was time to give up. Three years of my spare time straight down the drain. Time I could have spent writing about someone I admired, like Montgomery Clift. Or Rock Hudson."

"Perish the thought."

"R.I.P."

Sanjay missed the next part of the symposium because he was sent to help the servant carry plates. When he came back, the subject of the conversation had changed. They were talking about Mr Rochester. "I'm sorry to have missed Ted," said Mr Cuthbert. Sanjay knew what 'to miss' meant. It meant to be sad about someone not being with you. But he could not quite grasp why Mr Cuthbert spoke in the past tense, as if he had *stopped* missing Mr Rochester. Mr Cuthbert would rush on and Mr Desmond would argue with him in a way that made him rush on even more. He was also managing to absorb enough cool drink to ensure that he would rush on more loudly. But it was still possible to start another conversation elsewhere in the room. Sanjay ventured to try out some advanced English on Gupta, whose attention had obviously wandered. "Mr Desmond," said Sanjay, "punctuates Mr Cuthbert's personality."

"Well said," said Gupta. "Where do you learn things like that?" Sanjay would have been more flattered by Gupta's question if it had not been framed in Hindi. After some time Sanjay noticed that Mr Desmond was following their conversation. It was a trick he had: he could talk in a perfectly collected manner to one person while listening to someone else. The party went on until very late and Gupta was the last guest to leave.

"I have a feeling Gupta might inherit you from me," said Mr Desmond. "You could do worse. He's wasting a fine brain being a

134

businessman. And he's a bit of a cold bastard. But he has good connections. The prospect takes some of the sting out of saying goodbye. Not all of it, though. Not all of it."

"Mr Cuthbert seems very clever," said Sanjay, to ward off embarrassment. To hold it.

"Ian is a very clever man," said Mr Desmond, reaching to stroke the scar in Sanjay's eyebrow with his fingertip. "But he's sterile, and the brilliantly sterile always feel threatened by creativity. By creativity and by innocence. We take it as a reproach."

Later on Sanjay had a shower, a luxury he always took pains to enjoy. He soaped his behind gingerly, feeling sore. Mr Desmond had used rubber, the way he always did on the nights he wanted something extra. When Sanjay went back into the bedroom, he was wearing a towel like a sarong, the way he had seen Chunky do in one of the magazines. Mr Desmond was holding Sanjay's trousers in one hand and with the other was holding the gold piece to the light of the bedside lamp.

"Can I keep this?" asked Mr Desmond without looking at him. "I'll give you twice as much as it's worth. I'd like to have a little something to remember you by, and this is *very* little. Our little secret."

The last word, secret, he only half pronounced, because Sanjay had hit him on the side of the head. Mr Desmond fell against the headboard of the bed and the gold piece fell on the carpet. Sanjay had retrieved it and put it back into the secret compartment in the waistband of his trousers before he began to worry about what he had done. Then he worried a lot. It was too late to stop the quarrel. He couldn't hold it. Mr Desmond's ear was bleeding. He was shocked and angry and sent Sanjay away.

Back in the slum, Sanjay locked himself into his room and slept badly. His friendship with Mr Desmond was due to end anyway, but to let it end in rancour had been foolish and probably expensive.

The next morning there was a knock on the door. Sanjay, only half dressed, opened it. There stood Mr Desmond, flanked by a struggling small crowd of curious people. Sanjay ushered him in and shut them out.

"Finding you took a lot of asking," said Mr Desmond, with uncharacteristic awkwardness. He had a patch of white sticking-plaster on his ear. "Is this all you have to read? You should have told me you needed a proper mirror. I suppose I could have found out."

Sanjay said nothing. He didn't know what to say. Mr Desmond had taken the top magazine from one of Sanjay's several neat stacks and opened it at random.

"I should have done more for you," he said, shutting it and putting it back. "I should have taught you to read, the way Valmiki taught the sons of Kama in the *Ramayana*. When they came to him for refuge. Did I tell you about that?"

Sanjay shook his head. Mr Desmond, though he had always kept his cultural references local just for Sanjay's benefit, had never fully realised that his ward was just as ignorant about India as he was about anywhere else.

"No. Because it didn't suit me. Forgive me. I find friendship . . . difficult. I have manners instead of love. It's all locked up. The way it is in you. But one day *you* will break loose. Will you come with me to the airport?"

Sanjay said he had to go to work.

"And what kind of work is that, I wonder? Hell, it's your business. I was going to give you this when we got there. I may as well give it to you here. It looks like this place could use it."

It was a thick sealed envelope.

"Buy yourself a mirror, sweetheart. You should see yourself every day. You're a sight to behold."

There was that word 'hold' again. Mr Desmond held him for a little while and then went. Inside the envelope was Gupta's telephone number and a startling amount of money.

14

THE AUSTRALIANS were the first television crew in Sanjay's experience who were not making a programme about Bombay's poverty. They were making a programme about Bombay's film industry instead. On the way to Film City Sanjay sat in the front seat beside the driver and listened to the talk going on behind him. The Australian front man had a name half Italian and half something else: Wayne Calvino. Confusingly, he was talking about American films.

"It takes talent to make a really lousy picture. The Indians just make lousy pictures. But for a *really* lousy picture you need Hollywood. You need a huge budget and lots of talent. *The Last Tycoon*, for example. The Indians could never make that."

"Didn't Jack Clayton make that?" asked the producer, a young woman in overalls called Robin. "He was English, not American."

"No, that was *The Great Gatsby. The Last Tycoon* was directed by Elia Kazan."

"Wasn't he Czechoslovakian or something?"

"American. You're thinking of Karel Reisz. It was an American picture. Produced by Sam Spiegel. Written by Harold Pinter."

"Now *he's* English."

"Still an American picture. Starring Robert de Niro. Don't quibble. We've got an important issue here."

"OK, OK. Get on with it."

"Kazan, Spiegel, Pinter, De Niro. What could go wrong? *Everything* went wrong."

"I saw it," said the cameraman, a stocky, heavily bearded man called Darryl. "I thought it looked good."

"It looked all right," said Wayne. "But so does a turd if you light it properly."

"I had to once," said Darryl. "It still looked like shit." Everyone laughed, so Sanjay joined in, although he didn't quite see the point. A turd *was* shit, so why was that funny?

"Let me tell you what's wrong with *The Last Tycoon*," said Wayne.

"We'd better let him," said Robin. "He's got it all rehearsed."

"What's wrong with *The Last Tycoon* is the women," said Wayne. "First of all there's Jeanne Moreau, playing the big foreign star. But she has to play it in English and she can't *speak* English. So she learns her lines phonetically and they all come out with the em*pha*sis in the *wrong* place."

"For example?" asked Robin.

"Like, she says 'I'm having trouble with my *frigging* hair.' As if carefully pointing out that she's got some special kind of hair she uses just for frigging. She also says 'Nobody likes me or *something*.' Infallibly emphasising practically the only word in the sentence that shouldn't be emphasised. Imagine Pinter's face when he sees the rough cut and finds out his delicately balanced lines are all coming out back to front."

"Cop this over on the left," said Darryl.

"Jesus," said Wayne, with the impatient anguish of a man who has been forced to interrupt his train of thought. "What do you call this place, Sanjay?"

Sanjay, who had once called this place home, said the name of the road.

"Jesus," said Wayne again, "there's miles of it. Anyway, it all happened because Kazan fell for the girl."

"What was her name?" said Robin. "I'm damned if I can remember."

Sanjay tried to shield one side of his face with his hand when he caught sight of his mother. He lowered the hand when he realised that she would not recognise him even if she saw him. Then she was gone again, a spark that had jumped unusually high from a low-burning oblivion. Not looking much older than when he had seen her last because she had already looked exhausted then, still standing in front of what had once been his house, she crossed the rear-view mirror and vanished like a ghost blown on a wind of light.

"I can't remember either. Some semi-famous model who had never acted before. Good-looking girl if you don't mind them with faces shaped like a TV set and shoulder blades like little extra boobs going backwards."

"Sexist bastard," said Robin. "She was lovely."

"Exactly. Was. On her one and only appearance. Never seen again, and all because they made her run before she could walk. Walk? She couldn't even *stand*. With those little norks going in both directions you couldn't tell which way she was facing until she spoke. And when she did, you wished she hadn't. Her line readings made Jeanne Moreau sound like Glenda Jackson. Even De Niro looked as if he was giving her elocution lessons. Every time they were together the picture turned over and sank. Poor kid, it must have destroyed her. She must have cursed the day she was ever talked into it And how did it happen?"

"*You* know how it happened," said Robin. "We can tell."

"Kazan was mad about her. Old man in love. It doesn't matter how long they've been at it or how many Oscars they've won or how wise and wizened they are, finally a woman will warp their judgment. Bella Darvi did it for Zanuck. Jennifer Jones did it for Selznick. Why are we suddenly surrounded by all this mulga?"

Sanjay hadn't heard this word before but guessed that it must mean scrub. He ventured to say something.

"At the top of the next hill we will be there."

"He's right," said Robin. "We've got a treasure here with Sanjay. He's been around."

"Yonder," said Wayne, "lies the castle of my father."

Rising above the trees as it had once done long ago, suddenly there it was: the Silver Castle. And there it wasn't. In Sanjay's mind, memory and perception abruptly boiled like the intersection of two wavelets on a flat beach, the thin, far-flung edges of the next wave coming in to compete with the exhausted remains of the first wave going out. The castle was more extensive now, but somehow not so huge. New sections had been built on; it covered more ground; yet it

139

had lost its monumental integrity. It was silver now only in places. A lot of it was white, and the turrets were all different colours. Some parts of it were not even plausible: Sanjay could see struts of undressed timber holding up façades. Unreality had become real, yielding up its depth by doing so. What was happening to Sanjay, as the van covered that last half mile, is what happens to all of us when we go back physically into spiritual time: a conscious moment in the long unconscious process of leaving imagination behind. It was a tribute to Sanjay's adaptability that he was not floored by the shock. The boiling edges of the second ripple overwhelmed the first and flattened out. By the time the van stopped under the trees he could climb out untroubled, even though he knew he had once sat on this very spot with the shining man and eaten a cheese roll.

The film starred neither Miranda nor Rahul Kapoor. They were both busy with their careers elsewhere. The stars today were Shubash Kumar Tak and Divya, in a film about a fleeing princess restored to her throne by a bandit chief who himself turns out to be a prince in exile. All the Australians went inside the castle to film the film being filmed. Sanjay spent the morning helping the driver to mind the van. It had been a long time since Sanjay had done just minding and he felt underemployed. He talked with the driver for as long as he could stand the boredom. Like most drivers, this one suspected, correctly, that Sanjay was being paid almost as much for not driving. The driver expressed his disapproval through taciturnity. When at last the hooter sounded for lunch, the Australians came out again, carried by the flood of a hundred extras in search of shade and the principal players heading for their pavilions. Sanjay handed around bottles of authentically sealed water fresh from the styrofoam cold box which the Australians confusingly insisted on calling an Eskie.

"Shit, that tastes good," said Darryl the cameraman, his shirt drenched with sweat. "Thanks, Sanjay. I drank half a bottle of that orange stuff in there and I'm still farting through the mouth. How do they get it so warm and sweet?"

"They piss in it," said the sound man. It was the first time he had said anything.

Wayne went off to talk to the Indian director, the famous Prakash Ghai. Robin followed him with her kindly eyes.

"I hope Wayne isn't going to send them up," said Robin. "I think Divya is the most beautiful thing I've ever seen."

"Divya is not as beautiful as Poojah or Mumtas but she has been in better films," said Sanjay, with sensible quietness. It was the start of a long conversation in which he was able to demonstrate his knowledge about the stars. He could tell Robin was impressed, by the way she asked questions. After ten minutes she started taking notes.

"We should put some of this in the com," she said. "What was that about Shubash again? He's been married *how* many times?"

"Only once," Sanjay explained. "Now he lives with her sister. It's a dream team all right. But hold it. His wife lives with the head of the Greater Bombay Film Company so Shubash has signed no films with them for two years."

"This is terrific stuff," said Robin. "Keep going."

Sanjay kept going, being careful not to overdo it, while they all ate the sandwiches and hard-boiled eggs packed for them by the hotel. When Wayne came back, Robin had some lines ready for him to say.

"That director might as well be David fucking Puttnam," said Wayne. "He just mumbles in his beard. We can forget about interviewing *him*. Hey, this is good. Where did you pick all this up?"

"Sanjay's got it all in his head."

"Good on you, digger," said Wayne, without taking his eyes off the piece of paper. "You've just been promoted to assistant scriptwriter and technical adviser." The driver had guessed enough of what was going on to make him look even more sour than before, as if sucking a bad tooth.

From then on the driver had to mind the van all by himself. When everyone went back into the castle Sanjay tagged along. Apart from helping with the odd point of pronunciation he was not asked to contribute much except his presence, so he had ample opportunity to observe. Wayne spoke the new lines into a bulbous microphone while the camera pointed at him and the film went on being made in the background. Sanjay was pleased to recognise the process. Everything was still being done ten times. But if the process was the same, most of the physical details were not. The terraces of the courtyards had lost their balustrades. Small trees in pots grew there instead. There was a fountain in the middle of the courtyard where the main dancing had once taken place. Now it took place around the fountain and up on a wide staircase with steps deep enough for giants, a line of dancing girls on each step. Divya wore glittering trousers instead of Miranda's draped skirt. Divya had no jewel in her navel. Sanjay could see into it. The skin inside it was as smooth as the skin around it, as if she was starting again in there. He had the same feeling about himself. Everything was similar, but it was all going somewhere else, smaller but with more detail. The main camera on its rails, the camera that had once loomed like a monster, he could now see as a machine composed of many parts. Sanjay's erstwhile fascination had become curiosity: a less intense thing, but more penetrating. Piece by piece, his eyes focused on everything. There was no total impression to stun him: just innumerable points of interest to lead him on.

Sanjay spent the best part of a week working for the Australians. Though he soon discovered that Wayne had only been joking about his promotion, the tips he picked up on top of his basic minder's fee compensated for any disappointment at his lack of official status, and meanwhile he was acquiring all kinds of useful experience. The most interesting part of the engagement was a night shoot in a specially built street near the breakwater, only a mile or so from the slum where he lived. The street had been built by one of the film companies. It looked just like an ordinary street but it was rigged so that lights could be aimed into it through windows and the camera could swing on a huge crane. The street was thronged with people helping. They ran and shouted. When the whistle blew, they all crowded to the side of the street behind the camera, leaving the space in front of it free for the actors. The piercing tweet produced silence and emptiness. Then the action erupted, like a dance only different.

This time the dance was deadly. The film being made was about gangs. The story was that the sister of the leader of a gang was kidnapped by the leader of the other gang and fell in love with him. The stars, Chimpoo Kapoor and Vijayashanti, were not present for the night scene. It was a stunt scene. Members of the two gangs fought a battle in the street. They punched each other and some of them fell off the roof. They fell into cardboard boxes in the street below. Sanjay guessed from the angle of the camera that it could not see the boxes, so it would look as if the men had fallen to their deaths. One of them almost did. The cardboard boxes he landed on collapsed instantly beneath him, forming too thin a mattress to absorb all his momentum. There was a loud thump and he had to be carried away. Nevertheless Sanjay was acutely interested in what the stunt men did. It was not the same as being a star, but it was a kind of acting. He had read in the magazines about how some of the tricks were done, but he had not been able to deduce how much preparation it took. Now he could see that it was a full-time job. He vaguely wondered how people got into it. He had never seen himself as a star, but he could see himself falling off a roof. It was like one of his dreams.

The Australian crew had been filming when the man who fell off the roof was injured. Not long afterwards, Wayne said something to the camera about the criminal lack of air-bags, whatever that meant. At the end of the night's work a representative of the production company insisted that the exposed film should be handed over. Darryl refused. The police came. Threatened with endless bureaucracy and a possible day or two at the police station, he reluctantly gave in. Later on, in the van back to the hotel, Robin consoled him.

"Never mind," she said. "We did the right thing. We would never have got on the plane."

"We'd better pray we do before they develop that roll," said Darryl. "There's nothing on it except some of the spare stuff we squirted off at the beach. Ten thrilling minutes of waiting for that guy buried in the sand to stick his head out."

"Jesus," said Robin. "You mean you gave them a dud roll?"

"Course he did," said Wayne. "They'll never get around to looking at it in less than a week. But it might be smart for everyone to be unavailable tomorrow night. We'll go out for a late dinner at that place where they beat the lettuce against a rock. What was it called again?"

"The Jewel in the Crown," said Sanjay. The last time they had all gone there he had heard about it only the next day, and had marvelled at their equanimity. The magazines were full of The Jewel in the Crown. It was the world-renowned gourmet restaurant in Juhu where all the famous people of the film industry went to eat and be photographed.

"That's the place. You're invited, Sanjay. We'll be gone next morning and we ought to say goodbye properly. Our shout."

Sanjay didn't know what 'shout' meant in that context, but from the tone he judged that it must have something to do with not worrying about the expense. Outside the window of the speeding van, the edges of the roads were still crowded after midnight with thousands of people who would never enter the doors of The Jewel in the Crown. That night he hardly slept.

Next day they filmed poverty. Wayne and Robin wanted it for contrast. Since few people spoke good English where they were going, it would have been usual for Elizabeth or one of her colleagues to join the party as fixer, but apparently Elizabeth told Robin that Sanjay would be able to handle the fixing on his own. Her faith was justified. Marshalling beggars for the camera, paying off street vendors and shooing away too tall, insufficiently cute children who would otherwise insist on ogling the camera at the wrong time, Sanjay was at his helpful best.

They wrapped at six o'clock, which gave Sanjay an hour and a half to go home, change into his best clothes and come back to the hotel. He spent a long time washing as carefully as possible before putting on his best shirt, trousers and shoes. The shirt was his special pride. He had first seen it illustrated in *Stardust* magazine. "Charagh Din present an absolutely new range of their Designer Shirts . . . the hand-painted Exclusives!" Three shirts had been featured and he thought one of them in particular struck the difficult balance of meeting Pratiba's criteria for subtlety while simultaneously conveying a sense of luxury. Basically white, it had soft splashes of mixed grey and pink at the shoulders and on one sleeve. Available only at the showroom of Charagh Din, the Shirt People, it had cost a heart-stopping couple of hundred rupees plus. The packed shirt had been too bulky to allow the possibility of snaffling a duplicate, so he had been unable to defray the expense. The shirt had stayed in its packing until this moment. Unpacking it took more time than he had anticipated. There seemed always to be another pin.

Sanjay handled the shirt as if the air might tear it if he moved too suddenly. The trousers had been worn many times before but looked all the better for it: fully washed and pressed, they had, he thought, the timeless urbane look that doesn't wear out. He transferred the gold piece to them as if pinning on a secret *boutonnière*. The shoes were satisfactory. A better pair for best would be his next big purchase. But for now he had deployed the maximum of his resources. He looked into his fragmented mirror and it all cohered. "Image incarnation," he thought.

All the way back through the slum to the main road, Sanjay walked with care, avoiding puddles and rivulets. On all the pavements of the route to the hotel he avoided the merest patch of dust and took elaborate steps not to brush against people. On arrival at the entrance to the hotel he found the spruced Australians no less radiant than himself but far more raucous.

"Jesus, cop that shirt!"

"It's Snake-hips Sanjay, the Beast of Bombay!"

"How's his rotten form?"

"Do we dare to put *this* man among *women*?"

"They'll tear him to bits!"

"I'll look after him," said Robin. "I'll sit on his lap."

"You can stop all the other sheilahs from sitting on his face," said the sound man. It was the second time he had said anything.

"Ignore them all, Sanjay," said Robin. "You're totally gorgeous, and tonight you're mine."

Sanjay was aware that this was only a joke. Robin was not pretty and he did not think of her in a desiring way. Nor did Robin seem to think in a desiring way about him or any other man. But she was kind and funny. That night, like the men, she had taken special care of her appearance. Just as they had put on lightweight jackets, she too had a jacket to go with her trousers. It was of pale blue light cloth with big shoulders. Sanjay had to be careful not to press against one of the shoulders and crumple it when he sat between Robin and Wayne in

145

the back seat of an A/C car. She was wearing a perfume that made it delightful to breathe the same cool air. The pretty but silent production assistant sat beside the driver. All the others got into another A/C car that followed on. The two cars travelled in convoy from the Tajma to Juhu, along the brightly lit main roads thronged with people. At Juhu the entrance portico of The Jewel in the Crown was even more brightly lit than the street. There were small trees in wooden pots on the pavement and tall men in turbans to ward off undesirables. This made Sanjay feel desirable. He felt taller than usual as he walked into the restaurant with the Australians. The crowded interior of the restaurant was like a gossip spread from *Stardust* magazine, or from *Tinsel Town*. Straight away he could see Raveena, Karisma and Mamta, sitting at separate tables with their respective circles of influential friends. At a table on the far side of the restaurant, near the orchestra, sat none other than Dev Anand, surrounded by beautiful women. The Australian party was given a good table. Robin told Sanjay where to sit.

"Sit where you can see the action, darling. If anything's going on you can let us know."

"It looks a bit more glam tonight," said Wayne. "We must have been here on the wrong night last time."

"Must be pay day," said Darryl. He was wearing a bow tie. "Lucky I trimmed my beard."

"Is that what happpened to it?" said Wayne.

Sanjay said nothing. He looked like someone watching an eclipse of the sun who had been told it would damage his eyes but didn't want to believe it. From the angle opened up to him from where he was sitting, he had just seen, at a special table hedged in by plants in the dark far corner, Mumtas. She was wearing a low-cut western-style white dress encrusted with silver filigree and her thundercloud hair was done in a strange, wonderful way that made it look wild and windblown yet somehow heavy, as if it had been rinsed in cream and then photographed while it was flying. She was laughing. Sanjay didn't even blink.

"Wait a sec," said Robin. "Sanjay's seen something he likes." She

146

turned to look in the direction of his gaze. "Wow!" she said. "Who's *that*?"

But the waiter had arrived to interrupt. They ordered drinks before starting the long task of consulting the menu. Sanjay was painfully aware that on this point he could not be of much help. He scarcely recognised the name of a single dish, even though the names were written in his own language as well as in French and English. When Wayne and Darryl asked him something he was at a loss. Robin helped him out of his embarrassment by changing the subject back to what it had been before. Sanjay was grateful to her all over again.

"Come on, Sanjay. Who's your dream girl?"

"That is Mumtas."

"Aah!" This was the extended, swooping musical sound that Robin sometimes made and Sanjay had found so hard to copy. "She's the one who's even more beautiful than Poopot."

"Poojah. Yes, Mumtas is the most beautiful. But she does not want to be branded as just a body," Sanjay went on. "So she gives voice to her daredevilry as well." Sanjay did not reveal that he was quoting this from the best thumbed of all his magazines, a copy of *Stardust* which had long since broken up into separate pages and had to be kept together in a plastic bag.

"Don't stop now," said Wayne. "Fill us in."

"From Randhi Kapoor to Juhi Chawla to Yash Chopra to Sudhakar Bokade, they have all borne the brunt of her fury. The girl has wounded many a heart with her 'they can all go to hell' attitude. But at least there are no half measures to this Maharashtrian beauty."

"No bull?" asked Darryl strangely.

"When attacked, she claws back with devastating results."

"I'll bet she does," said Darryl, sitting almost backwards in his chair. "She can claw *my* back any time."

"She's everything you say, love," said Robin. "What a heart-breaker."

"We definitely came on the wrong night last time," said Wayne. "This is the right night to be here. We should have been shooting this."

"They'd never have let us light it," said Darryl.

147

"Yeah, I know. Who else is here, digger?"

Sanjay started the long job of telling them all he knew. His stream of information made him the hit of the dinner. For once he forgot himself and talked too much, but with the Australians that did not seem to matter. Often they would make their own additional comments on what he said and break out into laughter, but he could tell they were not mocking him. They were being affectionate. He was being affectionate himself, aided by a generous share of the delicious cool white wine. By the end of the meal they were all singing along with any western tune the orchestra played. When it played an Indian tune they would improvise their own lyrics. Darryl made up a very funny lyric about Randhi Kapoor. Astonishingly, the sound man was the one with the best voice. People at other tables looked as if they were enjoying the uproar. Their table was the centre of attention. When Mumtas and her party got up to leave, they came past the Australian table on the way out. It could now be seen that Mumtas's low-cut filigree-encrusted white dress was not a dress at all, but only a top, worn over tight faded blue jeans and high white American cowboy boots. She swayed as she walked. A powerful-looking dark-suited cigar-smoking man who was the head of their party said, "Thanks for the show."

"Any time, cobber," said Darryl. Mumtas said nothing. She did not even smile. But as her glance swept their table it stopped for a second at Sanjay's face. Then she and her entourage moved on.

"You're in like Flynn," said Darryl.

"She put a tag on you and threw you back," said Wayne.

"Leave him alone," said Robin. "Don't put ideas in his head. That goon with the cigar looked dangerous."

"What about the ideas in *your* head?" asked Wayne.

"She certainly is gorgeous," said Robin, shaking her head. "That *skin*. I could eat her."

"Taste better than this shit," said the sound man, who had not liked his dessert. It was the third thing he had said, apart from what he had sung.

The evening declined into maudlin confession, unforgivable frankness and awkward goodbyes. Sanjay was given a fat envelope,

148

which, in his usual discreet manner, he pocketed without opening. All were agreed that Sanjay should get out of the poverty business and make himself available to foreign television crews as a walking compendium of knowledge about the film industry. Sanjay, uneasily aware that he knew little about it except gossip, had no trouble being modest about his qualifications. Nevertheless he felt that his life, to at least some extent, might change in that direction. That had been the real invitation in Mumtas's glance: to dare. More decisively than that he found it hard to think. When they got up to go he had trouble walking.

With immense generosity, the Australians, when they got back to the Tajma, let him keep one of the A/C cars to take him back to the slum, where he arrived in glory, observed by several of its awed residents as he stepped from the car and fell to his hands and knees in a patch of mud. A small spatter of mud joined one of the coloured patches on his shirt to provide an unplanned counterpoint. Image incarnation. He slept long, woke choking, and hurried back to the hotel to find his friends already gone.

15

SANJAY'S PROGRESS towards a career in films was only gradual. He was short of contacts. Though the economy had at last been deregulated and Bombay had been officially declared India's boom town in several different fields, most of the foreign television crews visiting the city were still interested mainly in poverty. Elizabeth could always be relied on to recommend him as their van minder. When it was a simple job she would recommend him as the fixer and not even come on the job herself. He would split the extra fee with her and count himself lucky. He needed the money. Gupta was rich but not very generous, even though he was by far the most wealthy Indian Sanjay had yet encountered. The renegade son of a renowned cosmopolitan plutocrat, Gupta was doing brilliantly well out of the new economic freedom. With a Cambridge education, perfect English, and valuable connections abroad, he knew what to import and how to get it. He knew how to persuade the government agencies to put up the risk capital for a new enterprise: the idea for microwave ovenettes was his, but the seed money was theirs. As the consumer markets expanded, the clothes and expensive toys favoured by famous young people like Mamta and Mumtas were all brought in by people like Gupta, and none of his competitors could match his nose for a fad. He was famous himself. You could see him in the group photographs in all the glossy gossip magazines, the only one not smiling, a serious presence, a 'dark horse'. He lived in a palatial triplex penthouse apartment on the point at Malabar near Raj Bhavan, with glass walls, a swimming-pool, and a collection of East Asian sculpture that experts pronounced to be of museum quality.

The experts came to his parties, along with prominent people from business, politics and sport. Unlike Mr Desmond, Gupta did not often betray his proclivities by restricting his guest list. Sanjay was rarely invited to a party unless extra help was needed. When he was, he felt out of place. The conversations were bewildering. Often they were in English even when few foreigners were present.

"Go to Aspen," said a splendidly suited young man wearing a Rolex. "You're wasting your time in the Alps."

"Maybe you're right," said another splendidly suited young man wearing a Rolex. "I certainly never want to see Gstaad again. The red runs were scraped clean. It rattled my teeth. The moguls were the size of Volkswagens."

"Never happens at Aspen. On Ajax they don't even allow snow-boards. The trails are like ballrooms. You can cruise for miles and never feel a bump. It's bliss."

"When do we go?"

Sanjay didn't know what they were talking about. When Mr Desmond had talked about Moguls he was talking about history. But what kind of moguls were these? It was not much fun being at one of Gupta's parties. The people were not sufficiently artistic to suit Sanjay's taste. On the other hand, being alone with Gupta was not much fun either. Gupta said the minimum. He kept his best thoughts for his friends. He was not generous with his mind as Mr Rochester and Mr Desmond had been. He was not generous with anything. Sanjay could not afford to take it easy with his work. The only bright note was that he was able to extend his range as a van minder. He was no longer confined to the poverty circuit. He also became first choice as a van minder for the foreign television crews covering the Bombay film industry. Robin had passed the word along. There was usually an Indian fixer. When it was Elizabeth, she would happily leave him to do the minor fixing while she went off to arrange the big interviews. Even when the fixer was not Elizabeth and insisted on doing everything, Sanjay still made himself invaluable as a source of information on the stars. As a result, tips were plentiful. But he did not make very many useful contacts. The film industry people, the actual Bollywood personnel, thought of him as something of a pest. In his own language, so as to avoid the possibility of being overheard by some member of the foreign crew he was working for, he would ask if there were any openings going for a stunt-man. All too often he was laughed at or rebuffed abruptly. But eventually, when he had almost given up hope, the day came when he was given advice instead of abuse. A kind second assistant director told him not to waste his time by trying to be taken on as a stunt-man. No one could be a stunt-man without training. The way in was to be taken on as an extra. The man even gave him an address where he could apply.

The time came when he had three clear weeks between jobs. Wearing his second-best shirt, he found his way to the hiring hall for bit-part players and extras. It was only a mile or so from Victoria Terminus but hard to find, at the end of a chain of crowded alleyways. There was an anonymous door you had to knock on and then you had to talk your way in. Sanjay had a letter from Elizabeth that proved he was connected to the agency providing help for foreign television companies and was empowered to do research on their behalf. He used this letter to talk his way past the doorkeeper and after that he quietly made himself part of the scenery. The scenery consisted almost entirely of men; men of all ages and conditions. They sat in tiers along both sides and one end of an enormous room with a dirty cracked concrete floor and a high corrugated iron ceiling that capped an unclear clerestory of dusty glass. At the other end of the room was a sort of gallery reached by a ladder. In the gallery sat men with telephones. The atmosphere was one of waiting. Sanjay found a place in one of the only empty spaces in the second tier on the far side of the room, quite a distance from the gallery. He sat still and thought of other things.

He sat there for a long time. Near the end of the first day, an older man sitting beside him told him that he would not even be called for an interview in less than a week. The older man said he had spent most of his career waiting in this room. He gave Sanjay all kinds of tips on how to arrive and leave in a conspicuous manner, how to sit always where the sunlight fell most brightly, and how to talk to one's neighbours in a way that would show animation and energy. "You must remind them of your personality," he said. "Even when you go out to the toilet, you must walk in a vigorous manner." Sanjay privately decided that if the older man had spent so much more time waiting than working, his advice was probably not very good. Sanjay decided to arrive, sit and leave as inconspicuously as possible. Events proved this to be a wise tactic. On the afternoon of the third day a man wearing a spectacular floral shirt and an improbable hairstyle parted low on the side climbed down from the gallery, walked the length of the room, stood in front of him, and beckoned with a crooked forefinger. He was being called to the gallery.

Sitting quietly in the hiring room had been hot work but the gallery was hotter still. There were several men sitting up there looking important. It was easy to see which of the men mattered most. He had a small electric fan and two telephones on his desk and was enormously fat. The only way you could tell he was sitting in a swivel chair was that he swivelled. Almost bald, with a huge head that shone like good furniture, he turned his whole body towards Sanjay and looked up at him where he stood. Sanjay tried to show the appropriate blend of deference and self-possession. When doing this he always found that it helped to think about Sabbandra. It gave him the look of an apologetic but fundamentally confident pupil.

"Your name?"

Sanjay gave his name, using his first name twice.

"Previous experience?"

Sanjay said he was just starting. He thought it best not to lie about that. This man must know a lot.

"It is a nice change to hear a confession of ignorance. Usually they tell me they are Shashi Kapoor's cousin. Say a line to me."

Sanjay asked him what line he meant.

"Any line. A line of dialogue. Make it up if you must. Pretend that I am a beautiful woman. Make love to me."

"You can claw *my* back any time."

"That is not bad. Your voice is clear. What do you want to do?"

Sanjay said he thought he could do stunts.

"Nobody begins as a stunt-man. People are very lucky to start as an extra. But you have proved that you have the patience to wait.

153

Being an extra mainly consists of waiting without going away. Usually I would have made you wait another few days, just to be sure."

Sanjay took this as a good sign.

"You have a good face. A pity it has been injured. But it will help you look like somebody tough. You will be one of a group of tough-looking extras in the film *Barj Barj*. That name means nothing. They will change it later, after filming is completed. It starts on Friday of next week and you will work for two weeks at Film City. You will not need a suit. It is a costume drama. Mr Mehta over there will arrange your payment, which you get at the *end* of the film, not the start. You understand?"

Sanjay smiled a small smile to show that he understood.

"Don't smile when you get there. For this part you must look tough. When you smile you look like a baby that has been beaten up. Meanwhile I will put you on the register so you do not have to lie to get in here."

Sanjay nodded, concealing his delight. It was only after the formalities were complete and he was walking home along the crowded pavements that he began to tackle the problem of how he could start his next scheduled job for Elizabeth when there would still be another week's work to complete at Film City. He decided not to tell her straight away. He decided not to think about it at all, for the moment. Instead, he bought an ice-cream: a rare indulgence. Like all home-grown brands of ice-cream it was well supplied with stiffeners to delay the certainty of its liquefying in the heat, so several minutes passed before he had to stop walking and lean over in case drops from the last few mouthfuls descended on his shoes. A few small street children gathered to watch him, as if he were a Chowpatty side-show. He gave them a tough look.

For most of the ensuing week he practised looking tough in front of the mirror. When he walked the streets of the city, he walked them toughly. Thinking of Dilip helped. People recoiled from Sanjay's path. He went to visit Urmila in Falkland Street. He climbed the stairs very toughly. When he found her with dead eyes and drowsy with smoke, however, he did not know how to express his toughness. The truth was, he was afraid of the people there. He could bargain with them, but he did not see himself threatening them. If they could do these things to her, what would they do to him? He felt a similar timidity about telling Elizabeth of his plans. He let time go by. It was not that he was nerving himself up: he just avoided the issue. He spent evenings talking and smoking heroin with Sunil and his friends on the toilet roof, under the floodlit canopy of the enormous trees, with the crowds milling below. He spent half an afternoon just killing time on Chowpatty beach with Ajay: they watched the boy going into the box and coming out of the sack, the man who bent spears by leaning on their points with his throat, the men who whipped themselves. He spent a whole afternoon playing cricket in Azad Park. Finally, far too late, he faced the fact that if he did not tell Elizabeth he might never mind a van again.

"Why did you wait so long to tell me?" she said in the hardest voice she had ever used. They were in her little office in the street of the sari shops. It had taken him an hour to walk the length of the block, looking in every shop, convincing himself he was fascinated by the racks of colour.

"You must have realised that the later you told me the worse it would be. Didn't you realise that?"

Elizabeth had all kinds of postcards pinned to the board above her desk. The postcards came from all over India and other parts of the world. There were several from London, where she had lived. He recognised the big red buses. There are some big red buses in Bombay too, but the background is different.

"The Japanese crew have the same assistant producer as before and he remembered you. He asked for you especially. Calling from Tokyo. And now I have to tell him he will have to use someone he doesn't know for the whole first week. While you are off dressing up as a gangster. I had better not tell him that, had I?"

Her eyes were very big and white around their black centres. She was finely made, Elizabeth, but he had never found her beautiful. His charm did not work with her, and so her good looks did not work with him. She made him uncomfortable. She reduced him infallibly to silence.

"If I was in my right mind I would replace you for the whole shoot

155

and let you get on with your mad new career. But I suppose I will find a substitute for the first week. Mohandas can do it. He has the brains of a cow but at least he is honest. If *he* was going to be a week late he would tell me."

The appointments were made and the agony was over. Sanjay left with the mixed feelings he always took away from a meeting with Elizabeth. She made him feel awkward, uneducated and inferior. On the other hand he recognised that there was a kind of compliment in the way she valued his work for itself, without placing any value on his winning ways. She treated him as an erring adult: that was what was so uncomfortable. He preferred to be treated as a gifted child. Sometimes he was sorry he had ever met her. But now he was walking briskly. This time he did not pretend to look into the sari shops. He preferred to look at the saris in the street, the ones with women inside them. He was alive again. He was on the road to a new adventure, with his old job waiting for him if the adventure failed. He had worked the trick.

Once it finally started, the adventure was not much to get excited about. It was lucky that he gave himself two whole hours to get out to Film City, because the bus journey featured, at an early stage, a full half hour stuck in a traffic jam on the flyover, with nothing to do except struggle silently for an extra inch of standing room by breathing deeply. Fortunately he was close enough to a window to get a good view of the work being done on a tall building nearby. They were putting up a big electric sign for Pepsi Cola. It was a talisman of deregulation, a token of Bombay's booming, bustling new economy that they were talking about in the magazines. When the bus finally proceeded and the road sank back to ground level it was possible to detect what had been holding up its progress. As another token of the booming, bustling new economy, the road was being refurbished. Hundreds of workmen were each carrying a bucket of sand or gravel very slowly, while hundreds more, with almost equal slowness, carried empty buckets in the other direction. The bus crawled past them with similar dynamism. Finally it speeded up. Sanjay consulted his watch by looking up at his wrist. The watch was his latest acquisition. It was not a famous brand, but at least it was stolen. Only the stolen watches, Dilip had told him, were worth buying. It had the plain look which Sanjay, from studying the society photographs in the magazines, had deduced was desirable. In all other respects he was glad that he had worn only his second-best clothes. Although he rarely sweated, he was close to it, and the people around him were certainly very close to him. When the bus went up the last long stretch of road to Film City, the house where he was born was somewhere behind his back. He was not sure that he would have looked at it anyway.

At the castle he handed in his work chitty and was given a costume to change into. There was a red turban, a sort of wraparound red blouse, and a pair of baggy pants. The cloth was coarse and hot. None of it flowed like Chablis. The only sign of real toughness was the black belt, which had silver studs and a curved dagger in a sheath. He tested the curved dagger. It was made of some soft metal that bent and stayed that way until you bent it back again. There were no shoes. A busy man who had fifty other extras to look after found just enough time to say that Sanjay could wear his ordinary shoes today: if his feet were ever needed in shot he would be issued with boots. Thinking ahead, Sanjay had already solved the problem of what to do with his gold piece. He had purchased a thin money-belt with a small pouch just big enough to hold his personal effects, including the new watch, which he had correctly guessed he would not be allowed to wear when in costume. The money-belt was already in place under his street clothes, so after he had finished changing in the extras' communal dressing shed, everything he could not afford to lose was safely on his person, instead of dangerously left with his neatly folded kit. He noticed that he was one of only a dozen extras dressed in red. Dozens of others were dressed in yellow. From their facial features he guessed that the men in red were going to be the tough ones and the men in yellow were going to be not so tough. But at this stage the different colours were jumbled together as they all moved out into the sunlight and made their way, marshalled by a man with a megaphone, into the main courtyard. Sanjay felt awkward in his ordinary shoes, as if his feet came from the twentieth century and the rest of him from Long Ago. He really would have felt better with some proper boots. But it was already all too evident that nobody

157

cared very much about how he felt. To the organisers he was just another extra and to the extras he was just another competitor standing between them and preferment. Some dark looks from the men in yellow, indeed, were clearly meant to inform him that he had no right to be dressed in red without having done his time in yellow first. He concluded that it was a privilege to be dressed in red.

The privilege consisted of taking part in an individual shot. The men in yellow formed such a large group that they were never all in shot at once unless the camera was high up on a crane. The men in red stood or moved as a body. They were required to move menacingly. Usually they stood or moved behind the actor playing the bad bandit chief. The good bandit chief, the hero of the film, was being played by the celebrated Anupam Ghai, who was treated as royalty at all times, whether the camera was turning or not. The bad bandit chief was of lesser importance and was consequently played by a character actor. But the bad bandit chief and his men in red still had to participate in at least one scene every day, and since there was no telling when their scene would be filmed, they all had to stand by in costume. There was a great deal of waiting. Then, when the scene finally happened, there was a great deal of hurrying. The bad bandit chief and his men in red would arrive, look menacing, and leave. When the bad bandit chief had lines to deliver, his men in red would look menacing in the background. It was only towards the end of the first week that Sanjay noticed he was always further in the background than anybody else. It occurred to him that the other men in red were engineering this. At the start of the second week he started to insinuate himself closer to the front. In the middle of the second week his efforts were rewarded with a pair of boots.

"Cut," said the director, who was not a sympathetic man. "The one in the second row on the right. I can see he hasn't got any boots. Put him at the back."

"It won't match," said the assistant director. "He's already there in the wide shot."

"Give him some boots, then. Quickly, please."

So Sanjay got his boots, plus some dark looks from the other men in red, and still darker looks from the men in yellow who had been looking at him darkly since the first day.

At the end of the second week, Sanjay overdid it. They were filming up on the battlements. The bad bandit chief and his men in red had just scaled the walls and were looking down menacingly into the courtyard. The shot of them scaling the walls had not yet been done. They were doing the menacing look shot first. The camera was a long way away, down on the ground on the far side of the courtyard, aiming up. Because the camera was a long way away, Sanjay put some extra emphasis into his menacing look.

"Cut." The camera operator was talking to the director. The director picked up his electric horn and aimed it upwards. Sanjay felt that it was being aimed at him. He was right.

"You. The one second on the right. What is your name?"

Sanjay hated to raise his voice. His father had beaten him once for talking loudly enough to wake him up. But this time it seemed politic to do so, so he shouted his name.

"The same name twice? You've got your own echo. Listen to me. The camera is far away but the lens is *close*, you understand? So stop trying to win the Academy Award. Do it the same way you did it in the rehearsal. Film stock is expensive. You understand?"

Sanjay shouted yes, though he would have preferred to take the curved dagger from his belt and cut his own throat with it. He had never been so embarrassed since Sabbandra had caught him with his hand down Pratiba's blouse. Later on, however, the assisant director was very kind. "Don't worry," he said. "At least he noticed you. And it shows you were thinking of the camera, even if you got it wrong. Most of these idiots don't even know whether they're in shot or not." Sanjay took some consolation from that. Another unexpected consequence of his public humiliation was that some of the other extras started to talk to him during the lunch break. Sometimes the shared bottle of warm Thums Up even gravitated his way.

On the day that the bad bandit chief and his men in red scaled the wall, Sanjay distinguished himself. A team of stunt-men did the actual scaling in the wide shot, but there was a mid shot in which the bad bandit chief and his men in red scaled a section of wall lying flat on the ground. As he scaled, Sanjay cast some grimaces towards the camera which were meant to combine menace and effort. Apparently they were successful. The assistant director, who was in charge of the shot in the absence of the director, looked pleased. "That was good. You're coming on. You've got an idea of what the camera can see. Just don't spin it out, OK? Keep it simple and quick."

Luckily Sanjay was given this praise when none of the other men in red could hear it. Almost fatally, however, it inspired him to bigger things. Towards the middle of the third week, with the filming almost over, the bad bandit chief and his men in red were due to be wiped out in a big fight scene with the good bandit chief and his men in yellow, who had superior numbers on their side. The big day had been preceded by two and a half days of waiting while the open-air sections of a big dance number were slowly blocked out, rehearsed and filmed. The dance number revolved around the two stars of the film. The celebrated Anupam Ghai had been joined by the illustrious Sushila. It was the first time Sanjay had seen her in the whole of the filming. Though she was not one of his favourite actresses, he was fascinated by her professional approach. He had plenty of time to observe this professionalism. Most of the extras were outside the castle trying to find some relief under the trees from the hot sunlight. Sanjay had found himself a place in the terraces where he could be safely out of shot while he observed. What he observed was dedication. Sushila had none of the artistic temperament that the magazines always mentioned when they talked about Mamta or Mumtas or the other young actresses. Sushila was not precisely a young actress any more, but she had a schooled grace to make up for it. If he had not already known from her magazine profiles, Sanjay thought he would have been able to tell that she had been to Cathedral School, followed by St Xavier's Senior College and further education abroad at the famous finishing school called Swiss. If there had to be another take, she moved back into position quickly and without protest, so as to save time and energy. When the dancing mistress showed her the next step, she learned it in at most three tries. A blown take was never her fault. Any suggestion she made was instantly adopted. Sanjay deduced from this that her suggestions must be reasonable, because the director was an irascible man who despised idle chatter and always thought he knew best. Sushila worked harder than she was asked to. She gave more. Giving more, she got more. The make-up and lighting people were especially attentive to her. Sanjay decided that there was a lesson here.

Unfortunately he overinterpreted the lesson. In the fight, the men in red were handicapped not only by their inferior numbers, but through having only their curved daggers with which to do battle against the straight swords of the men in yellow. Sanjay thought he did quite well in the wide shots. It was another extra, one at the back wearing ordinary shoes, who ruined a take when he could not get his dagger out of its sheath and wandered off in search of help. It was pleasant to hear the director vent his amplified wrath on someone else. It made Sanjay more confident: always a dangerous condition when in a strange environment.

For the closer shots, some of the men in red had to die more spectacular deaths. The team of stunt-men were brought in. One by one they received sword thrusts to their vital parts. Clutching these, they threw themselves backwards in a spectacular manner on to the ground, alighting in various postures. It took most of an afternoon. Towards the end of the day one of the stunt-men failed to get up again after a rehearsal. He had sprained his wrist so severely that the muscles of his forearm were upside down, as if it had been incorrectly drawn.

"We need another death," said the director, in the same tone he had used previously when asking for a bottle of water.

"He will not be able to do it," said the fight arranger. "He cannot break his fall with his hand. His wrist is gone." Sanjay was almost sure that the fight arranger was the same person who had once, long ago, picked him up and carried him. But in those days, if Sanjay had ever been told the name, he had failed to register its significance. Now Sanjay knew who the man was. He was the famous Rajiv Bharati, memorably described by the magazines as the scarred veteran of many a fracas. After he had fallen off more than his fair share of battlements and exploded through many a window made of real glass, he had graduated to organising action sequences in which

161

young men had to do the same. He tried to keep the casualty rate as low as possible, not just to avoid paperwork but out of real compassion. Finally, however, what counted was getting the scene done.

"Somebody has to die," said the director. "We are losing the light."

Sanjay was suddenly discovered to be standing in the right place.

"You are willing to do this?" asked Rajiv. "You have done falls before?"

"Yes, I have," Sanjay lied.

"Don't lie to me."

"No, I haven't."

"OK. That's better. This is comparatively easy but there is a trick you must remember. Drop your dagger and clutch your wound with the same hand, like this. But use your other hand to smack the ground when you come down. You understand?"

"Quickly," said the director. "No rehearsal." The camera operator was looking at the sun through a filter.

"Slate," said the assistant director.

"Action," said the director.

Run through under his right arm by the straight sword of a fiercely shouting man in yellow, Sanjay screamed, threw himself into the air in a spectacular manner, dropped his curved dagger, clutched his wound, and smacked the ground when he came down.

"Cut. Good. Got it. Not bad."

Sanjay tried to get up again as lithely as possible but Rajiv the fight arranger had to lend a helping hand. Under the peak of his American-style cap his eyes were concerned.

"You are hurt?"

"No."

"You are lying. You have to smack the ground *before* you land. It breaks your fall. Otherwise all the shock goes into your back. Can you breathe all right?"

Sanjay pretended that he could.

"You are lying again. In this kind of work you must tell the truth all the time or you will get badly hurt and I will have to spend hours

162

filling out forms. This is not Hollywood. In Hollywood they would prepare the ground. They would make it soft. This is unprepared ground, baked hard by the sun." Rajiv stubbed the ground with the toe of his American-style trainer shoe. "If you do not break your fall first you will bruise the little bones in your back and end up walking with a limp. Can you breathe better now?"

Sanjay tried to say yes without wheezing.

"You are lying *again*." Rajiv looked annoyed. "Tomorrow is the last day. Don't volunteer for anything else. Just walk through it with the others. If you make me fill out any forms I will make sure that I never have to worry about you again. Now go and get changed. Go home."

Sanjay tried to walk upright as he walked away. That night he woke up whenever he rolled over on to his back. When the usual clamour outside in the passage woke him up at dawn he had trouble getting out of bed. But once again he made the long journey to Film City. The last day was pay day. The men in red had only a couple of scenes to do. In the morning they lay still being dead bodies while the prince and the princess met among the heaped corpses and stared lovingly into each other's eyes, on the point of kissing as the massed ranks of men in yellow cheered. At lunchtime Sanjay was invited to sit down under a tree and eat his roll with two of the stunt-men. They each had fish paste for their rolls and one of them shared his fish paste with Sanjay.

"A very convincing fall yesterday," said the stunt-man who had given him the fish paste.

"*Very* convincing," said the other stunt-man.

"Don't try it again," said the stunt-man who had given him the fish paste. He was tapping Sanjay on the knee with the end of his white plastic knife. "You could get hurt badly next time. This work is for professionals. You understand?"

"There is no room for amateurs," said the other stunt-man.

Sanjay said nothing. He was examining his knee. There was a trace of fish paste on it.

After lunch the men in red worked outside the castle. They ran towards it while the camera filmed them from the battlements.

163

Running towards a death that he had already died, Sanjay would have been impressed all over again by the remorseless logic of film-making, but he was afraid of having to do too many takes. It hurt him to run. He did his best not to show it, of course. He tried to stay up near the front even though it would have been easier to drop back. Rajiv was up on the battlements with his own megaphone, giving instructions to the stunt-men who had to be hit by arrows. When it was all over and Sanjay stood in the queue for his pay, Rajiv came over and took him aside.

"Don't worry, you will not lose your place in the line. You feel better today?"

Sanjay managed to say yes without wheezing.

"Lying again. But at least you are determined. You really want to go on with stunt work?"

This time Sanjay did wheeze when he said yes.

"You have no qualifications for it at all. Except one qualification. You think if somebody else can do it, you can do it. And you are not bad looking. OK. On your next film you can have junior trainee grade. You know how that works?"

Sanjay shook his head.

"At last an honest answer. It means we show you a few things to do but you don't get the full pay, and you have to work as an extra as well. You understand?"

Sanjay nodded.

"OK. Next time you go to the hiring room you hand in this chitty. And don't forget to practise telling the truth. Otherwise you will have a bad accident."

Sanjay pocketed the chitty with as little fuss as possible. Rajiv did not exactly smile, but he nodded approval of Sanjay's discretion.

"Make sure that is the only form I ever have to fill out for you."

With his pay safe in his money-belt, Sanjay went slowly back to town through the rush hour in a bus jammed with extras. The pressure of the people around him made the pain in his back hard to bear, but he was still happy. Something had been achieved. When the bus got stuck on the flyover, he had enough of a view through the window to see that the work had been completed on the Pepsi sign.

This fact in itself was evidence of the new economic tempo. In the past it had been a rare building project which was ever completed quickly enough for people to remember when it started. The bus stopped there, locked in the honking traffic, as the sky grew darker. To gasps of admiration from those passengers who could see it, the sign came on, like the sudden dawn of a new era.

With his back at last hurting a little less, Sanjay picked up his minding work with the Japanese. The assistant producer, Yoshida-*san*, was glad to see him. Apparently his substitute had been merely satisfactory. Sanjay tried to live up to his reputation, but his heart was not in it. The previous Japanese presenters had been dignified men speaking in solemn tones. This time the presenters wore bits and pieces of different military uniforms, with epaulettes that reminded Sanjay of photographs of the white American entertainer Michael Jackson he had seen in the magazines. The chief Japanese presenter was called Soho and he jumped and yelled all the time. The producer had decided on a combined treatment of both the film industry and the poverty. Soho would turn away from the film dancers, point back at them, and snort knowingly into the camera. Oddly enough, he would do the same when his subject was poverty. The camera would pan off a little boy pissing in the street to reveal Soho crouching, snorting, pointing and laughing. Sanjay was deputed by Elizabeth to do some of the fixing as well as the minding. He did a smooth job, but he felt that he was prostituting his talent. There was also the consideration that opportunities to drop into the hiring hall were few, and although he now had his precious chitty working in his favour, it was still advisable to be there waiting. You had to be seen. Nobody would think of you if you were absent.

Yet Sanjay disliked the idea of being driven to a choice. It was all too unsure. He felt the same way about his friendship with Gupta. The friendship was not very friendly, but its advantages could not be gainsaid. It yielded a certain amount of steady income, even at the cost of humiliation. Gupta could be counted on to humiliate him at some stage, either when they were alone together or else in the middle of a large party, but the situation in which Gupta seemed determined to humiliate him from the outset was when they were

165

surrounded by a small group of Gupta's like-minded friends, lounging in the square array of pale blue velvet couches in the centre of Gupta's vast living-room, which would have made Sanjay think of an art gallery if he had ever seen one. One of these friends, an economist of rich background who spent most of each year in California, treated Sanjay as part of the furniture. Sanjay felt that if he did not stay alert he would be used as an ashtray.

"And you know," the economist said with his habitual impatience and scorn, "her folks are only Brahmins by the skin of their teeth. What right do they think they have to pull her out of the marriage? They should count themselves lucky. She is good looking, but I could get her bride price if I sold my bloody Porsche, let alone one of my really good cars."

"You have to see their viewpoint or you won't get what you want," said Gupta. "She is here, waiting. You are over there running around with an American actress. They heard about it. If they hadn't heard about it there would have been no problem. You should have run around with a waitress."

"I don't screw waitresses. You do. I don't."

"What waitress have I ever screwed?"

"Him. An Untouchable."

"Sanjay is not an Untouchable," said Gupta, but Sanjay knew better than to think a compliment was coming. "Sanjay is an Unthinkable. An Indescribable."

"He does not know his place."

"He has no place to know. That's the whole point. We are entering a new world. What was so marvellous about the old one?"

When everyone else had gone, Sanjay tried to plead backache. He was hurt all right, but it was not his back that was hurting. He felt that he had been humiliated. There was no point saying so, however, because he had long ago guessed that for Gupta the infliction of mental anguish was part of the thrill. It was lucky that he did not feel the same about physical anguish.

"You're no use to me if you come here injured. I don't want you moaning and groaning. Not in that way, anyway. You had better think hard about this new profession of yours."

166

Sanjay said he was thinking about it.

"Well, go home and think about it. Don't think about it on my time. Here. Take this much for serving the drinks."

With a lot less than half of his usual subvention, Sanjay walked home. He could have taken a taxi, but perhaps it was time to save money. Sooner or later he would have to decide whether this friendship was worth it. A letter from Mr Rochester vividly reminded him of what generous treatment had felt like. With his dictionary beside him he could understand the letter's warm tone, if not all its detail.

Dearest Sanjay, my Kim, my jewel,

Words can't describe how I miss my darling boy. I never told you that of all the other loves I had in my damned life before you, there was actually one who matched you for his delicacy, his charm, and his gift for embodying the essence of the culture from which he sprang. He was a Japanese boy that I knew in London. But my rapport with him was doomed to remain merely spiritual: an *amitié amoureuse*, as you might say. With you, *Gott sei dank*, the dream came entirely true. Strangely enough, that makes the memory more dream-like than ever. You are a nonpareil, a singleton, an avatar. What a cruel paradox that the only thing sustaining the many-layered society which gave birth to you is its inability to comprehend and value the uniqueness of your unrepeatable individuality. The base Indian threw a pearl away worth more than all his tribe.

I heard from dear Adrian that you met my old and loving friend Ian Cuthbert. I wish I could have been there to see how he impressed you with his mind. We were on the same stair at Selwyn and have known each other for ever. Being so grotesquely tall he always felt that the good things in life were placed beyond his reach, but downwards instead of upwards. Nevertheless he has a great gift of happiness – or had, until he went to Argentina. What an irony that he was hoping to meet some rough trade, as we say. Something that he always dreamed of but never dared. Well, he certainly met some, the poor forked creature. He probably told you that he found a true friend with whom he might have built a life at long last, but that the friend's sister was picked up by those devils in dark glasses and so vilely treated that she died. The friend – how natural to use the term that Ludwig II lavished so appropriately on Wagner, don't you agree? – fell into a melancholy, and from there into a metamorphosis, and there was nothing Ian could do except rail against fate. So now all that fine energy of his expends itself in . . ."

Sanjay gave up at the word 'metamorphosis' and decided to save the bulk of the six-page letter for later. It was miracle enough that it had reached him. The people who had taken over Mr Desmond's flat had given the letter to Elizabeth. She had handed it to him by way of compensation after breaking the news that there would be no minding or fixing work for another month. Sanjay made a promise to be available at that time, but the same thing happened as before. He waited for a week in the hiring hall and then he was given a job.

"You are coming up in the world," said the casting master. "You can be junior stunt-man in a film about gangsters. Chunky is the star. A very important film, with six songs and eight murders. You will have to do box-falls but no broken glass. Can you do box-falls?"

Sanjay said he could.

"You see on your chitty there is this little square drawn here with a circle inside it? That is a secret message from the fight arranger saying that you lie a lot. Can you do box-falls?"

Sanjay said he couldn't.

"Much better. But you will learn. Work starts in one week and lasts for three weeks. You have a suit? Careful now."

Sanjay said he would buy one.

"You can make it a good suit. It will not get damaged because when they throw you off a building they will give you an old suit the same colour. With pads."

Sanjay went off to start looking for a good suit. It would be difficult to steal one. He would have to pay. He was worried about what that would do to his currency reserves. He was also worried about

Elizabeth. Once again the filming would overlap with his next minding job by a week. Once again he put off telling her. There was too much to think about. Finding a good suit in his price range took several days. It came from one of the several western-style tailor's shops within a few blocks of the Tajma. Since the light fawn and sand-coloured suits were expensive, he settled for a dark blue suit, which anyway, he thought, looked more western, and went with his new lace-up black shoes. He did not see himself supplementing those with brown shoes: not at this stage. To buy a suit with a zip was breakthrough enough. The expense was already disturbing. Feeling disturbed about that, he decided to put off feeling disturbed about Elizabeth. There was also the matter of his unfriendly friendship with Gupta. That had always been disturbing, and on one particular evening it became more disturbing still. It was one of those unpleasant occasions when only a few of Gupta's friends were present: all businessmen, all talking about their wealth, and all treating him, Sanjay, like a deaf-and-dumb servant, a machine combining the virtues of an ashtray and a drinks trolley. It was especially galling because for the first time he was wearing his new suit, in the hope of being accepted as some sort of equal. Instead, he was ignored. He was not even the object of sarcasm. He was just an object, like the objects they were talking about, although obviously far less valuable.

"So what happened to the Lamborghini?" asked Gupta, in the way he always had, when he asked a question, of not being able to care less about the answer.

"Oh, the insurance people are fixing it," said a man in a blue suit. The blue suit had fine white lines on it and Sanjay could see that it was a better suit than his own.

"Pity they can't fix the woman," said Gupta, with a smile.

"Which woman is that?" asked another friend.

"Didn't you hear about it?" asked Gupta, with his first real sign of animation. "In Bayswater Road that flying saucer of his hit a woman on the pavement and smashed her legs."

"Her fault for standing there," said the friend in the suit. "It was

169

damned lucky I had diplomatic status. I would have been in real trouble."

"You were in trouble from the moment you bought that thing," said Gupta. "A Lamborghini in London makes no sense at all. Those fat wheels are just for decoration. They can't possibly absorb all that power. For London or Paris you should have a Mercedes 500SL with an automatic top."

"Too pretty," said the friend in the suit. "I like something that looks the part. Like my Cobra. My dear fabulous amazing Cobra. What a brute. With a big bulge on the hood. *Boom!*"

"You have a Cobra?" asked the other friend.

"Used to have."

"Where is it now?"

"Last I saw of it, it was in a window in Los Angeles."

"For sale? Can I buy it?"

"No, not that kind of window. The window of an antique shop. I hit a patch of oil. It's time we went."

Gupta's friends left early. They were going to a fashion show at the Hilton. The mysterious name Givenchy had been mentioned. Sanjay heard them leave but did not see them. He had long ago made his escape into Gupta's books. "I am in his good books," thought Sanjay, wishing he could say it to Pratiba. Unlike Mr Desmond, Gupta did not allow books or any other written material into his living-room. His books were in a special room of their own, called the library. They seemed very advanced. The word 'philosophy' kept cropping up in the titles. The ones Sanjay tried were very hard to read, even when they were in English. Some of them were in languages he didn't even recognise.

"Where the devil did *you* get to?" asked Gupta with more than usual asperity. "Some of them wanted a last drink. I had to do it myself. If I'd known you were going to spend the evening improving your bloody Greek I wouldn't have given my man the night off."

"What does this one say?" asked Sanjay, who had taken down another book at random and was pretending to consult it, hoping to head off Gupta's bitterness.

"It preaches the virtues of an unrestricted free market. The value of the sweatshop. You just happened to pick the one book that helped me to realise I'd wasted fifteen years of my life reading all the others."

"*The Road to Serfdom.*" Sanjay had pronounced the book's title with something like success.

"Bravo. But it's 'serfdom'. The same sound as the surf you swim in. Not that you've ever swum in any, I expect."

"What *is* serfdom?"

"Nothing for you to worry about. Come on, let's go to work. We can have a bite to eat later."

Sanjay went to work, but could not quell his restlessness. When Gupta lay replete on the wide bed – it was the only time he ever relaxed – Sanjay was gazing intently out of the window at the city lights and the sea. The Pepsi sign was brilliant and only half broken. The sea had lights too. They were the lights of the fishing boats. Sanjay remembered what life had been like under the wharf. Suddenly it seemed close behind him. The effect was to urge him further forward. He felt he was on the verge of a great risk.

"Are you trying to tell me something?" Gupta murmured.

Sanjay told him that it was perhaps time for their friendship to end.

"Get out then. Put on your pathetic clothes and go. And don't take anything with you. I know where everything is and what everything is worth."

Sanjay knew it was the truth, but after he had dressed and left the bedroom he still lingered a while in the huge living-room, looking at the objects. Even the very smallest were lit up individually where they lay in their cases or stood on their velvet plinths, adding their reflections to the intricate interplay of indirect light on the white silk drapes that covered the glass walls, a personally planned aurora shutting out the chaotic night. There were miniature jewelled daggers, gods shrunk to the size of pebbles, polished wooden squatting Buddhas that could have fitted inside an ivory tennis ball. Some of these objects were very small indeed: pocket sized. Sanjay knew that he could sell any one of them for as much as he could make in a whole year and that he might even be able to brazen it out with the police. After all, he had a job now. He was a junior stunt-man. And Gupta would have to explain why he had received such a visitor

171

and how he had known who his visitor was and where he lived. But Sanjay had hesitated for too long. His souveniring instinct was overcome by a growing determination to be quit of Gupta and all his works. The man he wanted to hear about life from now was Rajiv, the famous fight arranger, scarred veteran of many a fracas. Sanjay contented himself with taking an apple from the silver bowl of fruit on the crystal table that he had so often barely avoided walking into. On the way down in the elevator he took a bite out of the apple. A mixture of juice and saliva dribbled unexpectedly from his mouth. He only just managed to bend forward in time to avoid staining the lapel of his new suit. The dribble hit the floor of the elevator. It gave him an idea. When the elevator doors opened at the ground floor he pressed the button to close them again and held it while he unzipped himself with his other hand and copiously pissed, aiming to cover as much of the floor as possible without endangering his shoes. Gupta might suspect him, but would not be able to prove it.

16

WHERE GUPTA WAS concerned, Sanjay had burned his boats, if that is the appropriate metaphor for saturating the floor on which one stands. It might be better to say he had painted himself into a corner. He had never earned enough from Gupta to make it worthwhile paying Ajay a commission, so he had never admitted the friendship. But his reasons were not just financial. Nor was Gupta's coldness the decisive factor. Sanjay had simply – gradually but simply – grown sick of that way of life. The film world, with all its consuming purity of purpose, had taken him over. He had even concluded that if it came to a rupture with Elizabeth he would not try to repair the damage. As it happened, Elizabeth took the decision for him. She was not severe with him – or at any rate no more severe than she always was – but she was disinclined to argue.

"Well, you must have known that I would find it unacceptable if you tried the same trick again. You know what that means, 'unacceptable'?"

"It means you are angry."

"No, it means I am *not* angry. It means I am just going to write you off. But I expected it. Your ridiculous film magazines have driven you mad."

Sanjay stood silent.

"Do you think you are going to be a big star? Do you think your face is going to be up there on the buildings? You with your broken nose."

"I will not do love faces. I will do tough faces."

"Well, maybe all those brainless women will love your tough face."

173

Then she did a strange thing. She reached out and touched his scarred eyebrow with her fingertip. "Tough face," she said. "Go on, then, tough face. Come back to me one day if it all goes wrong."

He thought she was giving him a chance to kiss her. He moved forward with his arms prepared for an embrace. "You're beautiful when you're angry," he murmured.

"What are you *doing*? Go on. *Go*!" Sanjay, feeling silly, turned and left her little office. But only a short way down the street of saris he heard her calling.

"Hey, tough face!" He turned. She was standing at her doorway, still half inside it but leaning out. "Good luck."

It was a message he needed. His first day on the new film he was thrown in at the deep end. More accurately, he was thrown off a balcony, at night. It was the same permanent street set where he had previously gone with the Australians, but it was a different film and this time he was in it. On the first afternoon of filming he was meant to be a sort of glorified extra, a member of a gang. All he had to do was fight with his fists. Rajiv was not there. It was an assistant fight arranger with an American cap worn backwards who took five minutes to show him how to throw a short punch and how to react when apparently struck. Sanjay got it right first take. This was a dubious triumph because when the night scenes started he found himself promoted immediately to the status of a gang member falling off a roof. "This is a very simple box-fall," said the assistant fight arranger through his chewing gum. "You are only a junior so you don't have to bounce off the awning. You just fall into those boxes down there. You can do a somersault?"

Sanjay did not precisely know whether he couldn't, so he nodded.

"Good. Just turn over a bit on the way down so you hit the boxes with your shoulders."

Sanjay asked if his padded suit was ready.

"There are no padded suits in your colour. But you will not need one. It is a very simple fall. Just remember to let the other man fall first and bounce off the awning. The camera is coming up past him in a long panning shot and then it sees you as you go straight down.

174

Nothing to it. But whatever you do, you must go. If there has to be a retake, you will not be in it. Understand?"

Sanjay understood. And indeed there was nothing to it. He and the other man were up there on the roof with lights behind them. The Pepsi sign, which the camera could not see, looked pale in the far distance. Down in the street there were more lights to illuminate them as they descended. On the other side of the street, behind the line of the camera, were all the people of the crew and its attendant services. Even the actors who were snacking or changing costume were looking up in expectation. So there was no choice. When Sanjay saw the other man bounce off the awning he had a powerful impulse to go home, but the thought of having his new career terminated on the first day was too much to bear, so he closed his eyes and dived. He forgot all about turning over and went straight down head first into the boxes. They absorbed nearly all the impact. The contact between his head and the pavement was minimalised by the multiple layers of suddenly compressed cardboard. He was almost fully conscious when the assistant fight arranger helped him up.

"Not bad," said the assistant fight arranger. His sharp voice was joined by another, deeper voice.

"Clever stuff. It looked real."

"That was the director talking," said the assistant fight arranger. "He was impressed. How many fingers am I holding up?"

Sanjay guessed. It had to be fewer than four and it looked like more than one. He said three.

"Pretty close. OK. Medical examination completed. Go and get something to drink. In half an hour we'll do a set-up on the roof where you two chaps get hit before you fall over the edge. Then there's just a couple of easy shots that show your gang making plans. No action. All easy. You're having a good first day."

When they wrapped at midnight, Sanjay was thinking clearly enough to realise that his first day had indeed been good. Just before he left he heard the director talking about him to the script editor. "Good face, that kid. Very tough. Injured beauty. The women like that."

"We could put him next to the gang chief," said the script editor.

175

"He could be the silent, brooding lieutenant. With a death wish because of his lost love. Ready for any danger."

"Any danger," said the director reflectively. "Yes, I like the sound of that. Write him in. No words, though. Just the face."

It was almost a part. Sanjay did not have any lines, but he had been given a character. He was even given a girlfriend, to whom he was meant to be indifferent. It was easy to be indifferent to her because she was a silly person with the apt name of Chatterjee. But it was nice to be granted so much attention. Unfortunately he was not granted any more money. In his new elevated role he was excused work as an extra. This proved to be a mixed blessing. Over the next three weeks he had to turn up when he was on call, but he was paid only for those days. As an extra he would have drawn a day's pay for just waiting. Now he was marked for payment only on the days when he did something. He never knew which days those would be far enough in advance to take work on another film. Stars and feature players with proper contracts and schedules could work on three or four films at once. The lowly had to be on hand. His pay scale as a junior stunt-man was double that of an extra but he was marked present for only two-thirds of the total time, so he barely came out ahead. The magnitude of the financial risk he was taking was brought painfully home to him. It was almost as painful as his bruises. The assistant fight arranger was, effectively, the fight arranger. Rajiv was hardly ever present. Rajiv was working on another film, at the Silver Castle. The exteriors for the film Sanjay was in were shot at another location, over the next hill, where nothing could be seen of the castle except two pointed towers with flags on them. The exterior set for the gangster film was a big modern house, or anyway it pretended to be. In actuality it was just a lot of separate walls around a courtyard in which the chorus of gangster girlfriends could dance to playback. In the façades and half-built rooms round this courtyard there were staircases to fall down and windows to be thrown through. Sanjay was excused from being thrown through windows. Only the fully-fledged stunt-men were required to do that. Sanjay lost some of his eagerness to try it when the assistant fight arranger filled him in on the facts.

"In Hollywood they always use toffee glass," said the assistant fight

176

arranger. "The glass is made of candy. It can't hurt you even if you go through it face first. But here we can afford the toffee glass only for the big stunts. Mostly we have to use real glass and you have to know how to go through it with your arms up and plenty of padding. Very professional work. Maybe next year you can try it. Not now. I don't want to be filling out a lot of forms."

Sanjay was relieved. He found it hard enough just falling down short flights of stairs. The stairs were padded but they still scuffed his good suit, which was looking less good by the second week, and in the third week had to be replaced for filming. Sanjay was not fond of the substitute suit that he was issued. It was brown and too tight under the arms.

"His suit is a different colour," said the director, a bearded mouth under a large-brimmed black hat tilted casually forward.

"We can assume his character had two suits," said the ever-resourceful script editor. "I have checked the early scenes and there is no problem with matching. Maybe some of his mid-shots will have to come out."

Sanjay did not enjoy hearing this. He had already learned that the closer the shot, the more desirable it was to appear in. At his level he could not expect to be given any individual close-ups, but in several mid-shots of the gang he had featured prominently. He was disappointed at the prospect of losing them. He was also disappointed at how rapidly his good new suit had been converted into something that looked much less impressive even after it had been cleaned at great expense. So from barely ahead on the deal he had graduated in the reverse direction to being considerably behind. Preoccupied with his sufferings, he added to them on the last day of shooting when he forgot to duck a punch. The stunt-man who threw it was one of the group who had warned him off on his previous film. Perhaps the man threw the punch an unnecessary distance. But Sanjay should have jerked his head back earlier. His lip was split quite badly. When the camera cut and all the bodies picked themselves up and dispersed, Sanjay was left there looking at the blood on his fingertips.

"I like the way he looks now," said the director. "That is very good make-up for once."

177

"That is real blood," said the assistant fight arranger. "Vikram must have connected."

"Real blood. I like that even better. Let's get a close-up."

"We are losing the light."

"They can pump it up in the lab. I must have that blood."

Sanjay was encouraged not to touch his lip during the short time it took to adjust the set-up. Because he was still in shock, it was easy for him to stand still and wait. Quite often the director allowed his assistant to deal with the fight scenes. This time he looked through the eye-piece personally and even called for some lights on stands to be re-angled so that Sanjay's bloody lip would show up to greater effect.

"Don't move," said the director. "Just keep looking stunned the way you are doing now."

"Running," said the operator.

"Keep running," said the director to the operator, walking to one side. Then he raised his voice to talk to Sanjay. "Now just use your eyes to look over here at me. Don't move your face. That's it. OK . . . Cut! Put a mute end-board on that."

Sanjay was led away to have his lip dabbed with something that stung. After a while, with everyone else going home, the assistant fight arranger joined him. "The director has been talking to the producer about you. He was saying how good you looked with the blood running down your chin and the look of pain in your eyes. It might lead to something, you never know. How many fingers am I holding up?"

"Three," said Sanjay with some difficulty. He could see all right, but had trouble enunciating.

"Medical examination completed. Don't forget to draw your pay."

Sanjay's mashed lip healed with a sinister bump, adding an extra point of interest to his face. His lip had plenty of time to get better. The monsoon had come again. Since most films of violence required a large amount of exterior shooting, there was a long time without work. It was not a good time for the lavatory roof so Sanjay visited Sunil in his slum room. There they would exchange magazines and smoke. There was a new magazine, *Debonair*, which featured bare female breasts. These demanded a lot of concentration, for which intense smoking was only appropriate. Sometimes they would smoke heroin, always performing the traditional elaborate ceremony with the silver paper. But their camaraderie was not what it had been. Sanjay got the sense that Sunil thought his erstwhile protégé nowadays required an extra size in hats. Sanjay did his best to talk down his achievements. Expressions of humility were, after all, soundly based. He hadn't done much except get hit in the mouth. His income, averaged out over time, was less than before. Because he had broken his connection with Gupta without first lining up another protector, he would have found it hard to get back into that way of life even if he had wanted to. Sunil and Ajay might have arranged some casual work for him but he did not see himself in that role again.

He saw himself in a film role, as a tough face. Yet even here, when auditions started again, he found himself with weeks stretching ahead before the next violent films were scheduled to begin shooting. Lacking funds to go out, and reluctant to touch what was left of his nest-egg, he spent a lot of time in his room studying. "Speaking about *Shashi Kapoor*," said Smart Alec in his excellent Good Oil column in *Cine-Blitz*, "I recently saw his *Jab Jab Phool Khile, Aa Gale Lag Jaa* and *Trishul* and how I went into a depression, darlings! Couldn't believe that this irresistibly charming man had wrecked his physique so drastically. It's truly sad to see one of our most good-looking heroes in such awful shape. Perhaps that's the reason why his role as the despairing Urdu poet in *Muhafiz* has a similar poignancy. Hope someone drills some sense into him. We really miss the Shashi Kapoor of yore."

Having looked up 'poignancy' and 'yore', Sanjay took comfort. Even the greats had slumps in their careers. On the other hand it was galling to read about aspiring young actors already in the midst of an exciting life. "Recently bumped into *Saif Ali Kahn*," said Smart Alec in another instalment of his fascinating column, "and let the lad know I'd heard that he's played cupid between *Kamar Bose* and *Raveena Tandon*. Guffawing at my suggestion, he exclaimed that one needn't play cupid to a guy like Kamar. Maybe he's right. Is it any wonder then that *Sharon Prabhakar* found Kamar just right for her sexy man ensemble in a recently conducted poll? Phew!"

Though it was undoubtedly a healthy sense of 'why not me?' that helped spur Sanjay on, uncontrollable personal envy was not among his failings, but after he had looked up 'guffaw' he found it hard not to be envious of Saif Ali Kahn. It must be satisfying, he thought, to be in a position where one could guffaw at a distinguished, talented writer like Smart Alec. Sanjay looked into his fractured mirror and practised guffawing. It would have been easier if he had had someone to guffaw at. To his dismay, he now found that he himself was more likely to be the object of derision. The first film that he had been an extra in was released for the screen. Sanjay went to the Palace with Sunil's gang for company. When they saw him climbing up the castle wall, everyone except Sunil guffawed. In the crowd outside afterwards, Dilip appeared. Dilip managed to guffaw and sneer simultaneously.

"We didn't see much singing and dancing from you," he said. "But you fell over quite well. You always were good at falling over." Sanjay knew what he was referring to and felt the usual shame of the victim. Sunil tried to encourage him on the way home.

"Don't listen to that kind of talk," Sunil said. "It all comes from jealousy. Dilip would like to be the one meeting Raveena, you can bet on that."

"I never met her," said Sanjay candidly. "I hardly ever saw her. She was working on two other films as well, so she would just arrive and leave."

"Oh well," said Sunil. "You looked almost as natural as the others." Sanjay correctly took this to mean that Sunil had thought his performance unnatural. What neither of them knew is that to see an acquaintance from your real life up on the screen is always to be struck by embarrassment at the incongruity. The opinion that matters is the one formed by all the people who *don't* know you: the public. As yet unapprised of this important fact, for the time being Sanjay was invaded by a disabling self doubt. It was all he could do to haul himself down to the hiring hall every morning. But eventually he was called up to the gallery, where a remarkable new turn in his fortunes was announced.

"Apparently," said the casting master, "Talat Anand was pleased with a close-up he took of you in his last film. He wants you specifically for the new film he is directing. A very important film with seven songs and nine murders. No title as yet. But the female lead is the great Miranda. A particular favourite of mine. You will be one of her bodyguards. It is a very small part but there is three weeks of work all told. You will have two lines. One line is 'Bow when you address the princess.' Can you say that?"

"Bow when you address the princess."

"Quite good. With a bit more of a snarl, perhaps."

"What is my other line?"

"Bow when you address the princess, son of a dog."

This time Sanjay gave it more of a snarl. "Bow when you address the princess," he snarled, "son of a dog."

"Excellent."

"I can do it with a guffaw also."

"That will not be necessary. Shooting starts in ten days. Here are the details."

For ten days Sanjay addressed his fractured mirror each morning, when his brain was clear and his imagination was at its height. "Bow when you address the princess, son of a dog." He frightened even himself. His confidence was already coming back. He treated himself to a new haircut and a carton of imported cigarettes. He decided to tell Sunil nothing as yet. Better to make sure it all happened. His only worry was about whether he should, or should not, try to remind the great star that he had met her earlier in her career. On this subject his emotions were oddly turbulent. He harboured an urge to avenge himself upon her for her betrayal. On the other hand he well realised that these vengeful feelings would be less acute if she had not once represented for him his ideal of beauty. As many of the magazines so cruelly said, she was no longer in the very first flush of her youth. They said that her famous poise had become staid, that she was a prude, that she had been outstripped ('literally', said Smart Alec, with characteristic wit) by Dimple, Karisma, Mumtas and the other wild youngsters who could not keep their shirts on and did not want to. But she still had a lush warmth that struck Sanjay as the acme of opulence. It was just that it was so difficult to contemplate her image, or even her mere name, without arousing that powerful memory of being shut out. It was her fault that he had been banished from the Silver Castle. Now that he was back, should he raise the subject? She had probably forgotten all about it. Perhaps it would be wiser to talk about something else. He imagined speaking to her. As an aid to inventiveness, he addressed her photograph in one of the latest issues of *Stardust*. The interview that began opposite the full-page photograph was suddenly of vital interest to him personally.

"Your hang-up about your age is showing," said the *Stardust* questioner in bold type. "How come you accept only roles that require you to look youthful? Younger actresses have no problems playing mother but with you it is a 'no-no'. Come clean!"

"The allegation is absolutely false," replied Miranda in ordinary type. "I lied about my age when I came into films, so that I wouldn't be rejected by producers. I was thirteen but told them I was eighteen and my mature figure led them to believe me."

"Your comeback film *Aadmi Khiladi Hai*," the questioner continued, "bombed at the box-office despite being helmed by the same director J. Om Prakash who once made your biggest hits like *Aasha, Arpan* and *Apnapan.* The much hyped *Bedardi* vanished without a trace. Can't you take a hint or don't you realise what is happening? In other words why are you forcing yourself on the audience? Get real!"

"This is ridiculous," Miranda answered. "Are you trying to say that I am no longer wanted in the industry? If that were correct how come I am still being offered films? In fact the offers never stopped coming in even after marriage."

Sanjay agreed that the imputation was ridiculous. Nevertheless he found the interview admirably thorough. There were full details of Miranda's unsuccessful second marriage to a younger man. There was an implication – a puzzling one for Sanjay, in view of his memories – that she had been romantically involved with the shining man, Rahul Kapoor, at the time of her first marriage and his first divorce. Now, it was clear, she was once again in search of emotional sustenance, even as she strove to re-establish her high profile. "A sudden interest in looks," Sanjay read in the summing-up. "Crash diets, aerobics, specially imported Jane Fonda video workouts to get that plump figure back to its original effortless svelte shape. Queening it as of old at her legendary dinner tables. Sudden visibility at social dos." In the photograph next to the summing-up there seemed nothing especially plump about her figure, except, of course, in the region of her celebrated bosom. She looked svelte enough to him. He had looked 'svelte' up. As so often, the guide to pronunciation read like a misprint, but it was a useful word to have. He rather fancied the idea of being svelte himself. Meanwhile there was some comfort to be obtained from evidence that Miranda's current position in the film industry was less than dominant. In the memorable words of the headline on the interview, things were 'far from hunky-dory'. There would be no reason to feel intimidated when he finally met her again.

Nevertheless he was, thoroughly. The film's exteriors were shot first. The location was the Silver Castle. He had a week to play himself in before she appeared. This was lucky, because there was an unsettling development, or lack of it. The director Talat Anand who was supposed to be so enthusiastic about him treated him as a stranger. Sanjay was just one bodyguard in a team of six. Dressed in curled shoes, baggy pants, armless open jackets over their bare chests and strange flat turbans, they had to jump off a wall together while flourishing their swords and then go into a dance. Sanjay knew very little about dancing beyond what he had seen in the movies. Now that he was dancing in a movie himself, he was sorry to discover that it was hideously difficult. He did not shine. After the dancing mistress had shown them the next step, everyone else picked it up faster than he did. The bare-footed, toe-belled dancing mistress having holy status, she was not supposed to look impatient, but when she looked at him she could not be said to smile. He could have told her that he was fairly sure she was the same small large woman who had once smiled at him years ago. But he was only fairly sure, and not sure at all how the information would be received. So he persevered in silence, often breaking into an unaccustomed sweat. The director looked frankly impatient at the hold-ups. The sequence was finally completed only on the third day. Other sequences had been shot too, of course, but there was no blinking the fact that Sanjay had slowed the dancing sequence down. When, with the last light looming, it was at last secured, the director said something which Sanjay greeted with mixed pride and shame, glad to be remembered but sorry about the circumstances.

"Tomorrow it is action. At least you know how to get hit."

To Sanjay's great relief, Rajiv the fight arranger, scarred veteran of many a fracas, was present the next morning to supervise the battle. "At least you didn't lie about your dancing abilities," said Rajiv. "That would have been a big mistake." In the battle sequence, the bodyguards were to protect the princess, who would be filmed at a later time. She had to be protected against a gang of assassins. Twenty men fiercely dressed in brown, the assassins ran up the castle terraces in drilled formation. They were met by the bodyguard and a fight ensued. Rajiv choreographed the fight. Standing somersaults by the bodyguards were doubled by acrobats, but Sanjay and his colleagues still had to do quite a lot of leaping, falling and rolling. Bruises were the inevitable result. The assassins were mown down in spectacular fashion. The same acrobats doubled their back flips, but once again the actors had to absorb a lot of the impact. The twenty assassins were soon reduced to eighteen. That was judged to be a sufficient number. Rajiv was very active and the director had so many instructions to give that the assistant director had to do all the shouting. The scene took two full days to shoot. It culminated in medium close-ups of the individual bodyguards wheeling to receive the approval of the princess. On the first day of the second week of shooting, she arrived to bestow it.

Sanjay was flabbergasted. Under the bright sun, her hair stirred by the gentlest breeze from the wind machine, she looked more beautiful than ever. To start with, she was wearing much less than when he had first met her. Films having moved on in the interim, her costume was more revealing than he remembered it. Now he could see not just the swell of her breasts, but their sweet division, and her jewelled belt was slung so low that he fancied he could see where hairs had been plucked. What really rocked him was the light in her eyes. He had kept her face in his mind, but memory had stylised it. Here was the actual, vivid thing, the intensity of spirit that no still photograph could reproduce, because it was generated by her vibrant movement; and that no film image could ever fully capture, because it would translate her, into a sphere she fitted, from the real world that she outshone. Even in repose, she radiated energy. Not bothering to disguise her boredom when she was shown her marks for the thousandth time in her life, she still glowed. When the shot was rehearsed, she caught fire. The camera was behind the bodyguards. While they knelt, it would shoot past their obedient backs to observe her conferring imperious, unaccustomed thanks on her brave servants.

"You have done well. But I expect no less. To guard me is your . . . what's the next line?"

"To guard me against evil is your task," said the script editor in a raised voice.

"You have done well. But I expect no less. To guard me against evil is your task."

After final checks the shot was secured on the first take. Sanjay could hardly believe it: he was in the same shot as the great Miranda. Admittedly he was pointing in the wrong direction, but the chances were that his face would get into the same shot with her eventually. If only he could study the script. Like every participant below the level of star he would never see even the small portion of it containing his own scenes. The script editor himself carried only the portions of script currently being shot. It was hard to know how big your part would be or how long you would stay alive. In that respect, the director was a god, and even he had other gods, the producers, somewhere behind him. Sanjay felt like a toy of fate. But for as long as he was near her he was a happy toy. He had decided to forgive her. The only question was whether he should tell her about it. To do that, of course, he would have to be alone with her.

Three days later the opportunity came. Unfortunately grief came with it. They were filming beside the fountain. The camera could not see the fountain's plastic lining and rusty pipes. The princess rehearsed beneath a canopy to protect her from the sun. Her singing handmaidens were in attendance, pouring water from silver jugs and decorating the air with strewn petals. An envoy from the bandit chief arrived. He strode towards her but was stilled by the upraised hand of her deputy chief bodyguard. That was how Sanjay found out that he was the deputy chief bodyguard. He was the one deputed to raise his hand. He was also given a medium close-up in which to deliver one of his two scheduled lines. All his practising, however, had been to small avail, because the rehearsal went badly.

"Bow when you address her. She is a princess."

"That isn't right, is it?" Miranda asked the director. "I'm not *a* princess. I'm *the* princess."

"Yes," said the script editor. "That line was wrong. 'Bow when you address the princess.' That is the right line. He was told."

"You can remember that?" asked the director impatiently. "Let's go for a take straight away." But Sanjay was flustered.

"Bow when you address the princess, son of a dog."

"Cut. Good."

"No, not good," said the script editor. "That line comes next week, when the bandit chief is brought in as a prisoner. This time it should be just 'Bow when you address the princess.' He is trying to pad the part."

"You were given the line, weren't you?" asked the director, even more impatient than before.

"I haven't got *time* for this," muttered Miranda. Her words stung Sanjay like a bad memory. On the next take he got lost altogether.

"Bow, son. Bow when you address a. The. Princess."

"Cut."

Miranda burst out laughing. Sanjay thought the world was coming to an end. The director was looking at a patch of bare earth in the scuffed lawn and shaking his head. Sanjay expected to be fired there and then. At that moment Rajiv the fight arranger arrived out of nowhere and took him aside.

"Breathe in," he said.

Sanjay breathed in.

"Now breathe out slowly."

Sanjay breathed out slowly. He was glad to see that Rajiv was smiling. A smile hurt much less than a laugh.

"Now say the line to me."

"Bow when you address the princess."

"That's it. Now forget everything else and do it."

Sanjay, for a mercy, got it right on the next take. He felt no sense of elation. Lunch was called. He seriously considered walking away and never coming back. He had been betrayed again. Outside the castle he lined up for his plate of food, shook some saffron on it, and walked away to eat it alone.

"Hey. Bodyguard."

It was Miranda. She was sitting with her entourage of women at a folding table erected beneath the awning of her caravan, in the partial shade of the trees.

"Over here."

Sanjay walked over, feeling very young, as if it were the first day he had ever been to the Youth Club and he could hear the yells of children being washed.

"I apologise to you," she said. "I was rude. I know how hard it is, the first time. Or at any rate I should have known. You forgot your line but I forgot my manners, and for that there can be no excuse. You did well. Your voice is beautiful."

"A poor thing but mine own."

"And in English! This is wonderful. Sit down and eat with us." The women who had been staring into their food, he now realised, had been trying not to laugh, but suddenly it didn't matter. Nervous about his manners but glad to be present, Sanjay sat quietly while Miranda and her retinue gossiped. This they did shamelessly. The dancing mistress was there, chiming and chinking when she laughed. The retinue dished dirt about other film stars while Miranda professed to be shocked. Sanjay could tell that this was only a pose. They were telling her what she wanted to hear. Some of it was very scandalous.

"So when her husband turns up," said one of the retinue, a plump woman whose double role was to brush hair and speak the unspeakable, "she is still in her caravan with both the young men."

"No! I don't believe it. She must be crazy," said Miranda.

"No, she is smart. Because her husband breaks off the lock with one twist of his hand and comes bursting in and one of the young men has only just finished getting his pants back on. She says 'We were rehearsing.' Her husband screams 'You call *this* rehearsing?' And she says 'Yes, I can prove it. Because *he* is here too.' And the other young man steps out from the other end of the caravan."

"Complete with pants?" asked Miranda, a plum half way to her lips.

"With pants firmly in place. A chaperon, you see? So her husband has to accept it."

"He should not have done all that shouting before he broke in. He would have caught them at it." Miranda was smiling wisely.

"If he was that smart she would never have betrayed him," said the dancing mistress.

"Betrayal is her nature," said Miranda. "The only thing she has never betrayed is a hint of talent." She bit into her plum. Everyone laughed except her. It was her technique. She liked to be the still centre. But she was still smiling, her lips moist with juice, and Sanjay was pleased to find that the smile included him. It was almost as if he were her only audience.

"Are you shocked by this kind of talk?" she asked unexpectedly. Sanjay had his mouth full so he merely shook his head.

"You ought to be. These women are scandal-mongers. They continually disgust me with the filthiness of their minds." Then there was a lot more of the same sort of conversation until it was time to go back to work.

"You may walk with me," she said as she rose. "You are my bodyguard and that is what bodyguards do. In fact you can stand by my chair when you are not in a scene."

"Are you sure he is handsome enough for you?" said the plump speaker of the unspeakable.

"Be quiet. It will not hurt to have a man beside me I can trust. It will be a nice change."

Back inside the castle, the beginning of the afternoon was slow for Sanjay. Apart from having to leap off a low wall a few times he could spend most of his time standing beside Miranda's chair.

"What is this?" asked the director during an idle moment while the assistant director was blocking out a scene.

188

"My bodyguard is practising," said Miranda.

"Make sure he practises his dialogue too."

"Practise your dialogue," said Miranda, after the director had wandered away.

"Bow when you address the princess, son of a dog."

"Very good. What else can you say?"

"Tell me when you want your chair moved and I will carry it for you."

"The grips do that. But I will let you do it if you like." She said this with her eyes closed and her head tilted back while one of her women was touching up the paint on her eyelids.

"I have done it before."

"Who for?"

"For you." This was the moment.

"Never. When?"

"Long ago. When I was a boy."

"Hello, what are you now? Oh. Wait a second."

The tiny paint-brush was withdrawn and she turned her open eyes to him. "My goodness. It's you. I remember."

Sanjay said nothing. Her voice was so troubled that he was sorry he had spoken.

"My God, you were such a perfect little boy. A perfect sparrow bathed in dust. Now I really *do* owe you an apology."

Sanjay did not know how to respond. It turned out not to matter, because her conversation was with her own memory.

"I have had you on my conscience ever since. That thug Rahul Kapoor and I were fighting the way lovers do when they should never have parted. Especially when they should never have met in the first place. I'm afraid you got caught in the battlefield. Like dear dead Prakash. My favourite director. But it was shameless conduct on my part. I was younger then." She closed her eyes again, this time, it seemed, for no other reason than that she did not want them to be open. Or perhaps she was gazing within. "My God, how much younger I was then."

"We all were," said the speaker of the unspeakable.

"Be quiet, Ghita." And Ghita, because her name was used, knew that the admonition was meant.

From that time forward, Sanjay was one of Miranda's party. When he was not required for a scene, he stood near her, and bodyguarded her chair when she was in front of the camera. His new role caused much giggling among her retinue of women, and the opposite of giggling among the other male bodyguards. Never before in his career had Sanjay been the focus of quite so many annoyed stares. He didn't let it matter. An episode of his life was being repeated, only this time it was going right, which made it a different episode altogether. Towards the end of the following week, he was even allowed to live out his fondest wish: his face and Miranda's were in the same shot. The captured bandit chief knelt before him. Sanjay delivered his line without a hitch.

"Bow when you address the princess, son of a dog."

It was Sanjay's inspiration to cap his line by placing his right foot on the bandit chief's head and forcing it down between his shoulder-blades.

"Cut," said the director.

"He was not supposed to do that," said the script editor.

"It looked good, though," said the director. "Let's do another take and hold it a bit longer. Mirry darling, if you can do a bit more of the approving look, that would be nice. Bit of electricity between you and the cruelly handsome bodyguard, I like that."

So Sanjay was actually filmed with Miranda giving him an approving look. If this ever gets into the film, thought Sanjay, Sunil will never talk to me again. Dilip will probably kill me. Somehow it didn't matter. He had come a long way and it was worth it. This was the last day he and Miranda would be on set together. He had used his time well. None of it had been wasted. It was enough for him. He was not expecting more. But there was more. Miranda took him aside.

"I am giving my team drinks at my apartment this evening," she said quietly. "I think you deserve a drink too, after all your hard work. After you get changed, join us at my caravan."

Sanjay's nerve failed. He would not know how to behave.

190

Everything he had learned with Mr Desmond and Gupta, all the manners he had acquired, would not be enough. What would he say? He shook his head.

"Bow when you address the princess," she said, "son of a dog." But her smile was the real command. So he stopped shaking his head and started nodding it, feeling as awkward as he ever had in his life. It was like having Pratiba's hands on his back, while looking at a policeman flexing his cane. It was very confusing.

17

ALTHOUGH SANJAY had another few days of shooting to walk through, in his mind the film was over from that evening, and a new episode in his life began. Miranda's entourage, with him included, drove in a fleet of cars to her apartment in Juhu Beach. The director came too, and later on the producers turned up, with their own retinues of legal people and lackeys. High up in one of the tallest buildings, the apartment was more than big enough to hold everyone concerned. Sanjay sat drinking cold mango juice with the plump speaker of the unspeakable and three more of Miranda's women in a set of soft, peach-coloured, calico-covered chairs grouped around a glass table near the sliding glass doors leading to the terrace. The glass doors were open, a gentle breeze came in, and the sea began to glitter beyond as the exhausted sun prepared to join it. Miranda's women were talking scandal as usual. Sometimes the subjects of the scandal were in the room. Miranda's women did not have to moderate their voices. The accumulated chatter in the vast apartment amounted to an uproar. In the distance, Miranda moved among her guests, leaning on the arm of her director, who still had his hat tilted forward over his eyes. Groups of men arrived to pay court to her. One of the men Sanjay recognised as the famous Kamar Bose, the very man selected, according to Smart Alec, for Sharon Prabhakar's sexy man ensemble in her recently conducted poll. He wore a white suit with a black shirt and dark glasses. His hair was magnificent, a creation in black lacquer, piled and whorled like soft ice-cream.

"He would like to have her on his *curriculum vitae*," said one of the lesser women at Sanjay's table. "It would be a real sign of arrival."

"She will never go for him," said the speaker of the unspeakable. "He is too pretty-pretty. That hairstyle of his should have rear-view mirrors. How can he see out of the sides?"

"They say that his . . ." said another of the lesser women, but she put her hand beside her mouth and whispered so that Sanjay could not hear the rest of it. There was a cascade of giggles. He didn't mind being left out of the joke. He felt included enough already: more so than allowed him to be fully comfortable. At the moment of sunset he rose as if to leave.

"Where are you going?" asked the speaker of the unspeakable.

Sanjay said it was probably time for him to go home.

"No, you mustn't. She would want you to stay. You stay right where you are." The other women were suddenly studying their glasses of mango juice. Later on, as the party began to thin out, Miranda, in a break from doing her social rounds, momentarily joined them.

"No, don't get up," she said to Sanjay as she approached. Sanjay, who hadn't been getting up, half got up. Her hand on his shoulder pressed him back into his seat. It was the first time she had touched him. He would have to remember about getting up. Mr Desmond and Gupta had never made him do that. He deduced that it should be done for women. Thrillingly she shared the chair of the woman nearest to him so that she could lean forward and talk to him as if they were alone.

"So, are you enjoying your party?"

Sanjay indicated that he was.

"You must stay for dinner." She saw the fear in his eyes. "Don't worry. It will be just me and a few people. Very relaxed. We have had a hard last day. Are these women looking after you?"

Sanjay indicated that they were.

"You are the sort of man that women enjoy looking after, I think. Now I must begin to throw people out. Starting with that posturing jackass in the dark glasses. Otherwise they will all be here until dawn. Would you like a proper drink?"

Sanjay indicated that as far as he was concerned mango juice was a proper drink. Then she was gone again, having touched his wrist in farewell.

"You see what you get for looking natural?" asked the speaker of the unspeakable. "If you were wearing a white suit like a glass of milk she would not look at you twice."

"I wonder what else he will get?" giggled one of the lesser women.

"Be quiet, Indira. You will frighten him."

Dinner was not quite as the hostess promised. It was indeed a relaxed occasion, but there were a dozen guests, with others coming and going. They all sat on chairs, western style. Two servants were constantly on their way between the table and the double doors. Sanjay was at the far end of the table from his hostess and could not always hear her speak. People spoke in small groups. Sanjay had no trouble keeping his end up in the conversation because the people near him demanded only a listener, not an interlocutor. They interrupted each other constantly while he turned his head attentively from one to the other and copied the way they ate. The director sat nearby, addressing two producers and a journalist. The speaker of the unspeakable sat between the two producers. Even she, like Sanjay, was reduced to merely turning her head. The director and the journalist did most of the talking.

"That Oliver Stone movie about JFK, what was it called . . . ?"

"*JFK*," said the journalist.

"Did you *see* that thing? I saw it in Los Angeles. You know what it made me feel? It made me feel nostalgic."

"Nostalgic for what?"

"For when I thought *Elephant Walk* was a bad movie. When I see such horrors I am almost glad we are making our own silly stuff. Hollywood is turning into something awful. Badness has grown wings."

"The best lack all conviction, while the worst . . ."

"Have budgets of thirty million dollars and up."

"You could make fifty films for that," said one of the producers, finally getting a word in edgeways.

"With you producing, a hundred."

They were all drawn away again into separate conversations. The only person who was allowed to speak to the entire table was apparently the editor of a great newspaper. Of a certain age, with a polished high forehead, he spoke wondrously well. Sanjay, though he could not understand a lot of what was said, knew by the attitude of his audience that it must be good. Sometimes they let the man speak for a whole minute without interrupting.

"The maturity of a social system", said the editor in his low but commanding voice, "is whether it can survive the assassination of its great men. That is why we know the Weimar Republic was weak. It could not do without Rathenau. Its last years were one long hopeless lament for the loss of a genius. Pity help the nation that needs heroes. Brecht said that."

"Yes, but what are *you* saying?" said one of the producers. "You are talking about Gandhi. Come out with it."

"Yes, I am talking about Gandhi. But I am talking about Indira Gandhi too."

"All the Gandhis," said the other producer.

"Indira was not a Gandhi," said Miranda. "She was a Nehru, poor creature. Like that late and unlamented smiling idiot son of hers. But come on, Naveen, what are you saying here, really?"

"I am saying that Chaudhuri was right about Gandhi."

"Chaudhuri!" said the first producer. "But this is preposterous. He is an expatriate traitor."

"He is worse than Rushdie," said the other producer. "Chaudhuri is not a baby in a beard. He is an old man who knows what he is up to. Selling us out abroad."

"He is our greatest writer even if he lives in England," the editor pressed on. "And he was right about Gandhi. The Indian intellectuals had a cult of Gandhi. They always have the cult of the leader, a *Führerprinzip*. Or else they have a cult of history, which is the same thing. The wave of the future. They worship success. In the war they longed for the defeat of Britain even though it would have meant the Japanese would have killed us by the million. And Gandhi was right with them. The Quit India movement in 1943 would have meant the suicide of our country if it had succeeded. But they were all for him then. They joined him in his mad fetish about rejecting western influence. And now the same sort of people have a fetish about

195

accepting it in all its worst forms. The only thing that has changed is the form of the power worship. The form of the defeatism. But defeatism it still is. And still it hungers for a redeemer."

"This is too sophisticated for me," said the first producer. "Surely now we have the greatest opportunity we have ever had. Secularisation. A free market. At last we can grow."

"Secularisation", said the editor, "will mean nothing without tolerance. What we want from the West is their *tolerance* for belief, not their lack of belief. Under the old Empire the British left recruitment for the army to the tribes and castes, and look what happened. The movement towards tolerance was nipped in the bud. With bayonets. And now this new secularisation is the biggest threat to tolerance there has ever been."

"How is that?" said the second producer.

"Because it will leave each religion prey to its own fanatics. It will strip each religion of its reasonable people and leave only the mad bombers who really have had only one religion all along. That is fundamentalism. Whose only expression is terror. The biggest threat we face. The great world threat of the next century, and it is already here."

"So we are a modern country after all," said Miranda.

"In that respect we are," said the editor, "sad though I am to say so. But in our incurable longing for a great man or a great woman, we are not modern at all. We are a throwback still. We are a backwater."

"Well, all I can do is disagree," said the first producer. "What about Margaret Thatcher?"

"My point exactly," said the editor. "Look at the mess Britain is in now, and all because they hail any strong leader they can get as a new Churchill. But we should no longer be thinking about Britain. We should be grateful, as Chaudhuri says. But we should be grateful and move on. We should be thinking about Norway or Sweden. Successful countries whose prime ministers we cannot name."

"Olof Palme," said Miranda. "My mother knew him well."

"The only famous one," said the editor. "But when he was assassinated they survived it. All right, let's say that we should be thinking about Iceland. Any country that enjoys honest, working, durable institutions. No dramas. We should lower our sights and lengthen our breath. We should settle down for the long haul, as the Americans call it. And above all," he thumped the table with a rhetorical fist, "this above all . . ."

"What above all, Naveen?" asked Miranda with a smile. "Out with it. And watch out for my table."

"You are saying India is like *Iceland*?" It was the second producer, but the editor ignored him.

"This above all. We should not make a fetish of the free market."

"Why not?" asked the first producer.

"Because the first thing it will produce is more poverty," said the editor, and what had been a discussion turned into an argument that lasted an hour. Some of the men tried to win by shouting. Sanjay, who had understood little of the symposium except the emotions involved, shared the only available silence with Miranda. From the other end of the table she sent him a smile of delighted complicity that propelled them both into a separate world. Later, when almost everyone else had gone home except for her immediate retinue of women, she sat him down beside her in one of the great couches while coffee was brought.

"So," she said, "I thought you put up with the noise level very well. Were you impressed?"

Sanjay said he had been.

"Deafened too, I expect. But Naveen can be very eloquent when there are fewer people present who get his goat. He is turning into a bit of a bore in his old age but he is generally right. He has a mixed marriage, you know. His wife is a Muslim. Did you know that?"

Sanjay shook his head.

"With my parents it was the same thing. It gives you perspective."

Sanjay nodded, guessing that perspective was a good thing to have.

"But he is seduced by Bombay. His hopes are too high. This has always been a tolerant city, relative to the rest of India. A few bombs now and then but nothing much. That is why I came here from Calcutta. The life of my parents was a nightmare. You cannot imagine the horrors they saw. How are you getting home?"

Sanjay said he would walk.

"I will send you in a car. But I want you to come back tomorrow and stay with me here as my bodyguard and general equerry. Would you consider that?"

Sanjay indicated assent as well as someone can who has stopped breathing.

"You will not have to go everywhere with me. But it would be a comfort to have such a strong-looking individual around the house. Life is not always perfectly safe for someone in my position. With your fighting skills available I will feel a little more secure."

Sanjay, who knew that his fighting skills were largely illusory, decided not to protest. If the illusion convinced her, it might convince her potential assailants.

"There is a little room upstairs which might suit you. Perhaps you should see it. Ghita!"

The speaker of the unspeakable was suddenly in attendance.

"Would you show our young man the little room upstairs and see what he thinks? And wipe that smile off your face."

Sanjay had had no idea that there was another floor to the apartment. The polished wooden staircase up to it was wide enough for four people and the little room could have fitted his own room into it twice. It had sparse but proper furniture and a carpet on the floor. The bed was covered with a woven spread. A window looked away from the sea and across the city, far beyond the Pepsi sign, in the direction of the Silver Castle. Perhaps, in the daylight, he would be able to see it shining.

"You are a very lucky young man," said the speaker of the unspeakable. "There is many a man who would like to be offered this little bed. Men of all ages and nations. There is a bathroom next door and you can put your laundry in this bag at any time. Cleanliness is next to godliness. Especially where *this* goddess is concerned. A word to the wise."

When she led him downstairs again, the arrangements for the car had all been made. Miranda was talking on the telephone. She stopped only long enough to lift her spare hand, give the smallest of waves, and mouth a word that must have meant tomorrow.

18

Sanjay had been installed in the little upstairs room of Miranda's vast apartment for almost a week and he still had hardly seen her. He had not given up his room in the slum, of course. He had brought with him only his best clothes, his dictionary and the barest few of his favourite magazines. Keen to pick up on the resurgence of her career, Miranda was working on two new films simultaneously, and one of them involved night shoots. Sanjay was three more days completing his part in the film which he would remember as the one in which he had met again the ideal woman of his youth. The problem now was to meet her in the reality of her home. Like the Silver Castle – which he thought, but could not be sure, that he could catch a glimpse of from his window – she was both there and not there. He would have felt foolish hanging around the apartment in the daytime after his part finished. Wisely he hung around the hiring hall instead. He was gratified to land a role as a man of menace in an upcoming all-singing, all-dancing modern thriller with seven love scenes and eight murders. The film would start in only another ten days. He was told that he would commit one of the murders and later on be murdered himself. The casting master was most flattering.

"You are in demand. It is because of your close-up in *Huzor Huzor*. Also your box-fall was very good. Show me your fear at being murdered."

Sanjay showed fear.

"Not so craven. The fear of a man of menace who realises that his career is over. A more tough fear."

Sanjay showed tough fear.

"That is not bad. It could be better. You should go and see *Huzor Huzor* and see how you look."

Sanjay went to see the film and was quite impressed with himself. He took care, however, to be out in the sunlight before the closing titles. He preferred to avoid meeting anyone he knew. That evening he hung around Miranda's apartment. Platoons of her servants and assistants wafted in and out, looking plausibly busy during her absence. They could not be trying to impress each other. Probably they were trying to prove to him that they had something to do. With nothing to do himself, Sanjay studied her bookshelves. She had many hundreds of books, in English and other languages as well as her own. Except for the picture books, he had no idea where to start. Even the picture books were forbidding. *The Art of the Great Hollywood Portrait Photographers* was a disappointment. He did not recognise a single face. Who was Rita Hayworth? On one of the glass tables there were magazines as thick as books, with thick paper so white that it glowed from within. The prose was basically in English but the captions to the photographs of women were in some language he could not read. A tall short-haired woman stood beside a swimming-pool. He could partly see through her pale blue dress, which was an interesting effect, but the caption was worse than a disappointment: *Versace*, it said. One word and he could not understand it. It felt like a reproof. Taking with him the stuffed bun prepared for him by Miranda's cook, he retired defeated to his room, where he fell with relief on his newly-purchased latest issue of *Debonair*. The Centresprea was sensational as usual. He was still worried about the word Centresprea: there was a capital D underneath it which made him think that the word might possibly be CentrespreaD, but he could not find this word in his dictionary. He was starting to get sick of his dictionary, which all too often answered mysteries with mysteries. In this case, however, the words hardly mattered beside the pictures. The girl was wonderfully naked, with extraordinary nipples. The bit of the nipple that actually stuck out was quite small in circumference, yet the bit surrounding it was large. Unaccountably the girl in possession of these treasures seemed annoyed instead of glad. Sanjay argued with her sullen gaze for a while, became inopportunely hard, and moved on to the caption. "Funny how the stars in your eyes melt at dusk," she was saying, "to reappear as sparks of desire in my veins." This, he considered, was English prose at its most poetically resonant. After the captions to the Centresprea, his favourite part of *Debonair* was always the Erotica section. In the current issue it surpassed itself. Entitled 'Is This Real?', it was the work of the very talented Protima Roy. The voice was of a woman talking to herself while being made love to. "He's at me again. His face between my legs. His tongue working up a wetness, slipping, sliding. It's like he's grown roots. I wrap my legs around the back of his head and rock to an explosion. Later, as he rests on one elbow and watches me recovering, I get up, turn around and almost swallow his cock."

Sanjay took pride in knowing what this last word meant. In his earlier days with *Debonair* he had neglected to check all the definitions of this word in the dictionary, so for a while he had been under the impression that the lovemaking involved the participation of a domestic fowl. Now he knew better. But he was still puzzled about precisely what kind of explosion was meant. Something to do with digestion? Were they being attacked by robbers? It scarcely seemed erotic. These considerations, though unsettling, were not enough to put him off. After a slow, contemplative bath, he took a hand towel, turned out the light, lay down and attended to himself. He thought of the Centresprea girl and her intoxicating caption. He did not dare to think of Miranda. He did not think it was really possible that he would ever be allowed to touch her as she touched him, but if there was such a possibility, however remote, he did not want to spoil it by presumption. He was still a child in that way, not thinking of the wished-for thing in case whatever forces that might grant it would deny it.

Finally they were at home and awake on the same evening. She sent everyone away – or as far away as everyone ever goes in the home of a prominent actress – and laid out a salad for two, with dips and warm thin bread that tore like scorched parchment. Sanjay had no means of assessing the prodigies of modern liberalism she represented by sharing soft food, an activity which in the old days was taboo even between degrees within a caste, let alone between castes.

201

She was giving him her imagination. They ate it on the terrace, under the stars.

"So," she said, "you're mine at last. You are supposed to drink that wine, not just study its surface. Are you a scientist or something? What are you thinking?"

Sanjay did not know precisely what to say, so fell back on his time-honoured sources of inspiration. "I was thinking, funny how the stars in your eyes melt at dusk."

"But it is long past dusk. There is no dusk. We have no dusk. Where do you get this stuff from? Everything you say is like dialogue. When you say anything at all. Why not say what is in your heart? Just be yourself. It's an attractive self to be, you know. You are very handsome."

Sanjay shook his head.

"You are. Not pretty-pretty like most young men who want to be actors. Your face has been lived in. Things have happened to it."

Thinking of some of the things that had happened to his face, Sanjay could only smile. It was exactly the right thing to do, as it turned out. She took him to her bed as naturally as if she was showing him her books and paintings. As so often in his life, Sanjay's luck had come to help him at the key moment. Her reproof had silenced his mouth. Thus he was saved from the folly of trying to find words where they would surely have been inadequate, and might well have put into reverse the revelation of her gift for him. It started when she undressed. In the low light provided by the candles she had lit, the walls were hard to see beyond the white screens of muslin. The bed melted upwards into the dark over hills of cushions. She was darkness herself. He had to feel for her. He could not have felt more. When she kissed him he tasted plums. There was music coming from somewhere: a low, deep purr rising to a sigh, a high, soft sigh sinking to a purr. It was coming from her. She helped him to undress, kissing the skin that she uncovered. Then she lay down with her hair spread on the pillows. She held up her arms to guide him down. He felt her legs open underneath him and before her toes touched him in the small of the back he was already inside her. He hadn't expected to be held there so firmly. Urmila had been languid inside as well as out.

202

This was different. This must be what Pratiba would have felt like. How could anything so yielding and moist be so tight and crisp? He was burning his way in like a hot knife through halvah. But when he pulled back, the destruction repaired itself, chasing his retreat, asking to be destroyed again. He obliged. He was conferring a blow of grace. Confirmation of his mercy came from her cries. He was reminded of Pratiba, but with the urgency extended into time, and infinitely modulated. The purrs and the sighs had been joined by sobs. Finally they were joined by words. Amazing words. How dare she? At last he realised it was a trap. She was not going to let him rule over her ruin. As her thighs lifted and shook, she held the back of his neck, lifted her head, and kissed him so deeply that the pleasure in his mouth would have done for him all by itself. She seemed to gasp a different note at his every pulse of release. As if knowing that it would be too much, she ceased to work at him from the centre. Only her fingertips and toes continued a slow, rhythmic stroking. They settled into stillness. Her breath subsided. She had the last word. "Perfect," she said. "What a talent."

"A poor thing but mine own," said Sanjay, in a voice bereft of breath. She hummed a laugh. It was a vocalised smile. He could feel it. For long minutes he could feel her every murmur resonate in the bones of his own face. He could feel everything. Three feet from his eyes, a drip of hot wax from the high plateau of a candle fell past the escarpment of its length and splashed into the dish below, where he felt it cool and stiffen. Already he was stiffening again himself.

"My goodness. He wants more."

Sanjay did want more. He liked the idea of being talented at this. Actually, although he was not to know it, this was his best language. Speaking this nearly silent tongue, he was himself, told fewer lies, and his knack of listening reaped rich rewards.

"Where did you learn to do this?" she asked him at one point. "From your magazines, I hope."

He told her she was right. It was almost true. Really he had little experience. He just had the right instinct. His body found out what her body demanded and made sure it was supplied. Combined with his light but strong shape, it was a gift bound to make him popular.

He was a long time over her in their second round. Those amazing things all happened to her twice more, and the last time she wept, which would have worried him if he had not been able to see her face in the candlelight. In his eyes, the transformation of her face had already become the supreme blessing of this activity. Heroically he contrived not to come himself when she did. He supposed that this was what the various writers of the *Debonair* Erotica section must mean when they used the word 'explosion'. He resolved to control his own explosion to the fullest extent possible. She caught him at it.

"Stop trying to impress me. Just lie beside me for a while and let me rest. I am not quite so young as you."

He lay beside her and looked. She had her hands above her head, lost in the pillows. Her eyes were closed. She was letting him look. Her raised breasts were astonishing. They were still there when she was lying down. They were extremely there. Her nipples had gone soft now, although he had been struck by their hardness before, when they were underneath him. He touched one with his tongue.

"No. Let me rest. In a minute. Then you can."

On his knees, moving down, he checked to see if those hairs had been plucked. It was hard to tell in this light. He blew on the hair to see if it would shift.

"That will be lovely a bit later on. It's too soon. Give a girl a break."

Her legs were far enough apart to let him look. Some of the moisture, he decided, must be his. Fine hair was matted together into the paintbrush tips of the miniaturist he had once seen at work against the railings of Mahapalika Marg, a few mats on from the pavement dentist's pitch, towards Mahatma Gandhi Road. He touched with a fingertip. There was no protest, so he touched with his tongue.

"Beast." She had erupted. "Get on your back. Here comes some of your own medicine."

He had been inside a mouth before, but not this mouth. This mouth was for him. Her fingers did unfair things. There was no question of controlling the explosion. But he fought her off before it came, pinned her on her back with her wrists beside her shoulders,

204

and set out to have it inside her. She was laughing at him in a way he did not mind. It was the first time anyone had ever done that in circumstances like these. He managed to hold back just long enough, however, to ensure that it happened to her as well: more softly this time, and with less abandon, so she was able to watch his face. It was her turn.

"Ah. You liked that."

"Yes."

"Now lie beside me and stay still. Please. Don't kill me all in one night."

He was almost as tired as she was. It must have been an hour before his sleeping arm woke him up. One of the candles was flickering.

"I shouldn't have let you do that."

For a moment he was afraid that it was all going to be withdrawn from him just as it had been achieved.

"No, don't worry. I meant I shouldn't have let you hold me while I slept. It's all a myth that lovers can sleep in each other's arms. You just get cramps and pins and needles."

"*Such* skin," said Sanjay, tracing the line of her hip with his open hand.

"Where did you get that?"

"Get what?"

"What you said. Dialogue again. Something someone else made up. It makes you sound inauthentic. All my life I have dreaded being involved with someone inauthentic."

"I made it up myself," said Sanjay, who did not like the idea of being thought inauthentic, even though he was proud of having deduced the word's meaning the moment it was uttered.

"Made it up. Precisely. That is just what frightens me. The way you make things up. Have you made up your love for me?"

He kissed her for an answer.

"That's better. Better than the dialogue. You don't have to do all that stuff. Just be natural. You *are* the most natural boy in the world, you know. A force of nature."

"Am I?" asked Sanjay, fishing for compliments.

"You must know you are. But your instincts are miles ahead of what you say. I would like to help you there."

"You are helping."

"No, this is for me. Although I suppose it's for you too. You are one of those lucky, lucky men. There are men who love to take pleasure from a woman. And there are men who love to *give* pleasure *to* a woman. They are the lucky ones, because the woman gives more pleasure back. I suppose you feel powerful when you make me go mad like that. Do you?"

"Yes."

"I suppose it's just another way of being a bastard. A kind of sadism. Inflicting pleasure instead of pain. But it feels like love. I suppose that's all that matters."

"It *is* love."

"What do you know of love? You're just a ball of dust who wandered into my castle." But she was smiling and he did not mind. In fact he was further encouraged. He went to taste her properly between the legs but she put her hand there. Catching the candlelight, her painted fingernails looked amazing in that setting, like shells in seaweed.

"Next time. Now you must go back to bed."

"I'm *in* bed," said Sanjay. He thought it a rather good joke. For once, it was all his own.

"No," said Miranda, "this is *my* bed. But tonight it was heaven. Now off you go. Out, out. And get dressed properly. And if you pass anyone, try to pretend you were visiting the kitchen."

The last he saw of her that night, she was sitting up smiling, the same way she had smiled from the other end of the dinner table, or across the parched grass at the Silver Castle, long ago.

19

MORE THAN A MONTH had gone by since Sanjay had visited his room in the slum. He went back only to pay the rent and to pick up his mail. There was one letter. It was from Mr Rochester. In reply to Mr Rochester's previous letter, Sanjay had sent only a single page with one paragraph on it, dealing mainly with a more reliably specified version of his own address. His principal reason for doing this had been in the hope of being sent some money. Mr Rochester's new letter was fat enough to encourage the impression that this hope had been fulfilled. Unfortunately there was nothing in the envelope except six thin pages closely filled with handwriting on both sides. One of the early paragraphs seemed pertinent.

So I wasn't Assistant Editor any more. I was something called a Roving Editor, which as we all know means one step ahead of the boot. *Tant pis*, I thought. I still have my beautiful memories, not to mention the odd book contract and my modest private income. One could scrape by, *nicht wahr*? It was at this point that I was vouchsafed the revelation of what a glorious privilege it was to be a Name at Lloyd's. It turned out that I was in the worst syndicate of the lot. There wasn't a disaster since Krakatoa that it wasn't liable for. I won't bother you with the gory details, high finance not being precisely your *chose*, but it appears that from now until the millennium I'll be paying for oil rigs that blew up, tankers that sank, and entire litigious American families who cleverly chose to live in houses constructed exclusively from sheet asbestos. All these things had been insured for billions with my paltry few thousand. The last straw – way beyond the last straw in fact, the camel being already prostrate on the desert, maggots licking its skeleton clean – was a colossal claim from some antique dealer in Los Angeles whose front window full of Ming vases had been atomised when one of your countrymen drove his sports car into it. So much for my grand plans to fly you here and install you in my eyrie, looking down on the Guildhall School of Music. I'll be lucky to be looking out on a rubbish dump. Probably I'll be looking up through it. My personal liability is so laughably high that I honestly don't know whether I can afford a stamp for this letter. If only I could afford to deliver it personally! If only I could be with you in your little room and never come out! People of my class used to call it Going Native. You can't imagine what it does to me when I think of our solitary moment of love. It makes me think of all the fleeting, blessed conjunctions in history when those meant for each other found each other across barriers of time and circumstance. It makes me think of that scarcely believable, incandescent occasion when Nabokov danced with Pavlova. It makes me think of . . .

There was a lot more about what it made him think of. Sanjay read some of it and half promised himself to read the rest when he got back to his dictionary. 'Vouchsafe' looked like an interesting word. But when he returned to what he now thought of as his home, he put the letter amongst his minor belongings and forgot it. The day was too perfect for regrets. He undressed and as usual put his neatly folded trousers on his chair. He never hung them up when the gold piece was in them, in case it fell out. Then he had a shower, wrapped a towel around his waist, went downstairs and leaned on the rail of the balcony to her bedroom. The sea crinkled under the afternoon sun. Down on the beach, a team of beachcombing children moved, scavenging towards the city. One of them stopped and looked up. Sanjay waved. Yes, he thought, it must be the same balcony. It must have been her that day. Behind him, one of her servants moved busily about. She would be home early this evening. Sanjay went upstairs, got dressed, and returned, this time to the terrace off the living-room. He settled down with a cigarette and a glass of chilled mango juice to continue with the book she had insisted that he try to read. His first whole book in English, it was called *A Passage to India*. He was finding it tough going. His dictionary was taking punishment. But there was a lot he would do for her, because she had done so much for him. He was not without gratitude. It paid. Beyond that, or perhaps beneath it, there was genuine affection. In the person of Miranda, his previously fragmentary experience of women had to some extent become whole, or at least coherent. She had the beauty of Urmila and the vivid passion of Pratiba. She also had, despite her superior position, an encouraging readiness to treat him as her equal. She enjoyed commanding him, but he believed her when she said that it was always for his benefit; and in the moments that mattered she allowed him to command her. She welcomed being told what to do. Put your hands above your head. Lift your knees. Point your toes. Say this. Say that. He stirred at the thought of it, wishing that there was not a dinner party tonight. He would have to wait before he got her to himself. Some of the novelty had worn off, but a lot more of it would have had to wear off before he ceased looking forward to the freedom and fulfilment of being alone with her. She made a man of him, just as he made a girl of her. He could tell that that was one of her main reasons for valuing him. She was almost frank about it. She felt threatened by the younger actresses. The gossip columnists were saying so with increasing frequency. There could be no doubt that her suggestively yet discreetly clad voluptuousness did look a bit old-fashioned compared to the new wave of actresses who were prepared to reveal almost all for the magazines, let alone compared to the clusters of bare breasts in *Debonair*. Now that deregulation was at last here, the level of the permissible was going up all the time. On the screen, kissing was back after a long exile. Sanjay had read an excellent scholarly article on the subject in the latest issue of *Gladrags* magazine. What had it said again? Sanjay put down his book, went up to his room, and came back with the magazine. He would just read it for a while and then return safely to the book before she got home. "And then came *Phir Teri Kahani Yaad Aayi*," said *Gladrags*, "with a kiss as long as its name. With a kiss that was aired on the national network. With a kiss between two unmarried people, walking up a staircase. With a kiss that actually involved the exchange of saliva. Hear that sound? It's the sound of lips meeting. It's the sound of barriers crumbling at long last."

Sanjay was especially fond of this issue of *Gladrags* because it mentioned him. He turned to the relevant page. It fell open easily. There was an item in one of the gossip columns that mentioned his name in connection with Miranda. "Passion brewing? Often to be seen standing near Miranda's chair as she desperately strives to rebuild her career is a handsome young man about whom there has been much buzz in tinsel circles. This column is able to reveal that he goes by the name Sanjay. Not Sanjay Dutt, naturally! Just Sanjay. That name and no other. He comes from nowhere, but industry wise guys are tipping him for the top. Insiders who have seen him around Miranda's lush Juhu duplex are tipping him for something else as well. What could it be, we puzzle? Toy-boy joy? Surely not! And yet . . . Our brow furrows, and we bet yours does too." Sanjay admired the prose style of the columnist, Highbrow. In Sanjay's opinion, Highbrow was almost in the class of Smart Alec, although not quite as witty. Yes, it was an excellent issue. He had been wise to buy three copies while stocks lasted. On the cover was a particularly shameless full-face study of Mumtas, looking as if she had been ravished by a typhoon. He was still studying this when he heard the sudden bustle of Miranda's arrival. Half a dozen voices erupted. He had no time to hide the magazine so he just put it on the table beside him and set his glass, packet of cigarettes and brand new green plastic cigarette lighter on top of it. He took up the book again and was reading it quite convincingly when she joined him.

"Thank heavens for a short day," she said, lying back on the steamer-chair opposite him. Having seen her well established, Sanjay settled back again into his own chair. Nowadays he always remembered about getting up.

"I see you are keeping your magazine mentions close at hand. For reference, no doubt."

Sanjay thought it best to make his smile rueful.

210

"They would have gossiped anyway. Most of that stuff is made up so nobody believes anything even when it's true. But if you are going to talk about your career I suppose it's about time you had a second name, for professional purposes. I thought of Nul. Sanjay Nul."

"What does it mean?"

"It means nothing. In French. A good name for the young man from nowhere. And it sounds a little bit Indian, without quite being it. Like *my* name. You know that my name is not Indian?"

"I know that no other woman is called by it."

"My father thought of it. A Latin word that means 'it must be looked at'. He was foolishly confident that I would be beautiful. Thank you, Ayesha. Take that away." She was pointing at Sanjay's empty glass. One of her women had brought tall glasses of cold clarity stocked with rising bubbles. Sanjay did not have to wait for Miranda to squeeze the slice of lime into the glass and then copy her. He knew what to do and did it at the same time.

"He was right," said Sanjay.

"You sound almost sincere. You are improving. At least my father's inspiration was plausible. Whoever thought up a name for *that* hooker was really pushing it." Without deigning to redirect her eyes, she had briefly inclined her head towards Sanjay's magazine where it lay on the table.

"Is her name thought up?" Sanjay could not believe that there was a fact about Mumtas he had not read in his research.

"Yes, didn't you know? She is named after the queen who is buried in the Taj Mahal. Her name was Mumtaz. All they did was change a letter. What a laugh."

"She is buried in the Tajma?"

"No, the real Taj Mahal. The one in Agra." This was Miranda at her best, because she did not laugh at him. Instead of scorn she felt a momentary sadness, and did not even show that. "The great Mogul emperor Jehan loved her so much that he built the world's most beautiful shrine to her memory. One of those gangsters who look after your dream girl must have read a book. And they didn't even mind that there was already another actress called Mumtaz. I used to know her. An older actress, of course. But quite famous once. The bastards."

211

"She is not my dream girl."

"I don't mind, as long as she stays that way. I wonder what you would have been like," she went on, as though talking to herself, "if you had been brought up in a house like mine. The walls were made of books. Cliffs of them. My grandfather was the last great poet of Bengal. He knew Tagore personally. And my mother's father was the great Urdu poet of his generation. All his books were in our house. Satyajit Ray would come to tea in our house. You have heard of Satyajit Ray? Don't pretend."

Sanjay did not pretend. She wasn't even looking at him. Her head was back and her eyes were closed as she took in the last of the sunlight.

"No, of course not. Most of India has never heard of him. The world has, but India hasn't. One of the greatest film directors who have ever lived. And instead of his great works of art, we have *our* great works of art. The princess runs away. She is captured by the bandit chief. The bandit chief is a prince in disguise. They sing. They dance. On and on and *on*. What a disaster. Heaven help us, we have colonised ourselves. How are you getting on with the book?" She was talking to him again.

"I have almost finished it."

"Are you enjoying it?"

It was an awkward question. He thought it best not to give a direct answer. It would be smarter to ask a question of his own.

"What happened in the caves?"

"Nobody knows," she said, smiling. "That's supposed to be the point. The shocking, sensual mystery of outrageous India. Perhaps he put his hand up her dress."

"Perhaps he tried to steal her wrist-watch," said Sanjay, with a smile of his own.

"Perhaps. Do you still want me? Is it still an urgent adventure for you?"

"Yes." It was more or less the truth.

"Liar. There is something about you that always wants more." But her eyes were sparkling again so he thought it best to proffer no denials. Her eyes sparkled like the cold, clean, clear water spiked with lime. The sea had begun to scintillate under the sidelong bombardment of the setting sun. It was a dream come true. He should have been content. He attributed his unease to the imminent dinner party. He knew how to behave by now, but the proceedings would still be largely beyond him, and in no interesting way. What had once been daunting had become tedious.

The editor was there again and unfortunately he was in good form. "That is one thing Chaudhuri was right about," he told the assembled company.

"You always say Chaudhuri is right about everything," said Miranda. Resplendent in a white sari seeded with pearls, she showed by her delighted smile how she loved to tease him. "So how can he be right about one thing?"

"He is right about how we forget our heritage by trying to make it exclusively ours. He is right about provincialism. Think of the troops who died for us in the Arrakan and we have forgotten them because they were commanded by the British. Think of the two thousand troops we lost at the Dardanelles in the first war."

"Did we?" asked one of the producers. "I didn't even know we were there."

"We were there. We were fulfilling our duty to an Empire from which we had benefited, the Empire which made possible a united India. But the Australians have made the whole thing theirs. The Australians don't even mention that the English lost three times as many troops in that campaign."

"I saw the film," said one of the producers. "I saw it in London. Mel Gibson was in it. That was before he had big hair."

"But if *we* remembered the troops we lost there," said another producer, "and if *we* forgot to mention that the British lost many more, and if *we* used that to say that the British were just exploiting us, wouldn't that make us the same as the Australians? That would be just as provincial, wouldn't it?"

"No, it would not," said the editor. "Let me explain." And he explained at length, but this time he had some formidable opposition lying in wait for him, because Gupta was among the guests. Sanjay was glad that Gupta was sitting at the other end of the table, at

213

Miranda's right hand. It had been awkward earlier when Gupta arrived, although Gupta, to do him credit, had silently condoned Sanjay's manoeuvres of avoidance, confining his signals of recognition to a mere nod and a half smile. During the long reception before everyone sat down to dinner, Gupta had spent most of his time with the producers, and Sanjay had heard, from conversations elsewhere in the room, that this was a good sign because it meant that Bombay's most famous entrepreneur was at last about to make good on his long promise to acquire a stake in the film industry. In a year of riots, with nearly six hundred Muslims slain and film production cut by almost half to fewer than three hundred and fifty films, this would be an act of faith in the city, the initiative of a visionary. Gupta was making a quiet but unambiguous show of being there to learn. For most of the meal he had stayed silent, allowing people to talk across him in the separate conversations at his end of the table. When, as always, the separate conversations reached the stage of coalescing into a general discussion that erupted into an argument, he was content to let the august editor be the focal point. But finally he spoke, and it was immediately apparent that this famously loquacious table had acquired a new epicentre of authority.

"With all due respect," he began, and made a gesture to prove that his respect for the editor's wisdom and seniority was real, "I have to say that your wish to acknowledge the importance of our British heritage is necessary but not sufficient."

"How not?" asked the editor, and for once he really seemed curious to hear another opinion, such was the commanding timbre of Gupta's voice, although the thought of so much money in the background might have had something to do with it.

"Because the question *now* is not about how we relate to the past, it is about how we relate to the future. Morbid nostalgia for our safe days as a glorified colony would be as dangerous as to deny it ever happened. I admit that it is a powerful memory, a fruitful memory. There are moments when I can still see myself in the courtyards of Trinity, walking the same flagstones as great Indian mathematicians and economists for whom their time in Cambridge was a liberation.

214

And eventually men like them helped to liberate us all from the colonial yoke, or whatever you want to call it."

"I would not want to call it that," said the editor, but he was not really interrupting. He was just playing bass.

"Of course not. The conquerors gave us our freedom. If it was against their wish, it was in line with their culture, and without the binding influence of that culture we would have remained split, at war among ourselves for ever. But that was then. This is now. What we must join now is the world. Already, right here in Bombay, in one of my companies, hundreds of bright young people are working on computer software that will make us part of an unimaginable tomorrow."

"An unimaginable tomorrow?" asked Miranda, looking away from him as she supervised a servant threatening to overdo the refilling of her wine glass. "I'm not sure I like the sound of that."

"Nobody likes the unimaginable. But one thing we *can* imagine. If we do not exploit it, we will be exploited. Exploited *again*, and this time worse. And it is too much to expect that the brilliant young people who give us the future will have the time and the attention to educate themselves in our complex heritage. I don't mean that they have to be rigid, narrow nationalists. They won't even be that. They just won't care. They will think only of one world."

"And will they think of the poor people in the street?" asked Miranda. "Will they think of those human wrecks in the street that your chauffeur had to steer through to bring you to my door tonight?" Sanjay was pleased that she did not seem to like Gupta at all.

"I know *you* think of them," said Gupta. "Your charitable works are famous. But the truth is that only prosperity will save them."

"Aha!" exclaimed the editor triumphantly. "Only when the few have too much will the many have enough. An old story." The older man, good at old stories, was back at centre stage and did not relinquish it for half an hour at least, but Gupta, in Sanjay's judgment, had made a powerful impression. Sanjay even had to admit that he had been impressed himself. Later on, with sweets and candies and coffee being brought to the table on a relay of silver trays, Gupta even managed to be funny, something Sanjay had never heard

215

him be. It made Sanjay jealous, in the way we often are when we find that someone with whom we have been intimate has lavished on others a gift he has withheld from us. Miranda had teased Gupta about his Savile Row suit. For Miranda to tease Gupta instead of just contradicting him might have been enough to ignite Sanjay's jealousy anyway, but the way Gupta capitalised on the provocation made the thing certain.

"A good guess, madam. Your eye is legendary. But in this case you are not quite correct. This suit does indeed come from London. But not from Savile Row. It comes from Selfridges."

"From a department store? I don't believe it. It's too well cut. It must have cost lakhs of rupees."

"No, it just looks like it. And I'm sure you will agree that in matters of clothing the look is everything. This suit is made in Italy by the firm of Sidi."

"Seedy? An unfortunate name."

"Only in English. Selfridges ought to change that. But what matters is the tailoring, and the point is that there *is* no tailoring. So the suit costs only three hundred pounds."

"Three hundred pounds? No."

"Three hundred pounds with an extra pair of pants thrown in."

"How is that possible?"

"No tailoring. The material is so soft that it drapes by itself. You can buy it off the hook and you can fold it up in a bag. It doesn't even crush. Here, feel."

Miranda inserted her fingertips into his proffered cuff and rubbed with her thumb. Sanjay's jealousy, already bubbling, would have boiled over if it had had a sexual element. It meant salvation to know that Gupta was a pervert. "It's like a sari," said Miranda, with an astonished little laugh that Sanjay found artificial. Who was being inauthentic now?

"Let me assure you, gentlemen," said Gupta to the entire table, "that the old colonial dream of being tailored in Savile Row is over. English tailoring was never worth a damn in the first place."

"Oh, come on," said one of the producers, shooting his cuffs,

"Don't tell me I've been wasting my money. It's too much money to waste."

"You have. You have. The English tailors tailor to your figure. That's the last thing you want, unless you're an Adonis. They meticulously measure your every fault and then make a suit that reproduces it exactly. The Italians think only of the ideal. They make a suit the shape you *want* to have and then you slip inside it. I promise you that the man inside *this* suit is just a bag of bones." Sanjay knew that it wasn't so. Gupta was actually quite athletic. He could ride a horse. But Sanjay could tell that Gupta was pleasing his audience. This displeased Sanjay more than he would have believed possible.

"Now I can reveal that I wore this suit to prove my point," said Gupta, with a smile to indicate that he was mocking the editor in a friendly way. "I brought it as evidence that we must take from the world and give to the world."

"How can I get a suit like that without flying all the way to Selfridges?" asked the producer.

"Right on cue," said Gupta, producing a leather cigar case, extracting a cigar from it and raising a supplicatory eyebrow at Miranda, who replied by gesturing to a servant. The servant instantly approached with a long, lit match but had to stand there while it burned, because Gupta would not be hurried in his ritual of preparing the cigar for smoking. While he did so, however, he went on talking, this time to inform rather than entertain "You can buy one from us, right here in Bombay. One of my companies has done a direct deal with the Italians and we've already brought in a thousand suits as a first shipment. You'll be pleased to hear," he added, emitting his first draught of aromatic smoke in the direction of the editor, "that a full page of advertising will be offered to your paper at the end of the month. To be renewed each week thereafter. We'll be running the campaign in all the principal publications for a full year."

"All for a change of clothes," said Miranda.

"All for a change of consciousness," said Gupta. They were smiling at each other. If Sanjay's jealousy had been visible, he would have fumed like that cigar. What on earth was an Adonis?

As if to prove that there was no end to the agony, more people

217

began to arrive. Miranda rose to greet her after-dinner guests. There were more film people, more businessmen, more journalists. There was also Pratiba. Sanjay could hardly believe it. If he had not been feeling so wretched, he would have embraced her. It would have been something to show Miranda. As things were, he was pleased enough to have someone to talk to: someone who would not pitch everything so far above him. The Dardanelles. Trinity. Savile Row. Adonis. Rita Hayworth. Versace. Satyajit Ray. If Pratiba had puzzled him with these things, she would have helped him to laugh. She would have made it matter less.

"What have you been doing? You look wonderful," said Sanjay. He had learned this latter expression from Miranda, having noticed that it worked particularly well on people who didn't. He sat down with Pratiba on a banquette in a corner, under one of those modern paintings that he was supposed to appreciate. There was hubbub all around them but they were safe in the past. It was as if they were in their schoolroom again, yet with no danger of the door bursting open under the flying weight of an angry Sabbandra.

"Well, where can I start? I spent a year in London. I grew up. I got married."

"You are married? That's wonderful." She was wearing a sari and looked less blatantly shapeless than she once had. She looked more at home.

"Yes. No thanks to you. He got his virgin. But I was lucky too. He is an accountant. Not handsome but kind. And very modern. He lets me work."

"You have a job? That's wonderful."

"Yes, everything's wonderful. You are already sounding like a record with the needle stuck. But you are right, it *is* wonderful. I have a job with that man over there, the man I came with. The great Zulfighar Desai. He is editor of a film magazine and I work for him."

"What magazine is that?"

"*Cine-Blitz.*"

"*Cine-Blitz*! That's . . ."

"Wonderful. I know. I work on the Smart Alec column."

"*You* are Smart Alec?" Sanjay's astonishment had escalated to awe.

218

"No." She laughed. "I am *part* of Smart Alec. His left elbow. There are six of us. But some of the items are written by me. Who knows, I might even write about you. You seem to have fallen on your feet."

"I have not fallen."

"That's what I meant, dummy. Falling on their feet is what cats do. It means you are doing better than ever. You know, there are so many rumours that she is really flat broke. But look at this place. Those miniatures in the panels of those folding doors, they are only one step down from real Moguls. And the saris she covers the walls with are all her grandmother's, did you know that? All classics. And then she just hangs paintings on them. So bold. She has so much taste. Such a perfect throwaway style. And she is *so* beautiful. Just look at her over there."

"I don't have to look at her. I already know." The truth was that he did not want to look. He knew that she was still talking to Gupta.

"Are you sleeping with her?"

He smiled a smile for which he had got the idea from a magazine article about the great foreign actor Charles Bronson. It was a smile meant to convey a willingness to let people believe what they wished. It was known as an enigmatic smile.

"I don't blame you for being mysterious," said Pratiba. "That *Stardust* piece must have driven her crazy. Everyone says you are sleeping with her but they would rather believe you aren't. I believe you are but I will say nothing. You can trust me. For old times' sake."

The awkward silence that threatened to fall as they both thought of old times was headed off by another voice. Gupta loomed above them.

"I'm heading home after a perfect evening," he said to Sanjay. "But before I went I wanted to tell you how good it was to see you again."

Sanjay nodded. He had just seen Gupta's shoes. They were black but gleamed like glass.

"Will you take this card? It has the name and numbers of the organisation that will be marketing our Italian suits. If you get in touch with the second number on the right they will be expecting your call. For the film magazines you have the right face. A dangerous face like yours would be exactly right."

"I am very busy in films," said Sanjay.

"You will be busier yet, I hear. But having your face in a prestige advertising campaign could scarcely hurt. And anyway you owe me one, as the Americans say."

Sanjay was genuinely puzzled.

"For the elevator."

Sanjay was still forming an enigmatic smile when Gupta had departed.

"Wow, that was cool," said Pratiba. "You *know* him. You were so *cool* with him. And he is a real bastard, that one. He didn't even *pretend* that he wanted to meet me. I can see that I *will* have to write something. Cool and dangerous Sanjay. Whose shirts have improved out of sight."

"Sanjay Nul."

"Is that your name now? I like it. How do you spell it? And what was that about an elevator?"

Pratiba and the great Zulfighar Desai left after only an hour. Other people were slower to clear out. Sanjay sat alone on the terrace. For a while Ghita, the speaker of the unspeakable, sat with him, but she found him even less forthcoming than usual so she left him alone again. He sipped his drink, smoked, and watched the lights of the fishing boats. He didn't show it, but he was still annoyed. When Miranda at last joined him, he showed it.

"Thank God *that's* over," she said, fanning her face with her hand to indicate the effort it had all been. "I'm sorry they lingered so long. Why the long face?"

"You talked to him the way you never talk to me."

"For heaven's sake. I have better ways to talk to you."

"You talk to all of them about things I have never heard of."

"It is not my fault that there are things you have never heard of. And they are not important things. Nothing is important beside the language we speak together."

"What is an Adonis?"

"A beautiful man, if you want to know. But *you* don't *need* to know. You *are* one."

Sanjay had begun to be mollified. He lit another cigarette.

"You are smoking like a chimney. Make sure you rinse your mouth before you kiss me. And make sure you kiss me to death. Who was that girl? Someone from your past?"

"A girl I once knew, yes."

"You think *you* were jealous when I talked to that swine of a suit salesman? When I saw you talking to that girl I could have *died* of jealousy."

"How could you be jealous? She is not beautiful. You are the most beautiful woman in the world."

"Nobody *feels* beautiful. They have to be told. They have to be attended to. I promise you that when you gave that poor dumpling your attention she turned into Princess Caroline of Monaco. You never told me that you knew Paramal Das-Gupta Kanwar."

"I met him only once," said Sanjay, sensing danger.

"Once is too often. He is a notorious pederast. A total shit. Dear God, I'm tired."

But she was not. As usual, an evening on stage had given her extra energy. He had extra energy to match. For both of them, jealousy, by restoring the familiar beloved to the pristine status of someone who might choose another, had worked its brutal trick of renovating desire. Sanjay stripped her, threw her on to her bed, scattered his own clothes all over the room, and fell on her.

"What are you, a wolf?"

He growled and kissed her.

"A wolf who has been smoking. Ugh."

So he kissed her elsewhere. She interrupted her own moans to call out. "Ghita! Get out of that corridor! Go to bed!" There was a scuttling of sandals outside. Miranda laughed, but not for long. Wet with her juice, his mouth sealed hers again.

"Well, at least that tastes better. Does it? Do you like that ta . . ."

He turned a word into a gasp with one stroke. With a few strokes more he changed her face. This was a situation he could control. For as long as it lasted, and he made it last a long time, he even managed to be grateful. Pouring his resentment back into its cause, he remembered his luck. It was only afterwards that he forgot it.

20

FROM THE TERRACE of the Gymkhana Club Sanjay looked down at the cricket. Another monsoon had come and gone. The sun was hot but the grass was green. So much grass and only one cricket match! Azad Park, where he had once played in two matches at the same time, was only a mile or so away, but here was a long way from there. This, he had been told, was where the *sahibs* had once played. The players below were all dressed in white, as if the *sahibs* had never gone away. Sanjay had only the haziest notion of where they had gone to. The Gymkhana Club was a sufficiently foreign country for him. All the men at the other tables exuded wealth. Some of them were losing it to others as they played cards. It didn't seem to bother them. The sums mentioned made him feel poor. He *was* poor. But his new friend had promised to fix that. His new friend was called Aziz. With easy familiarity, Aziz commanded the waiter to bring another round of the club's special lemonade. In the shade of the veranda, cool in his pale thin clothes and comfortable in his cushioned chair, Sanjay politely sipped the cold bitterness of the special lemonade while he listened to the nattily attired Aziz predict a golden future.

"What we need to do", said Aziz, "is keep the momentum going. We have to maximise the . . ."

Sanjay was pleased to hear that there was some momentum to be kept going. With the long hard plastic swizzle-stick he stirred the ice cubes in his tall glass and looked down again at the cricket while Aziz droned on. So this was real cricket. He had seen something of it on television at various times. Not that he had ever possessed a television set of his own. (Now *there* was a dream begging to be realised.) He had seen some cricket on a television set in an Arab's hotel room once. He had seen a few minutes of cricket on Mr Desmond's television set until he had been caught at it and made to switch channels to something more improving. In Miranda's apartment, during the nowadays mercifully less frequent afternoons when he was not on call and she was, he had watched television: hours of television. Mostly he watched MTV, which in less than two years had become a big sensation, bigger even than the film magazines. But occasionally he had seen cricket. Here, however, was the actual thing. Now he could see how fantastically good they were. They bowled like the wind and hit the ball for a mile. He could tell by the sound of the bat that the ball was heavy. It fizzed on the grass. He could feel the sting in the hands of the fielders who had to catch it. A real cricket ball was nothing like the ball he had once bowled. There was no connection. He had missed out on the whole event. Look at that grass. It was all green, with no patches of bare earth anywhere. He decided not to become interested in cricket, the same way as he had decided, belatedly but firmly, not to become interested in history and the arts and that stuff Miranda called literature. You had to have the education. He had learned that there were limits to what you could learn by yourself. There were too many words that could not be found in the dictionary. They were the common property of those who had grown up with them, and if you had grown up alone, too bad. It was too late. But the Gymkhana Club: now that *was* interesting. Such luxury. He always had time for more of that. The way Aziz was talking, there was more of that just around the corner, perhaps even a proper apartment of his own: somewhere where he would feel less cooped up, somewhere where he could watch MTV whenever he wanted to.

He had met Aziz at the cinema. Not the old, huge, packed-out Palace Cinema he used to go to. This was a special small cinema where people in the film industry could watch new films. Breathing cool air, sitting in special soft seats with an ashtray built into the arm-rest, they could watch films that were not even out yet. At the invitation of the director, he had gone to see the film in which he had been Miranda's bodyguard. Miranda was there too, of course, but

223

they had arrived separately, she coming from the set of her new film and he from his. At the screening he had not been encouraged to sit beside her. She had sat between the director and the producer. It was one of Sanjay's resentments, the way they never seemed to appear in public together. Everyone had been impressed with the way Sanjay spoke his line. When they were shooting the film he had spoken two lines but in the finished film there was only one.

"Bow when you address the princess, son of a dog."

On the screen, Miranda had looked at him as if suddenly impressed: a meaningful look full of promise. After the screening she merely congratulated him briefly. She was too busy receiving adulation from the producer, the director and the financier, all of whom had an enthusiastic entourage of their own to add to hers, the most enthusiastic of all. The cries of approval were still in the air when she swept out, giving him barely a smile. Aziz had been much more attentive. He had introduced himself and predicted that Sanjay's face would soon be making a big impact.

It was true in a way, but it was all so frustratingly gradual. Doing the photographs for the Italian suits took almost a week, and then it was months before the first magazines carrying them appeared on the stands. Sanjay bought three copies of each one. He liked the way he looked in the suit. It punctuated his personality and incarnated his image. But he could not understand why his name had not been used. Nor could he understand why the money was not immediately forthcoming. Aziz explained that it was because of deferred payment. Sanjay could not understand the explanation. He had not even been given the suit. Finally Aziz had given him a roll of bills. The sum was certainly enough to tide him over, but it was not a fortune. He could pay the rent on the slum, buy himself some more clothes, and even eat out in a good restaurant if he wanted to, but without Miranda's hospitality he would not be able to live well. And the hospitality was all she had to offer. She never gave him much money apart from his agreed salary for being a bodyguard. Being so dependent, with so little negotiable reward, no longer suited him. He wanted to – what was Pratiba's expression? – spread his wings. Some evenings, when Miranda was out working late, he would sit alone at a small table in

The Jewel in the Crown, spending a fortune while he tried to look cool and dangerous. People had not come up to him the way they came up to the stars. He had not signed even one menu.

"We can thank Smart Alec," Aziz droned, "for helping to make your name. But that is just the beginning. What we must do now is to connect the name to the face. The film-going public is beginning to know what your face looks like. The magazine-reading public is beginning to recognise your name. But the two images are like separate fragments which . . ."

Sanjay's name had indeed been cropping up in the gossip columns with gratifying frequency. Often the mentions were awkward because they put Miranda down. They talked about her as if she had taken him on simply as a weapon against the younger actresses, as a way of regaining an equal footing with Mumtas, Mamta, Dimple and the rest. Sanjay, of course, minded this less than she did, but he had learned that when such items were published it was wiser not to allude to them even in a helpful way. She preferred to ignore their existence. Her entourage cooperated by doing its best to ensure that no magazine containing such an item ever reached her. Smart Alec, on the other hand, was always as kind to Miranda as to him. Smart Alec correctly pointed out that it was only a few short years since Miranda had been in the same position as Mumtas, that Miranda had achievement behind her and not just promise ahead, and that Miranda's beauty in its full bloom of maturity left the upstarts looking like awkward schoolgirls. Sanjay guessed that these items had been written by Pratiba, who knew all there was to know about being an awkward schoolgirl. He could detect Pratiba's inventiveness in the prose. "You'd better believe it, hons, that this thing between the divine Miranda and her cool and dangerous sidekick Sanjay Nool is a mutual admiration society. Oh baby, you were never lovelier! But we know it isn't the old one-two. It's the praise he gives your art. And your talented pupil is going places, we hear. He ain't a star yet, but he'll soon be climbing the feature list the way he used to go up castle walls when he was just a lowly stunt-man. We don't need a photo of him here because he's all over page 26. Yes, the hard face in that soft, soft suit is none other than Mr Cool, Sanjay Nool. No wonder the

225

gorgeous Miranda won't let him sign that new film with Mumtas. He wouldn't be the lead, but he'd be on the same set with the main threat – and the great lady would wear *that* the same way she'd wear a cactus bikini. Not that she's jealous. No way. She just thinks that the chick with the four shiny cheeks can't act for toffee. So the claws are out and the bars are down, darlings!"

Sanjay could recite the whole item from memory. He had even thought of showing it to Miranda, because it praised her so much. He had been held back by the mentions of Mumtas. On the subject of Mumtas, Miranda invariably lost her sense of humour. Really she was being irrational. Sanjay was regularly cast now in junior roles as one of the hero's lieutenants or even as a chief gangster. Quite often he had lines. It was inevitable that he would end up working with all the actresses at one time or another. He had already worked with Sridevi, Mamta and even Dimple. With Dimple he had exchanged actual dialogue. "You will never hold me," Dimple had said, struggling in her bonds. "I have ways of holding you that you would not believe," Sanjay had replied, staring at her thinly-clad breasts where they jutted between the tight ropes. Then the hero had burst in and thrown him out of the window. One film had led to another until the point had arrived when he was working on three of them simultaneously. He never had to go down to the hiring hall anymore. Casting masters came to him, through Aziz. Finally the inevitable occurred and he was offered a small part in the new big musical film starring Mumtas. Naturally he had not been shown the script, but he had been assured that it would have ten songs, twelve murders, and a whole scene for him in which he would defend Mumtas single-handed against the gangsters before dying gloriously. It was a mouthwatering project. Unfortunately Miranda found out about it. It didn't matter how. What mattered was how she behaved: unreasonably.

"The bitch will try to steal you," she had said.

"I won't let her."

"You won't even be consulted. She can fuck a fakir. I have heard all about it."

"It is a good film for my career."

"It is the worst film in creation. The same as any other film. Tell me what happens. Do you save her from the bandits?"

"I save her from the gangsters."

"From the gangsters. How very up-to-date. Merchant Ivory, move over."

Sanjay didn't understand. Worse than that, he felt misunderstood. It was midnight, they had both come in late, and they were far apart. They were lying in her bed but the space betwen them was like space.

"Ghita! Get out of that bloody corridor!"

This time there was only the patter of sandals. There was no laughter. They had not made love. She had not even made a gesture. Sanjay said nothing.

"Sometimes those silences of yours sound just plain dumb. Cool, dangerous and dumb, Mr Nool. Nool! You can't even spell it."

He was hurt.

"I'm sorry. I shouldn't have said that. Listen, maybe it would be better if you left me alone now. And while *you're* alone, please figure out whether you really want to do this to me. To us. You'll be doing it to us."

So she had withdrawn her favours. Perhaps it was a way of making him feel the weight of the key in his pocket. He would certainly have suffered had that been withdrawn too. But she might have been surprised to learn just how indifferent it left him to be denied her bed. Too much resentment had neutralised desire. He had been frustrated for some time by how they never went out. Her idea of a night out was a night in. Once that had been an education: eating with the great star, drinking with the great star, sleeping with the great star. But education was like school in the end. The first time she had read to him from Tagore while they both lay naked, he had been carried away.

Love is taking poison with open eyes . . .

He liked himself as a poisoner. A poisoner sounded cool and dangerous. But one Tagore poem was pretty much like another, and the sad truth was that even making love could grow repetitious. She offered him more and more. There was almost nothing she would not do, and no lengths to which he could not drive her abandonment. He could make her shout. He could make her rave. Next day her servants would look at him as if he had descended from the clouds on a staircase of marble. He could make her face change into a weeping wound. But he could not change her into someone else.

It especially annoyed him that he could not change her into someone who would go out dancing. On MTV the young people were dancing all the time. The girls wore jeans and halters with nothing underneath, so that you could see their nipples under the cloth, being stroked by it as they hopped and shook. Even the hostesses, Sophiya and Anul, were dressed for desire. One night Mumtas was right there on the screen with them. While she stepped and swayed and shivered, the camera attacked from ten different directions. In the close-ups on her face she looked as if she was coming. He had to hold himself down while he watched. All the magazines had stories about what was going on in the nightclubs. They called it grooving. Occasionally he went to a nightclub and observed. He went to the Nineteen Hundreds, the best one. A girl would recognise him and make him groove. He found he could do it. One night there was a girl he would have liked to take home. But he had no home to go to. He couldn't take that kind of girl to the slum. There was nothing there except the occasional letter from Mr Rochester. The very occasional letter. One letter in the last six months. "I don't know how to tell you this," it had started. "It seems that I am very, very sick. Just when I thought that I could have no more troubles, it turns out that my troubles will soon be over. *La peste.* There are people who go out on Hampstead Heath every night and never get it. And here am I with my tiny, occasional, pathetically genuine love affair. I have already told Adrian and I thought that I had better tell you. We never did very much, but who knows? I couldn't bear . . ." Sanjay had not bothered to finish reading it. The usual unfathomable rigmarole. Brilliance could add up to boredom. He wanted to hear no more fancy names. Nothing more to leave him out. He was sick of being shone on. He wanted to shine. He wanted to go where the young people went. He wanted to go where they danced. How they had danced at the Nineteen Hundreds! If Miranda had been with him, he would have had all that fun, all those flashing lights, and her starlight. It was cranky of her to miss out on it all. And she was making him miss out on it as well.

"I know you have good reasons for not signing this film," Aziz was saying. "But you have to look at it careerwise. The worst that can happen is Miranda will throw you out. And if she does, it is a story. It links you and Miranda. It gives you good coverage. And coverage helps the film and the film helps you. Because you will be right up there with Mumtas in the same shot."

Down there on the lush grass, the batting team needed only four more runs to win. The star batsman, who had already scored a century, was looking around at the fielders while the frustrated fast bowler added to the red streaks around the crotch of his white trousers before turning to start his long run-up.

"And it does not matter that you have delayed so long. It is a good thing. It has only made them more keen. The offer is still open. They have extended it again. You can sign this afternoon. Any time before six o'clock. They have told me."

Before the ball had finished fizzing to the boundary the hero was already walking in, taking off his gloves. His studied casual walk was better than a swagger. Everyone was clapping. Aziz was clapping too, but he was still talking.

"Sign this film. Think of yourself."

Sanjay had been thinking of no one else.

"Yes. I'll sign it."

It was not a very good office. There were grander offices elsewhere, for the stars. But it was an office. It was not a shed with a corrugated iron roof. And there was a real contract and a real pen, produced from a suit pocket by a man whose horn-rimmed spectacles had been made for him, instead of bought from a stall in the street. Aziz pointed to the right place. Sanjay Nool had been practising his signature for weeks, so he needed only a few seconds to write it down.

21

MIRANDA DID NOT throw Sanjay out because of Mumtas. She decided
to make a joke of it. This was made easier for her by advance
knowledge. She was tipped off by Pratiba, of whom she had made a
friend. It would have been in Miranda's interests anyway, to befriend
a promising gossip columnist and bring her close. But the fact was
that she and Pratiba liked each other enormously right from the start.
Miranda was only fifteen years older than Pratiba but the gap was
enough to let them play mother and daughter as well as sister and
sister. They spent hours on the phone to each other late at night,
often to Sanjay's annoyance. He would be shunted aside, turfed out,
and sometimes even denied access altogether. It was during one of
these comfortless banishments to his own room that Pratiba told
Miranda the big news about Mumtas.

"You know her manager, Subash Chakraborty?" asked Pratiba, as
one asks a preliminary question so as to prepare the ground for a
smooth unfolding of a revelation.

"He is an old horror," said Miranda. "I knew him fleetingly at one
stage, when he was managing Rahul. Before Rahul caught him
milking the contracts. Awful manners and very vulgar."

"Don't forget violent. He is also that. He arranges accidents for his
enemies. Anyway, she has just started sleeping with him."

"With *him*? No. I don't believe it. He is too old and ugly."

"She is mad about him. It is a burning passion. With all those
billionaires she could get she goes and gives herself to this low-rent
thug. No wonder she is desperate to keep it a secret."

"Only stupid billionaires," Miranda pointed out. "No smart ones would touch her. Her conversation consists entirely of bird noises and the squeal of small animals. I have heard her. Yes. It would play hell with her image if the news got out."

"Yes. Anyway. She is head over heels for this vulgarian, and always he has gone after every woman he could get. So she is not only desperate to keep it secret, she is desperate to keep him interested."

"She is flirting harder than ever."

"She is flirting harder than ever with every handsome young man she meets."

"How very interesting."

If Sanjay had known all this it might have saved him from certain misapprehensions. When he turned up on the set for his film with Mumtas, almost the first thing he encountered was her burning glance beamed in his direction. He was already riding on a crested wave of possibility before he got near enough to her to see down her cleavage. From close to, her beauty had the force of nature. Not even the way she flaunted it could detract from it. Learned articles in the magazines had made the absurd claim that she had copied her pout from some western fashion model married to a magician. Juxtaposed photographs purported to prove this theory. Sanjay could see straight away that there was nothing in it: Mumtas's pout was all her own. She could pout with her mouth closed. She could pout with her mouth open. She could pout while she was singing. In the first day on set Sanjay had little to do beyond jumping off the occasional balcony, so he could stand around and observe her while she flirted with her leading man, none other than Kamar Bose, whose dark glasses worn indoors Miranda had found so ridiculous. He was wearing them again now. Sanjay would have liked to find him ridiculous too but could not help envying him his status. His entourage was the size of a small army. He could sit down without looking and never had to lift a finger to light a cigarette. Above all, he had the attention of Mumtas. While waiting between takes she would drape herself around him for support. Sanjay, seeing how she always managed to clutch one of his thighs between both of hers while absorbing one of his biceps between her breasts and breathing in his ear, wondered how the poor man kept from bursting out of his leather pants like a charging tiger. But

Sanjay's jealousy was tempered by the certainty that whenever Kamar was not on the set, Mumtas would transfer her attention to himself. Sometimes she would do this even when Kamar was there. It was heavily rumoured that Kamar was already mad for her and was facing death threats from the brothers of his latest lifetime companion, Sparkle Bhatt. Sanjay could see how Kamar would think the prize was worth the risk. The beauty of Mumtas was its own reality. In her vicinity all possibilities altered.

By the end of the first week, Kamar, when he was required to be on set, whether in the studio or at the location, was accompanied always either by Sparkle in person or by her mother. Mumtas retaliated by keeping Sanjay close to her at all times when he was not throwing punches or going backwards over balconies to land with a crunch in the cardboard boxes below. On several occasions he was almost alone with her in her caravan while she learned her lines. This she did with difficulty, because even her most elementary lines necessitated rapid rearrangements of her pout. Sanjay, serving as a model, would hold his face close to hers and say the line so that she could study his lips. She did not quite kiss him, just as, when she brushed against him or leaned on him for support, it was never quite an embrace. But it was more than enough to make him believe that it would be only a matter of time before his would be the spoon chosen to stir the smooth immobility of that lovely face into a raging whirlpool of insupportable pleasure. It was half happening already. There was a particularly promising moment in her caravan, in the afternoon of the last shooting day of the week, just after she had been called back to the set. There was nobody else present except her hairstylist, who was busy repacking a bank of curlers.

"Come, we must go," said Mumtas. It was a long speech for her to attempt without a script, but her body, as always, was eloquent. As she brushed past him, she pushed a hot upper thigh against his pleading groin, crammed a perfumed soft breast into the hollow of his heart, and passed her pout so close over his open mouth that he caught her breath. Sanjay was in such a state that he could not follow her. He had to stay behind for a couple of minutes and pretend to the hairdresser that he knew how to mend the plug of her curling iron.

News that Mumtas was vamping both Kamar and the new unknown Sanjay Nool was soon in the gossip columns. Sanjay was expecting a sticky reception at home. He was defiantly ready to counter an attack. It never came. Miranda persisted in being sweetly reasonable. That, in Sanjay's mind, was the most unreasonable aspect of her conduct. She was patronising him. At another of her damned dinner parties she even dared to mention his relationship with Mumtas.

"Now take our young friend here," she said, tilting her head fondly towards Sanjay with everyone watching. "He is in love with one of our young film stars. He thinks she is a princess. And why not? That is the way our films work. Princesses instead of people."

There was a British journalist among the guests. Apparently he was a prominent film critic who also appeared on the famous BBC2 television to talk about films. He wore strange eyeglasses: they were two dark circles no bigger than bottletops. His hairstyle was stranger: it stuck straight up like the bristles of a brush lying on its back.

"That's the most striking thing about the whole scene here," said the British film critic loudly, not looking at Miranda or anyone else, as far as could be ascertained. "I mean the *discrepancy* between the films and the people who make them. I mean it's an absolute *gulf.*"

"That is because", said Miranda, "there is a discrepancy between the people who make them and the people they make them for."

"You must forgive me if I find that attitude cynical. It presumes that most of the population of your country is less intelligent than you."

"I presume no such thing," said Miranda, with a smile that Sanjay could identify as a sign of impatience. "The people are not less intelligent than we are. But they are incomparably less well-informed. In Uttar Pradesh women are still daubed with cow dung after childbirth so as to prevent infection. Daubed with cow dung and washed with urine. That is only one instance among millions. It would be useless to show them Satyajit Ray films. You think they need an Ingmar Bergman festival? They want their princes and princesses. After all, you have yours."

"I take your point," said the film critic, not looking very much as if he did. "And I suppose any genre can have vigour. Hong Kong churns out thousands of kick-boxer films and they're all technically inept as well as totally mindless. I mean, they aren't even any good on their own terms. But John Woo came out of all that."

"Thanks for the comparison," said one of the directors. "You're telling us that if we study hard we'll get a chance to go to Hollywood."

"Sorry," said the film critic, not looking very sorry. "I only meant that any genre can be redeemed by a product of sufficient energy. It's just hard to prove it. Hard from my angle, I mean. I mean . . ." He hesitated.

"What *do* you mean?" asked Pratiba without hesitation. She was sitting only two places from Miranda and had often, during the course of the evening, acted as a spokesperson.

"I mean that as a writer I didn't have much trouble proving that *The Bonfire of the Vanities* was a lousy movie. But I *did* have trouble proving that *Alien Nations* was a wonderful movie. It was tightly written, well acted, brilliantly directed. But it came from a bad genre: science fiction. And really what you've saddled yourselves with is a bad genre: crazy musical melodramas where people sing and dance instead of kiss."

"Oh, we're a bit beyond that now," said Miranda, signalling for the coffee to be brought. "Some of the young ones are giving us their all. Being dragged through the village naked."

"We call it exposing," said Pratiba. "They expose."

"You should hear the lyrics of *Meri pant bhi sexy*," said one of the producers.

"Sing it, Akim," Miranda ordered. The producer rose to his feet so as to give himself room for the appropriate hip movements while he sang his version of the new hit song that had scandalised the country. Pratiba translated, to hilarious effect. An evening that had threatened to drown in solemnity was saved. But nothing could save it for Sanjay. He had grown indifferent to conversations in which he could not participate properly. The unknown was no longer a goad. He had come to realise that it had no limits and could not be attained. There was an infinity of unknowns. There was no end to learning about

234

history and geography and Ingmar Bergman Festival, whoever he was. Sanjay's curiosity had at last revealed to him the impossibility of its ever being satisfied. He had made his choice. There was a course open to him that he could master. It led by way of Mumtas into the world of MTV. There he could find his path and there he could grow. He was thinking all these things while the party drew to its protracted end. His mind was elsewhere. When all the guests had gone and even Pratiba had been packed off into the night, he was still abstracted. His thoughts were present only to the extent of apprehension that Miranda might follow up her sarcasm about Mumtas. But Miranda seemed to have preoccupations of her own. She reached for him. Glad to avoid a scene, Sanjay relaxed into her bed. It was, after all, familiar ground. It was just that this setting no longer satisfied his daydreams – or, rather, that by satisfying a precise set of daydreams it had made them change. Now he took it for granted, even took it for his right, that he should be lying here using her bosom for his pillow while she talked into the candlelight.

"What a rude prick that film critic is," she said to the shadows. "But he is more than half right, that's the hell of it. Ismael Merchant will make exactly one film here this year. The only film made by a proper production company about an Urdu poet. I know all about Urdu poetry. I can *read* Urdu. I am the right age, the right looks. But Shabbana Azmi gets the role. She is a good actress and very beautiful. She deserves it. And she is very intelligent, I have to admit it. I suppose she would have felt the same if I had got it. Frustration. There are so few opportunities to work seriously. You can't know what it's like, to have your gift wasted."

Sanjay had long ago grown tired of being told what he couldn't know. She must have sensed this, because she was talking to the ceiling. He could tell that without looking, from the way the muscles of her neck felt against his cheek. She felt and tasted warm and sweet as always, but he was not inclined to make love to her for a second time. It was a relief when she put on a video-tape of the episode of *The Bold and the Beautiful* whose transmission they had missed during the dinner party. *The Bold and the Beautiful* always brought them together. It was doing the same thing for the whole of India.

Everyone who had access to a television set was watching it. By the time the episode was finished the two lovers were so friendly that Sanjay felt it incumbent upon him to be passionate all over again.

"I am the bold and you are the beautiful," he said after he had brought her at last to rest.

"I'm afraid that both titles belong to you," she said with the smile he liked best, the one with the half-closed heavy eyes. But she spoiled it all again by talking about things he was never going to catch up with.

"I love it when we lie together like this," she said softly. "We are like the two lovers in a marvellous Polish film I saw over and over when I was very young in Paris. *Ashes and Diamonds*. She lets the young man make love to her because he comes out of nowhere and he will be gone tomorrow. But he falls in love with her and that is the end of him. He dies wrapped in a sheet."

"A sad story."

"But beautiful. He was a very beautiful young man, like you. Made more beautiful by his awful past. He wore dark glasses all the time so you could not see his eyes. It made you look at his mouth. The most beautiful, sculpted mouth. More sensual even than hers. More cruel. Sensitive only to its own pleasure. Your mouth is like that. In France they would call you a savage infant."

After all this publicity for his mouth he thought he had better kiss her with it, but really he was annoyed. He didn't want to hear about Polish films if he was never going to see them. He could not go back with her into the past, to Paris, to the ashes and the diamonds. So why was she bringing all that here? Why was she heaping it all on him? Recrimination might have unmanned him. Luckily he had done his duty. He left for his room, resolved to advance his claims on Mumtas during the following week's filming. He was forgetting the warmth of Miranda's body even as he climbed the stairs. He met Ghita, the speaker of the unspeakable, coming down them.

"If you throw all this away," she said, "you're an even bigger idiot than I thought. Don't you realise that you're hurting her? Is that your gratitude?"

"Ghita. Go to bed." He had copied Miranda's cadence exactly.

And so he went to bed himself, by himself, and honestly convinced that she had as much reason to be grateful to him as he to her, so the accounts were square. Such was the irony that made a rarefied illusion out of a friendship in flesh and blood. Neither of them ever realised that the gap separating them was so wide the opposite edges were invisible. Miranda, with the encouragement of Sanjay's taciturnity on the subject, thought that Sanjay's past life must have hurt his character merely by the absence of good things: she never suspected the presence of evil ones. Sanjay thought that the gulf between them was social. He thought that he had placed and crossed a bridge between his inferiority and her superiority. It had never occurred to him that Miranda's superiority was genuine, extending far beyond her social position. He cherished her intensely as a type and a symbol. When he penetrated her body he took possession of an ideal. But he never penetrated to her individuality. The unusual integrity of her personality remained a mystery to him, because his own personality had no integrity of its own. It was fragmented, and so could never focus its appreciation.

Had things been otherwise, however, there still could have been no guarantee that the most stable relationship of his life would have lasted. Mumtas was a powerful destabilising force. In the course of the following week's filming, Sanjay's suspicion that he would soon be regaled with the universally coveted favours of the Indian film industry's most sumptuous young star grew to a certainty. He would stagger out of the crushed ruins of a box-fall to find himself bathed in her glance. She would insist, when he was not required on the set, that he stand beside her chair so that she could drape her arm around his waist and rest the swell of a breast against his thigh. A new speciality, when they were both watching a scene that included neither of them, was for her to embrace him from behind with sleepy casualness, seemingly resting her helpless fragility against the spine of his manly strength. Mumtas being clearly possessed of tireless energy, this pose was unconvincing, but Sanjay was in no position to question it. He could not see what was going on back there. He could only feel it. Her breasts were in his back like hot cushions, the soft swell of her lower belly treating one or other of his reflexively tautened buttocks to a comprehensive sponge and press. Her breath torched the nape of his neck and the back of his ears. He needed every trick of his mind to control an incipient erection. He conjured up memories of being caned by a relay of policemen. He ran slow-motion replays of Sunil breaking his nose. The presence of his old enemy Vikram, who was choreographing most of the fight scenes, usefully helped to remind him of how his lip had hurt when it was healing. Recalling the exemplary thoroughness with which his father had thrashed him worked for a while. But finally the tricks ran out. His embarrassment was well developed when he was called to the set. He unwrapped Mumtas's arms from around his waist and turned away as if he had a small errand he must first complete before he went into action. Mumtas chose that moment to trail her hand across the front of his trousers. She looked away from him as she did so, but the flare of her nostrils and the rush of air through her pout were flagrant signals of desire. He had to back into the scene bent over, pretending to be looking for something he had lost. The director's amplified voice was sympathetic but no comfort.

"Are you hurt?"

Sanjay shook his head.

"We can shoot this later if you are hurt."

Sanjay shook his head again. He was ready. A few seconds later he was reeling backwards under a flurry of punches from the hero's best friend. The last punch sent him over a parapet which would later be matched to the top of a building he had already fallen off. This time he had only to roll over it backwards and lie on a mattress. As he lay there he saw Mumtas looking at him as if he had just dived out of an aeroplane to save her from the sharks. It was at that moment that he decided it was worth the risk of asking her out. He might lose the protection of Miranda. He might attract the sinister attention of Mumtas's manager's notoriously heavy friends. The only bright spot was that Mumtas's manager obviously did not mind her provocative behaviour, otherwise she would not have reserved her most blatant manoeuvres for when he was somewhere in the vicinity. If a man as powerfully ugly as that had threatened to turn nasty, Sanjay might have had sufficient reason to think again. As things were, he decided to go ahead.

She was ahead of him. She said, in a variation on her usual succession of fledgling bird calls, that she and a few of her friends had plans to go dancing at The Tiger Hunt in Juhu. Would he care to come? At the thought of grooving with Mumtas, Sanjay almost ejaculated on the spot. He was going to see those nipples stroked by cloth: actually *see it happen*. Her eyes promised that much else would happen too. Sanjay's mind was made up. At the end of the day's filming he went home to change, determined, if Miranda was there, to tell her – simply tell her – that he was going out dancing. She wasn't there. He was told that she had left suddenly and would be gone for the whole weekend at the very least. Gradually convincing himself that he was sorry not to have had the chance to breathe defiance, he showered and dressed with fanatical care. He felt svelte. When he descended the stairs to the living-room, Ghita, the speaker of the unspeakable, was there to bathe in his radiance.

"She will hear of this."

"Go ahead and tell her."

"You are a very foolish young man. There is something for you to eat in the kitchen. I hope you choke on it."

From Miranda's apartment building to The Tiger Hunt was a short distance but a long way. It was a different kind of life. The noise was as devastating as the entrance fee. He was glad he had eaten already because nobody was eating here. They were scarcely even drinking. They were just swallowing things in the toilets. Mumtas arrived with her manager and an augmented entourage, including one of the most prominent male models, a figure of enviable elegance against whom she flung herself rhythmically in time to the beat of a song by Madonna. Sanjay was starting to see the point of Madonna. Previously he had thought her to be suffering from a deadly combination of abbreviated legs and bad teeth, but if this kind of music could inspire Mumtas to such a frenzy then there must be something in it. One member of Mumtas's entourage lamented the absence of something called techno-punk but Sanjay declined to be daunted. He was in the right place. Suddenly Mumtas's hip was against his groin again and this time there seemed no limit to what might eventuate. Surely the way her manager bit the end of his cigar could only be a gesture of approval. Sanjay gave himself up to the event. Dancing backwards in front of him, Mumtas drew him by the cupped magnet of her body heat into the booming, shrieking depths of the dance floor where the light splashed and split. He danced like a man whose prayers were in the process of being answered. He danced like a rain dancer who could already taste the rain.

He danced the same way the next night as well. Mumtas had moved into The Tiger Hunt and set up shop. It was her place. All present were her possessions. Unfortunately Sanjay's plans for possessing her kept on not quite coming to fruition. She would touch him, stroke him, breathe into him. She would give her manager her lighted cigarette to hold while she sighed smoke into Sanjay's mouth from a millimetre away, undid his shirt buttons with her frosted nails, brushed her thinly encased breasts against his chest, and drew him back into the dance floor by the tips of his collar. Everyone in Juhu had heard of how she was dancing with him. The gossip columnists were already shuffling their clichés into unprecedented combinations. Yet somehow the promise of the night was never fulfilled.

Nor was the promise of the day. On the free day before shooting started again, Mumtas and Sanjay lay on adjacent sun-loungers beside the swimming-pool at her house. Her imported pale blue swimming costume was an incitement to violence. It was cut high at the sides and when she walked Sanjay could see in detail the form of the plush divide that he was designed to fill. But there were always at least half a dozen other people present including her manager, who was constantly on the telephone. The most Sanjay received, apart from a light lunch on a glass plate, was the by now dubious benefit of a comprehensive course of titillation. Mumtas rubbed oil into his back as he lay face down. She rubbed oil into his upper thighs. Her oiled hand slid in between. His erection threatened to pierce the lounger and punch into the concrete like the bit of a pneumatic drill. She could not have been more blatant. But once again the occasion petered out. In the late afternoon Mumtas changed clothes, climbed into the passenger seat of her manager's colossal BMW, and was quietly transported somewhere out of reach. If it had been going to happen, it should have happened here. Perhaps she wanted to be taken away. Sanjay wondered if he might not have already clinched it, if he had known where to take her. But the slum would not do and Miranda's apartment was impossible. Too many people would know.

Shooting resumed next day and so did Mumtas's teasing campaign. She had a new refinement: licking his ear lobe. He could not go on like this. His mind was not on the job. Falling off balconies was already tough enough without having to counteract the effects of a throbbing groin. Sooner or later he would have to make a drastic decision involving money. He would have to rent somewhere suitable to take her. He arrived home that evening to find that the decision had been forced on him. He had plans for a slow, careful primping before he advanced on the nightclub for a concerted attack on Mumtas's final defences. The first thing he was looking forward to was a shower. The first thing he ran into was Ghita, the speaker of the unspeakable. Just inside the main door of the apartment, in the foyer, she was aligning large plastic bags full of clothes beside his solitary suitcase.

"She is on the terrace. You had better see her straight away. And don't say I didn't tell you."

Miranda was standing up beside the coffee table on the terrace. In a yellow sari against a divided background of pale blue evening sky and silvering sea, she reminded him of a wrathful goddess on the back of a fateful card already being plucked at by the divinatory parrot. She did not sit down and did not invite Sanjay to do so either. There was a large book on the table, almost covering its surface. It was called *Bombay Blues*. Without lifting it from the table, Miranda opened it.

22

No, MIRANDA DID NOT throw Sanjay out because of Mumtas. She threw him out because of something else. "I could have stood the way you're making a fool of yourself with this floozy," said Miranda, looking, he thought, sad rather than angry. Well, that was a relief. Anger was never nice. He thought it best to hang his head while he tried to figure out what she was going to accuse him of. If she could stand the business with Mumtas, what was it she couldn't stand? Had he left a piece of scorched silver paper in his room? Had they realised how many cans of Sprite were disappearing from the refrigerator? It was while he was asking himself this question that he belatedly recognised what was depicted by one of the photographs displayed in the open book.

"I suppose I should be grateful that you at least had the decency not to bring her here."

Sanjay, who had forborne not out of decency but expediency, took the opportunity to nod.

"Eloquent as usual. I could even forgive *this*. This *is* you, isn't it? Screwing in some toilet in Falkland Street? Screwing some disease-ridden tart with a bucket of shit standing in the corner? That *is* you, isn't it? The same young man I allowed to touch me?"

"She was not a tart."

"Yes, I dare say it was a great romance. Look, it probably was. I can see she might have been pretty. And I am certain she was deprived. I am certain you both were, God help me. But I am not bringing our friendship to an end because of this."

Sanjay could not begin to guess what else there might be. Unless

242

Pratiba had talked. Yes, that must be it. Well, he could soon talk her out of being jealous of Pratiba. And nothing had ever really happened.

"What I can't bear is that you sold your body to perverted men. You did *that* and never told me."

So that was all. He could not see why she was making a fuss about that. It was long ago and it had nothing to do with her.

"Do you know where I have been in these last few days? I have been in London. Having my blood tested. By some miracle it turns out that I am all right. God knows whether *you* are. You will have to find out by yourself. But if I had gone to a doctor here the gossips really *would* have had something to go on. This is the world's biggest small town. Why do you think I brought you out here on the terrace? *Because no one must ever know about this.* No one. Do you understand? That much you owe me. Even Pratiba must never know. They must think it is about that birdbrain Mumtas. Or about this disgusting book."

"Who told you?"

"About the men? Gupta. Who else? It is his idea of pleasure, to tell someone news as unpleasant as that."

"He is lying."

"He is not lying. You are. You lied to me from the beginning. May heaven forgive me, I thought I was moulding you. I even had dreams of sending you to school. And you were already formed, all along. Formed into a pervert and a liar and a cheat."

"You're beautiful when you're angry." Sanjay tried this with a wry smile, but to no avail.

"Yes, well. That will be enough of that. I have put some money in your suitcase. One of the cars will take you back to the city."

"Goodbye," said Sanjay. He had realised that there was no use fighting. He might have fought if he had really cared. But this episode was over.

"Goodbye. I blame myself for all this, you know. We were both dreaming, but I had no excuse. Can you carry all that stuff?"

Sanjay said that it was no problem. As he bent over to pick up his bags, he could feel the edge of his money-belt against his lower chest.

In the money-belt was his gold piece. As long as he had that, his luck would hold. Nothing else mattered and nothing else was certain.

"And for God's sake, see a doctor," was the last thing he heard from her. He heard it as a whisper. Clearly no one else was meant to hear. She seemed unusually self-effacing on this issue. He couldn't imagine why. He had never been sick, except for the usual things that everyone got, and that were all over after a few weeks of pain.

He took all his gear back to his room in the slum but he knew he could never live there again. He could never bring Mumtas to a place like this. He would have to find somewhere decent, even if it meant getting into debt. Aziz would advance him some money against his future earnings. For now, he had a certain amount of money in the bank. Next day, taking only some of his best belongings in a small canvas bag, he drew out more than half the money and used it to pay cash in advance for a whole week in a room at the Tajma. He had hoped to be asked for only a deposit but as a man without documents he was not surprised to be asked for a full half of the amount, a sum which effectively emptied his money-belt. The balance, he was told, could be paid at the end, along with his extras. His room, although the smallest available, was still magnificent, with its own TV, a separate bathroom full of towels, and a refrigerator crammed with beers and soft drinks stacked in rows and layers. He rolled one of the chill bottles of Limca against his forehead. The nervous strain of checking in had brought him close to sweating and the air-conditioning took time to cool him down. He ran a bath, using all the green gel in the sachet. He imagined Mumtas in the bath with him, her breasts suavely drenched with suds like that girl's in the *Debonair* anniversary issue's free fold-out calendar. He imagined Mumtas on the bed, making love with him the way she danced, frenziedly creating a succession of spaces into which he hurried to fit himself with thrusts of his hips and lungings of his chest, chasing her pout with his panting mouth. Imagine doing all that while being actually inside her! And it was going to happen. It had to happen now. Heroically declining to ease the pressure in his groin, saving it for the actual moment, he dressed with great care, taking out of its flat box a Charagh Din long-sleeved shirt he had never worn. The shirt was so luxuriantly packed

244

that the pins had globular heads. There was always one more pin. Finally, after he had checked himself out against the full-length mirror, he went down to the foyer, out through the sobbing glass door, and instructed one of the turbaned giants to call him an A/C car so that he could arrive at the studio in style if not on time. He had seen guests of the hotel do these things and all he had to do was copy them. It was that easy. It was all so simple.

But once again there was nothing simple about Mumtas. She was not in that afternoon's scenes because she was already busy on an overlapping film, so he never even saw her. The next day she was there but did not want to go dancing in the night because she was going to a fashion show at the Hilton. Sanjay would quite like to have gone to that but was not asked. The next night she wanted to go dancing. She danced like a tigress in heat, but when Sanjay suggested, shouting in the thunderous dark, that she might like to come back to the Tajma for a drink, she said perhaps tomorrow. This would have been a crushing disappointment if she had not accompanied the postponement with a double nipple-thrust to his chest and a multiple stroking of his swollen member with her mons pubis, whose shape was so clearly detectable through her clinging miniskirt, and flagrant in her tight white panties when the miniskirt whipped up around her vibrating waist. There was also the encouragement provided by her way of communicating through the noise. She inserted her pursed lips into his ear and piped what she had to say like a musician. The word 'tomorrow' echoed wetly because she had licked his ear drum first. For a moment Sanjay forgot his hotel bill, ticking like the meter of an enormous, fatal taxi. This was the apex of his life. He felt as if he were about to burst from pent-up potential. He particularly felt like this below the waist, where his entire genital apparatus conveyed the impression that it had been carved from hardwood by a master craftsman and lovingly polished over a period of years.

On the afternoon of the next day Sanjay had to do a complicated fight scene. The great Rajiv, scarred veteran of many a fracas, had been brought in specially to supervise it.

"You have come a long way in a hurry," said Rajiv in an aside.

"I had a great teacher."

"Cut the flattery and watch out for Vikram when I'm not around. He doesn't like you. You know the way this one works?"

"I spin from the first punch, stiffen up at the second punch, fall back straight so my behind pivots on the wall, and then go over."

"And keep going over. It's only a few feet down but you want to hit the mattress on your front, not on your head. Your habit of landing on your head used to worry me a great deal. It was a miracle I never had to fill out any forms for you."

"Maybe today."

"Tomorrow. When Vikram's in charge. Let *him* fill out the forms. Is it true about you and Mumtas? I've got a bet going and I have to know."

"Yes, it's true. Almost true. True soon."

"Maybe for once you are not lying. Don't land on your head. OK, let's rehearse the camera."

Mumtas, flanked by her manager and surrounded by her entourage, was watching when Sanjay and the other heavies were defeated in battle. Sanjay was distracted by her fond regard. The second punch, instead of fanning his jaw, actually clipped it. His behind hit the top of the wall at an angle that threw him skewed into his loop. He didn't land on his head, but if he had not got his arms out early he would have had to kiss the mattress before embracing it. Rajiv helped him up.

"You aren't concentrating. Stop thinking about that delicious pussy or you'll never live to get it." But the slightly dazed Sanjay was looking across to see if Mumtas seemed suitably concerned. Yes, she did. It was going to be all right. Comforted, he did the real one perfectly. Mumtas applauded and blew him a kiss. It flew into his face like a hot bird.

It was in the night that things got out of hand. Once again he was close beside her as her small army forced its way through the photographers and spectators on the brilliant pavement outside The Tiger Hunt. In a scoop-necked white top, tight jeans and white cowboy boots, she actually held on to his arm as she pirouetted and posed, aiming a pout at every lens. Inside the club she danced as if during all previous evenings she had been under doctor's orders to

246

convalesce. As usual she went to the toilet every twenty minutes. This time she appointed Sanjay guardian of the toilet door. The corridor, though jammed with impatient women, was incomparably more peaceful than the dance floor, so he chose that setting to remind her of her promise to come back with him to the Tajma for a quiet drink. She said she would. In the course of time she did. Unfortunately her manager and half a dozen other people came with her. It took two cars to get them there. Sanjay's room was already jammed before Aziz invited himself over with a friend. Sanjay had to call room service for a second bottle of champagne. The refrigerator was soon emptied of its bottles of beer. Mumtas turned the television set to MTV. She wanted to dance. Dancing made her want to go to the toilet. She started a separate party in the bathroom. Sanjay had to order a third bottle of champagne. Dimly aware of what could be done to a hotel bill by the phenomenon known as extras, he was rather hoping that Mumtas's manager would offer to pay for all this, but the manager gave no sign of feeling generous. Instead he looked rather strict. Eventually, very late, everybody went. Everybody included Mumtas. Sanjay was alone. He couldn't believe it.

He couldn't, but he should have. Mumtas had caused Sanjay to lose his wits. This was a serious deprivation. All his life, a naturally cool head had been his only sure defence against peril. He could afford to forgo it only for a while, and not a very long while either. His infatuation might have been an amusing foible if he had commanded greater resources. He didn't, so he was playing against a stacked deck. There was nothing remarkable about what happened on the set next day. In the context of the Indian film industry it was an all too typical event. Vikram was in charge of the stunt. If Rajiv had been on duty, instead of busy on another film, he might have coached Sanjay more effectively, but there is no telling. Later on, some people associated with the production spread the rumour that Vikram had been out to get Sanjay. Later still, when Mumtas's manager left his wife, kidnapped his own children and the whole thing became a colossal scandal, informed insiders persuasively argued that he had put Vikram up to it so as to get a young rival out of the picture. Like most conspiracy theories, these had the merit of fitting the facts, but the drawback of turning a plausible accident into an elaborate plan, in a country where elaborate plans are the very kind most likely to come unstuck and least likely to remain secret long enough to be put into effect. The truth was that Sanjay, at the precise moment when he should have been thinking exclusively of his work, was thinking of something else. He had to jump through a big window to escape Mumtas's bodyguards, who had arrived to rescue her from her bonds. Mumtas, the bonds and the bodyguards would be present next day. For now nothing mattered except Sanjay and the big window. He couldn't complain about lack of attention to detail. Rarely for a locally made film, a toffee glass window had been provided, which could be jumped through in relative safety. Sanjay rehearsed a couple of times with the window frame empty. He ran up the ramp and hurtled through the frame. The camera would see him burst through the glass, fall six feet, and hit the ground running.

"When we do the real one," said the director, "give it plenty of expression. Cruel and defiant, as if you are doing something dangerous but don't care about the consequences, because of the anger in your soul. Lots of that. We'll be close on you and then zoom out in slow motion with the exploding glass." It was a tricky shot for the camera operator. He needed the rehearsals. For Sanjay one rehearsal should have been enough. He ought to have been ready when the toffee glass was put into the frame. As things turned out, however, he got the take so badly wrong that it could not be used.

"What's *wrong* with you?" asked the director, right there in front of everyone. "You had no expression on your face at all. We are on your face before we zoom out. You are supposed to look cruel and defiant. You looked as if you were opening a set of curtains."

"There is no more toffee glass," Vikram told the director. "That was all we had."

"We will have to go with real glass," said the director. He turned back to Sanjay. "You have done this through real glass?"

"Yes," said Sanjay, telling the lie of his life. "I have done it." What else could he say? How would Mumtas react if she heard that he had said no? He was her daredevil, her champion, her knight in shining armour. The director nodded and walked away, leaving Vikram in charge of the preparations. Vikram, to do him credit, tried to tell Sanjay to keep his arms up so that his padded sleeves would make the first break. Sanjay tried to take in the advice. But by the time the window was ready for another real one, Sanjay was distracted again. Too much talk about the cost of the toffee glass had set him thinking about the cost of his hotel room. It wasn't so much the remaining half of the basic charge. It was those extras. He was worried about those long phone calls she had made from the bathroom extension. Standing waving her glass of champagne while she piped and squeaked, she might have been talking to anywhere in the world. He thought about the way Mumtas drank champagne as if it were water to wash down pills, and that set him thinking about her mouth. Thinking about the way her mouth opened set him thinking about the way her legs divided, that clearly defined opulence. He wondered if she, like Miranda, became so wet with her own cream that she dripped. These are not things to be thinking and wondering when you are about to jump through real glass.

On the word 'Action!' Sanjay ran up the shallow ramp towards the big window. For real glass he had been provided with flesh-coloured gloves to supplement the padding under his sleeves and his trouser legs. He had checked the window pane and judged it sufficiently thin to be easily shattered. When he hit the glass, however, he didn't get his arms right. He had them up and to the side of his face so that the camera could see his expression, but he didn't have them far enough forward. His face was already badly cut before he fell. The glass proving much tougher than he had estimated, it slowed him down. His back foot caught on the bottom rail of the frame. He pitched forward at too great an angle to land on his feet. A big piece of glass had landed on its edge in precisely the right position to slice through the padding on his right forearm and do fearful damage from his elbow all the way to his armpit. Worse than all this, his head hit the corner of a wooden rostrum with such force that the indentation in his temple could be plainly seen when they turned him over, even though his slashed face was already awash with blood.

The shot of Sanjay exploding through the glass turned out reasonably well. The director and the producer wanted to keep it in the film, so the script editor was instructed to write Sanjay out at that point. More or less the same thing happened in real life. While Vikram got on with the long job of filling in all the forms, Sanjay, weak from loss of blood, was checked into a private ward in case some gossip writer tried to reach him. They did their best at the hospital, even though Sanjay did not rank as a very important man. His chance of ever being one of those had just ended. Nevertheless there is no reason to blame the prentice ministrations of a newly qualified anaesthetist. Sanjay's concussion was enough to work the cruel trick. When he regained consciousness, he did not regain his full intelligence. His once fine wits were dulled. Perhaps it was a blessing. His face had been sewn up but there was a limit to what could be done. When, after a long time, he was finally shown a mirror, he would have found himself a terrible thing to see had he still possessed his famed acuteness. As things were, he could only wonder. He found it hard to pay attention. When Rajiv came to visit him, Sanjay recognised him but couldn't think of anything to say. Miranda, though she was still angry with him, would have paid him a visit if she had known, but she was on holiday in Goa, with Pratiba as confidante and lady-in-waiting. Neither of them heard about Sanjay's accident until much later. But even if they had turned up, it is doubtful whether he would have had much to talk about. A doctor bent over his bed and told him, among other puzzling things, that his blood had been tested and found to be all right. Sanjay remembered that someone had told him to see a doctor. Well, now he had seen a doctor. It was a man in a white coat, blurry at the edges. When other memories came, they came slowly. It was only on the day he was due to leave that he remembered he should have a money-belt. Some kind of residual panic made him search frantically for it when he was handed his clothes, which the film company had kindly sent over from the dressing shed. For Sanjay as he was now, a frantic movement was slow, but it was still troubled. There was still some money in the belt, along with the key to his padlock. More importantly, his gold piece was still in its secret compartment. Verifying the fact was particularly awkward because he had only one workable hand to hunt with, and it was his bad hand. The people at the hospital, speaking slowly and emphatically, had told him that he must come back one day and have the stitches taken out of his face. They had also told him that his right arm would never work again. It was folded across his body and had no sensation in it below the shoulder. The hand was bent inwards at the wrist and the fingers were half folded shut. If he had not had help to get dressed it would have taken him half the day.

Not being quite certain where he was coming from, and with fogged memories of where he was going to, Sanjay was a long time getting back to the slum. He found it so difficult to unlock his padlock with one hand that at one point he gave up and wept. He wept very easily now. Eventually an old woman helped him by holding the padlock. It was probably a good thing that he forgot all about the Tajma, where his bill reached a fabulous figure before they wrote it off: in the course of time the manager had to answer to the board of directors for overseas phone calls totalling more than a thousand US dollars. With enough cash left to pay his rent until the monsoon was over, Sanjay lay on his bed for weeks, going out only to buy simple food. If he had bought some film magazines, he would have noticed that the gossip columns printed the pictures of him with Mumtas, wondered where he had disappeared to, and then forgot him. But he didn't buy them. It didn't occur to him. He knew that his bank book was the source of more money but he couldn't remember how to use it. He could only remember that he had to go to the bank and write something. At the bank they looked at his face and didn't believe that he was who he said he was. They said he had stolen the book. He had to run away. The stitches in his face badly needed to come out. Luckily a kind man passing in the street said he was a doctor. The doctor opened his little bag, took something out of it, and relieved Sanjay of his festering stitches right there on the pavement. A small crowd gathered to watch. The doctor also dabbed on some liquid, which stung. There was no charge. Sanjay was still left with the problem of his bank book. He remembered where Ajay lived and went to call on him. Ajay was not there, or anywhere else. Eventually a common acquaintance revealed that Ajay had caught a very bad disease and would probably not be coming back. Sanjay could not

251

find Sunil either. Some of the boys at the toilet said he had gone on a trip. Fearing that his friend might be avoiding him because of his face, Sanjay checked up on the story by hanging around outside the Palace cinema. He had guessed correctly that there was no fear of his being recognised. Sunil never appeared. Dilip did. Sanjay remembered that Dilip was no longer his friend. Something bad had happened once. But the memory of their friendship was earlier, deep set and more intense. So he asked Dilip to help him with his bank book. Dilip pronounced himself delighted to cooperate. "Was she worth it?" asked Dilip strangely. He answered his own question. "Doesn't look like it." At the bank Dilip arranged everything. All Sanjay had to do was sign. With his bad hand he did it awkwardly, but apparently it was enough. Then Dilip gave him some money. By the time Sanjay had realised that there was much less money than there ought to be, Dilip was gone.

When Sanjay could no longer pay the rent for his slum room, he was obliged to leave. He left behind his magazines and his dictionary. He could no longer concentrate on all that. His fragmentary mirror he left where it was on the wall: since his face had come to reflect it, instead of the other way about, he no longer liked to look into it. He took only his suitcase, clumsily packed with his remaining clothes. In the course of weeks, one item at a time, he had to sell them or barter them away. The suitcase was nearly empty when he at last reached the road where he was born. His memories were deep so he had no trouble finding his house. His father was gone. His mother was still there but very sick. All the possible breadwinners were missing. The family had split up, in the modern fashion. There was no one left but the halt and the lame. Sanjay, with the help of one of his sisters, broke up the suitcase and incorporated the pieces into the roof of the house.

23

SANJAY WENT BEGGING but did not prosper. He covered a wide territory, often walking as far as Juhu so that he could haunt the rich cars at the traffic-lights. The clothes on his back, the last clothes he had, were rags by now. He looked the part. Unfortunately there were lots of other beggars who looked the part too. They would surround a car so that you could barely see it: you could only hear it honk feebly like a hunted animal. Once he thought he remembered where Miranda's apartment block was, but he must have picked the wrong one, because the few people at the entrance who could bear to look at his face did not want to let him in. He cried, because he knew that if she could see him she would give him some money. When he cried they chased him away. So he went back to the traffic-lights and continued with his begging. He was given the odd blue note and on one occasion a brown one, but nothing wonderful. His problem was that although his damaged face registered well enough, his immobilised arm was hard to believe. He might have just been holding it like that. The competition flaunted injuries and deformities whose authenticity was unmistakable. In the late afternoon he would limp home discouraged. His household was not doing well. Even a few annas would make a difference. He had one thing left to sell. It would have to be sold to some effect. It would have to be an investment.

To walk back all the way into the heart of the city took a long time. It had to be done. That was where he would find the only man who could help him. The man was still there, squatting in front of the railings on Mahapalika Marg with Azad Park behind him. He was still hemmed in by snarling sets of teeth arranged in ranks. It was the

253

pavement dentist. Slowly, having trouble with some of the words and sometimes mixing his languages, Sanjay explained what he wanted. The dentist did not seem shocked. Pavement dentists are hard to unsettle with a tale of woe. They are practical men. The dentist demanded to see the colour of Sanjay's money. It was the colour of gold. For much of his waking life Sanjay had allowed no other hand but his own to touch the gold piece and he was not going to relinquish it now, so he was the one who held it close to the dentist's expert eye. After nodding agreement, the dentist told Sanjay that what he wanted could not be done until just before dawn, but they would need to start walking at least an hour before that. Rather than make a complicated rendezvous he allowed Sanjay to lie down on the mat to sleep the night until the appointed time. Very tired, Sanjay soon slept the untroubled sleep of a man whose dilemma is resolved. The last thing he saw before his eyes closed was a silent convocation of lipless smiles.

When the dentist left he took all his kit with him but kindly left the mat, calculating that nobody was going to steal it out from under his client. The dentist returned to find that somebody *had* stolen the mat. The dentist was unmollified by Sanjay's assurance that he had not felt it go. This was a bad start to their deal. There was nowhere to go but up. As they walked beside the railway tracks in the mild night under the stars, the dentist gradually restored himself to a good humour. He told stories of teeth gone by. Sanjay occupied himself with his own memories, such as they were. He knew that there were blanks. What bothered him most was that there might be blanks he didn't know about. Eventually, after they had walked for an hour, the dentist announced that this was the spot. He put down the little bag that he had been carrying and set out some instruments on a cloth, only a few feet from the tracks. Then he demonstrated the way he wanted Sanjay to lie down. Sanjay had trouble doing it. The dentist said that they would have to hurry because the first train would be along soon. The dentist helped to get Sanjay's dead hand into the correct position across the rail. Because Sanjay's arm was cramped against his body, it meant that he had to lie face down very close beside the rail. He had barely got into the correct position before the train came. Perhaps that was another stroke of luck. It meant that there was less time to think about it. With so little sensation in his arm, Sanjay hardly felt the hand go. He was much more struck by the noise and the vibration. The dentist, who had pinned him down so that he would not be dragged along, helped to roll him out of the way as soon as the job was done.

It was only the first part of the job, of course. That was why the dentist was there, to make sure the amputation was properly tidied up. The dentist wanted the gold piece before he started. Too shocked to argue, Sanjay could only comply. He fumbled at his money-belt. He pointed to the secret compartment. The dentist took the gold piece, held it up to check it in the light of the rising sun, and put it in a pocket of his own. Then, an honourable man, he got to work. Sanjay fainted, which was probably just as well. His last conscious thought for some time was of how wise he had been always to keep the gold piece safe, until the day came when it could make the difference between life and death.

24

SANJAY WAS RIGHT. The gold piece had made it possible for him to do the only thing that could save him. There were people who wanted to help him after they heard about his accident on the film set, but they were too late. When Miranda and Pratiba got back from Goa, Pratiba heard about it from her contacts in the minor purlieus of the film world. She told Miranda, and Miranda immediately sent her to find him. Pratiba thought that she remembered the way. She did indeed remember where the slum was but once she got into it she was soon lost. It was enormous. There was no end to it. Her enquiries were useless. So she brought back the packet of money Miranda had given her and the two women discussed what to do. Finally Pratiba tracked down Aziz and for a consideration wormed Sanjay's address out of him. Armed with that, she went back to the slum. This time she knew what to ask for. But she was too late. There was a whole family living in Sanjay's room, including an older female relative who, if not yet quite dead, was certainly no longer among the living except in a technical sense. Elizabeth, when she arrived independently a few days later, found the same scene, minus the older female relative. Elizabeth had some money with her too. It might have staved off the inevitable, but not for long. Sanjay was a child of the streets, and the children of the streets are on their own. They have to be strong. If they are injured, and need charity, they have to be stronger still. A windfall might only have robbed Sanjay of the determination he needed to do what was necessary. Anyway, no help reached him. He helped himself, and did it. His right hand had lost its cunning. It offended him, so he cut it off.

He became a more successful beggar after that. The competition was still fierce, but now he had something to show. When he had recovered from shock and infection, he went back to work at the crossroads at the bottom of the hill, where the main road comes in from the coast. Some of the cars and buses visiting Film City still turn there to start the long shallow climb to the gate. Beyond the gate, back in the low hills, the Silver Castle has been rebuilt and replaced so often by now that it has small resemblance to the edifice Sanjay knew when he was little. There is still the occasional adventurous street child who emerges from the bushes to see it and believe it, but for Sanjay it is not even a memory. He has enough to worry about. Any of the cars and buses might contain the rich person with the spare annas, or even the spare rupees. He has to approach, press his face against the window, tilt his upper body, and hold up his stump as best he can before the intact faces inside can turn away. He doesn't do as well as the mothers with children, and nothing like as well as the children with babies. But he does better than the man with the twisted legs on the little trolley, or the man with no legs at all. Sanjay is higher up, moves more quickly into position, and he has his tears. Once, when he was young, working the trains and boats, his tears were schooled. Now they are spontaneous. Ever since his accident he has cried a little all the time. It is something to do with the nerves in his face. He is a sight to touch the conscience. Foreign television crews on the poverty tour have filmed him several times. Elizabeth was with a Dutch crew on the way to Film City. They stopped to film Sanjay beside the road. So Elizabeth gave Sanjay ten rupees without knowing who he was. Nor did he know her. His eyes were wet, the light was behind her, and his head hurt with the heat. Elizabeth had once been a little bit in love with Sanjay's face, and love for something perhaps makes it harder to recognise when it drastically changes. Also she knew nothing about what had happened to his hand, and he walked with a different posture. There is also the consideration, although it should be put with care, that she lived locally, and the inhabitants of Bombay are less likely than visitors to look closely at a beggar. The price of habituation is a certain indifference, and it remains terribly true that the most deserving cases are out of sight, wasting away in a dark silence.

Sanjay will never go back now to the heart of the city. It is too far. Once he tried, in the dim hope of finding Urmila, but he was barely a third of the way there when he was stopped by a giant roadside sign with a strange word on it. The sign said 'Häagen-Dazs'. The completeness with which he did not understand this word left him desolate. He turned for home. So now he is stuck there at the fringe, in the same area where he was born. But for someone who started from nothing he got a long way. A few steps more and he might have been a legend. As things worked out, he is remembered only by those who knew him, but they remember him well. There aren't many street children who go so far, and few indeed who go further. Sunil, uniquely subtle, was one of them. Using all the money he had so carefully saved, he got all the way to England. He entered the country in a sealed container and was one of the lucky ones who were still alive when it was opened. He even managed to obtain a job, at the Ganges Sporting Club in Birmingham. He kept the job until his character was called into question. Now he works at other things related to the Indian community, but must always face the problem that most of the work available is legal. He will probably overcome this difficulty. He has the talent. It would have been nice to say that Urmila, too, managed to escape her circumstances. A more romantic God would have rescued her to become a catwalk model or a film star. Unfortunately she was without the inner resources. When they were through with her at Falkland Street, she retraced her always graceful steps to her old home in the alley, and there she still is, a mouth to feed that tries to pay its way by cleaning the pot in which the food is cooked.

One of the opulent cars to which Sanjay daily makes his mute appeal might have been Miranda's by now if she had gone on with her career. But she had seen the writing on the wall, in twenty different Indian languages, and given up. There were no good films waiting for her, and too many bad ones. She married Gupta. He had probably been planning it already when he told her about Sanjay. Gupta wanted the right woman – beautiful, distinguished, intelligent

– as a front. He had political ambitions. Miranda disliked him but could not help admiring his power. She was approaching bankruptcy, a condition which makes power easier to admire. Also she was approaching the age when any man was likely to betray her eventually, so she chose a man who would betray her from the beginning, without draining her of love and trust. Miranda is in a new phase of her life now. She spends much time in London and New York and her beloved Paris. When Gupta makes his elaborate deals, she presides at his dinner tables, not just flattering and cajoling but personally and truly representing that rich civilization which her great country has always held waiting within it, and which will soon contribute to a wider world, the unimaginable tomorrow. Gupta's booming home-grown legitimate computer program enterprise in Bombay would have been hardly possible if the Bangalore software pirates had not first been tamed; the government regulations that tamed them would not have been possible without pressure from the American communications giants; and it was Miranda, with the aid of her personal assistant Pratiba, who showed the American lawyers how to frame and address their letters of protest so that the bureaucrats of Delhi could not bury them in the pending tray. Miranda is better than Gupta at that kind of thing, and he knows it. His charitable works were his own idea, but it takes her enlightened chairmanship to make them plausible. Gupta has improved under her tutelage. He is no nicer, but less proud of being ruthless. At least he is natural. There are one or two men in India who are richer than he is. Based in Britain, Sri and Gopi Hinduja count as two of the richest men in the world. There is at least one Indian tycoon based in India who is richer than both of them put together. But he believes in fairies and flying saucers. Gupta has a clear mind, even if it is cold. He is not everything that India needs, but he is certainly something. Miranda also advises him closely on his growing interests in the film industry, and it might be that from his studio, under her cultivated influence, the kind of films will finally come she should always have been in. A new Satyajit Ray might emerge. Why not? He did before, and in circumstances far less propitious. Meanwhile, working as long a day as her driven husband, Miranda is very busy. But she is alone in the night, and lying in the dark she often thinks of what she ought to have done for Sanjay that she did not do.

It is kind of her. Though afraid of time and ruled too much by her fears, she is a good person, and her guilt is misplaced. Long before he met her, Sanjay was already condemned. Even as she groomed him he was on the slide. Lately our biologists and philosophers have begun to reach something like agreement on the nature of human consciousness. Apparently it is fragmentary, and we have no central mind making sense of everything. Coherence is an illusion: a necessary illusion, but an illusion nevertheless. Time and experience oblige us to accept that the things we know do not form a complete picture. They are just bits of a puzzle. But we have some idea of what the puzzle is. We can see its edges even though there are whole patches of sky, sea and earth missing, and we can guess the subject even though there is a whole heap of pieces at our elbow that we will never have the time or the aptitude to make fit. It is a picture of a lost ship, called Western Civilization; of a radiant long cloister called the Grace of God; or of a glittering, variegated procession called the Ascent of Man. There is a unity, even if it is only suggested: a congruence of hints. But the young Sanjay, even at his brightest, could see no edges. For him there *was* no picture. The pieces of the puzzle were never together on the table in front of him. They were never in the same room, or even in the same house. They were scattered through time and space, never to be joined even potentially. In view of that cruel fact, he did well, and his story, though sad, should give us cause for hope. There was nothing and no one to form his character, yet his character, though of necessity opportunistic, was still much more benevolent than it might have been. He was a thief but no murderer. Hurt often, he seldom hurt other people. When he did, he hardly did it out of calculation, and still less from pleasure. There was a tenderness to him, and it was inbred. It is a comfort to believe that tenderness can be instinctive. Miranda, who valued his light touch and helped him to value it in his turn, was right to regard it as his best gift. If Mumtas had given herself to him she might have learned something.

Mumtas is the biggest star of all, for now. There is talk of flattening the Silver Castle so as to make room for a multilevel set – built out of real metal scaffolding – for the first Indian cyberpunk movie, in which she will star. She will stand poised in midair, magnificent in studded leather, holding her pout in profile against the hot sky. There is talk of her going to Hollywood. No Indian film star has ever flourished when thus transplanted, but there is always a first time, and Mumtas certainly has the drive. She is a princess. A princess must take her destiny in her own hands or she will be destroyed by the dreams that the rest of us have on her behalf. Mumtas is not the wisest princess that has ever reigned over the Indian film world. Nor is she the kindest. But she is one of the loveliest, and in that respect she is a fitting representative of a form of art that matches a way of life, that gives something to people who have nothing, and that might not survive in so foolishly innocent a form. For the next Sanjays who come trekking in from the beach or from under the wharf, the dreams on the screen will never again so exactly supply the deficiencies of their real lives. Generated on computers in the shadow factories of Los Angeles, detached even from the sunlight, the techno future will be a less comfortable dreamland to escape to than Long Ago. The techno future might come true, for some. The enchanted past never could, for anyone. That was its point. Deprivation was shared. There was a democracy of longing. It was the one thing that everyone had been given in common. No doubt it would be better if everyone could go to school instead, but such an elementary requirement might be a long time on the way. Before the new way of life comes, there is an old one to be lost. It had something to it. If you visit Bombay soon, you might just be in time to see the last of it before it goes.

Sanjay is only one person among many millions waiting for the first scraps of the new free enterprise society to come drifting down. There are signs that the situation is at least no worse, or at any rate bad in a more promising way. There is less corruption in the public services. There are only half as many people who have to be paid off if you want to get anything done. They have to be paid twice as much, but at least you save time. It would be nice to think that time did not matter, but fine talk about eternal India should not be allowed to obscure the fact that it does. The poor live with tight margins. When the subsidies were removed from kerosene and cooking oil, feeding a family got harder, not easier. As a direct result of deregulation, lentils and chappati bread got dearer, not cheaper. There is no sense, and no decency, in saying wait to people who can't. Young economists may spout confident jargon about the trickle-down effect and the eventual certainty of the benefits kicking in. They had better be right. Meanwhile the poor don't just wait, they increase in numbers. In the country villages they go on having as many children as possible so as to gather things in. When all the things are gathered in and gone, the families leave their wasted districts, come to the big city, and join the population of the pavements. It has all been going on for a long time and the chances are – overwhelmingly are – that it will go on for a long while yet. That is why it is such an education to go to a city like Bombay for even a little while. The poverty in the streets is not like a disaster in the past. When we see the train tracks in Poland and think of the little children, or when we see the dreadful photographs from Cambodia of the torture factories where the victims were hurt worse if they screamed, we say it is impossible to bear but we don't quite mean it, because we *can* bear it: it is in the past, the situation altered, it is over, it won't happen again. In Buenos Aires, when the Mothers of the Disappeared parade each Thursday in the Plaza de Mayo, the photographs of their missing children that hang around their necks are terrible to see. That beautiful daughter who was going to be the scientist could have been *your* daughter. It could have been *your* daughter who was raped and tortured and thrown alive out of an aeroplane into the hungry ocean. But the children playing in the square, the next generation, are healthy and safe: it is not going to happen to them. And the children in the street of Ho Chi Minh City, the children known as the Dust of Life: one day, when the city is called Saigon again, those children might vanish, never to be replaced, because there is no irreversible reason for them to be there. And those terrifying African countries, the ones where the starving children swell up like cherry bubbles until pricked at last by the pin of death: those countries could all feed themselves if they were well governed, if the tribes would stop killing each other, and if the West could find a way of helping that doesn't hinder. Though it is a lot to

262

hope for, there are no irreversible reasons why those horrors happen. But in Bombay, for all we know, and for as much as we dare to guess, the reasons *are* irreversible. The impoverished are there with the all-pervading applicability of a natural law, like gravity or decay. Every advance in medicine or economics seems to bring more deprivation: deprivation of everything beyond mere sustenance. They don't starve any more, but they hardly live. Think of your own life minus all the things worth living for: wouldn't that be a kind of death? Well, there it is, no further away than the thickness of a car window.

Travelling through Bombay, you will see many Sanjays. If you go out to his area you might even see the man himself. Though he always looks in hope, he has still never seen, in the passing cars, anyone that he recognises. Whether you recognise him, if you ever pass that way, is for you to decide. We have to ask ourselves what our lives would have been like if we had had no advantages at all. It is harder to imagine than we imagine. We always put our character into the picture, as if we got it from nowhere. But the mighty, infinitely malleable Stendhal was right about that: we can acquire anything in solitude, except character. And Bombay, for all its inescapable propinquity, is the world's clearest proof that a great city is a great solitude. If you were alone, like the people of the streets, you too would be without the means even to conjecture that your true life, the life you were meant for, had been misplaced. Yet the picture of desolation is mercifully incomplete. There is not much violence that moves fast enough to be seen. That young beggar with the scarred face and the ball of rags for a hand might annoy you but will not attack you. It is not because he is too weak, or too afraid, but because it has not yet occurred to him to doubt that you are only someone else like him, on a different journey. Perhaps you will see that in his ruined eyes. You will look through him and see yourself reflected. If you do, the spirit of the city will enter into you, and Bombay will be with you always, for the rest of your life.